LW0016665

ELVI RHODES

OMNIBUS

ELVI RHODES

OMNIBUS

Opal

&

Doctor Rose

BANTAM PRESS

LONDON · NEW YORK · TORONTO · SYDNEY · AUCKLAND

TRANSWORLD PUBLISHERS LTD
61–63 Uxbridge Road, London W5 5SA

TRANSWORLD PUBLISHERS (AUSTRALIA) PTY LTD
15–23 Helles Avenue, Moorebank, NSW 2170

TRANSWORLD PUBLISHERS (NZ) LTD
3 William Pickering Drive, Albany, Auckland

Published 1992 by Bantam Press
a division of Transworld Publishers Ltd
Copyright © Elvi Rhodes 1992

Printing History – *Opal*
Century edition 1984
Corgi edition 1984, reissued 1987, reprinted 1987

Printing History – *Doctor Rose*
Century edition 1984
Corgi edition 1984, reprinted 1987

A catalogue record for this book is available from the British
Library
ISBN 0-593-02544-X

Typeset in Plantin by
Phoenix Typesetting, Burley-in-Wharfedale, West Yorkshire
Printed and bound in Great Britain by
Biddles Ltd, Guildford and King's Lynn

For my daughters-in-law, Christine and Margaret

I

Opal, carrying the child in one arm and a canvas bag over the other, came into the house and kicked the door to with her foot, but not quickly enough to keep out the thin cloud of powdery snowflakes which followed her. They settled on the doormat and, though the room was bitterly cold, were quickly melted and absorbed. The child started to cry, a thin, miserable sound.

'I know son. You're cold,' Opal said. 'Just let me set you down and we'll soon get things warmed up.'

She sat him on the black horsehair sofa which was partly covered by a large square of knitted patchwork.

'There!' she said gently. 'Now wait on. I'll be as quick as I can.'

The light had almost gone from the short February day. She found the box of matches on the mantelpiece and lit the gas, standing on tiptoe and stretching out her arm to the bracket, for she was only five feet tall. The gas popped and spluttered, seeming reluctant to settle down to its usual steady hiss. Its soft glow lit the centre of the room, enhancing the ruby-red plush tablecloth, picking out the odd patches of colour in the rag rugs on the stone floor, but not penetrating into the corners of even so small a room. The rugs were made from old clothes cut into strips, or 'tabs'. Everyone's clothes seemed to have been made in dark, serviceable colours, but whenever she had been able to get hold of something brighter, Opal had worked it into the rug in the rough shape of a flower. She loved colour, and nowhere in her life was there enough of it.

'We need a new gas mantle,' she said, kneeling down

to be on a level with her small son. His cry had changed to an intermittent whimper.

'Now,' she went on. 'Mam'll blow on your hands for a minute to warm them, then she'll light the fire.,' She cupped his small hands in her own, though hers were scarcely less cold, and blew her warm breath over them, gently chafing his fingers until he was comforted.

'There!' she said. 'Isn't that better?'

She took food from the canvas bag and put it into the oven, which always retained a vestige of heat. Then she pulled down the window blind and drew the heavy chenille curtain against the back of the street door. The door leading to the stairs was similarly curtained, for the house was full of draughts.

'When the wind blows from the north,' she observed. 'When it's blowing straight from the moor, nothing'll keep it out!'

The fire was laid. She took a taper from the jar on the shelf – for not even a match must be wasted – lit it from the gas and put it to the kindling.

'We'll soon have you warmed up,' she promised the child. 'See the smoke curling up the chimney? And the pretty orange flames, though you must never go near them. Now if you sit there and watch you'll see the black coals turn red and then we'll be really warm. But perhaps you'd better keep your coat and scarf on a bit longer.'

She talked to Daniel most of the time when they were alone together but, being not quite two years old, he seldom answered her. In any case he was a quiet child. He was dark, like herself, with large, solemn eyes which watched everything. She wondered what went on in his mind.

'I had hoped your Dad might have been home before us, got the fire going,' she said. 'I wonder where he's got to?'

At this time of the year the fire should be lit in the morning and be warming the house all day; but coal cost money and they had none. To be precise, she had twopence in her purse, which had to see her through until Friday morning. It was Wednesday today.

Every Wednesday she visited her mother-in-law, arriving before the midday dinner and leaving in time to have Edgar's tea ready when he came in from work. Though it was now six months since he had worked she kept to the same routine. No need to rub it in that time was no longer important to him . He could have gone with her, enjoyed a good meal, but he seldom did. Perhaps to visit his mother in the middle of the day was to underline his position and Opal did not press him. She enjoyed Sarah Carson's company. Her mother-in-law was a warm, fat, cheerful woman. Her house was warm too because her husband, Percy, was the local baker. Today's overheated kitchen, right next to the bakehouse, had felt like heaven.

Opal heard her husband at the door and went to ease back the curtain. He entered, bringing a gust of cold air and more snowflakes with him. Edgar Carson was not especially tall, but he seemed at once to fill the space in the small room, perhaps because of the breadth of his shoulders and the set of his handsome head, but really more because of some indefinable inner quality. Whatever it was it never failed to quicken Opal's pulse, to enliven her. Even when things were going badly his magnetism for her never lessened. He removed his cap, shaking the snow on to the floor, and revealed tightly-curled, light brown hair in need of cutting.

'My word!' he said. 'It's bitter out there! I'm perished!'

He looked it. The tip of his nose glowed red as a beacon in his white face and a few snowflakes had caught and stayed, too icy to melt, in his thick, fair moustache and heavy eyebrows.

'It's cold in here,' Opal said. 'I've only just lit the fire. We went early to your mother's – just after you'd left for the Labour Exchange – so as not to have to light it. Why didn't you come for your dinner, love? We had a lovely steak and kidney pie.'

'They sent me after a job.'

3

'And?' But she didn't need to ask.

The years immediately after the War had been good ones. Trade had picked up quickly and there had been an air of optimism everywhere. But it didn't last long. Edgar knew he was only one of thousands who'd been laid off in 1922, and prospects for 1923 seemed no brighter. Hope for a new kind of world, which was what had kept him going in the filth of the trenches, for he had hated every minute of being a soldier, had already died in him.

'There were twenty of us after it. There's a lot of weavers out of work, as well you know,' he said defensively.

'Oh I know all right,' Opal said. 'I know!'

She pushed past him to fill the kettle at the scullery tap, and then back again to place it on the hob. Hunger and cold had so numbed him that he seemed not to have the wit to get out of her way.

'Lloyd George promised us a land fit for heroes to live in,' he said. 'We believed him, simple folk like me. Well he's out of it now, and serve him right I say. But I see nothing better from this lot.'

Opal sighed. 'Politics! Politics won't fill our bellies! See to Daniel, will you love?'

Edgar moved to the sofa and took his son on his lap. There were days when his inside seemed to turn to stone, when his broad shoulders seemed unable to bear the almost physical weight of his depression. Opal, though he knew she tried, didn't understand how a man in his position felt.

'Don't take Daniel's coat off yet,' she said. 'Not until the house has warmed up.'

'All the same, you're wrong about politics,' Edgar said. 'They matter all right. It's Governments decide the way we live, you and me.'

'Don't forget there was a war,' Opal said.

'I'm not likely to,' he said grimly. 'But who caused that lot if it wasn't the politicians? Answer me that!'

'I can't.'

4

She sighed. He was in a bad mood again, working himself up to no purpose. She *did* sympathize with him, ached at his inability to get a job. Yet as the months went by a cold voice inside her too often asked why, whenever there was a job going, it never went to Edgar? His appearance was good. He was a competent workman. But the months of idleness were dulling him, resentment was taking hold. At a time when even good workmen were without jobs he lacked the spark which would have given him the edge in an interview with a prospective employer. She could see all that so plainly, but how could she tell him without hurting him further?

'Kettle's boiling,' Edgar said.

Opal made the tea and set it aside to brew. The longer it stood the more strength they would get from the spoonful of tea. She wondered if life was to go on like this forever. And to crown it all she was pregnant again, though she had not yet told Edgar, or indeed anyone. People who were better off preached that it was wrong and improvident of the unemployed to have children. Well, she wasn't overjoyed about the child she was carrying, either. She had no idea how they would manage. But what the well-off didn't understand – how could they? – was that sex was the only pleasure left which didn't need money in the purse; that in the warmth and darkness of the bed it blotted out reality. And that while it lasted, the coupling of the poorest man and woman could equal that of the rich.

But at its conclusion the worry always started again. Supposing I've been caught? We should have been more careful, stopped before the climax. 'Always take a towel to bed with you.' the women advised each other. 'Let him come on that!'

Easier said than done, so that after the earliest possible douching, uncomfortably carried out in the kitchen with a bucket of water and an arrangement of rubber tubing, one waited and prayed daily for the menstrual blood to flow again. And if the blood did not flow, then it was the large measure of gin, the raspberry leaf tea, the repeated jumping off the kitchen table – all advised to bring on an early miscarriage.

Opal had done none of that, nor would she. She was too afraid that if she tampered with Nature, then Nature might take its revenge and give her a deformed child. But she was three months gone now and she would have to tell Edgar, as well as his parents and hers. Also, she had this other matter in mind. Both subjects had to be broached. But better wait until they'd eaten. Food might raise Edgar's spirits.

'Your mother gave me a couple of meat pasties today,' she said. 'And currant teacakes to finish off with. I don't know where we'd be without your mother. My Mam's well-intentioned enough, and I know she'd help if she were asked, but somehow she doesn't think of the little things like your mother does.'

Perhaps, Opal thought, because her mother had been a servant in a house where there were no shortages, and since her marriage had lived on farms, where basic foods were more easily come by, it had never occurred to her that her daughter might be hungry. And Opal would not have hinted at it. She did not see her mother often and in her heart she knew that she neglected her.

She served the pasties, one each for herself and Edgar.

'I'll give Daniel a bit of mine if he fancies it,' she said. 'But he ate well at his grandma's today.'

She must visit her mother soon. The small sheep farm to which her parents had moved from Grandpa Derwent's place was four miles away across the moors, and it was a bad time for walking, but see her mother she must. She had a favour to ask of her.

'I'd like you to look after Daniel on Saturday,' she said to Edgar. 'I want to go to Highcliffe. He's a weight to carry and it's too far for him to walk.'

'Whatever do you want to go for in this weather?' Edgar asked. 'There's snow on the ground. It might not clear by the weekend.'

6

'It might not clear all winter,' Opal said. 'I can't wait until the Spring comes.'

She went to the kettle and poured more water over the tea leaves.

'I can squeeze another cup,' she said. 'There's no sugar. You'll have to manage without.'

'What is there that can't wait, for Heaven's sake?'

Opal sipped her tea. She felt better now. The room was warming up and the food had done her good. She was always ravenous these days.

'Well . . .,' she began hesitantly. 'There's two things I have to tell you, love. I reckon you won't like either of them.'

He stared at her. 'Well, what is it then?'

'The first is, I'm three months pregnant. The second is . . . I'm going to open up a house shop!'

'A house shop? What on earth do you mean?'

It was clear, Opal thought, which announcement had upset him most.

'What else can I mean, Edgar,' she replied patiently, 'than a little shop right here in the house? It's not uncommon. Other people have done it.'

'But why? Why you?'

'Why me?'

And then it was as if the poison of every bad feeling – of frustration, of hunger, of fear for the future – which for Edgar's sake she had strived to hide over the last few months, churned in her stomach, rose chokingly into her throat, and had to be spat out.

'Why me?' she snapped. 'Because I want sugar in my tea and butter on my bread! I want more to live on every Thursday than a twopenny packet of soup! And Daniel's growing out of his clothes and your boots let in the water!' Her voice rose to a shout and Daniel, frightened, began to cry. 'I can think of several other reasons, but will those do to be going on with?'

Edgar's hurt eyes met hers. To her horror she saw the tears rise in them and spill over. She felt as though she had taken a whip to him. But if crying was any good, she thought wearily, she'd have solved all their problems long ago. She never cried nowadays. As for a man doing so, as for Edgar doing so, that was weakness, and frightening. Now more than ever they needed each other's strength.

She picked up Daniel and held him in her lap, burying her face in the warm nape of his neck. Then eventually she stretched out her hand and took Edgar's.

'I'm sorry, love,' she said. 'I know you want to get work. I know you deserve to have a job. But it might be a long time before you do and we can't go on like this. Twenty-one shillings a week was bad enough for the three of us, but now you've run out of benefit and what the Board of Guardians allows us won't feed a cat. And another thing – I'm sick of Food Vouchers! Some Jack-in-Office telling me what I can buy and what I can't buy! Do you know there's a list as long as my arm of foods I *can't* get on the vouchers because *they* think they're luxuries? Not for the likes of us! No, Edgar, if I can make just a bit extra, a shilling or two a week, it'll make all the difference. I'm going to need new things for the baby, too.'

She was babbling. She knew it. But anything to wipe that look from his face.

Edgar wiped his eyes with the back of his hand. She was always so logical, so right. When they were courting and in the early days of their marriage he had admired her strengths, though they were different from his own. She was a wife who would help a husband to get on, spur his ambitions. He was a man who would work for his family, strive to do all that was expected of him, given the chance. But sometimes now, though she did not know it, Opal's strength seemed to diminish him. Sometimes he longed for a glimpse of some frailty in her which would excuse the weakness he knew in himself.

'You must see it's reasonable,' Opal said more quietly. She saw by the look in his eyes, the all-too-familiar look of defeat, that she had won. She would have her house shop. But the victory itself gave her no pleasure. How much better if the idea had been his!

'We don't have much room here,' Edgar said in a dull voice. 'Where will you put everything?'

'I thought I'd clear the top of the sideboard and set up shop there, and perhaps on a bit of the table. I could empty the sideboard cupboards, too. God knows there's not much in them. You could take the doors off for me and it would be like display shelves.'

'But what about the other shops in the village? Won't they object?'

'No,' she said. 'What little bit of trade I do won't affect them. I'll sell a variety of things so it'll only be a very little from each.' In any case she did not care. She had her own family to look out for.

'Where will you get money to buy stock?' Edgar asked. 'You'll need cash on the nail.'

'I know. That's why I want to go to Highcliffe. I'm sure Mam has a bit put by. Her egg money from the market and suchlike. If she'd lend me five pounds I could make a start.'

Edgar sighed. 'Well you seem to have it all worked out.'

'Oh I have,' Opal agreed. 'And I'll make it pay. You'll see. But you've not said anything about the baby!'

'What do you want me to say? These things happen. Of course I'm pleased. We didn't want Daniel to be our only bairn, did we? But it'll be harder for you than for me. Are you sure you'll be able to manage the shop as well?'

It was strange, Opal thought, that it never occurred to him that he might run the shop while she looked after their children and kept house. While he might not forbid her to go ahead with the scheme it would not enter his head to contribute. Running a house shop – selling needles and thread and sweets and groceries was, like housework, cooking, and bringing up children, women's work. It was beside the point that he had nothing else to

9

do except sign on at the Labour Exchange and attend a decreasing number of interviews.

But having told Edgar she felt the project was as good as launched. She was sure she could get the loan. For the first time in many weeks excitement stirred in her and with it came that other, more familiar feeling. It ran like fire through her body and tingled in her breasts. She wanted, needed, to make love now, urgently. If it had not been for Daniel she would have liked to have lain with Edgar on the hearthrug, naked in the light from the fire, now glowing red, instead of in the dark, chilly bedroom. But, though he knew how much she loved him, such desires of the body were not ones which she could put into words to Edgar. It was shaming enough that she, a woman, should have them.

'I'll put Daniel to bed and we'll have an early night,' she said. 'It'll save the gas.'

She began to undress Daniel. There was one thing to be said in favour of being pregnant; you could make love whenever you wanted to. When Daniel was in his night-shift she put him down gently on the rug. Then she began to remove the pins from her hair. It cascaded around her shoulders, thick, jet black, gleaming in the light from the fire. Edgar had always liked to see her hair loose. When they were first married he would take out the pins himself, slowly, one by one, watching the hair fall.

She lifted Daniel from the rug and went up to the bedroom, leaving the stairs door open behind her.

The main street of Milton ran down to the railway bridge, and just beyond that to the bridge over the river. The mill which gave the village its reason for being there (for it had not grown from early beginnings like other villages, but had been built all in one go) stood on a strip of land between the two bridges. Sir Henry Milton, in the nineteenth century, had carefully calculated the advantages of this position: the soft river water to wash the wool, the railway (in which he was a shareholder) to bear it away; spun, woven and dyed into the finest cloth.

Though the village was dominated by the mill and could not have existed without it, Sir Henry was a philanthropic businessman and had also built a school, a public washhouse, a chapel (in the grounds of which he now rested in his ornate tomb), a cottage hospital and several streets of small, terraced houses for his millhands, with a few larger ones for the Managers. It was because he worked at the mill that Edgar had been able, on his marriage, to rent the house in Acer Street.

This morning groups of men stood on the railway bridge. One of them called out to Opal as she passed.

'Good-morning Mrs Carson!'

'Good-morning Mr Holroyd. Cold weather we're having!'

They were standing there, she knew, because Saturday was a working day and they had been used to rising early and going to the mill. Though for most of them there was now no work, they felt better getting up, getting out of the house, meeting with their mates.

Beyond the river the cobbled street ended and the track through the woods up to the moor began, rising steeply from the valley. Opal enjoyed the climb. On the top of the moor the air was clear and dry, the sky unusually high for February. She was glad to get away from Milton for a few hours and was looking forward to seeing her family and hearing the news of the farm.

She had not always thought that way. When Edgar Carson had first called at the farm . . . he was returning over the moors from Ilkley with two friends and enquired if a ham and egg tea could be provided – Opal had answered the door to him . She knew at once that here was the man she had been waiting for to carry her away. And after that first Sunday he had returned often, sometimes with his friends and then, as time went on, more often on his own.

'It's clear what *he's* coming for,' Opal's mother said. 'Plain as a pikestaff!'

'Well I like him,' Opal said. She loved him, but that was too extravagant a feeling to express out loud, to her mother.

'So do we all,' her mother replied. 'He's an agreeable lad. And he did his bit in the war, there's no denying that.'

'So what have you got against him?' Opal demanded.

'Not against *him*. Not personally. It's just that . . . well, your Dad and me thought of something better for you. A farmer or a schoolteacher.'

'But not a weaver,' Opal said. 'Well, he'll not always be a weaver. He means to get on. And I don't see any farmers or schoolteachers queueing up for me, do you?'

'There's plenty of time,' Mrs Derwent said. 'Why is it you can never wait for anything?'

Then in the June of nineteen twenty Edgar had come one weekend to give a hand with the haymaking, working all day beside Opal, forking the hay stooks into the cart. The day's toil, the hot sun, the clover-scented, newly-cut grass, were powerful aphrodisiacs for both of them (had they needed such aids). Before nightfall, in the stone barn where they had stacked the new hay, Daniel was conceived. Benjamin and Hannah Derwent said goodbye to their dreams for Opal and in September the couple were married in the tiny Methodist chapel at Highcliffe.

Opal climbed the last short steep rise before the summit of the moor. From now on it was all downhill. The countryside, its contours softened by the deep covering of snow, reminded her of a picture of Switzerland she had once seen on a calendar. A mile down the hill she could see the hamlet which was Highcliffe, and on the edge of it her father's farm. The sheep, which in the summer were allowed to roam the hill, were now folded in the small field close to the farm-house, where they were handy for winter feeding. They huddled together against the cold. In a couple of months from now the fields would be freshly green and the low pastures would be dotted with new lambs.

She began to hurry down the slope, sliding and slipping in the snow. In spite of being pregnant she felt incredibly fit and healthy. She had no morning sickness, and wouldn't have now. But she was terribly hungry and hoped that by the time she reached the farm, dinner would be on the table. They didn't know she was coming but there was always enough for an extra person. The way she felt she could eat two men's dinners.

She was not disappointed. When she reached the farm and walked into the big kitchen the warm air was filled with the delicious smell of food. Everyone was there, including her brother Mark and his bride-to-be, Queenie Stone, and Opal's Aunt Garnet. They were at the table, already starting on the meal. Mary jumped up from her chair and rushed to embrace her sister. Only Mary would ever dream of giving such an effusive greeting, but they all looked up from their heaped plates, pleased enough to see her.

'Come and sit down, love,' her mother said. 'Mary, lay another place. You've not brought Daniel nor Edgar, then?'

'No. I thought the weather might turn bad. And Daniel has a bit of a cold.'

As her mother rose to fetch the meat pie which she had returned to the oven to keep hot, Opal thought how thin she was looking. But she sounded well enough. Her voice was strong.

'I'm starving!' Opal said. 'I could eat a huge helping!'

'You always could,' her father said. 'I don't know where you put it. You are not the size of two pennorth of copper!'

'Well you know what they say,' Opal retorted. 'They don't make diamonds as big as bricks.'

'She's like me,' Aunt Garnet mumbled through a mouthful of pie. Aunt Garnet was the middle one of Opal's father's three sisters. The three were named Pearl, Garnet and Ruby because Grandpa Derwent said they were his jewels. When his first granddaughter was born he expected the tradition to be followed, favouring Diamond or Emerald, but Hannah was against it and Benjamin reckoned it was the mother's privilege to name the baby. In the end, Hannah compromised on Opal. Her own mother said that that was worse because everyone knew that Opals were for tears. When it came to her second daughter and last child she chose the name Mary as being the most straightforward she could think of.

'I didn't expect to find you here, Aunt Garnet,' Opal said.

'No you wouldn't,' her aunt replied. 'But as you know, there's less to do on the farm in winter, so I gave myself a holiday. Father wasn't too pleased, of course.'

Aunt Garnet must be in her forties, Opal thought, and Aunt Pearl was older still. Unlike Ruby, they had never married but had remained at home on the dales farm, where Grandfather Derwent treated them like children.

Opal turned to Queenie and Mark, who were seated side by side and were so much in love that they held hands between mouthfuls.

'Have you fixed the date yet?' she asked.

'Saturday the second of June,' Queenie said happily. 'Only sixteen weeks to go! And I have a favour to ask you, Opal. Will you make the wedding hats? Mine and the bridesmaids? You're so clever at it.'

'You can do mine as well,' Aunt Garnet said.

'You're not having a white wedding, then?' Opal enquired.

'No. With Mother gone and father rather poorly, it seems best not.'

'Well of course I'll do them.'

'Our Opal was always gifted with her needle,' Hannah Derwent said. 'When she was little she didn't really play with dolls like other children do. She just made hats and dresses for them, and always in the latest style.'

'I'll make you a new hat, too, Mother,' Opal said.

'Nay lass,' her mother answered. 'The one I had for your wedding's as good as new. I've hardly worn it since, except to Harvest Thanksgiving and Whitsundays to chapel. It'll do me nicely.'

'You'll have to go with me to buy the material, Queenie,' Opal said. There was no way she could lay out a penny. She would earn a bit in the end, but not much since it was for family.

'Oh we'll arrange all that,' Queenie said. 'Shall we have a trip to Leasfield? Or Leeds or Bradford?'

Queenie's father was a prosperous wool merchant and none of his family were ever short of money, but Queenie was sensitive to other people's needs and perfectly understood Opal's remark.

When the meal was over Opal contrived to get her mother to accompany her upstairs so that they could speak alone.

'I wanted you to know before the others,' Opal said. 'I'm expecting. It'll be in August.'

There was a barely felt pause, a fleeting look of pain on her mother's face, but swiftly followed by a pleased smile.

'Well that's good news, Opal love!' She patted her daughter's hand, the nearest she ever came to a caress. 'It's best for little Daniel not to be an only child. But don't have a quiverful as the Good Book says. It's too big a burden. Oh I don't mean that any of you lot were,' she added quickly. 'Nothing like that. But with jobs so hard to come by . . . I suppose Edgar hasn't heard anything yet?'

'No,' Opal said. 'Which brings me to the next thing.'

She explained to her mother what she had in mind about the shop and asked for the loan of five pounds.

'I'll pay it back as soon as I can. A bit at a time, but you'll get it all,' Opal promised.

'Well if you're sure it's what you want to do, you can have the money and welcome,' Mrs Derwent said. She crossed to the walnut chest and took out a small bag from the back of a drawer.

'Here you are love,' she said. 'And ten gold sovereigns, not five. You'll do better with a good start. I don't want it

back. It's yours to keep. Only don't you go telling anyone
– not your father nor anyone. What's mine is my own and
it's up to me what I do with it!'

'Oh Mam! I don't know how to thank you!'

'Then don't! And now we'd best get back downstairs.
There's a mountain of washing up.'

Downstairs, Mary shooed her mother out of the
kitchen.

'You go and sit in the parlour and talk weddings with
Queenie,' she said.

'Mam's not well,' Mary told Opal when their mother
had left the room. 'But she won't rest. That's why Aunt
Garnet's here, only Mam doesn't know it.'

'What's wrong with her?' Opal asked. 'I thought she
looked thinner. Why didn't you let me know? I'd have
come sooner.'

'I was going to if you hadn't come today. I don't know
what's wrong and she won't see a doctor. She says it's
simply the end of the winter and she'll be better in the
Spring. Of course we both know she's never been the
same since George was killed. More than six years now,
but she doesn't get over it. George was more to her
than you and me put together!'

It was not to be wondered at, Opal thought. She, too,
had worshipped her brother. A light had gone out for all
of them when George had been killed on the Somme. For
their mother it had never been rekindled.

'I'm having another baby,' she announced.

'Oh Opal, you're not! Oh you are lucky! I do envy
you. Sometimes I think I'll never get married and have
babies yet it's all I ever want.'

Opal laughed. 'What *do* you mean? Of course you will.
You're only eighteen. There's all the time in the world.'

'I never meet anyone,' Mary said.

'You will,' Opal assured her. 'Perhaps someone will
come knocking on the door, like Edgar did.'

Too soon it was time to leave. Opal would have liked
to have stayed longer, wouldn't have minded in the least

16

walking back across the moor in the dark, but Edgar would expect her back and Daniel would no doubt be waiting for his tea.

'I'll walk along the bottom path with you,' her mother said. It was an unusual gesture, and even more strange that she should wave Mary aside, wanting to have Opal to herself. Yet as they walked she had nothing of significance to say. At the end of the level path where Opal must turn to start the walk up to the moor, she took both her daughter's hands in hers.

'You've always been a good lass to me,' she said. 'I don't forget it. Now get on, and take care of yourself.'

'And you do the same, Mam,' Opal answered.

She wondered about her mother as she climbed the hill. Was she perhaps trying to say that she was sorry for her concentration on her dead son and the exclusion of her living children? When she reached the top of the hill she turned and looked back. Her mother was still standing there. The two women raised their hands in a final gesture of farewell. But when Opal started on the downward slope her thoughts turned at once to her house shop. She began to plan what she would buy with the ten gold sovereigns in her purse.

On the Monday following her visit to Highcliffe she did the family wash; starching, blueing, mangling, drying, ironing – so that by bedtime everything had been aired off on the clothes horse by the fire and could be put away. On Tuesday she cleaned the living room, polished the sideboard, scrubbing the table top with coarse salt, blackleading the range until Daniel could see his face in the oven door.

'Why all the fuss?' Edgar enquired. 'If somebody wants a packet of pins in a hurry they won't care a tinker's curse whether the firegrate's clean or not.'

'Oh yes they will,' Opal contradicted. 'They may not realize it, but everything about the surroundings matters when you're trying to sell something.'

Edgar looked at her in astonishment.

'How do you know? You've never sold anything.'

'I just do, that's all. I know I'm right. I wish I had a few flowers to brighten up the place. When I'm rich I shall have fresh flowers every day.'

On Wednesday she made her usual visit to her mother-in-law and gave her the news. Mrs Carson was delighted about the baby. 'It was a sorrow to Percy and me,' she said. 'That Edgar was the only one.' About the shop she was dubious but resigned, even a little guilty that her son might have brought this upon his family.

'I'm sure our Edgar tries to get work,' she defended him. 'These are hard times we live in. We can't even afford to take a man on in the bakery, or there'd be a job for Edgar there. I just wish we could help you more.'

'No-one's been more helpful than you have,' Opal said. 'You've been a Godsend.'

'I daresay you'll make a go of it,' Mrs Carson said more cheerfully. She could never be downhearted for long. 'Though I'm sorry you won't be able to come here on a Wednesday any more.'

'With Wednesday being half-day closing around here,' Opal said, 'It's a good time for me to be open.'

The next day she was up early. Immediately after breakfast she set off for Shepton, pushing Daniel's empty perambulator. Ridley's was the wholesaler she intended visiting. She had seen the advertisement in the Argus and it looked as though they might supply everything she needed. She hoped for as many lines as possible, reckoning that by stocking all the different goods her capital would allow, she might attract more customers. A woman who came for a reel of thread might be tempted by a chocolate bar if it was under her nose. 'You can get it at Opal's,' was to be her slogan.

The wholesaler's was situated over a newsagent and tobacconist, in the middle of a row of dismal-looking

shops. 'Keenest prices, highest quality,' the advertisement
had said. Well, that was what she was after. She propped
the pram against the wall outside the newsagent's and
hoped it would be there when she returned.

'K. Ridley, General Wholesaler,' the door on the first
landing proclaimed. And below that a notice said 'Please
do not ask for Credit since a Refusal may cause Offence.'
She knocked and entered. The warehouse was larger than
she had expected. The walls were shelved and crammed
with goods from floor to ceiling. The man who greeted her
was a wisp of a man; scarcely bigger than she herself.

'Ken Ridley, Esquire, at your service,' he announced.
His voice was inappropriately deep and strong. 'I don't
know you, do I?'

'Mrs Opal Carson.'

'So what can I do for a pretty lady like you?' he asked.
Opal explained her errand.

'Well then,' he said. 'You'd best look around and see
what takes your fancy! It's all here somewhere!'

It was difficult to know where to start and even more
difficult to know when to stop. She chose reels of cotton,
reluctantly confining herself to black and white; cards
of white linen shirt buttons, pins, sewing and darning
needles, knicker elastic, grey darning wool. From the
confectionery shelves she selected small items which children could buy with a halfpenny: toffee bars, aniseed
balls, sherbert fountains, liquorice chews, fruit gums,
dolly mixtures, jelly babies, pear drops and acid drops.
And to tempt the mothers with a copper or two to spare
and a treat in mind, Fry's cream bars and Rowntree's
whipped cream walnuts.

'You'll find sweets a good line,' Mr Ridley advised.
The less money people have, the more they seem to
want to suck sweets. But save enough money for a few
packets of groceries. Baking powder, tea. And a few
medicinal items for the sudden upset. All obtainable in
handy sizes. Daisy headache powders, senna pods, epsom
salts, syrup of figs – if you'll pardon me mentioning

them. And Doctor Cassell's tablets. Magical for shell-shock, nervous debility, stomach pains. Take the one-and-threepenny box and sell them a couple at a time. You'll make a penny or two there.'

'I think I must have reached the limit,' Opal said eventually. She had been trying to add up in her head but had long ago lost count. 'But what I *would* like, even if I have to put something else back on the shelf, is a jar of Fortune's Whispers.'

'Ah!' Mr Ridley said. 'You're a romantic, like all the ladies!'

'No,' Opal said. 'I'm a realist. It's my intention to allow every customer for the first month to pick out a Fortune's Whisper, free. I'm relying on everyone else to be romantic, you see. To want to see into the future.'

Mr Ridley clapped his hands. 'Well I'll be blowed if you don't take the biscuit,' he chuckled. 'I'll tell you what, I'll do something which is against the rules of a lifetime. You can have the Fortune's Whispers on credit! Pay me when you've given them all away! And while you're at it, pick one for yourself. Go on! Let's see what *your* future's going to be! Come on, dip in. Close your eyes first!'

Opal put her hand into the sweet jar and extracted the small, flat, pastel-coloured sugar sweet, with its message printed on one surface.

'Well, what does it say?' Mr Ridley was all eagerness.

She read the words aloud.

'This could be your lucky day.'

'There you are!' cried Mr Ridley. 'I knew it!'

So did Opal. She felt it in her bones and was at once elated and awed.

Amazingly, the goods came to sixpence short of ten pounds. She would be able to eat.

'And I'll throw in a few little cards which might be useful,' Mr Ridley said. 'You'll find the customers appreciate them.' He gave her three oblong cards, threaded with string to hang on the wall. 'We Aim to Please', 'If You Don't see What You Require, Please Ask', and

'Thank You, Please Call Again'.

Before leaving Shepton she bought a plain teacake filled with boiled ham and spread with mustard, for fourpence, and an Eccles cake for a penny. Walking along the road, pushing the laden pram, she ate them greedily.

On Friday morning when Edgar had left for the Labour Exchange she spread her best tablecloth on top of the sideboard and arranged her stock. She placed an empty Oxo tin on the corner of the sideboard and hoped that no-one would require change. She had a float of one penny. Then she sat back, too excited to engage in any activity, and waited for customers. She had put the word around among neighbours and there was nothing more she could do.

It was a quarter before midday when the door opened and her first customer appeared – a small boy, the son of a neighbour.

'What can I do for you, Thomas?' she asked.

'Mam says do you sell Oxo cubes?'

'I do,' Opal said. 'How many would you like?'

'One.'

When he had paid her she proffered the jar of Fortune's Whispers. 'There's one for every customer who buys,' she told him. 'A lucky dip. Be sure to tell your friends, won't you? And because you're my very first customer, Thomas, you can choose something from amongst the sweets. Anything you like as long as it costs a halfpenny!'

She was in business.

2

Opal cleared the breakfast table quickly, then opened the door and shook the crumbs from the tablecloth to the sparrows waiting in the street. She glanced up at the sky; blue, with fleecy white clouds hurrying before a breeze. A perfect May morning. Earlier she had taken a cup of tea to Edgar but he had not yet come down. Well then, he must fend for himself when he did get up – which she hoped would be soon because she was going out and both Daniel and the shop were to be left in his care.

Each day now she made an early start with the shop so that she could catch the children's custom on their way to school. How, in these hard times, parents could afford to give their children a halfpenny two or three times a week, she just didn't know. But so long as they did, she wanted it to come to her. Mr Ridley had been right; the less money some people had, the more they spent on sweets.

She wished Edgar would get a move on. These last few weeks, except on his signing-on mornings, he'd taken to sleeping late every day, sometimes not coming down until after eleven. It seemed sometimes that the harder she tried, the less he cooperated. She went to the bottom of the stairs and called out to him.

'Edgar! It's time you were up! Don't forget I'm going to Queenie's.'

A grunt confirmed that he had heard her, but it was another quarter of an hour before he shuffled downstairs, rubbing the sleep from his eyes.

'I don't know how you can loll in bed the way you do,' Opal said.

'You wouldn't,' he replied.

Even after all this time he still wakened at six, forgetting for a moment, then remembering. Why couldn't Opal understand that to rise early only made the day longer. There was no purpose to it. Better to turn over and go to sleep again.

'You know perfectly well I have to take the hats,' Opal said.

'I'd forgotten. What about my breakfast?'

'I've left you some porridge. It's in the pan on the side. Don't use the milk. Daniel needs it.'

She ought to be drinking milk herself, being pregnant, but most of the half-pint a day which she bought went to Daniel. Perhaps before long she could order extra. She was now making a regular two or three shillings a week profit on the shop. A proportion of this was regularly put aside to invest in more stock, but some she did spend on food. Twice a week she bought fresh herrings, which were cheap and tasty. Every Saturday night she bought 'pie bits', or a rabbit from the butcher, so that they always had a good Sunday dinner. But also, though she had no clear idea why, she was trying to save a few coppers each week, in a toffee tin. One day she would know why she wanted them, and they would be there. Meanwhile the sight of the toffee tin gave her a feeling of security.

'How long will you be gone?' Edgar asked.

'I don't know. It'll be dinner time before I get to the other side of Leasfield. After dinner I have to set to and do the final bits on the hats. Mary and the other bridesmaid will be there and Mary's taking Aunt Garnet's hat back with her.'

'Aunt Garnet's not back at Highcliffe, is she?' Edgar asked.

'No. But they'll be stopping there on their way to the wedding.'

She wished her aunt could have been at Highcliffe, since her mother was no better. She had walked over to the farm a fortnight ago and had been concerned to see

23

her thinner than ever, and breathless after the slightest exertion.

Opal tried to fasten her jacket and found that it would no longer meet over her increasing girth.

'It's a good thing it's cut to hang straight from the shoulders,' she said. 'I can leave it undone and it'll help to hide me.'

She looked at herself critically in the mirror over the sideboard, adjusting her hat. It was a cream-coloured straw with a deep brim, the crown trimmed with green ribbon finishing in a large bow at the side. However little she had in her purse she tried never to show poverty in her appearance. Her clothes were always clean and well pressed and by clever alterations and small touches here and there she kept in fashion. Never, ever, would she be seen like the other women in Milton, with a shawl over her head to slip to the local shops. And when she went out she always wore gloves.

She gave a final adjustment to her hat and turned to face Edgar.

'Will I do then?' she asked.

'You look grand,' he said. 'Good enough to eat!'

She smiled happily, her good humour restored by his praise.

'What in *my* condition? Well I'll be off then.'

She gathered up her bulky parcels and bent to kiss Daniel.

'Now don't forget Edgar,' she said. 'There's some soup in the pan for your dinner and Daniel's. See that he has his afternoon sleep. I've set out the shop, as you can see. Try not to use paper bags, but if you really must, then use the smallest. Wrapping paper costs money. And don't forget . . .'

'All right, all right!' Edgar interrupted. 'Are you sure you wouldn't like me to do the washing and blacklead the fireplace in my spare time?'

'Well if you were me you might have to,' Opal quipped. 'Ta-ta then!'

It was generally supposed that the tram ran from Leasfield to a point quite close to Milton because Sir Henry and his descendants held so much power in both places. Also because when Milton was in full work the Miltonians flocked to Leasfield to spend their wages. In Leasfield there were large shops, two markets, two theatres, three cinemas and countless public houses. Opal took the tram into the centre of the town, then boarded another tram outside the smoke-blackened town hall, destination Barton, where the well-to-do lived.

Queenie's father, Henry Stone, had made his money in wool. His wife had died, leaving Queenie to look after her father and, when the time came, to inherit his wealth. Mr Stone would never have let Mark Derwent come near Queenie if Mark hadn't saved her life, Opal thought, climbing the steps of the large stone house, ringing the bell. He had seen her in difficulties in the river, near Milton, and as her boat capsized he jumped in and rescued her. It was love at first sight for both of them. Queenie would look at no-one else and her father could hardly turn away the man but for whom, his daughter assured him, she might not *be* there.

A maid showed Opal into the large, comfortable sitting room where Queenie stood with outstretched hands to greet her.

'Opal, how lovely to see you! Oh, how exciting your parcels look! I can hardly wait. But I must, and you must have a cup of tea after your journey. Or better still a glass of sherry. That's it! We'll both be quite wicked and have a glass of sherry! Come over here and sit on the sofa.'

Opal sank into the soft, springy comfort of the sofa, pushing one of the several down-filled cushions into the small of her back. Intent on getting here, she hadn't noticed until now how tired she was.

'There you are!' Queenie said. 'Finest Amontillado! It will put new life into you. Now tell me how you are. Oh, I can't wait to be pregnant!' She blushed. 'After I'm married of course.'

'I'm fine,' Opal said. 'And this May weather is perfect for me. Selfishly, I hope we don't have a hot summer.'

'As long as you'll allow me a fine wedding day,' Queenie said.

'You shall have a beautiful wedding day,' Opal promised. 'Now, do you want to take a peek at the hats before dinner?'

'Oh yes please. I can hardly wait. But bring them upstairs and I'll show you the dresses. Mrs Bassett has almost finished them. By the way, how is Edgar?'

'He's a bit low,' Opal replied. 'I suppose it's to be expected and I do feel sorry for him, but sometimes I think he should make an effort to snap out of it.'

'Poor Edgar!' Queenie said sympathetically.

In the bedroom Queenie opened the large mahogany wardrobe and took out her wedding dress, holding it with reverence.

'I know it's extravagant to have crepe georgette when so many people are poor,' she apologized. 'But it's the only wedding I'll ever have. I'm not beautiful like you, but I want to look my very best for Mark.'

'It's quite perfect,' Opal assured her. 'And so will you be. This soft lavender with your fair colouring is exactly right. And Mrs Bassett's made a marvellous job of the silver beading.' She touched the georgette lovingly. She had a feeling for fine materials.

'Hasn't she just! She still has to turn up the hem. The last few stitches won't be put in until the day, and I mustn't try it on, once it's finished, until I'm ready to wear it because that might bring bad luck.'

Opal laughed. 'Don't be silly!'

'I know it's silly,' Queenie confessed. 'But I daren't risk it.'

'Well don't let Mrs Bassett make it too long. Seven inches from the ground is quite long enough. Skirts are getting shorter all the time. Now, here's your hat, my lady!'

She unwrapped the hat carefully and held it out to

Queenie. The crown was deep, the brim wide, but narrowing towards the centre and dipping at the sides. The whole shape was covered in fine silk velvet in intermingling, finely-graded shades of pale mauve, deep lilac and cream. Queenie, eyes shining, cried out with pleasure.

'Oh it's beautiful, Opal! It's beautiful! Don't you think it's the loveliest thing you've ever made?'

'I think it might be,' Opal admitted. 'Especially when I've finished the trimming. I thought I'd use a little of the material left over from your dress to make the band, and embroider it with some of those silver beads. What do you think?'

'I think that would be perfect.'

'And here are the bridesmaids' hats. Lilac straw, trimmed with the rose-coloured velvet we found in Leasfield. They're smaller in the brim than yours because yours must be the most important; but don't you think they'll be pretty with the pale grey dresses?'

'Oh I do, I do Opal! Mary will look lovely with her dark colouring. And even dear Cousin Maud . . .' she giggled, '. . . will be enhanced. Oh I'm so grateful to you, dear Opal!'

'There's no need,' Opal said.

It was true. She would do almost anything in the world for Queenie. Although the Stones were well-to-do, Queenie had treated her like a sister from their very first meeting. Her love for Mark had spread out and embraced his whole family. Even Edgar fell under her spell and on the few occasions he was with her he became at once brighter and more cheerful.

'Will your father be well enough to attend the wedding?' she asked.

Queenie's face clouded. 'I don't know. He's not at all well and the doctor has advised him to take things very quietly. It will be sad for me if I have no parents at my wedding. But yours will be there and they are always so nice to me. Even your grandparents are coming, which is wonderful.'

'Which reminds me,' Opal said. 'I have to tell you that I can't come.'

Queenie stared at her.

'*You* not come? But Opal, why?'

'Well,' Opal said, 'I'll be seven months pregnant. I shouldn't really be appearing in public. But the truth is I shan't have a single garment which will fit me. Things are difficult right now. I haven't been able to make anything.'

Tears filled Queenie's eyes.

'Oh Opal how selfish I've been! I never thought . . . I expect because you always look so smart. But you must let me buy you something. Some nice material.'

'Thank you, Queenie, but I couldn't,' Opal said firmly. 'I really couldn't.'

'Then there must be something in my mother's wardrobe,' Queenie said. 'I haven't been able to bear to give away all her things. She wore voluminous clothes so there's sure to be something with plenty of material for you to make over. You couldn't refuse to have something of my mother's.'

'No,' Opal agreed, 'I couldn't refuse that.'

'Then we'll go and choose it before Mary and Maud arrive. No-one else need know.'

'It's a fine day,' Opal remarked. 'I knew it would be.'

She got out of bed slowly. If she moved too fast she might go dizzy again and have to rest, and today there was no time for that. She looked out of the window. In one way they were lucky. Acer Street ran north and south so that, though the street itself with its long rows of dark stone houses on either side was uniformly drab, from the bedroom window it was possible to see beyond the village to the moors on the horizon.

Every morning of her life now, Opal's first act after getting out of bed was to look towards the moors. When she'd married and come to live in Acer Street she had thought she was gaining her freedom. 'In any case we shan't be in Acer Street long,' she'd said to Edgar. 'I just know you'll be a Mill Manager one of these days and then we'll live in Park Road.'

Now it seemed as though she had simply flown into another cage; a smaller one with a heavier lock on the door. She felt trapped by poverty, by Edgar's failure to find work; by Daniel who needed her all the time; by the child she was carrying. Between them they imprisoned her here, and she knew she was born for something better. She was born to go somewhere, be somebody.

'It's time we were up and doing,' she said.

'Why? The wedding's not until two o-clock.' Edgar's voice came muffled from under the bedclothes.

'There's plenty to do,' Opal said. 'We're all to get ready. I've got to set out the shop and then clear it away again before we leave, or the mice will have it.'

Edgar sat up slowly, yawning. Daniel, wide awake, climbed from his cot on to his parents' bed, which he much preferred to his own. Edgar took his son in his arms and ruffled his soft, dark hair.

'You're surely not going to open the shop today, Opal?'

'For an hour or two this morning, of course I am. Whyever not?'

'I would have thought you could have given yourself one day off,' he said. 'It can't make all that much difference.'

'Oh yes it can,' Opal replied. 'That's just where you're wrong. People don't have all that much loyalty. It only needs a shop to be closed one day for them to take their custom elsewhere. I can't afford to risk that.'

'Then I wonder you haven't got someone to look after it while we're at the wedding.'

'I thought about it,' Opal admitted. 'But I'm not keen on neighbours knowing my business. So I'll keep open for most of the morning and if we're not too late back I'll open up again in the evening.'

Edgar said nothing more. He might as well keep his mouth shut, he thought, for all the weight his opinions carried.

After breakfast Opal took the kettle of hot water from the fire to the kitchen, closed the door and, standing at the sink, gave herself a good wash from top to toe. She had treated herself to a small tablet of scented soap especially for this day and she used it lavishly. As she rinsed and dried her swollen stomach, hating the sight of it, she felt the baby kick, and then saw the ripple of its movement across her flesh. She ought, she supposed, to feel pleasure, tenderness, but such feelings did not come as they had when she was pregnant with Daniel.

She dressed, for the time being, in a clean blouse and the navy wrap-around skirt which was all that would fit her. She would not put on her new dress until the last minute for fear of accidents.

She was pleased with the new dress and looked forward to wearing it. In the end, from the late Mrs Stone's wardrobe, she had chosen a long skirt in fine, cream gabardine, with a matching coat. There was so much material in it that she had been able to contrive a dress with plenty of fulness, and from the clippings she had made small flowers which she had appliquéd on to her brown hat.

'I dread to think what it's like up at Highcliffe, with Grandfather and Grandma and the aunts there and everybody getting ready at once,' she said, coming back into the living room. 'A good thing they had a bath put in. I'd like to live in a house with a bathroom. They say the new Council houses in Leasfield have them.'

'If all we lack is a bathroom we shan't do so badly,' Edgar said.

'Well one day we shall have a house with a bathroom, hot and cold water, electric light and a garden,' Opal said pleasantly. 'And it won't be a Council house either.'

She made him feel, Edgar thought, that it was his fault that she didn't have these things. That if only *he* was different, then everything would be all right. But they weren't the only people in their present straits, not by a long chalk.

'And what'll you use for rent money?' he asked. 'Shall you use monkey nuts?'

Opal smiled. 'Oh we won't rent the house. We'll buy it,' she teased.

And then suddenly her mood changed. In the act of setting out the shop, the children's sweets well to the fore because with luck they'd be coming in with their Saturday pennies, she paused, and looked at Edgar.

'Can't you see, can't you *see* Edgar, that the only way I can bear this rotten present is to look forward to the future. Oh I know it's not your fault, love – and I know my dreams are a bit fanciful, but can't you understand that?'

'I try,' he said quietly. 'I do try to understand, but I can't always share your feelings about the future. You leave me behind, Opal. I wasn't born with your imagination.'

'I know,' she spoke gently. 'Mam always said I had too much imagination and I daresay she was right. But sometimes it's what keeps me going, even if I don't believe every bit of it myself. I wish I could give a bit of it to you, love!'

She recognized, with a deep feeling of sadness, that what she missed most in Edgar, what more and more came between them even though she truly loved him, was not their poverty, not his lack of a job, but his refusal, his inability, to share her dreams. That was what mattered. That was what lay at the root of the loneliness she increasingly felt.

Shortly before noon they had a slice or two of bread to keep them going until the wedding reception, at which there would be a spread. They were ready for off when the door opened and a girl of about twelve walked in. It slightly irritated Opal that no-one around here ever knocked before entering, though she knew it was an irrational feeling in one who had set herself up as a shopkeeper.

'Oh Mrs Carson you do look lovely!' the girl said.

'We're off to a wedding, Milly,' Edgar told her. 'Mrs

Carson's brother. In fact we've just shut up shop.'

'Never mind that,' Opal said quickly. 'If there's something you want I'll be pleased to get it out for you.'

'It's me Mam,' Milly said. 'She says have you got a Daisy headache powder. Her head's splitting.'

'I'm sorry to hear that, Milly,' Opal said. 'Yes, I always keep them. Tell your mother I hope she'll soon feel better but should she need another powder I'll be back this evening.'

They reached the church in the nick of time. It was not possible to greet anyone for as they settled into their seats the organ music announced the arrival of the bride. How radiant and lovely Queenie looked! How clearly and eagerly she made her responses. Insofar as she ever addressed God, Opal prayed that marriage would not rob her new sister-in-law of that radiance and eagerness. But marriage changed people.

After the ceremony everyone except the bridal couple and the bridesmaids walked back to the house. Opal fell into step beside her mother. Hannah's pace was slow and her breathing difficult. She took her daughter's arm and though to Opal her mother looked slighter than ever, as if a strong wind on the top of the moor would blow her away, she leaned heavily upon her daughter. Opal, bearing the weight of her own pregnancy, found it difficult to support her mother, though not for the world would she have showed it.

'You should have gone in the motor car,' she said. 'This is quite a hill. In fact, should you have come at all, Mother?'

'Of course I should. I wanted to see Mark married.'

They were the last to arrive at the house. Queenie, standing beside her new husband, her eyes shining, cheeks glowing, embraced them in turn.

'Come and sit down, Mother!' She blushed prettily at her first use of the new title. 'You know, you *are* my mother now!'

'And pleased to be,' Hannah Derwent said. 'You're

looking very bonny, isn't she Opal?'

'She looks beautiful!'

'Well it's partly due to Opal if I do. Everyone's been admiring my hat, and the bridesmaids'. In fact, Opal, one of the guests is the sister of a lady who has a milliner's shop. She says you're just the person her sister's looking for.'

Opal glanced down at her figure. 'Not in this state,' she said ruefully.

'That's what I told her,' Queenie replied. 'And that you also had another child and a husband to look after.'

'Now that everyone's here,' Mark broke in, 'we can have the toast and then we can all eat. I'm starving!'

'We're to drink champagne,' Queenie said. 'Father insisted, though *he's* not supposed to touch it.'

'Is he feeling better?' Opal asked.

'Not really, though he's determined to get through the reception. He's over there, sitting in the armchair by the screen. Do go and have a word with him, Opal. He enjoys talking to you. He thinks you're much cleverer and more sensible than I am.'

'Rubbish,' Opal said. 'He thinks the sun shines on you.' All the same, she was pleased by Queenie's remark.

She moved to where her grandparents, parents and aunts stood in a tight group. Champagne was handed round and the toast was drunk to the newly-weds.

'Mmm! It's delicious!' Opal cried. 'I've never tasted champagne before!'

'Nor have I, and I'm seventy-three,' her grandfather said. 'And I reckon nothing to it. Here you are, Opal. You can have mine. I'd sooner have a glass of beer any day.'

'Oh, but, Father, do you think Opal should? In her condition?' Aunt Pearl said doubtfully. 'Alcohol!'

'Nay, it's more like fizzy lemonade,' her father said. 'What can that do except give you belly-ache?'

'Abraham! Do mind your words!' His wife's quiet whisper was anguished. 'You're not on the farm now. You're in a drawing room, and a very lovely one it is, too. She gazed appreciatively at the green flock wallpaper, the rosewood grand piano, the embossed velvet upholstery and the crystal chandelier. 'Fancy our Mark marrying into a home like this!'

Opal laughed. 'He's married Queenie, not the piano!' As for her grandfather, she thought, though his warm personality made him welcome wherever he went, the background of his farm suited him better than this room. It was a long time now since she had been up to Langstrothdale. Her grandfather was the fourth generation of Derwents to farm there and her own earliest memories were of the dale where she had spent the first five years of her life, before her father had moved to his own farm in the West Riding. It was a small, wild dale which saw the beginnings of the River Wharfe. The river was always the clearest thing in her memories of childhood.

'Do you remember, Grandma, that afternoon when you showed me how to dam a bit of the river with stones?' she asked. Her grandmother, in spite of the hard work of the farm, had always had time to spare for her.

'Aye, I do that,' her grandmother said. 'I mind it well. You enjoyed that bit of power didn't you? You thought you had it in you to change the whole course of the river!'

So I did, Opal thought. 'I'm going to talk to Mr Stone,' she said. 'I promised Queenie.'

Mr Stone seemed pleased to see her, though she thought how strained and tired he looked.

'Queenie talks a lot about you,' he said. 'She's very fond of you, you know.'

'And I of her,' Opal said. 'I hope she'll be very happy with my brother.'

'Young Mark'll have me to answer to if she's not,' Mr Stone said. 'But I wouldn't have offered him a job in my Company, let alone give him my daughter, if I hadn't thought highly of him – once I got to know him.

34

I hope you'll come and see them often when they're living here.'

'I will,' Opal promised.

She would have liked to have talked to him longer but other guests came and claimed his attention and she could see that he was weary. She left him and found herself a seat. She was desperate to sit down. Besides, food was being handed round; ham and tongue sandwiches, salmon patties, savoury things on toast – and on the table she could see cream trifles and iced fancies flanking the two-tier wedding cake. She was tremendously hungry. She took several items of food from the tray a waitress offered and settled down to eat in earnest. Daniel was being looked after by his Aunt Mary; Edgar was talking, with unusual animation, to Queenie. When she had eaten her fill she went over to join them.

'We must go soon,' she said. 'If we stay too long Daniel will get too tired, and then he'll be fractious. He's fine now, but it won't last.'

'I understand,' Queenie said. 'We're going to cut the cake now, and then Mark and I must leave.' The colour rose in her face again at the thought of the honeymoon. 'I hope you won't take it amiss, Opal, but I've asked Jane to pack you a basket to take home. It will be waiting in the hall for you and no-one will see it. There's so much food here and if someone doesn't take it it will go to waste. So you'll be doing me a favour.'

'I'm grateful,' Opal said quietly. It would probably feed them through the weekend and beyond. 'It's been a lovely wedding. I hope you have a wonderful honeymoon.'

Queenie and Mark looked at each other, their faces alight with love.

'Oh we shall,' Mark said. 'We shall.'

'Your mother looks none too good,' Edgar said when they were home. After the double tram ride they were hungry again and when Daniel, who had fallen asleep on the tram and had had to be carried home in his father's arms, had been put to bed, and the shop set out afresh,

Opal spread some of the contents of Queenie's basket on the table.

'I agree,' she said. 'I'm worried about her. Well, best come and eat.'

'Bits and pieces,' Edgar said. 'Bits and pieces. Not what I call solid food.'

'It's all delicious,' Opal said. 'I'd like to eat like this every day. And drink champagne!'

'You've got ideas above your station,' Edgar said, but not unkindly. Something, perhaps the champagne which he affected not to like, had put him in a good mood.

Only two people came to buy from the shop, a small boy for a sherbert fountain and a woman for a whipped cream walnut. 'As it's Saturday night,' she said. At nine-o-clock, though it was still daylight, Opal said, 'It's been a long day. Why don't we go to bed?'

She was nearing the end of the Monday wash when she heard the knock at the door. The whites, having been rubbed, boiled and starched, with a squeeze of Dolly blue in the starch water for added whiteness, were already drying in the sun, on the line which stretched across the street. On Monday mornings the whole length of every street in Milton was strung with laundry, like a village *en fête*. No cart of any kind could pass and even a pedestrian must dodge between sheets and shirts, shifts and blouses.

Opal straightened her body as she heard the knock. Pounding and twisting the peggy stick, in her condition, was painful. Thank goodness Edgar would help her with the mangle.

'See who's at the door, Edgar,' she called out. 'If it's a hawker he's out of luck, poor devil!'

'Why, Sam, whatever brings you here?' she heard Edgar say. Her stomach lurched at the greeting. Sam worked for her father on the farm and in the middle of Monday morning he could only be bringing bad news.

'What is it?' she asked, coming to the door. 'What's amiss?'

'It's Mrs Derwent,' the boy said. 'She's been took real bad. The Maister thinks you'd best come.'

Opal grasped Edgar's arm, trying to steady the world which had started to spin. And yet it was no surprise. She had seen it in her mother's face at the wedding, only two days ago. She had felt it in her mother's weight on her arm and heard it in her weakened voice.

'Steady on,' Edgar said. 'Sit down and I'll make you a cup of tea. Sam, you'll have a drink of tea?'

'Nay, I mun get back. Shall I tell the Maister you're coming, then?'

'Yes,' Opal answered. 'I'll be there as quickly as ever I can.'

'You'd best have a few minutes rest before you go,' Edgar advised when Sam had gone. 'It's a tidy walk. Do you want me to come with you, take Daniel to Ma's?'

'No. You stay here and look after him. I'll be all right. But I might not be back tonight. If there's nursing to be done I shall want to take my share. I won't wait for a cup of tea right now. Fetch my clean nightdress in from the line, will you. Quickly!'

Climbing the hillside, though there was some shade from the trees, was warm work. Sweat ran down Opal's face and around the collar of her blouse, which clung damply to her back. She would have liked to have taken a short rest but there was no time. In spite of the awkwardness of her body she walked quickly. On the top of the moor, away from the trees, it was hotter than ever. The sun, almost at its zenith now, beat down on her head. There was no shade anywhere and the out-croppings of rock seemed to reflect the sun's rays, bouncing them back into the air to heat it still further. But she kept up her pace, trying not to notice her fatigue.

She had neglected her mother. She knew it only too well. 'Dear God,' she prayed. 'Only let my mother live and I'll be better!' But would God make a bargain with someone who most of the time ignored him? The pain in her back was worsening. She wanted more than anything

37

in the world to lie down, but there was no question of doing so.

She was almost at the top of the moor now. The downhill journey would be easier. When she reached the crest of the hill and saw Highcliffe down below she felt a new rush of strength to match her urgency, and started to run. She never knew what tripped her up – perhaps a bramble root, perhaps a stone on the track. She fell to the ground and rolled over and over down the hill until a narrow, shelving plateau stopped her. There, for a second or two, she lay on the ground, her whole body shaking. But there were no bones broken and she must get on. She must hurry, hurry! She got to her feet and started down the hill again as quickly as her trembling legs would take her.

When she reached the farm the door was open. She passed through the empty kitchen and, with great difficulty, for she had neither breath nor strength left, went upstairs to her mother's bedroom. Her father, Aunt Garnet and Mary stood by the bed. It was Mary who turned towards her, the tears streaming down her white face.

'Oh Opal!' she sobbed 'You're too late! It's all over! She died not five minutes ago. You're too late!'

And then her sister and her aunt moved forward quickly as Opal, the pain searing her back and now embracing her belly with hands of red-hot iron, screamed as the world grew dark and she dropped to the floor.

It was almost a month before the doctor declared Opal fit to return to her own home.

'You'll be glad to get back to your husband and your little boy,' he said. 'But go carefully, my dear. You're not completely strong yet.'

In her heart she knew she was not, and never would be ready to return to Acer Street. Though it contained those she held most dear, Edgar and Daniel, the doctor's words sounded in her ears like a prison sentence. 'I condemn you to penal servitude for life!' If only they could get away! If only they could make a fresh start. But she said nothing of these feelings; not to her father, sunk in his own world of grief; not to Aunt Garnet or to Mary; not to Edgar when he came to visit her.

Her baby daughter, born before Hannah Derwent was in her coffin, had died less than twenty-four hours after the grandmother who never saw her. Aunt Garnet said they would meet in heaven and know each other.

'She was quite perfect,' Mary wept – though whether for the baby or her mother she was not sure. 'Such a darling little girl!'

'But too small to survive,' Aunt Garnet said. 'Our Opal's small herself, so at seven months what chance did the bairn have? And a rough passage into the world at that.'

It had been clear to all except Opal, to whom because of her pain nothing was real except the pain itself, that the child could not live, and the same clergyman who was in the house because of Mrs Derwent's passing, baptised the infant. Opal, rallying for a moment, chose the name Judith. Then the milk which Nature sent so liberally to Opal's breasts turned against her. When the small coffin followed the larger one out of the house, to be buried in the graveyard on the side of the moor, Opal was raging with milk fever, too delirious to know anything. For a while it seemed as though a third funeral must follow.

But as the days went by the fever subsided. She knew that she would recover but her spirits were low and she wondered, lying in the narrow bed which had been hers until she had married, whether she wanted to do so. Edgar came to see her frequently, sometimes bringing Daniel, more often leaving the child with his mother. She did not tell him how she felt but he was aware that something was wrong.

'You must make an effort, love,' he said. 'For my sake and little Daniel's. We want you back.'

'I'm being punished for my sins,' Opal said. 'I never wanted the baby and I didn't do enough for my mother. Now I'd give anything to have them back but it's too late. God is just! He's not merciful, but he's just. He gives punishment where it's due.'

'I don't understand about that,' Edgar said helplessly. 'I'm sure you'll feel better when you're a bit stronger. I've been keeping the shop going,' he added, trying to turn the direction of her mind. 'People have been very kind, asking after you. And I'm going to see Mr Ridley in a day or two. Perhaps you should think about what I ought to buy from him?'

In the end, though she did not come to it quickly, it was the thought of the shop which aroused Opal from her apathy. Yet even while she thought of it, sitting now in a chair outside the farmhouse in the July sunshine, looking up to the moors which were breaking into their covering of purple heather, she knew that it was not enough. She must do something, anything, to change her life, to change life for all three of them. And then she realized – it came to her quite clearly – where her hope lay.

When Mary came towards her with a cup of tea and a piece of fresh curd tart to tempt her appetite she asked, 'Will Queenie be coming at the weekend?'

'I think so. Why?'

'Well, since they'll come over from Leasfield in her father's car, I thought she might take me back to Milton. It's about time I was going.'

'That's a bit sudden,' Mary said. 'Oh I know Doctor Lee said you could, and there's Edgar and little Daniel to think of, so I daresay you're right. But it's been a comfort to me to have you here to look after.'

When Queenie arrived on Saturday afternoon Opal took her at once into the parlour. Queenie's grief for Hannah Derwent had been deep, but simple, and without guilt, so that the tears she had shed had comforted her, as Opal's could not. Opal wished that she could be more like Queenie; uncomplicated, kind and good. But it was not in her.

'Do you remember at your wedding you mentioned a lady with a hat shop?' she asked quickly. 'You said she might be wanting an assistant and her sister liked my hats.'

'Why yes, I remember,' Queenie said.

'Did she engage anyone? Is the job still open?'

'I've no idea,' Queenie said with surprise. 'I don't even know whether it was serious. But Opal you can't mean . . . You can't possibly do it! You're not yet strong enough. Besides, you've got Edgar and Daniel to look after.'

'Never mind that just now,' Opal said eagerly. 'Will you find out if there is a job? And if there is, will you put in a word for me?'

'But I don't . . .' Queenie sounded bewildered.

'Oh *please* Queenie! I beg you! I assure you it's what I need if I'm to stay sane! And the woman won't regret it if she takes me on.'

'I'm sure she won't,' Queenie said. 'But what will Edgar say? And what about Daniel?'

'I'll deal with that,' Opal said hurriedly. 'Don't mention it to Edgar, or to anyone else just yet.'

Edgar would hate it, that was certain. Even after all this time without work he saw himself as the breadwinner, the one responsible for supporting his family. She had no wish to deprive him of this role, but somehow he must be made to see her point of view.

Back in Acer Street, she paused inside the doorway. How small the room looked! How small and shabby; tidy enough but not clean. The fireplace was dull, and behind the lace curtains, which were badly in need of washing, the window was smoke-grimed. True to his promise Edgar had set out the shop, though not with her order and precision. It looked tatty. She doubted whether she could ever settle here again. One way or another, however long it took, she must get out.

She waited until they had had their tea and she had put Daniel to bed before she broached the subject which was burning inside her. In the end she could think of no subtle way of leading up to it, no tactful manner of introducing it. Her blunt announcement, she thought, sounded like an attack.

'You may as well know, Edgar, I'm thinking of going out to work.'

He stared, not believing his ears.

'What did you say?'

'I'm going out to work,' she repeated. She wished she did not sound so defiant. It was not how she had meant it to be.

'But I don't understand!' He looked confused. 'You're a married woman with a young child. *You* shouldn't be going out to work.'

'I want to. Please Edgar, I really want to!'

She watched the shadow pass over his face.

'You mean you need to. Because I can't keep my wife and family like a man should. That's what you mean, isn't it?'

She could have borne it if he had been angry, shouted at her, shaken her by the shoulders. It would have hurt her less.

She shook her head. 'You're wrong. It's not like . . . But you must admit that it would help?'

'So what makes you think you can get a job?' he asked. 'What can you do? You've no sort of experience.'

'Well I can make hats for one thing. And I can serve in a shop. I've proved that. So I shall look for something which combines the two. Of course I might not find anything.' But she would, she knew she would.

'And what about me and Daniel while you're out working?'

She was irritated by the self-pity in his voice, but even so she tried to speak reassuringly.

'You and Daniel have shown how well you can manage without me. You've looked after him very well. He's the picture of health.' She intended to say nothing about the state of the house. 'And I'm sure his Grandma will be pleased to have him when you have to sign on.'

'I see you've got it all worked out,' Edgar said. 'There's

not much left for me to say, is there? I suppose, then, you'll be giving up all this?' He motioned to the house shop, laid out on the table.

'Give it up?' Opal retorted, stung to an anger she could no longer control. 'No, Edgar, we'll not give it up! Why should we? You shall run the house shop, Edgar! There's no point at all in giving it up!'

3

'So there it is,' Madame Dora said. 'Since he's taking me to lunch, I can't be out when Mr Hessle comes. It's his last visit before he retires and he's bringing his nephew who's taking over from him. I shall want to meet him. So there's nothing else for it, Opal, you'll have to deliver the hats to Miss Taylor!'

Miss Taylor, though goodness knew she could be a nuisance, was one of their best customers. She seldom set foot in the shop (Opal had never seen her) but about once every couple of months she telephoned Madame Dora and asked her to bring a selection of hats up to the house, and she almost always bought one.

'Sometimes I wonder if I was wise to have the telephone installed,' Madame Dora said. 'But with a high-class business like this it's expected. It's not as if we were a sweets and tobacco or a greengrocer's.'

'I'm sure you're right, Madame Dora,' Opal agreed.

Her employer liked to be addressed as Madame Dora though everyone in the locality knew that she was really Dora Barraclough, widow of the late Asa Barraclough, pork butcher, who had died of the Spanish flu in 1919. Indeed, the very premises which now, carpeted in beige Wilton and tastefully decorated, housed Madame Dora, High Class Milliner, had once contained Mr Barraclough, surrounded by sides of pork, legs of ham, dishes of chitterlings, faggots and, on Fridays at twelve noon, a leg of succulent hot roast pork which could be purchased, thinly sliced, by the quarter pound.

Sometimes when she was hungry Madame Dora imagined she could smell that roast pork, taste the crackling.

Out of the whole business it was the only thing she had been able to stand. That, and the money her husband made. When he was taken she had genuinely mourned him, but she was glad to be rid of the butcher's shop and to put her inheritance into something more refined.

'Moreover,' Madame Dora said, 'I know Miss Taylor likes to see me personally. But you're more than capable of delivering the hats and you can tell her I'll call myself later this afternoon, even though it's early closing, to help her make a choice.'

'Supposing she wants to try them on while I'm there?' Opal asked.

Madame Dora frowned. She was aware that her assistant was more than able to help Miss Taylor choose a hat, and to trim it for her. She was the best assistant she had ever had in the salon. (Madame Dora never thought of it as a shop). In fact, what with her instinct for fashion, her skill with a needle and her interest in everything to do with the business Madame Dora thought that Opal might be a greater talent than herself. But, she comforted herself, clients did prefer the attention of the proprietoress.

'Well the customer is always right,' she conceded. 'If she does insist, try to sell her the velour. It's expensive – a guinea untrimmed – but she can afford it. Her father was Taylor's treacle toffee, you know.'

'I'll do my best,' Opal promised.

'And before you go, let down the sunblind. The September sun isn't as damaging as the Spring sun, but we can't afford to have the hats fade. In fact, I think you'd better bring the velvet toque out of the window. And cover the mauve felt with a sheet of tissue. Mauve's the very devil for fading.'

They waged a constant battle between the need to display the finest hat – though never too many at a time since both ladies agreed that that was common – and the propensity of every material to fade in the light. Sometimes a single, sunny morning was enough to ruin a hat. Opal took the toque out of the window and placed it on a stand in the shop.

'I don't suppose this shape will ever go out of fashion,' she remarked. 'Not as long as the Queen wears it.'

It was a beautiful hat and she alone had made it, though for herself to wear she preferred something more up-to-date.

'You did a good job on that,' Madame Dora said. She believed in giving praise where praise was due. When she had first set eyes on Opal – tiny, thin, her face white and pinched – she had not been impressed by her. Height was an asset in a shop assistant, as was a fashionable figure to show off clothes and a pretty face to enhance a hat. Opal's figure, since in spite of her slenderness she had well-rounded breasts, was unfashionable. She needed a good, tight bust band to flatten that area. Nor was she, in Madame Dora's eyes, strictly speaking pretty, though she had good cheekbones and fine, dark eyes. Nevertheless, Madame Dora recognized style when she saw it. It transcended many faults.

'I wanted to talk to you, Madame Dora,' Opal said. 'Could you spare me a minute later in the morning?'

'Well, we'll see how busy we are, shall we?'

She knew what it would be about and she was not worried. The labourer was worthy of his hire and she had no objection to giving Opal an extra half-crown a week.

'Right now you'd better be off,' she said. 'Oak House, Nab End Rise. Halfway up the hill.'

It was good to be out in the air on such a fine morning. Though Opal had often delivered hats to back doors she had not up to now been entrusted with an errand which might possibly take her inside a rich customer's home. In her two year's service she had done most tasks, from sweeping the shop floor and cleaning the plate glass window to making and trimming hats for quite important weddings and funerals. She knew how to start with nothing more than a length of millinery wire and finish up with a hat fit for a queen.

46

The only chore which she had never been allowed to touch was that of totting up the contents of the till and entering them in the ledger. This Madame Dora kept to herself.

'But I know the cost of all the materials,' Opal told Edgar. She talked to him regularly about her job in spite of the fact that he showed little interest. She doubted that he had ever forgiven her for taking it and she felt compassion for him that she had found a job so easily while he was still without.

'I know the cost of the buckram shapes, the linings, ribbons, feathers, flowers,' she told him. 'And I've a fair idea of the rates of the shop with the living quarters over. With the prices Madame Dora charges for hats she must be making a pretty good living.' It seemed to Opal that she deserved a bigger share of it than the ten shillings a week she was paid.

Her wages, though, had been a godsend. With them, plus the few shillings the house shop still made, and Edgar's dole money, they just about managed. There was still no sign of work for Edgar, nor for hundreds of others who formed long queues outside the Labour Exchanges. He seemed now to have settled down to a workless condition as if he had known no other. It worried Opal that he seemed interested in nothing, except for Daniel. Even politics no longer had the power to move him. He had not so much settled down, she thought, as succumbed.

As for any physical expression of love between them, well that almost never happened. Sometimes, aching with her own desire, and wanting also to give him comfort, in bed she tried to draw him into her arms. Too often he turned away from her, leaving her ashamed of her longings.

Resolutely she put Edgar out of her mind as she turned the corner into Nab End Rise. It was a road where people of substance lived in handsome houses set in large, tree-bordered gardens. Opal hesitated outside the large iron gates of Oak House, wondering whether she dare present herself at the front door. But that might be going too far.

'I'm from Madame Dora,' she told the maid who answered the kitchen door. 'Miss Taylor's expecting me.'

'That's right. This way if you please!'

Opal followed the maid along the stone-flagged passage to the other side of a baize-lined door. It was a different world here: a world of deep-pile carpets, gilt-framed paintings, embossed wallpaper, exotic plants in jardinières. The room into which the maid ushered her was grander still, with green silk curtains and a green and gold Chinese carpet. Miss Taylor, standing in front of the white marble fireplace, was tall, angular, and expensively dressed in a brown frock coat which did nothing for her sallow skin and grey hair.

'I'm sorry Madame Dora couldn't come,' she said. 'She knows what I like.'

'She's disappointed too,' Opal said. 'But such a severe stomach upset.'

It was the fiction they had decided on. It would never do to let Miss Taylor know that she had been passed over for a commercial traveller.

'I hope I may help you,' Opal ventured. 'Madame Dora thought that if you were to try on the hats while I was here I might be able to assist you in your choice.' She could always tell Madame that Miss Taylor had insisted.

'Well we'll see,' Miss Taylor said doubtfully. Opal wondered why she bought hats so often since she had a face so rugged and individual that there could be few hats which could actually adorn it.

'I suppose you had better come up to my bedroom then,' Miss Taylor said. 'We can't try on hats without a mirror.'

Opal followed her up the wide, curving staircase and into a large room with a dressing table set into the deep bay of a window. Miss Taylor sat herself in front of the mirror and waited for Opal to unpack the hats. They were not what Opal would have selected for Miss Taylor now that she had seen her, but she was here to sell and she must do her best. She was confident that she could change the nature of some of them with judicious trimming and she was glad that she had persuaded Madame Dora to let her bring a few things along. But the artificial flowers were out. Miss Taylor was definitely not the type to be flower trimmed.

She placed each hat in turn on top of Miss Taylor's sparse hair while the lady frowned at her reflection in the glass. Opal knew that the rust-coloured velour was far and away the most suitable, so she saved it until the last.

'You could wear any of them, Madame,' she said politely. 'But I think this is really you! I always think it's a pity,' she added thoughtfully, 'that we only see ourselves in mirrors, because that's not any of us at our best. Something to do with "reversed image". I don't understand it, but it's a fact that we all look nicer than we think.'

She held her breath while Miss Taylor gazed into the glass, frowning. Had she said too much, even though it was true? She was relieved when she saw Miss Taylor's expression soften, watched her lift her head and view her reflection with something like approval.

'I think you should have quite a severe trimming on this one,' Opal advised. 'A stiffish bow, almost self-coloured – I have the very ribbon here – and well to the side to add a little width.' Deftly, she formed the ribbon into intricate folds and held it in position.

'Yes,' Miss Taylor said. 'I think you're right!'

'Would you like me to complete it while I'm here?' Opal asked. 'I could do it quite quickly.'

'Very well then,' Miss Taylor agreed. She seemed amiable enough now. Not at all a bit of a Tartar. 'I daresay you'd like a cup of tea?'

Opal knew by the maid's down-turned mouth as she brought in the teatray that she did not approve of this gesture. Certainly Madame Dora had never mentioned tea, and surely she would have done had it happened?

The tea was pale gold in colour, delicate in flavour, served in rose-patterned china. It was quite unlike the brew she and Edgar drank every day.

When she had finished the hat Miss Taylor tried it on again. 'Yes,' she said. 'That will do nicely. You're a gifted young lady. But I supposed you'll give it up and marry some man and have hordes of children!'

'I am married,' Opal said hesitantly. There was a polite fiction that no young woman in a job was married. She was always addressed as 'Miss Carson'. 'I have a little boy. My husband is unemployed. He couldn't get a job, so I did.'

But it was not as simple as that. Something other than economic necessity had driven her to seek for work and now her job had become all-important to her. She enjoyed leaving the house each morning and going out into the world, even a world no farther away than Madame Dora's.

'What about your little boy?'

'His father looks after him very well. And of course I'm able to do better by him – give him better foods, clothes. Daniel doesn't lose out at all.' She sounded on the defensive and was cross with herself that she should. After all, where Daniel was concerned, she was the loser. She missed him so much, was painfully aware that she had shut herself out from a part of his life and tried to make up for it in the time they were together. She was unreasonably jealous of the close bond she recognized between Daniel and his father.

'Isn't it hard work, going out to a job and running a home?' Miss Taylor asked.

'Yes. I have to be at the salon at eight-thirty in the morning and I don't finish until seven at night.'

She could have added that to save the tramfare she walked the two miles each way from Madame Dora's to Acer Street, that on her half-day she cleaned the house, looked after the house shop and sometimes, usually taking Daniel with her, went to Ridley's for new stock. Also that on Sundays she did the week's washing, ready for hanging out on the line first thing on Monday morning.

'I think I should have liked to have had a job,' Miss Taylor said. 'But naturally I looked after my parents until they were taken. I don't know what I could have done, though. I'm not cut out for teaching and I could never have worked in a hospital. And what else is there?'

For you, since you're a lady, not much, Opal thought. For me, anything I can get.

'Tell me Miss Carson,' Miss Taylor said suddenly. 'What does someone like you think of votes for women?'

Opal flushed. 'I only know what I think,' she said pertly – and was then aware that she had spoken rudely to a valuable customer. But when Miss Taylor's sharp eyes met her own she saw, with relief, that there was amusement rather than anger in them.

'And what *do* you think?'

'That it's right and proper. That it's unfair that we should have to wait until we're thirty. We should be equal with the men.'

'What you mean is that we should have equal voting rights with the men,' Miss Taylor corrected her. 'I agree with that. But we can never be quite equal with the men. It's not in our nature.'

'I mean,' Opal began, but thought better of it. She knew what she meant; that women should have the same chances as men. She wondered if Miss Taylor would have liked to have been a man with – for those who were lucky – a man's opportunities? For herself she was glad to be a woman, but she wanted the opportunities too.

'Well thank you. I mustn't detain you any longer.' Miss Taylor spoke briskly, as if conscious that she might have spoken too freely with the milliner's little assistant. Perhaps it was to restore matters to their proper footing that she gave Opal a shilling as she was leaving.

Opal hurried back, from time to time restraining herself from breaking into a run from her joy at being out on so fine a morning. The shilling tip was most generous. She would spend it all on Daniel, perhaps even on a nice toy. She was glad she had sold the velour. It was important that she should please Madame Dora today.

When she reached the salon Mr Hessle had not arrived.

'So tiresome!' Madame Dora grumbled. 'I could have gone to Miss Taylor's after all. Still, I must say you've done very well.'

'As there's no-one in the salon at the moment, could I speak to you now?' Opal asked.

'Very well, Miss Carson. But if it's what I think it is you can save yourself the trouble. You've worked hard this last year and I've already decided to give you an increase of half-a-crown a week from the end of the month. There! Does that suit you?'

Opal hesitated. 'Not quite,' she said slowly.

'Not quite? Well I can assure you, Miss, I can't possibly give you more! I consider I'm being most generous!'

'Oh you are, you are!' Opal cried. 'I didn't mean that. It's just that what I had in mind was something a little different.'

'Something different? In heaven's name what?'

Opal took a deep breath.

'Well . . . . . if you could agree to it . . . . . . I wondered if I might have . . . what I'd like to have is a small percentage, oh a very small one, of the profits. Instead of a rise, I mean.' She was astonished at her own audacity. She could get the sack for less than this.

'A *percentage of profits*?' Madame Dora sounded as though Opal had spoken in a foreign tongue. 'A percentage of profits? Why, some weeks I hardly make a profit at all – and some weeks nothing!'

'Then on those weeks you would only pay me my ten shillings,' Opal said quickly. 'You would save half-a-crown.'

Her voice was steady, but inside she was trembling. Now that she had come out with the idea it sounded impossible. 'And I mean profits over a certain amount, naturally,' she continued. 'Perhaps over what they are

52

now. That way you couldn't lose. You'd only pay me extra if I earned extra first – and then only a small part of it.'

'What makes you think,' Madame Dora said slowly (though Opal could hear the interest creeping into her voice). 'What makes you think you could increase the profits?'

'I have several ideas,' Opal said eagerly. 'I've given it a lot of thought.'

'What ideas?'

'Well, for instance, I thought that perhaps we . . . I mean you . . . might introduce a few more lines. Not just hats, but other accessories – scarves, gloves, hosiery. Lots of people are wearing the new art silk stockings and since they last no time at all they have to keep buying more. And ladies underwear, or in our case, lingerie, for I know you'd only sell the best. They're beginning to sell it in the big stores. People don't make their own underwear as much as they used to. And no-one around here sells these items – at least not yet.'

'Well,' Madame Dora exclaimed, 'You certainly *have* been thinking about it, haven't you? I'm not sure that I can take it in so quickly!'

'And I thought you might change the name to "Madame Dora's Modes",' Opal said.

'Madame Dora's Modes, eh? Yes. But there's the question of space – that is supposing I were to agree to any of it in the first place. Have you thought about space?'

'I have,' Opal began.

She was interrupted by the arrival of Mr Hessle. Unlike some of their commercial travellers who crept into the salon as if uncertain of their welcome, his entry was that of a leading actor on to the centre stage. He was a large man, but it was more his air of bonhomie than his size which seemed to fill the shop.

'My dear Madame Dora! Dear lady! I do apologize if I've inconvenienced you in the slightest degree. We were unavoidably detained. Yes, unavoidably detained!'

In the Red Lion, Opal thought, smelling his breath.

'I have to blame my imminent retirement,' he continued. 'I had no idea, no idea at all, that I had so many friends in the trade. And far too many of them, I'm afraid, wanted to toast my future. But I've saved the best to the last, dear lady, and my time from this moment on is all yours. Wednesday afternoon, early closing, all the time in the world for a long, leisurely lunch!'

'I'm looking forward to it, Mr Hessle,' Madame Dora said.

'Capital! And now let me introduce my nephew Mr David Hessle, who will take over from me. David, step forward to meet Madame Dora! And her young lady assistant, Miss Carson.'

David Hessle was tall, all of six feet. He was well dressed in a light grey suit with a striped silk tie. On removing his silver grey trilby he revealed a head of rich, auburn hair. When he shook hands with Opal, with a grip that was firm and pleasant, he smiled directly at her and the smile extended to his grey-green eyes. Opal thought he looked a cut above any commercial traveller she had ever seen.

'Now unless there's anything you're particularly wanting – though we have a nice line in velvet ribbon which I *would* like you to look at – we won't concentrate on business today,' Mr Hessle senior said. 'Mr David will be around again in the second week in October and I know he'll have some new lines to discuss with you. But not today, Madame Dora! Today luncheon awaits!'

Over the top of Madame Dora's head David Hessle caught Opal's eye, and smiled. She wished she was being included in the party.

Opal took the iron from the fire, blew the ash from it, and spat on it to test the heat. Then, to help the iron glide over the cloth, she rubbed the hot sole with a piece of candle fat wrapped in a bit of cotton cloth.

'I shall have to have some stuff for a new work dress,' she remarked to Edgar. 'This one's getting very shabby.'

She would buy the new black material from the savings in the toffee tin and she would make up the dress to the same pattern – long sleeves, high round neck (with a white collar which had to be washed every day) – only this time it could be a little shorter. Skirts were knee-high in London though no doubt she'd have to be a little more circumspect. She reckoned that wearing a new dress had helped her to get the job with Madame Dora; that and the fact that she'd had her hair bobbed. It hung straight and heavy, with a thick fringe across her forehead and the sides curving on to her cheeks. Edgar hated it.

'You need a new shirt too,' she continued. 'I saw some in Tatham's window; cotton and flannelette, lined across the shoulder, for three-and-eleven three-farthings. You can get them cheaper but cheap clothes don't pay in the end.'

'I can manage,' Edgar said.

'No you can't,' she contradicted. 'It's important to be decently dressed. How much money is there in the savings tin?'

'I don't know.'

'Then count it.'

She didn't need him to do so. She knew there was thirteen shillings and fourpence, but anything to make him move, take an interest.

Reluctantly, he took the tin from the dresser drawer, spilled the money on to the table, and began to count.

'Thirteen and twopence,' he said.

'That's wrong! There should be thirteen and fourpence.'

He pushed the money away angrily.

'If you know how much there is why do you ask me to count it? And if you must know, I took twopence for a packet of woodbines. I'd none left. A man needs a smoke.'

Opal flushed.

'I'd have bought you extra if you'd said.'

55

Like most women she bought her husband's cigarettes along with the groceries. In work, the men handed over their unopened wage packets, out of work their dole money. The women handed back the man's pocket money and bought his cigarettes. It was the way things were done and there was simply no reason for the sense of shame Edgar's words had roused in her.

'Anyway,' she said, 'it's enough to buy some dress material *and* a shirt, and some socks for Daniel.'

She had never made a secret of savings in the tin. They were more or less common property. But what Edgar didn't know, and she was not sure why she had never told him, was that she now had her own bank account with the Yorkshire Penny Bank. There was not much in it but it was growing steadily. The Penny Bank boasted that it would gladly receive any sum, from one penny upwards, and she therefore felt no awkwardness in paying in her small amount each Friday as soon as she drew her wages. She enjoyed looking at the bankbook, watching the balance increase. She had made no withdrawals, nor would she unless for something so extra special that it had not so far even entered her mind.

She put the newly-pressed dress on a hanger and, striding over Daniel who was playing on the floor with a small wooden cart which Edgar had made him, she suspended it from the ceiling clothes dryer to air off. She smiled at Daniel. At four years old he was still a quiet child, undemanding, easygoing. Which was just as well, she thought, for much as she loved him she had little time to spend on him. There was always so much to do. It would be better for Daniel when he could go to school, be with other children of his own age.

'I took some hats to a customer in Nab End Rise this morning,' she told Edgar. 'It was a beautiful house. She gave me a lovely cup of tea and bought an expensive hat.'

'It's not right,' Edgar said.

'What isn't?'

'It's not right that some women can spend all that money on a hat.'

'I daresay it isn't,' Opal said mildly. 'All I know is that if she and her like couldn't, then I wouldn't have a job. It's no use *me* grumbling at the Miss Taylors of this world. I have to be thankful for them. Anyway, she was nice.'

She would like to be one of them. She would like to live in a big house with a garden and have a maid to answer the door. She would even like to be Madame Dora, with a nice little business and living quarters over. Or rather, not Miss Taylor, not Madame Dora, but her own self in a similar position. It was her circumstances she wished to change, not herself.

'Old Mr Hessle came in for the last time today,' she said. 'He brought his nephew, who's to take his place.'

But Edgar wasn't listening. He was staring into the fire. She wondered, fleetingly, if Edgar could ever get a job as a commercial traveller, just supposing she ever heard of one? He was good-looking, reasonably well-spoken, and in his navy blue suit which he now seldom wore, he looked as smart as the next man. On the rare occasions when they went out together she was always proud to be seen with him. What he lacked, what, try as she might, she seemed unable to give him, was confidence in himself. Now David Hessle, she felt sure, had that quality in abundance.

4

'It seems to me,' Edgar said, 'that you're none too pleased I've got the job!'

'That's ridiculous,' Opal objected. 'How can you think such a thing?'

But she felt mean that she hadn't shown more pleasure at his news, guilty at the lack of enthusiasm inside herself. Perhaps it was simply that she was so very tired. The week before Whitsuntide was a busy one in the shop and she had been on her feet since early morning.

'Well you're not saying much. Hardly a word. I'd have thought you'd have been as pleased as Punch!'

'I am, I am!' Opal protested. 'It's the shock. It's hardly five minutes since you told me. An insurance agent! I can hardly get it into my head!'

'I was dead lucky to get it,' Edgar said. 'I don't know that I would have but for the Reverend Atkinson putting in a word for me. It so happens that the District Manager is his churchwarden, and Ma knew that, you see.'

'How did you know about the vacancy?' Opal asked. 'Had you written to the Company?'

She thought that unlikely. He had written for nothing in the last two years, saying it was a waste of time and stamps.

'No, it was Ma! She came dashing round here as if her coat tails were on fire! Told me Jonah Ramsden had had a seizure on his way to pay out the insurance on old Grandma Battersby. He fell down in the street with the money on him, Ma said, and as likely as not they'd be paying out on him before the week was out.

'So get into your Sunday suit, and around to Reverend Atkinson to ask him to put in a word for you,' she said. 'And then off into Leasfield with you.'

'But it's more than a week since Mr Ramsden was taken bad,' Opal said. 'He died yesterday. I can't understand why you didn't tell me you'd been after the job!'

He'd had good enough reason for that, Edgar thought. He'd gone off to the interview without any hope whatever. After more than four years hope had died in him. So what was the use of telling Opal? When he didn't get the job it would be simply another failure to chalk up against him. She would never say it, but sometimes he saw it in her eyes. He knew he was a failure.

'Shall you be able to do it?' Opal asked. 'I mean . . . well, you've not done anything like this before.'

'I don't know till I try, do I?'

'Of course not,' she agreed. 'Anyway, if Jonah Ramsden could go it, I'm sure you can.' It was so good to hear hope in his voice. 'I am truly pleased for you, Edgar,' she assured him.

And now – he could still hardly believe it – he was a failure no longer. The slow, terrible, gut-rotting years had ended. From now on everything was going to be all right. And yet, he thought, if he had not gone after the job so quickly, urged on by his mother, he would never have got it. He could not have stood up to the competition once they had seen several other candidates. For him, to be an insurance agent was a step up.

'I suppose you'll have to go after new business?'

'I daresay,' he said. 'But people always want a bit of insurance. The worse off they are, the more they need it. Nobody's going to risk being buried by the Parish if a penny a week will pay for the funeral. It stands to reason.'

'I expect it does,' Opal agreed. 'But don't you have to put down money for an insurance agency?'

'Twenty pounds,' Edgar said. 'Ma lent me her savings. I shall pay her back as soon as I get on my feet.'

He could have asked me, Opal thought. But he'd rather take his mother's last penny than ask me. Well, though it said nothing good about the state of their marriage, it had its compensations. Now that she had the arrangement with Madame Dora she had been able to put a bit more by, but she had no wish to dissipate her savings because she had at last decided what they were for. Her goal was now as firmly fixed as the Pole star, though no-one beside herself knew anything about it. Under the top surface of her mind it occupied her thoughts from waking to sleeping. Sometimes it pursued her in sleep, and she had vivid, pleasurable dreams of the future. But she would willingly have given Edgar whatever he needed, if he had come to her.

'So I start next Wednesday, after the Whitsun holiday,' Edgar said. 'They don't want the payments to fall into arrears. I thought you might give me a hand with the books. You're good at figures.'

Where does he think I'll get the time, Opal asked herself.

'I'll make a cup of tea and see to Daniel,' she said, turning to her son.

'And what did you do today, love?' she asked.

'I did a drawing,' Daniel said. 'I brought it home to show you. Look! Miss Potter said it was the best in the class.'

Opal studied the drawing with interest. It depicted a street scene, in coloured chalks. Though the houses, the children playing, the horse pulling the coal cart, were all crudely drawn, the picture had great life and vigour.

'Well I think it's nice too,' she said, smiling at him. 'We'll pin it on the wall, shall we, where we can all see it? And now into the scullery and start getting washed while I put the supper on. And don't skip the back of your neck, my lad!'

At five years old he was capable and independent beyond his years and (for which she was truly thankful) with the capacity for enjoying himself for hours on end. He was never as happy as when he had a box of wax crayons and some paper to draw on. That he had talent she was sure, though she didn't know where he got it from. Also, he could now read. He was no trouble and she loved him dearly. He was part of all her dreams for the future.

'We shall have to make some arrangement about Daniel,' she said to Edgar when the child had gone into the scullery.

'I'm sure his Grandma'll have him,' Edgar said. 'It'll only be for a week, until you've worked out your notice.'

Opal, in the act of laying the table, paused and stared at him.

'My notice?'

'You'll be able to give it in tomorrow. The job's certain you know. From next week on, *I'll* be the breadwinner!'

'But . . .'

'Oh you can keep on the house shop if you want to. But no more working from morning until night, coming home too tired to lift a teaspoon. No, you'll be back in your rightful place. But don't think I'm not grateful for what you've done, love!'

Opal knew, now, the reason for the disquiet which had stirred her mind at the moment he had given her his great news.

'Edgar,' she said quietly. 'I can't give up my job.'

He leaned across the table and took her hand in what was an almost forgotten, loving manner.

'You're afraid I'll not succeed,' he said gently. 'Well I can't blame you. But I'm going to prove you wrong. I'm going to show you that all I needed was the chance.'

'It's not that!' Opal protested. In her heart she knew she had her doubts about him, but she would never show them. And what sort of a job was it? Where would it lead compared to what she had in mind?

'It's not that,' she repeated. 'I'm sure you'll do well. It's that I *like* my job. I enjoy every minute of it, even though I do come home tired. I'm good at it, Edgar, and it's what I want to do.'

Edgar's forehead tightened in a frown. His eyes, meeting hers, were hard and puzzled. He doesn't really understand at all, Opal thought.

'We can't talk about it now,' he said. 'We'll discuss it when Daniel's gone to bed.'

'As you wish,' Opal said. 'But you may as well know that I haven't the slightest intention of giving in my notice.'

Edgar jumped up from the table. She saw his neck suffuse with red where it bulged against his collar. He bounded to the window, turning his back on her, his broad shoulders hunched in anger.

'You'll give in your notice,' he shouted. 'You have a working husband now and it's your place to run the home and look after your child!'

She left the table and went into the scullery, to Daniel. Her whole body was shaking but she tried to speak calmly to her son. He was the witness, recently, of far too many quarrels.

'Have you finished, love? Let me see.'

She bent down and kissed his shining face. He smelled deliciously of the Knight's Castile soap which was especially kept for his delicate child's skin.

'Supper and then bed,' she said. 'It's time you were asleep.'

During the meal she and Edgar did not speak, though she kept up a conversation with Daniel. She was thankful when supper was over and she could take the child upstairs. He had his own bedroom now, about the size of a cupboard. She tucked him in and heard him repeat the prayers his grandmother had taught him, then she kissed him good-night and went downstairs again.

Edgar was standing with his back to the fireplace, his arms tightly folded against his chest, his head lowered as if he was about to charge.

'Now, Madam, let's get things straight,' he said grimly.

'Certainly!' Opal flashed back. 'That's what I want, too! For a start, I *do* look after my child, I *do* run the home, working or not. How much housework do *you* do, though you're home all day? When do *you* cook a meal?'

'That's not the point,' Edgar said. 'A woman's place is in the home. Everybody knows that.'

'Well I can assure you, Edgar, I am *not* giving up my job, not for you, not for anyone.' She spoke calmly, but inside she trembled and felt sick.

'Not even for Daniel?' Edgar said. 'I know you've got precious little time for me, but don't you care about Daniel?'

His voice was quieter, too, but it pierced her more than his temper could ever have done. He knew her vulnerability all right. It was the vulnerability of all who carry a child in the womb, bring it helpless and dependent into life. It was a pain of the heart more deeply felt than any bodily pain and she was no more immune to it than any other woman.

Convention had nothing to do with it. She didn't mind what people said, and no-one was going to tell her where her place was. It was what she herself must give up, must be prepared to miss, in the hours of separation from Daniel. That, and the niggling question as to what such a separation might or might not do to her son. She knew the risks, but the fight was for her own identity, for the right to do as she pleased with her own life. In spite of the doubts which remained in her – and perhaps always would – it was a fight she intended to win.

'You're being unfair!' she cried. 'It's not true that I've no time for you, and you know it. But you don't own me. As for Daniel, you're talking as though I have to choose between loving Daniel and going out to work. Well, I don't! I can do both.'

'Not properly,' Edgar insisted. 'You can't do both things well and we all know who'll suffer.'

But for all the strength which had come to him with the prospect of his new job, he was no match for this small, determined woman; this woman he loved but frequently did not understand. He had lost and he knew it.

'I promise you, Edgar, Daniel won't suffer,' Opal assured him. 'And now I'll go around and see your mother and we'll come to some arrangement. She'll understand.'

'I'm not sure I approve,' Mrs Carson said doubtfully. 'Oh, your wages must have been a godsend over the last three years, but now that Edgar's got himself a job . . . Anyway, it's not my approval you're after, is it? Of course Daniel can come here to his dinner every day. And if Edgar's likely to be out on his rounds he can come to his tea as well.'

'He'll love that,' Opal said. 'You know how he enjoys coming here.'

'Aye, well, that's settled then,' Mrs Carson said.

She admired her daughter-in-law – so competent, so ambitious – but she did not always understand her and in this case she couldn't enter into her feelings. But she would do anything for little Daniel. The way things were going he looked like being the only grandchild she'd ever have.

'I'd best be getting back,' Opal said. 'There's some ironing to do.'

'You work too hard,' Mrs Carson said. 'I should have thought you'd have been glad of the chance . . . But there it is. Anyway, I've got a nice apple pasty for you to take back with you. Fresh baked today.'

She wrapped the pasty carefully, taking pleasure in the sight of it. There were few situations that a nice, well-baked apple pasty couldn't improve.

When Opal arrived home Daniel was sitting in the armchair, wrapped in a blanket.

'He's been sick,' Edgar informed her. 'I brought him down and gave him a drink of warm milk.'

His tone of voice said that if she had been in her rightful place this wouldn't have happened. Oh Daniel, she thought ruefully, did it have to be now?

She knelt down by the chair and put her arms around him. 'It must be something you ate, love. Did anyone give you anything at school?'

'Dick Foster gave me some pink sweets,' Daniel confessed.

'Then that's it! Are you better now?'

'Yes.'

There was colour in his cheeks and his eyes were bright enough, the whites clear and blue.

'Well then, back to bed or you'll be too tired for school in the morning.'

'Carry me upstairs,' Daniel demanded.

'A great big boy like you?'

'Well I *was* sick.'

'All right then,' she said. 'Just this once. It'll have to be a piggy back.'

She changed the sheet and tucked him into bed. He flung his arms around her and they hugged each other tightly. Who could possibly say that she did not love her son enough? Then he lay back on the pillow and closed his eyes. She traced the fine arch on his eyebrows with her finger, touched his cool cheek. He was asleep before she left the bedroom.

'Supposing this happens when we're both out at work?' Edgar demanded. 'What then?'

'We'll meet that when it comes,' Opal said. 'It's no use, Edgar. You're not going to make me change my mind.'

By mid-morning it was really busy in the shop, but in this particular week that was to be expected. Everyone who could possibly afford it wanted something new for Whit Sunday, to wear to church or chapel, and perhaps afterwards to the brass band concert in the park. And if there was not enough money for a complete new outfit, then a new hat, and perhaps new white gloves, must do.

'We're selling a lot of white gloves,' Madame Dora said. 'I wonder if we should get another two dozen pairs when David Hessle comes in? Or is it too late? Will the rush be over? Thank goodness the General Strike's finished. If it had gone on even a day or two longer it could have ruined our Whitsuntide trade!'

'I think the rush is about over,' Opal said. 'But white gloves could sell right through the summer. What we must have, though, is more art silk stockings in that new beige shade. No-one wants lisle for best any more. Do you think he might make a special delivery?'

'He might,' Madame Dora said. 'Especially if *you* ask him.'

Opal bent her head over the deep drawer in which she was checking the hosiery stock. She had got on well with David Hessle from the start, but Madame Dora made too much of it. It was nothing more than a pleasant business relationship. How could it be otherwise, even if she were so inclined, which she was not. Though he was single, she was a married woman with a child. But she would not let Madame Dora see her irritation.

Her employer had been good to her, no doubt about that. She had agreed to all her ideas for expansion and had even moved the office and stockroom upstairs into her flat to free more space. They now did a good trade in gloves, scarves, hosiery, artificial flowers and sundry other items to adorn the female form. Lingerie had done well though it was falling off a little at present, this being the season for outward show. Hats, though, continued to be their mainstay. They had many more customers now, and if they were not quite as exclusive as they had been, well, their money was good. And since Opal now had two-and-a-half per cent of the extra profits she wasn't complaining.

'Perhaps you'd better telephone him,' Madame Dora said. 'Order what you think best.'

Her confidence in Opal grew all the time. The takings had doubled in the past two years. And Opal, though she didn't yet know it, was to have her reward. Not an immediate tangible reward. Madame Dora hoped it would not be reaped for a long time to come. But something for Opal to look forward to, in a manner of speaking. It would also be one in the eye for her sister, Millicent, Madame Dora thought with satisfaction.

'Don't let me forget I'm to see Mr Ratcliffe at twelve noon,' she said. 'I mustn't be late. Solicitors charge you for the time you keep them waiting.'

'I'll remind you,' Opal promised.

'When I get back,' Madame Dora said solemnly, 'I'll tell you all about it.'

Opal scarcely heard her. She was making a list of items required from David Hessle. It was important to achieve the right balance between having too little stock to meet the demand and thereby missing sales, and having too much when the season was over. She must also try once more to persuade Madame Dora to have a July sale. Sales were the one thing on which she dug in her heels. A discreet discount on an item which had been slow to sell was one thing; sales, with price tickets in the window, were quite another. As for advertising . . . ! Opal wondered if David Hessle might get hold of any special sale items. She completed her list and was about to unhook the telephone receiver when he walked into the salon.

'I was coming this way,' he said. 'I thought I'd call on the offchance.'

'You're just the man we wanted,' Madame Dora said. 'But I'm leaving you to Miss Carson. I have to see my solicitor.'

'What's that about?' David Hessle asked when Madame Dora had left. 'Not trouble, I hope?'

'I don't think so. She's probably changing her will again. She does it to spite her sister. She hates her since their father died last year and left everything in the house to Millicent. Have you any white gloves, sizes six-and-a-half and seven? And art silk hose, beige dawn, sizes eight-and-a-half and nine?'

Their dealing was interrupted several times while Opal broke off to serve customers. Hessle stepped back out of the way and watched her. She was so competent. She had exactly the right balance of deference and friendliness towards the customers, and the skill to guide them, without ever seeming to hurry, to a reasonably quick decision. She was damnably attractive too, but a hard nut to crack.

By the time the last customer had left and he had completed his order book it was five minutes to one.

'Come and have a bite to eat with me,' he said. 'I'm always asking you and you never accept.'

'Well I can't today,' Opal said. 'It's kind of you but, as you see, Madame Dora isn't back and we never close the salon over the dinner hour.'

'Always the ready answer,' he said with good humour.

She thought how attractive he looked. It would have been pleasant to have gone with him.

'Shall you be going to the band concert on Sunday?' he asked.

'It depends on my husband,' Opal said. 'It depends on what he wants to do.'

'Do you always defer to your husband?' David Hessle asked.

'Of course!' But her eyes, meeting David's, were not as demure as her words.

Ten minutes after he had left, Madame Dora returned.

'Lock the shop door!' she said. 'Yes, I mean it! And come upstairs. I've got something to tell you.' She had an air of great importance, but her eyes were excited, like a child with a secret to impart. Opal followed her upstairs and took a chair in Madame Dora's private sitting room.

'Now!' Madame Dora said. 'Prepare yourself for a shock! A pleasant one – a *very* pleasant one – but a shock!'

'I'm prepared,' Opal said. What could it possibly be? Was Madame Dora perhaps going to get married again?

'Well I've seen Mr Ratcliffe, and the long and short of it is, Opal – and I'm far too excited to beat about the bush –

I've changed my will and I'm leaving the business to you! There!'

'To *me*!' Opal gasped. 'You don't mean it! I can't believe it!' She felt dizzy with the news.

'I don't suppose you can,' Madame Dora said. 'It's not something that happens every day. But it's true. It'll all be yours one day; lock, stock and barrel. Or to be more precise, stock, fixtures, fittings and good-will. You deserve it and it'll be one in the eye for that greedy pig of a sister of mine!'

The world stopped spinning. Opal was on firm ground again. It was a kind gesture of course, but in practical terms it could mean very little to her. Madame Dora was forty-two and in the best of health. She would live another thirty years or more, by which time Opal was quite certain she would have her own business, far bigger and more important than this one could ever be. It was her goal, it was why she was saving her money. Any inheritance from Madame Dora – who in any case might change her mind half-a-dozen times between now and then – would be of small account by the time she could claim it. Now if it were to happen *soon* . . . She stopped her thoughts in mid-flight, horrified by the direction they had taken.

'Thank you Madame Dora,' she said. 'I appreciate it very much indeed. But of course I hope you're going to live a very long time yet, to enjoy Madame Dora's Modes to the full.'

'Shall we go to the band concert today?' Opal asked on Sunday. 'It's the Black Dyke Mills. You always like them.'

'I'd have thought you'd have been too tired for traipsing up and down in the park,' Edgar replied.

'A change is as good as a rest,' Opal said briskly. 'Besides, Daniel might enjoy it. If you don't want to go I suppose I could take him.'

'Well I daresay it would help to take my mind off things,' Edgar said.

As the time grew nearer he was increasingly nervy about starting his new job. Though little more had been said about it, Opal could sense that. She would have liked to have talked to him, tried to reassure him, but it was a sensitive area and she had no wish to provoke another quarrel. She had won her point and that was that.

'It would do that,' she agreed. 'But there's no need for you to worry, Edgar. You'll be all right. Especially as the Supervisor's going around with you for the first week. Anyway, do we go to the band concert?'

'I suppose we might as well,' he said.

'Then we must look our best. Wear your Sunday suit, and the tie I bought you.'

She changed into the cream gabardine which she had worn for Queenie's wedding three years ago. She had taken it in to suit her normal, slender figure, shortened the skirt, trimmed it with new braid, changed the buttons. No-one would recognize it and the material was as good as ever. She had borrowed a hat from the salon, which was allowed since it was good for trade. Daniel had a new suit, as befitted the time of year. They made a smart trio, she thought with satisfaction as they set off.

They took a tram to the park, sitting outside on top at Daniel's request. At the park entrance Edgar tossed twopence into the canvas sheet at the entrance, which entitled them to a printed programme.

'It looks like a good selection,' he said. 'Poet and Peasant, Gondoliers, Il Travatore. And a nice cornet solo. Shall we treat ourselves to chairs and concentrate on the music?'

Though the band concerts, which started at Whitsun and took place every Sunday until the middle of September, were supposedly musical occasions, everyone knew that they were also the scene setters for fashion parades. Those who really wanted to concentrate on the music could pay twopence to sit in a deck chair in a roped-off enclosure around the bandstand. The rest strolled, preferably in groups of three or four, up and down the wide avenues of the park. For them the music was a pleasant background to the more important business of seeing and being seen, especially by the opposite sex.

For no reason at all Opal suddenly wondered just how interested David Hessle was in music? For instance, would he sit in the enclosure? Then she dismissed the thought. She had not come here to see David Hessle.

'I think Daniel might get bored, just sitting still,' she said. 'It would be best to walk. But why don't you take a seat by the bandstand while I walk around with Daniel. I know you appreciate the music more than I do. I like to see what people are wearing.'

'I'll come with you,' Edgar said. 'Anyway it's a bit chilly to sit still, in spite of the sun. I don't know how some of you women keep warm in such thin dresses.'

'Pride keeps women warm,' Opal informed him.

All the same she was glad she was not wearing the flimsy voile which was everywhere around, pretty though it looked. The crowded avenue with people sauntering up and down looked like a summer flower bed moving in the breeze. The women's hats – by far the larger number of them of white straw trimmed with flowers – were interspersed by the men's fawn or grey trilbys or their cream-coloured boaters with striped hatbands.

'Your outfit's as smart as any, even though you did wear it to Queenie's wedding,' Edgar observed.

A great deal had happened to Queenie since that June afternoon. She and Mark had two little daughters and were now hoping that the new arrival would be the son they both wanted. Mr Stone had died, leaving a fortune to his daughter. But nothing could spoil Queenie's nature. She continued as simple and affectionate as ever, and every day more in love with Mark. She was the only person in the world Opal envied, and not for her possessions.

Daniel tugged at Opal's skirt.

'Can we go to see the ducks?' he asked.

Opal frowned slightly. The pond was out of earshot of the band and, except for children, the area would be deserted. Everything of interest was here.

'Perhaps later,' she said. 'Not just now. Mother and Father want to listen to the music and look at all the people.'

'Perhaps we *should* take him,' Edgar said.

'He can wait a little while. He mustn't think he can have everything the minute he asks for it.'

Edgar looked at her in surprise. 'You've changed your tune,' he said.

And then Opal saw David Hessle. He was walking towards her, and clinging to his arm was a pretty, fair creature. The floating panels of her ninon dress lifted in the breeze, which also caused her to hold down her fine straw hat with a small hand elegantly gloved in white kid. Good quality, eight-and-eleven three farthings, Opal noted automatically. Hessle's gaze was concentrated on his companion and he did not see Opal until he was almost upon her. When he did, there was no doubting the pleasure of his recognition.

'Why, Mrs Carson!' he exclaimed. 'I didn't expect to see *you* here! How pleasant!'

'My husband is very fond of music,' Opal said. 'We come whenever we can, don't we Edgar?'

'Allow me to introduce my cousin, Miss Dolly Simpson,' Hessle said.

They chatted amiably for a minute or two. Opal was aware that David Hessle missed nothing of her appearance, also that he approved. She was pleased that, for once, he had seen her in something other than her black work dress, even though her gabardine was not nearly as glamorous as his companion's flowered ninon.

'We must go,' she said after a little while. 'Daniel wants to see the ducks and we've promised him he shall.'

'If she's his cousin,' Edgar said as they walked in the direction of the pond, 'I'm the Prince of Wales!'

★   ★   ★

It was while they were waiting for the tram, close by the park entrance, that the accident happened. The concert was over, everyone rushing home to tea, crowds pouring through the park gates. Opal, standing in the long queue with Edgar and Daniel, saw Madame Dora among them. She was unmistakable in her elegance. Her wide-brimmed, yellow hat had been trimmed by Opal only a few days ago.

'There's Madame Dora!' Opal cried. 'How strange we didn't meet her in the park!' She let go of Daniel and raised her hand, waving to attract her employer's attention.

Eventually Madame Dora saw her. She returned Opal's wave and started to cross towards her. Afterwards, no-one in the crowd seemed to know where the motor-car had come from. One minute it was not in sight and the next it had hit Madame Dora when she was no more than three yards from the pavement. For a split second she lay terribly alone, the yellow hat on the ground a few yards away where the breeze had carried it. Then suddenly people gathered around her still figure. Opal, already running from the opposite side of the road, pushed her way to the front of the crowd.

Madame Dora was alive, though unconscious, when the ambulance came. By the time it reached the hospital Opal, travelling with her, clutching the yellow hat as if it might work a miracle, did not need to be told by the ambulanceman that she was dead.

What horrified Opal for a long time to come was the speed with which the thought came into her mind. She pushed it away again, but it was already too late. The words into which it formed itself burned inside her.

'It's all mine! The business is all mine!'

5

Opal looked up, frowning, as her new assistant rushed into the stockroom. The girl must learn to conduct herself in a more decorous manner. She was new, of course, and young – not yet twenty. But she would have to be trained.

'Oh Mrs Carson,' the girl began breathlessly.

'Calm down Miss Browning,' Opal admonished.

'Well there's a great big car just drawn up at the kerb, with a chauffeur and everything, and I think the lady's coming in here! You'd better come, Mrs Carson!'

Opal smiled; not the polite, upcurving of her lips which she offered to customers, but a smile of real pleasure which lit up her face and shone in her eyes.

'That will be my sister-in-law, Mrs Mark Derwent,' she said. 'I'm expecting her.' She rose and hurried to greet Queenie as she entered the shop. Connie Browning was surprised at the warmth of the meeting between the two women. Mrs Carson was such a cool customer, she wouldn't have thought she'd have had it in her.

'You're looking wonderful, Opal dear,' Queenie said.

'You too!' Privately Opal thought, in the kindest possible way, that her sister-in-law's expensive outfit would have benefited from being more up-to-date, but it was still true that she looked wonderful.

'Come along upstairs,' she said. 'Oh yes, this is my new assistant, Miss Connie Browning. She's been with us just a fortnight. Miss Browning, do you think you could possibly keep an eye on the shop?' She no longer referred to it as the salon, as in Madame Dora's day. 'If there's the slightest problem, the very slightest, call me down at once.'

She went in front of Queenie along the corridor and up the narrow staircase which led to the living quarters above the shop. She heartily disliked this approach to the flat. It was so cramped and dark. When funds allowed she planned to have it decorated in light and bright colours, with a plain green carpet on the stairs; but for the last two years almost every spare penny had gone into the shop, expanding the range of goods, building up the business.

The living room which they now entered was furnished almost exactly as it had been when Madame Dora was alive. Beige-covered sofa and armchairs, walnut table, brown curtains. Opal had inherited the contents of the flat along with the business and had lost no time at all in getting rid of almost everything which the Acer Street house had contained. Not that she liked Madame Dora's taste. She would have preferred more colour. But first things first and the shop was the most important. Except for Daniel, of course. He, she was pleased to think, now lacked for nothing.

'How is business?' Queenie asked.

'Very good. Very good indeed. As far as space permits I'm introducing new lines all the time. And the takings are well up on last year, let alone on what they were when Madame Dora had it.'

She had been surprised, and not pleasantly, to find how little money Madame Dora actually made. Her own small, regular share of the extra profits had seemed riches only because she was so used to having nothing. Studying the books after Madame Dora's death, she had at once seen several ways in which profits might be increased. The moment the lawyers had sorted everything out, dealing swiftly with Millicent's vigorous protests over her sister's will, she had started to put her ideas into effect.

'The trouble with Madame Dora was,' she said to Queenie, 'that she tried to make money by economising on everything, cutting back everywhere. I believe you have to use money to make money. Invest it in goods and increase the turnover.'

Queenie smiled, shaking her head in wonderment. 'I don't know where you get it from, your business sense, I mean. You sound just like my father used to!'

And look where it got him, Opal thought. Look what his success gave you. A chauffeur driven limousine, an ermine stole over your shoulders, diamonds and emeralds on your hands. But there was no animosity in her thoughts. Queenie wore her riches with such natural grace, with so little ostentation, as to disarm all criticism.

'I'd be glad to have half your father's business gifts,' Opal said. 'And I envy his training. It's what I lack.'

'Ah, but you have *flair*!' Queenie said. 'I'm sure that's worth even more. But where's Daniel? I expected to see him.'

'He's out with his father,' Opal said. 'Edgar thought he shouldn't be sitting inside on such a fine afternoon so he's taken him on his rounds. I don't really approve, but Daniel was dying to go.'

'It sounds a good idea to me,' Queenie said. 'What's wrong with it?'

'Only that . . .' She did not quite know how to tell Queenie that she disliked the thought of her son being taken around the poor streets, entering the poverty-stricken homes – probably none too clean – which made up the larger part of Edgar's round. In little more than two short years she had left that behind forever and as far as her son was concerned she would like him to forget that it had ever existed. She intended life to be very different for Daniel.

'You never know what's going around,' she said. 'Infections and so on. I wouldn't want him to catch something just as he's about to go to a new school.'

'Is he looking forward to going to Bishop Tanner's?' Queenie asked.

Opal was saved from replying by the sound of Daniel's footsteps on the stairs. He came running into the room, followed a moment later by his father. The boy's cheeks were flushed in his otherwise pale, bright-eyed face.

Edgar's skin was tanned from being so much in the open air, but in spite of this, Queenie thought, he did not look healthy. It was difficult to say why. He had plenty of flesh on his bones and his decent navy suit sat well enough on his muscular body. It was perhaps something in his demeanour, in his stance. He entered the room quietly, his shoulders hunched, his head down, as if he was not sure that he belonged. And though he had been in work for two years now, it was the previous four years of unemployment which showed in the lines on his face and in the dullness of his eyes. She had seen little of him for some time and she was moved, shocked even, by his appearance. He was twenty-nine and looked at least ten years older. But when he raised his eyes to hers his expression brightened.

'It's such a long time since I saw you,' Queenie said. 'You must tell me about your job.'

'There's nothing to tell,' Edgar said abruptly.

'I can tell you,' Daniel offered. 'We went to a lot of houses today and some of them asked us in. There was an old man in a bed downstairs. He gave me a cough sweet from under his pillow.'

'I hope you didn't eat it,' Opal said sharply. 'It's not fit!'

'It was quite nice,' Daniel said. 'Sort of aniseedy.'

'I told you to watch him, Edgar,' Opal said. 'You know I didn't want him to go in the first place. You never know what he might pick up!'

'He only ate a sweet,' Edgar said. 'It won't kill him. And it gave old Mr Sykes a lot of pleasure. You remember old Sykes in Maud Street? He wouldn't hurt a fly.'

'A sweet from under his pillow! It could be riddled with germs!' Opal protested.

Edgar shrugged his shoulders. He poured himself a cup of tea from the pot on the table and took it to a chair by the window.

'I came to see if Daniel would like to come to stay with us for the last week of the school holidays,' Queenie said, changing the subject. 'But it seems he's going to Grandpa

Derwent's at Highcliffe tomorrow. Well, you'll enjoy it on the farm, won't you Daniel? And Aunt Mary will be very pleased to have you for company, I'm sure.'

'Uncle David's taking us in his car,' Daniel said. 'He's got a Ford. It can go at forty miles an hour!'

'Uncle David?'

'He's a friend. A friend of the family,' Opal said. 'I can't think why you've never met him. He's a wholesaler and I buy a lot of my stock from him. He's always been very helpful to me.'

'So he's going to take you all to Highcliffe!' Queenie said. 'Well that's very kind. It's not an easy place to get to.'

'Almost impossible in the evening,' Opal said. 'And I can't leave the shop during the day.'

'And Father can't go at all,' Daniel said. 'He has to work on Friday nights because that's when people have the money to pay him.'

Miss Browning's voice came from the bottom of the stairs. 'Mrs Derwent's car has come back for her, Mrs Carson.'

'I must be off,' Queenie said. 'Thank you for the tea. I'm glad I managed to see all three of you this time. Couldn't you all come over for the day one Sunday? I know how busy you are, Opal, but surely you could take a day off?'

'I usually do the books and see to the stocks on a Sunday. And a thousand other things. But yes, we'd like to come. And we will, just as soon as I can manage it.'

'And you must let me know how you get on at your new school, Daniel,' Queenie said. 'Are you looking forward to it?'

'No,' Daniel said flatly. 'My friends won't be going. And they'll make me do a lot of arithmetic and spelling and things. I only like to do drawing. I don't suppose they'll do much drawing.'

Opal put her arm around him. 'Of course they'll do drawing,' she said. 'And painting. I especially asked.

They do it every Thursday. And, you know, you can't get through life without arithmetic and spelling.'

'Why not?' Daniel demanded.

'Well you'll never be successful,' Opal said. 'You want to be successful don't you?'

Queenie drew on her gloves and went downstairs, accompanied by Opal, and by Daniel who wanted to inspect her car. Edgar watched them go. If only all women were like Queenie! Gentle and yielding. There wasn't an ounce of hardness in her. Of course she wasn't half as clever as Opal, and no-one worked harder than his wife. She had earned her success. But what she couldn't understand was that not everyone was cut out to be successful. She thought that it was simply a matter of putting your mind to it. Well, even if he had a mind as clear and decisive as Opal's, and he knew he never would have, what was there in his job to put it to?

He had quickly come to hate his job. It was not that he disliked the homes into which he had to enter, though his patch was one of the poorest, but he hated collecting coppers from people who could scarcely scrape them together. And when they could no longer keep up the payments, which happened all too often, he was embarrassed by the meagre surrender value which the Company offered. It was always so much less than had been paid in and sometimes, if they hadn't made enough contributions, it was nothing at all. Oh, he knew all the Company's arguments, and they sounded reasonable enough. Nevertheless they grew richer and richer, and he saw where the money came from.

He was no good at the job. It didn't need Mr Hardaker, the Supervisor, to tell him that. The main idea was to get new customers to replace those who were so frequently lost, and at this he was hopeless. It was bad enough pushing in where new babies had been born, persuading the mother to do her best for the child by taking out an insurance she could ill afford, but it was not as bad as intruding on the bereaved, advising them, even in the act of paying out on the deceased, to take proper precautions against their own demise by investing in more insurance. He had been reminded more than once that if he was to keep his job he must do better.

'The trouble with you,' Mr Hardaker complained, 'is that you're not Company minded! I'm not at all sure that you're cut out for insurance!' It was true enough. But what was he cut out for? Was there anything in the world he was good at? He doubted it.

'Mother says to tell you she'll be down in the shop until closing time,' Daniel said, coming back into the room. 'And she says I can have two custard cream biscuits.'

'Oh! And what does she say I can have?'

Daniel laughed. 'She didn't say. I expect you can have the same as me.'

Never, Edgar thought. I'm not in the same class. Everything for Daniel. He pulled himself up sharply. What was he coming to, to begrudge the boy? He cared for his son with a love at least as deep as Opal's. It hurt him that he couldn't do the things for him that she could. If he'd been capable at all of getting new business, as the Company wanted, he'd have done it for Daniel. But Opal took care of it all. Paints, drawing paper, toys, clothes – anything the child wanted. And now a fine new school, the fees for which, had he been required to contribute, would have taken every penny he earned.

Daniel sat at the table painting. There wouldn't be another word out of him. Edgar stood and stared out of the window. In the street a September wind blew up the dust. He disliked the autumn because it led so quickly to the winter, and here the winters were long. Before he knew it he would be trudging from house to house in the snow and the sludge.

It was a quiet afternoon in the shop. Summer being only just over and the autumn a fine one, no-one was prepared to buy for the winter. Thankfully, most of the warm weather stock had been shifted in the July sale. It had been a good sale, Opal thought. The items she had bought in specially – hosiery, gloves, lingerie – from a bankrupt stock in Leeds, had all sold out. The marked-down goods from her own stock had gone well too. Everything had been sold at a profit, if sometimes a small one, and, more important for the future, she had many satisfied and appreciative customers. The sales at Madame Dora's – she had had half-a-dozen over the last two years – were now acknowledged to be something special.

'All we need now,' Opal said to Connie Browning, 'is for the weather to turn cold for a day or two so that people will come in and buy their thick stockings and winter night-dresses. In the meantime I think we should dress the millinery window with hats suitable for wearing to the Harvest Thanksgiving services. Browns, rusts, reds, I think. Autumn colours.

'Yes Mrs Carson,' Connie said. 'Shall I empty the window?'

'Good gracious no!' Opal replied. 'Never have the window empty while the shop is open. You can clear it just before you leave and I'll dress it again right away.'

She searched through the millinery drawers, looking for hats which would suit her theme.

'When I first started here,' she remarked, 'I used to make hats starting with nothing more than a length of millinery wire twisted into a ring – building everything up from there.'

That was ages ago, now. It was five years to the week since she had started here, but it seemed twice as long. She had soon known that one day she would have her own business, though she had never expected it to happen the way it had. Sometimes, against her will, she recalled the thought she had had when Madame Dora had told her about the inheritance. 'If it could happen *soon*'. But she had never wished her to die. She had had nothing to do with it, it was pure accident. And every year on Whitsunday she visited the cemetery to place fresh flowers on her late employer's grave.

But I've not come all the way yet, Opal thought. Not by a long chalk. This shop was far from the summit of her ambition, in fact she felt she had already outgrown it. She wanted something much bigger, preferably in Leasfield itself, and she knew she would get it in the end. As well as putting money into this business she was saving hard, still paying her weekly visit to the bank but no longer depositing coppers or the odd shillings as she once had. When the opportunity for expansion came she would reach out and grab it with both hands.

'Who taught you to make hats?'

Opal was aware by the loudness of her assistant's voice that she was repeating the question.

About to say 'Madame Dora taught me,' she stopped and considered. In fact Madame Dora had taught her very little. She had provided the tools and a place in which to use them, but in their use Opal had outstripped her employer in no time at all.

'I suppose you could say I taught myself,' she said. 'But you won't need to learn all that because I've moved away from bespoke hats, except for a few old customers like Miss Taylor. There isn't the profit in it. Ready-to-wear hats are the thing now. One can always change the trimming to put up the price. The special orders I *do* take I can cope with quite easily.'

'By the way, Miss Browning,' she continued. 'I want to get away in good time tomorrow evening. Mr Hessle is kindly taking Daniel and me to my father's. Daniel's going to stay on the farm for the rest of the school holiday.'

A smile spread over Miss Browning's face and her blue eyes sparkled. She really is quite pretty, Opal thought, in a conventional sort of way.

'Oh I do like Mr Hessle,' the girl said. 'He's a real Prince Charming! Ever so handsome. I'll bet he's a right one for the ladies! Why, he even made a pass at me and I've only met him twice, both times here in the shop. He's not backward at coming forward, I must say. Of course he's too old for me. He must be pushing thirty.'

He's twenty-eight, the same as me, Opal thought. But men did not have to worry about age. What did the girl mean by saying he'd made a pass at her?

'That will do, Miss Browning,' she said in a cool voice. 'Now get on and check the glove drawers. I want to know exactly what we have and in what sizes. And please remember for the future that I don't allow gossip. In any case, I'm sure you must have misunderstood Mr Hessle.'

Miss Browning jerked open the glove drawer and began to count. Oh no I didn't misunderstand, she told herself. Do you ever go to the pictures was what he said to me and I don't need anyone to tell me what he meant. As sure as eggs is eggs, Madame is jealous. But better to tread carefully. Jobs were not all that easy to come by and she quite liked this one.

Later, after Miss Browning had departed on the dot and she had arranged what she thought would be an eye-catching display of hats in the window, Opal locked the shop door, emptied the till and went upstairs.

'Time for bed, love,' she said to Daniel. 'Clear your things away now and I'll poach you an egg for your supper. If I know your Auntie Mary you'll be having a week of late nights. She spoils you.'

Her sister spoiled Daniel by giving him unstintingly of her time. Opal was aware that Mary was never too busy to play with Daniel, or walk up on to the moors, or down to the village for sweets, however much work there was in the house. She does all the things I don't have time for, Opal thought. But it's all very well when you're not a parent. And I give him all the rest. He understands. He knows I love him and that I'm working for him, she consoled herself.

'A bit of spoiling never did anyone any harm,' Edgar said.

'I daresay I shall be back latish tomorrow night,' Opal said. 'Dad will be disappointed if we don't stay for a bit of supper and we can't rush away straight afterwards. But David will see me back safely.'

'I don't see why it couldn't have waited until Saturday morning,' Edgar protested. 'I could have taken Daniel then. We could have made a day of it, walked over the moors. We'd both have enjoyed that.'

'It's too far for Daniel to walk,' Opal answered. 'Besides, I want to see Dad and Mary.'

'Then the three of us could have gone on Sunday,' Edgar persisted.

'In any case,' Opal said finally, 'Daniel wants to go in David's new car. I'm going tomorrow evening to please Daniel.'

There was nothing more to be said. Edgar picked up the newspaper, though he had already read it. It was full of petty crime, social chit-chat, politics – which had once interested him and now no longer did. But there was nothing else to do. Opal had already opened her account books and was engrossed in adding up figures.

'I must go upstairs and finish Daniel's packing,' Opal said to Miss Browning towards the end of the busy Friday. 'We must be ready to leave the minute the shop closes. In fact if we don't have customers in I might just close a few minutes early. Mr Hessle should be here any minute. Ask him to come straight upstairs will you?'

She wondered, as the girl obviously had silly ideas in her head, whether she should wait in the shop until David came. But there was too much to do. Edgar was out working and Daniel could not be trusted to get himself ready entirely without supervision. But how silly she was being! David, she was sure, had scarcely noticed the girl. Notwithstanding, as she packed Daniel's case she kept an ear open for the sound of the shop bell. When she heard it, but David did not appear, she went downstairs again. Most likely it was a late customer. She might be needed, if only to sell her something quickly and get her off the premises.

There was no sign of a customer. Miss Browning was stretching up to a high shelf and David Hessle was standing close beside her.

'I heard the bell several minutes ago,' Opal said. 'I thought it must be a customer.'

'It was,' David said quickly. 'She was leaving as I came in just now.'

'Were you not able to help her, Miss Browning?' Opal asked.

The girl hesitated. 'No. That is . . .'

Of course there had been no customer. The girl's manner gave her away. But how silly of David!

'Very well Miss Browning, you may go now,' Opal said. 'And by the way, when you can't reach the high shelves, remember there's a step ladder. That's what it's for.'

She knew at once by the swift smile which David could not conceal that she had said the wrong thing. If there was one thing more attractive than another about Miss Browning it was her long, shapely legs beneath her short skirt. What man would not be pleased to watch her climb a step ladder?

'Good-night Miss Browning,' Opal said firmly. 'Be on time in the morning. We're hoping for a busy day.'

There was hardly any traffic on the moorland road. On either side, and as far as the eye could see, the heather was still in bloom, a blazing reddish-purple in the light of the setting sun. By the time they reached the farm the daylight had gone, leaving only a strip of dark blue in the western sky. As David drove into the farmyard Mary came out of the house to meet them. Daniel, who had fallen asleep despite all his efforts not to do so, wakened as the car stopped.

'We can't stay long,' Opal said, following her sister into the kitchen. 'It's going to be late as it is when we get back. I have to make an early start on Saturday mornings. It's good of you to have Daniel. I know he'll enjoy himself.'

'It will be a lovely change for me,' Mary said. 'Nothing

ever happens here. You don't know how lucky you are, Opal. Anyway, you must have a bite of supper.'

'Where's Grandpa?' Daniel asked.

'In the stables, seeing to Victor.'

'Can I ride Victor tomorrow?'

'Of course you can. Providing you go straight to sleep tonight.'

If she had a son, Mary thought – if ever she did, which seemed unlikely since she was stuck here on the farm without the slightest prospect of marriage – she would like him to be just like Daniel. But even if the chance of marriage came, how could she ever leave her father? He depended upon her entirely. Yet all she had ever wanted was a husband and children, and time was passing. She was already twenty-three. Opal had married at eighteen.

Ben Derwent came in from the stables, washed his hands at the sink and sat to the table.

'You look well, Dad,' Opal said.

He looked much less tired than Mary, but it was she who bore the double burden, that of deputy wife and of daughter. In the five years since his wife's death her father's duties had not changed. Opal knew that she could never have been as unselfish as Mary, she would have had to get out long ago, found her father a house-keeper. But Mary was not like that.

They ate supper; lamb from the farm, salad from Mary's garden, freshly-baked bread. After supper Opal wanted to leave at once but the two men were immersed in conversation.

'It's gone ten, David,' she reminded him.

She could not think what he could find to talk about with her father, though it was part of David's charm that he could get on well with anyone. Even with Edgar, if Edgar would only let him. But she knew that her husband – though he never said so – hated David Hessle.

She went upstairs to Daniel but he was fast asleep. She kissed him gently, hating to part with him even for a week. She loved him so very much, had such plans for him. At half-past ten David allowed himself to be dragged away. When they left the farm the night was clear and fine, with an early September nip in the air. The wide sky was navy blue, and star-filled. She looked forward to the drive back through the peaceful countryside.

6

At first they drove in silence. The moorland road was narrow, not built for motor traffic. It stretched out before them like a silver ribbon, in the light of a moon so brilliant that, in patches here and there, it coaxed a pale lilac colour from the dark heather. Except for a rabbit or two, momentarily transfixed in the headlights, they had the road to themselves. It was as if they were in some magic country on the edge of the world. Would she like to be suspended there forever Opal asked herself. She thought not. In spite of having been brought up on a farm she was not at heart a countrywoman. She preferred the hum and bustle of the town. She felt more a part of what went on there; the production of fine clothes in the mills, the buying and selling. In no time at all her mind was back in the shop. But with the thought of the shop came the niggling memory of Miss Browning.

'You seem to have made quite an impression on my new assistant,' she said, breaking the silence.

David laughed. 'She's an attractive kid. Lively too, I should think. You've made a good choice there.'

'She's pretty enough,' Opal agreed. 'But immature. She'll need a lot of training. By the way, she seems to have ideas about you! I wonder what put them into her head?'

David did not reply and his silence goaded her into a remark she regretted as soon as it was uttered.

'I would rather,' she said, 'that you kept off my assistant. She's young and silly. If you're going to turn her head she'll be no use to me.'

David, without answering, stopped the car by the side of the road and turned off the engine.

'What are you doing?' Opal demanded. 'You know we're in a hurry to get back. Edgar will be worried.'

He was looking straight ahead, his strong, beautiful profile etched in the moonlight. She wondered if he knew how attractive he was, and suspected that he did. But when he turned to face her his eyes were hard, his finely-curved lips unsmiling.

'Let's forget Edgar,' he said roughly. 'And Connie.' (She noted in spite of herself that he called her 'Connie'). 'Let's forget everyone except you and me.'

'What do you mean?' She had never before seen him in this mood, so remote from his cheerful, well-mannered self. She felt a frisson of fear, tinged with elation.

'You know quite well what I mean. If you don't, you're not the intelligent woman I took you for – though some-times I wonder if you're not all intelligence and no heart. But that's not true either. The fact that you're jealous – yes I said jealous – of Connie Browning shows that somewhere under that efficient exterior there is actually feeling.'

'What are you trying to say?' Opal asked.

'I'm trying to say – I am saying – that it's you I'm head over heels for. I think I have been ever since the first day I walked into Madame Dora's with my uncle. And now at long last I think you might just care a bit about me. So will you admit it?'

Was it true, what he said, she wondered suddenly? If not, why did his words not surprise her? She was fond of him, there was no doubt of that. She enjoyed his company, looked forward to his visits, missed him if he didn't come. There was a warmth in David, had been from the beginning, that was lacking in the rest of her life, especially in her marriage. There was none, any longer, in Edgar, nor did he want any from her. Whatever she offered, Edgar refused. She realized, then, that she would have liked to have been in love with David. And that even though she was not, she would like to throw discretion to the winds, to take whatever he offered and be thankful for it. But it was impossible.

'I'm married,' she said flatly. 'I'm a married woman with a child.' She was not sure whether she was speaking to David or reminding herself.

'I'm talking about your feeling, not your circumstances,' David said. 'Don't pretend to me that your marriage means a row of pins to you. I've seen you with Edgar, watched you together.'

She turned her head away from his searching look. Was it so plain to the world, the failure of her marriage? Did her hunger for physical satisfaction, which was by now almost entirely denied her, show in her face? Tears came into her eyes and she raised a hand to brush them away. David turned her face to his. His touch was gentle, his eyes compassionate.

'Don't worry,' he assured her. 'It doesn't show. Except to me because I care. Oh Opal, I want to give you so much!'

His arms went around her and his mouth sought hers. She did not resist, she had no desire to do so. In that awkward embrace, in the front of the little car, the longings of weeks and months, years even, rose up in her – though whether they were for David himself or for what Edgar would not, or could not, give her, she didn't know. Nor did it matter. His strong yet gentle fingers caressed her breasts. Wild delights and desires swept through her body. She knew that not far from here was the point of no return.

'Stop!' she cried. 'Stop! It's impossible!'

He held her more tightly, stopping her words with kisses, his hand now caressing her thigh. She felt the hard urgency in his body and the desire equally in her own. Then she jerked her head away from his and twisted and turned in his arms fighting to free herself.

'We can't David! We can't.'

He let her go, and for a moment looked at her as though

he did not know where he was, who she was. His face was full of anger.

'We can,' he said. 'I love you. You love me. Don't deny it because I shan't believe you. I felt it in you just now. You can't go back on that. Your marriage doesn't mean anything, you know that. Leave Edgar and come to me. It's as simple as that.'

She looked at him in astonishment.

'You can't be serious, David.'

'I am serious.'

'And what about Daniel?'

'I'll care for Daniel. Edgar can see him whenever he wants to. He'd never be denied that. And I'll care for Daniel as I care for you. He won't suffer, I promise you.'

'And the shop?' Opal asked. 'Oh David, who will patronize a woman who has left her husband, gone to live with another man? Even if I was divorced, and we married, it would never do.'

She was surprised by the astonishment of his face. Surely he understood that?

'The shop?' he said. 'You don't have to bother about the shop. I can support you. I can give you a good life. The kind of life you deserve. Come to me, Opal!'

He took her hands in his, gently now, and in the silence which followed his words, in the pause while he waited for her answer, she could feel his body trembling.

'I can't,' she said at last.

'Why can't you? Why not?'

'I don't love you, David.'

'I don't believe you.'

'And if I did there would still be Daniel.'

It was the truth, she told herself, but in her heart she knew that it was not the whole truth. The truth included Daniel, it included her hopes and plans for the future; it included Edgar, though she was not sure why.

'You don't fool me,' David said slowly. The hardness of his voice stabbed her. 'You're using Daniel. I think you would use anyone to get what you wanted. It's the business isn't it? You can't give it up. You can't relinquish the power.'

'It has nothing to do with power . . .'

'Oh yes it has. I know you better than you know yourself.'

Right now, she thought, that could be true. In the conflict inside her she hardly recognized herself.

'David, I swear to you . . .'

'Don't,' he said roughly. 'Don't, because you'd be lying. You can't stifle your ambition, can you? You have to be the one with power. Well, long may it serve you!'

'I recognize that I'm ambitious,' Opal said quietly. 'I can't help that. I can't change it.'

He turned on the engine, put the car into gear. 'It's the same old story,' he said bitterly. '*You* can't change, but others must – to fit in with you.'

'Being ambitious doesn't make for an easy life for a woman,' Opal defended herself. 'But right now I'm just desperately sorry and I wish I could comfort you.'

'Well don't let that worry you,' David retorted. 'I promise you I won't lack for comfort!'

He pressed his foot hard on the accelerator and the car leapt forward, racing along the moorland road. The moon was covered by clouds, now, and the roads and moor were a sheet of blackness pierced only by the headlights from the car. Opal put a hand on David's arm.

'Please slow down, David!'

He seemed not to hear her. She sat beside him in terrified silence until – and it seemed a lifetime later – he stopped the car at her door.

Then he said, 'I'm not sure that I can stop loving you, Opal. But the next move, if there's to be one, is yours. And don't expect me to wait forever, or to behave like a saint while I'm waiting. It's not in me.'

When he had driven away she let herself in through the shop entrance, locked the door behind her and dragged herself wearily upstairs. She was so tired.

As she expected, Edgar was waiting up for her. He had, unusually for him, been drinking. There were several empty beer bottles around the room and the small bottle of brandy which she kept for emergencies was on the table, half empty.

'So you decided to come home?' He spoke with slow, deliberate articulation. 'You actually remembered you had a husband?'

'How could I forget?' Opal said wearily. She was drained of emotion. All she wanted was to be on her own and to sleep.

'Easily enough I daresay. Do you know what time it is? Do you know it's after midnight?'

'We were late leaving,' Opal said shortly. 'Dad kept us talking.'

'I expect that wasn't all that kept you. I'm sure your fancy man wasn't averse to lingering!'

'You're drunk,' Opal said. 'Otherwise you wouldn't talk like that.'

'Yes I'm drunk,' Edgar said. 'Why not? What else is there? A sod of a job. A bitch of a wife who doesn't give a damn!'

She felt his words like a slap on the face. They were undeserved. In the last half hour the thought of Edgar had been strong in her mind.

'For God's sake stop it,' she flared. She hated it when he was in a maudlin, self-pitying mood. 'If you don't like it here why don't you get out? Nothing I do suits you. You're no support to me at all. What do you ever give me?'

She felt weak now; in need of a man's strength, a man's arms about her, not in passion or sexual love but in comfort and security.

'I give you all I've got,' Edgar said. 'It's not enough for you. You don't want me or what I can give. You haven't for years.'

'That's not true and you know it,' she said. 'You're the one who holds back. But I repeat, if you're so unhappy why don't you just go? Ours isn't a proper marriage any longer. Perhaps we'd be better apart. Go and live with your mother for a while.'

'You'd like that wouldn't you?' he shouted. 'Me leaving the field clear. Well there's no way it's going to happen. There's no way I'm leaving Daniel – though God knows I'm not much use to him either!'

He knew too – it was more clear to him because he was slightly drunk – that as long as he lived he could not leave Opal. Though sometimes he almost hated her, he could not envisage life without her.

'I'm very tired,' Opal said. 'I'm going to bed.'

But upstairs she went into Daniel's room. There was no way she could bear to be near Edgar tonight. She was unutterably weary, tired of everything and everybody. Something must change soon. It must, it must.

At five minutes past one on the following Wednesday Opal locked the shop door after Miss Browning and went upstairs to put on her hat and coat. From time to time on a Wednesday afternoon she took the tram into the centre of Leasfield to look at the shops. Leasfield's early closing day was Thursday. It was not so much that she wanted to buy anything, more that she wanted to see what other people were buying. Leasfield was in advance of its neighbours in fashion and by carefully studying the shops there she could often judge what to buy for her own. Sometimes she would buy items in the Leasfield sales and sell them at full price at her own shop. And today, she thought, seeing her pale face in the mirror as she adjusted her hat, the expedition might cheer her up.

She had not seen David since he had left her at the door on Friday night. He was due tomorrow and she both dreaded and looked forward to his visit. By Saturday morning Edgar had seemed his usual self; quiet – but then he was always quiet so it was difficult to judge. They had carried on their normal, sparse conversations as though Friday night had not happened. But she had not returned to his bed and he had not commented on the fact. It was a state of affairs that, in the two-bedroomed flat, could only last until Daniel returned. After that she supposed they would resume their usual condition – miles apart in the same bed.

She took the tram to Leasfield, alighting in the centre of the town, from whence it was no more than a five-minute walk to Miller's fashion store, her venue for the afternoon. As always, she walked slowly and carefully around each department, noting everything of interest. An evening dress in lace, with insets of chiffon in the skirt, caught her eye. The saleswoman moved in on her as she studied it.

'It's the very latest from Paris, Madame,' she said. 'We had it copied. You see the new hemline, just dipping a little at the back?'

'I suppose it had to come,' Opal said. 'Skirts have gone about as high as they can. It's really quite pretty.'

She moved on. She had no room on her premises to stock dresses. It would mean fitting rooms too. But what she had been wondering about was cosmetics. Most women now had abandoned the paper powder leaves in favour of real face powder, kept in a pretty box with a swansdown puff. Many used lipstick, discreetly applied. Rouge she was not sure about for her class of trade; but why not, if a woman wanted it?

There were several items on the toiletries counter she thought she might be able to sell: lavender water, eau-de-cologne, talcum powder – as well as make up and the pretty containers to keep it in. Altogether, it need take up no more than a couple of drawers and a shelf or two. She must find out the best wholesaler for such goods.

She climbed the stairs to the balcony tearoom on the next floor, choosing a table with a good view of what went on below. The waitress came at once.

'I'd like a pot of china tea and some buttered toast,' Opal said.

While she waited to be served she watched a constant, if steady, stream of customers at the toiletries counter.

They took their time about their purchases but seldom left without buying.

'I've been watching the toiletry counter,' Opal said when the waitress brought her tea. 'Is it always so busy?'

'I don't get much time to watch,' the waitress said. 'I suppose it is. They sell what we all want, don't they? Something to make us feel a bit better.'

'That's true,' Opal agreed.

She wished she was near enough to see exactly what the customers chose. She was sure the enterprise would be a good one for her and she wondered why she had not thought of it sooner. She hoped she was not getting slack. She tipped the waitress, paid her bill at the cash desk, and left.

No daylight had penetrated into the store and she had forgotten how bright the day was outside. Perhaps, rather than taking the tram all the way, she would walk the first mile or two. She enjoyed walking and did it too seldom. She had walked about a mile when she saw the building. She could not imagine why she had never seen it before until she realized that the buildings around it had been pulled down, thus rendering the one which remained more conspicuous.

It was three storeys high, solidly fashioned in an ornate, Victorian style with a small, square tower rising from the roof above the main entrance. Along the front, at ground level, were eight, large plate glass windows. It must surely, once, have been a retail store? For what other purpose than to display goods would one need such large windows? Now, though, they were fitted with grimy venetian blinds, as if the building might have been more recently used as a warehouse. The paintwork was shabby and peeling but, as far as she could see, the woodwork and the stone were sound. Surely this building was not to be demolished with the rest?

She walked along the front, trying without success to peer in through the blinds. When she reached the centre door she found a notice fixed behind the glass. 'Enquiries

to Davies and King, Estate Agents, Hart Lane, Leasfield.'
She knew at once, without the slightest shadow of doubt, without considering anything for or against, that she must see them. She did not even wish to walk around to view the rest of the building from the outside. Only let her get to Davies and King and the rest could come later. Directed by a passer by, she found them easily enough.

'If you'll tell me what it's about,' the clerk in the front office said, 'I'll find out if our Mr King can see you.' He returned two minutes later. 'Luckily,' he said, 'Mr King is available. Please come this way.'

'Please tell me Mr King,' Opal said without pre-liminaries, 'was it originally built as a retail store?'

'How observant of you,' Mr King said pleasantly. 'That is exactly what it was. But some years ago now. I under-stand – it was before I came to the neighbourhood – that it was a nice store, but a little old-fashioned. Didn't move with the times. And then it's just a little too far out of town for a retail business. Almost a mile, you see. They couldn't make it pay.'

'And what is it now?' Opal asked. 'Or what was it before it was empty? It is empty, isn't it?'

'Oh quite. Except of course that most of the shop counters and suchlike are left. No-one ever bothered to move them. It's been such as a warehouse, on and off, for a few years now. All clean stuff, of course. Garments mostly. The last tenants moved out to smaller, more modern premises, when their lease ran out.'

'I notice that some of the buildings around have been pulled down,' Opal said. 'Is that likely to happen to this one?'

'Oh no,' Mr King said. 'I don't think there's any question of that. It was small, back-to-back houses which were pulled down. No loss to anyone. The tenants have been moved into Council houses with baths and gardens and that sort of thing.'

'And what would be the rent of the place?' Opal asked.

'Well now, that depends on how much space you would

require,' Mr King said. 'If you would ask your husband to call in and discuss what he has in mind, we could perhaps put a figure on it.'

'My husband isn't the interested party,' Opal said coldly. 'I am. I'd like a price for the whole building, though it's possible that at first I'd only be able to rent one or two floors. Even so, I wouldn't take any of it without an option on the whole.'

She heard the words, like an echo, as she spoke them, but it seemed impossible that they were issuing from her mouth. Had she taken leave of her senses?

Mr King leaned back in his chair, surveying this small, neat woman, with clear bright eyes which met his without blinking.

'I see,' he said doubtfully.

Poor man, he doesn't see at all, Opal thought.

'I can't imagine the rent would be high,' she said. 'The place looks very run down. And naturally I'd like to see the inside. In fact, now, if that would be convenient. I have business commitments which prevent me coming to Leasfield often.'

'Perhaps you would tell me what you propose to use the premises for?' Mr King said. 'My clients would naturally want to know that.'

'Of course,' Opal said. 'I propose to open a retail store.'

'A *store*? But as I've just told you, my dear lady . . .'

'A fashion store. Ladies and children's clothing. Millinery, materials, gloves, haberdashery, cosmetics, hosiery and footwear. To start with, that is. I would hope to diversify later.'

'But how . . . ?'

'Leave the how to me, Mr King,' Opal said with more conviction than she felt. 'All I want from you right now is to see over the premises and have a figure for the rent. Of course any structural defects – worn stairs, plumbing and the like – would have to be made good by the owners before I could consider it. But I'm sure that would apply to any tenant. Shall we go?'

Mr King, as if mesmerized, called to his assistant for the keys.

'Could we open a few blinds?' Opal asked. 'It's all rather dark.'

Mr King, who without quite knowing how it had come about realized that he had surrendered his will to this commanding young lady, did as he was asked. Light flooded in.

'That's better,' Opal said. 'Oh dear, it is a dirty mess isn't it? And everything such dark paint. I'd have a great deal to do on this floor before I could even attempt to use it.'

But she had noted that the paint, though grimy, was not flaking, and that the counters which had been left behind would be quite adequate when well polished. There were also plenty of drawers. Opening one or two, she found that they ran smoothly. No damp, she thought.

The staircase which ran through the centre of the building to the two remaining floors was as solid as a rock, though the carpet which covered it was worn, and would have to be thrown out. But no matter. Good oak treads which these were, were quite adequate. On the first floor the windows were smaller, but more in number, and without blinds, so that everything seemed brighter. As on the ground floor, there were counters and other fittings, and a certain amount of carpet, which she thought might clean up well. This would be the floor for gowns, coats, millinery. One day, perhaps, she would sell furs.

'Now Mr King, what about the second floor?'

'That has never been fully developed,' Mr King said, leading the way. 'A certain number of offices and, of course, stock rooms.'

'I see,' Opal said. 'Yes, it is rather makeshift, isn't it?' But she saw no sense in giving overmuch space to offices. Offices were non-productive. If one was to make a business pay, then every foot of space must be calculated

99

to show a profit, and those which could not must be kept to a minimum.

'What's this small staircase here?' she asked.

'That leads to the tower room. A folly, I think you could call it. Typically Victorian. It leads nowhere and has no especial use.'

It could be my private office, Opal thought.

When they had seen over every inch of the building she demanded that they start again at the beginning, and only when everything had been seen twice did she declare herself satisfied.

'But when I say "satisfied",' she amended, 'I mean that I would be, provided that the owner would make the repairs which you have noted down, and that the rent is reasonable. The figure you suggested is undoubtedly too high. Not many people would be interested in such a property, would they? Especially surrounded by derelict land.'

She hoped he would not call her bluff on that one, for the spare land she saw as a real asset. When the time came she would buy it, build on it, expand even further.

'Well, my dear Mrs Carson, *you* are interested for one,' Mr King said smoothly.

'And how many others?' Opal asked. 'Anyway, let me know within the week. You have my telephone number. And in the meantime, thank you for showing me over.'

She left him, and walked to the tram stop. To take a tram was to return to the real world after the fairy tale world she had inhabited for the last hour. But the real world, the world of rents and rates, of goods and wages – in short, of money – was what she now had to contend with.

She needed David's help. Not only his practical help, though she had marked out in her mind what he could do for her in that area, but his interest as a friend, his opinion as a businessman, his reassurance that she was doing the right thing. How much had she forfeited his friendship since the events of Friday night? She could only put it to the test. At seven-o-clock in the evening she telephoned him.

'He's out,' his sister said. 'He came in and went out again. There's no telling when he'll be back.'

'I see. Well, when he does come in, will you ask him to telephone me? No matter how late.'

Edgar was also out, which suited her. She had no intention of telling him anything until her plans were more settled. She was certain of his disapproval. When he came in and saw her, sitting at the table, head bent over columns of figures, it was nothing new to him.

'I suppose you had a profitable afternoon in Leasfield?' he said.

'I believe so,' Opal said. 'I think it will turn out to be quite profitable.'

At midnight she decided that David was not going to telephone. She went to bed but, lying in Daniel's narrow bed, found no sleep until it was almost time to get up again. At half-past seven in the morning she went down into the shop to telephone.

'David! I expected to hear from you last night,' she said. 'Can you come over this morning? It's important.'

'It must be for you to ring at this hour,' he replied. 'What's it about? Is anything wrong?'

'Nothing. I can't tell you about it on the telephone.'

'Very well,' he promised. 'I'll make you my first call.'

Miss Browning arrived at half-past eight, pale and yawning.

'You look half asleep, Miss Browning,' Opal remarked.

'I am,' Connie Browning said. 'Had a late night. Went to the pictures and out to supper afterwards. My Ma didn't half create a fuss when I got home after midnight!'

Her smile, as her wide blue eyes met the direct look from Opal's dark ones, was one of triumph. It was a pity it would be unwise to tell Madam just who had kept her out so late. She'd have liked to have had the pleasure. Bosses were all the same; thought they could rule your life twenty-four hours a day. Well, she was definitely one up now! Come to think of it, Madam looked a bit odd this morning. Sort of excited. Surely *she* couldn't have been living it up?

'Well it's too bad you don't feel at your best,' Opal said briskly. 'I've decided to start stocktaking today. So will you please begin by measuring all the ribbons, then count the hosiery and gloves. Write down the quantities and sizes and put the price per yard or per pair at the side. I will do the extensions.'

The bold look her assistant had given her had not gone unnoticed. It taunted her, as it was meant to; but no matter how strong her suspicions were, and she felt quite sure that the girl had been out with David, there was little she could do about it. She did not care to risk jeopardizing her own friendship with David any further. She was still unsure how matters stood between them. When he arrived, however, an hour later, his manner towards her seemed the same as always. He gave Miss Browning no more than his usual polite greeting, but this did not prevent her from looking like a cat which had found a rich source of cream.

Little fool, Opal thought. She's quite transparent. He won't like that. But she had more on her mind this morning than David's flirtation.

'Will you come into the office?' she said to him.

The second she had closed the door she began to tell him about the empty store, and almost as quickly, he stopped her.

'Wait a minute! Opal, there's no way you can do this! Have you taken leave of your senses?'

'Don't!' she cried. 'Don't say that yet. I asked you to come this morning because I wanted to tell you about it before anyone else. You are, I hope, still my friend? In spite of everything?'

'Yes,' he replied. 'In spite of everything. Perhaps against my better judgement. Do you want to talk about that?'

'No,' she admitted. 'Not now. I just wanted to know.

David, will you do something for me? And not form any opinions until you've done it? Keep an open mind?'

'What is it you want?'

'It's not difficult. All I want is for you to go into Leasfield and look at the place. Not with me. In fact, you're not to let on that you know me. This is what I want you to do. Now listen.'

'I still think you're mad,' he said when she had finished.

'But you'll do it for me? And you'll go today?'

'Very well.'

'And you'll come back right away and tell me what happened?'

It was late afternoon when he returned.

'What did you think?' she asked eagerly. 'Tell me at once!'

'Well there's one thing sure,' he said. 'I didn't have to put on an act for the benefit of the estate agent. It's hopeless! Oh, I agree the place is basically sound. But it's far too big, even if you only opened a floor at a time. How would you stock it? How would you manage for staff? You can't possibly consider it, Opal!'

'That's not a decision you have to make,' Opal said quietly. She did not feel the slightest bit discouraged by his words. 'But thank you, David, for doing as I asked. With you turning it down so flatly they might think seriously about my offer. What a pity I can't get half-a-dozen people to do the same thing!'

'I was pretty forthright,' David said. 'I told them I wouldn't touch it with a bargepole – which is the truth – and that I couldn't imagine anyone who would!'

'So I have every hope that they'll accept my offer,' Opal said. 'And if they do, then I shall go ahead and try to raise the money.'

'But *how*?' David asked. 'How can you *possibly*?'

'Well not through you for a start, since you don't have faith in me!'

'Of course I have faith in you! If you'd suggested taking a bigger shop – even twice the size of the one you have

– I'd have said go ahead and good luck to you. But a department store! In any case, I haven't any money. All my money is in my warehouse stock.'

'I know,' Opal said. 'But if you do want to help me there is one way you can. Would you let me have long credit on your lines? I've always paid you promptly. Would you trust me a bit further if I managed to raise the money for rent and wages and so on? And could you give me introductions to other wholesalers who might do the same? Or vouch for me if I give your name as reference?'

'I'll do whatever's in my power to help,' David said. 'You know that.'

He felt quite safe in his promise. It would never come to fulfilment. There was no possible way that Opal could raise the money.

7

It was the first time, Opal reflected, that she had ever set eyes on a bank manager. They were creatures beyond her ken and until now her affairs had been so simple as never to need one. Mr Harper was not how she had pictured him on her way to the bank this Friday morning – tall, well-made, venerably greying, avuncular. He was a thin, hungry-looking man, the top of whose head, as Opal noted while he bent over the accounts she had given him, was bald except for a few wispy, black hairs.

'There's no doubt that you've got a good little business here,' he said, looking up. 'And you've built it up in a surprisingly short time. I commend you on your business acumen!'

'Then you'll back me?' Opal said.

He leaned back in his chair, clasping his hands together as if about to lead in prayer, and smiled a slow, gentle smile.

'Alas, my dear Mrs Carson, it's not quite so simple!'

'Why not?' Opal asked. 'You've seen my accounts, verified by the accountant. You've heard my proposals, to which I've given a great deal of thought. It's not a new idea to me, Mr Harper; not something thought up on the spur of the moment. It's something I've dreamed of for a long time. But not only dreamed. I've planned, too.'

'And most interesting your plans *are*,' Mr Harper conceded. 'Though some of them, I must say, are a little . . .' He struggled for a word. '. . . Well, shall we say *innovative*? Yes, innovative.' Having found the word, he rolled it off his tongue with enjoyment.

'They're all feasible,' Opal assured him.

'But of course there's more to it than that . . .'

'Such as?'

'Well in the first place I think what you propose would be an unwise move on your part. You're doing very nicely now, Mrs Carson. Why not build on what you've got? It doesn't do to be over-ambitious, you know. A young lady like yourself. A prosperous little business such as you have, easy to handle, not many staff, is much more suitable for the fair sex.'

'Would my ambition be more agreeable if I were a young man?' Opal asked swiftly.

'Now you're putting words into my mouth!' Mr Harper said pleasantly. 'But, naturally, ambition is more to be expected, and indeed more necessary, in a man. Though even a man might hesitate to take on what you have in mind. I suspect your husband would agree with me there.'

'Oh I'm sure he would,' Opal answered. 'But as I've already told you, my husband wouldn't be involved. I would be running the business myself.' And that remark will *not* have helped me, she thought. 'But do you mean you have a different policy towards a *man* who wants a loan?'

'Well . . .'

'Why?'

'It stands to reason, dear lady. Here you are, a young married woman.' He gave her a look which told her she was also attractive in his eyes. 'You have one child. Who is to say – and I hope you will forgive me for being so plain spoken – that you will not be blessed with more children? And what would happen to your business then?'

He spoke with calm confidence, almost with benevolence, as one who has made an unassailable point. Opal's reply was equally confident.

'It would carry on. Being a mother, though I admit there are certain practical matters I would have to sort out, would not stop me any more than being a father would stop a man.'

'More easily said than done,' Mr Harper said. 'Now if you were a widow . . .'

I would be a widow first and a woman second, Opal thought. And I would suddenly be capable of running a business. But she did not say it out loud. Nor did she consider herself as unlikely as any widow to have another child. It was clear, in spite of the polite smile which had not for one moment deserted him, that she had antagonized this man. Well, he antagonized her. He was a patronising idiot.

'And there is another matter, equally if not more important,' he continued. 'You see, you have no collateral to offer me. The Bank must have security, you know. We owe it to our shareholders.'

'But I've shown you my trading figures,' Opal protested. 'You've seen what I've done in the time I've had Madame Dora's. Doesn't that count?'

'But surely, Mrs Carson, if you were to move into something bigger, Madame Dora's would have to go? If you failed in your new venture the bank would have nothing at all to realize on!'

Opal rose to her feet. Anger flooded through her so that she could have beaten her fists against this man, wiped the everlasting smile from his face. She was furious with herself, too, that she could not hold back the tears which filled her eyes. It was exactly what he would expect of her. But she managed to keep her voice steady.

'So that's your last word?'

'I'm afraid so, Mrs Carson. Though of course if by some means you *were* to get the new business off the ground, if it *were* to be successful . . .' The tone of his voice said that the possibility was as remote as the farthest star from the earth. 'If at any time you wanted to expand a little, don't hesitate to consult us. We're always ready to listen!'

He held the door open for her, watching her as she

marched out of the bank into the street. A pretty little thing. Lively. Quite clever too. He must ask his wife if she ever patronized Madame Dora's.

Opal walked quickly, looking neither to right nor left. She admitted to herself that, angry though he had made her, she was not entirely surprised by the bank manager's attitude. Banking was a man's world. Well, no matter. She was not beaten yet, not by a long chalk.

The shop was empty of customers when she returned but evidence that there had been some lay strewn around in the form of gloves, hosiery, scarves. She bit back the sharp reprimand which rose to her lips as she saw Miss Browning standing idle amid the disorder. It would be necessary to absent herself from the shop, to leave it in Miss Browning's hands, on more than one occasion in the near future. In the last few days Opal had become curiously unsure of her assistant's temperament. That she was capable of taking charge of the shop for short periods Opal didn't doubt. But there was a boldness about the girl which suggested that she would not be driven.

'You've been busy I see,' Opal said, keeping her tone level.

'Nothing I couldn't handle,' Miss Browning said.

'I'm glad about that. It so happens that over the next few days I might have to leave you in charge for the odd hour or two now and then. I have some business to attend to. Shall you be able to manage?'

'I daresay,' Miss Browning answered.

She really must find out what these mysterious absences were about. But if she was persuasive, and she knew exactly how to be persuasive, David Hessle would tell her. He was sure to know because he and Madam were as thick as thieves. Well, perhaps no longer as thick as thieves since she was sure Madam hadn't an idea what he was up to. You'd be out on your ear otherwise, Connie Browning, she told herself. As a matter of fact she quite liked being left on her own. She got to serve the customers, which she enjoyed, and didn't do so often when her employer was around. Also, she could use the telephone when she felt like it, even though David had told her not to 'phone him.

'That's good,' Opal said. 'And now perhaps we should tidy things away while we have the chance.'

By which she means *I* should do it, Miss Browning thought. Correctly.

'It all sounded so mysterious on the telephone,' Queenie said, seating herself, drawing off her gloves. 'And so unlike you to summon one! An important matter to discuss, you said. Oh, Opal, I hope there's nothing wrong! It couldn't be anything to do with Edgar, could it? I mean . . .' She hesitated. 'I mean . . . you and Edgar?'

'Why of course not,' Opal said. Her sister-in-law was more perceptive than she seemed. 'It's got nothing to do with Edgar. Not in the way I think you mean. There's nothing wrong. It's just that I have something of import- ance to tell you . . .

'Opal, you're not – you're not *expecting*? Oh, Opal!'

'Of course not, Queenie dear! I've told you before, I've got my little Daniel and I love him dearly – but I've never wanted a large family. I leave that to natural-born mothers like you.'

'Then whatever can it be?' Queenie asked.

If only you would give me the chance to tell you, Opal thought. But one could not rush Queenie. In any case she was far too fond of her to be really impatient.

'I'm about to tell you,' Opal said. 'And if what I have in mind comes off, then it will be the best thing that's happened to me, and to Edgar and Daniel too. But I don't think I can do it at all without your help.'

She sat down beside Queenie and told her what she had in mind. She told it, not in outline as she had done to Mr Harper, but in detail; in colourful scenes which she could so easily picture. And as she talked and Queenie listened, Opal felt the store come alive, as vividly as if she were standing in it, surrounded by her merchandise thronged by customers. And she thought that if she could not have it she would die of disappointment.

'So you see why I need the money,' she concluded. 'Quite a lot, I'm afraid. Needless to say, however generous you are – and I know you *are* generous – I couldn't do it all on a loan from you. It's my intention to approach, also, an old and very rich customer. She's already agreed to see me.'

'Do I know her?' Queenie asked.

'I don't think so. And I'd rather not tell you who she is without her permission. I thought that if she would act as guarantor for the rent, lighting and so on, and you would lend me the money to start the alterations – which I shall keep to a minimum – and to help with stock – then I could manage the wages out of the profit I make and with what I get for this place. To start with, that is.'

'I must admit, you seem to have it all worked out,' Queenie said. But from the tone of her voice it was impossible, Opal thought anxiously, to tell what she really thought about it.

'Oh I have,' she said. 'I really have. And I'm sure I can do it, only given the chance. You'd get your money back, every penny and with interest. How quickly will depend on how quickly the business takes off. I have to be frank with you and say that I would need to give priority to paying wages and buying stock. It might be five years before you were paid. But you would be paid, I promise you! Oh, Queenie, what do you think? Please put me out of my misery and tell me what you think!'

'Opal dear, you mustn't rush me,' Queenie said gently. 'It's all so new to me. I have to take it in. Could we possibly have a cup of tea, do you think?'

Opal jumped to her feet.

'Of course! How remiss of me, Queenie. I'll put the kettle on at once.'

In the kitchen she set about making the tea. Her hands trembled as she laid the tray, so that she thought she would drop a cup or spill the sugar. When she carried the tray into the living room her hands shook so much that it was difficult to pour.

'Just look at me!' she said. 'I'm so nervous. But then I'm not used to asking for loans, not even of family!'

She remembered, suddenly, the winter Saturday, all that time ago it seemed now, when she had asked her mother for the loan of five pounds and had been given ten. Was that a good omen?

'Well,' Queenie said thoughtfully, sipping her tea. 'It's no secret that my father left me a lot of money. Anyone who reads the *Leasfield Argus* knows that. And Mark is doing well in the business, so we never touch my money. Of course, even though the money is my own to do with as I wish, and Mark never questions what I spend, I shall have to consult him. I shall show him your figures and I daresay he'll have some questions to ask. But apart from that . . .' She put down her teacup and stretched out her hand to take Opal's.

'Yes, Opal dear, I'm agreeable to lending you the money!'

For a moment Opal stared at her. She couldn't believe it! It was her dream, and it was beginning to come true! Then she fell to her knees and buried her face in Queenie's lap, not trying on this occasion to keep back the tears.

'Oh Queenie,' she said at last. 'There's just no way I can thank you!'

'I'm your family,' Queenie said. 'Why shouldn't I be the first to help? And I remember how much my father thought of you. He said you were a very clever woman. I'm sure he'd have approved of my decision, just as I'm sure Mark will.' She laughed. 'Anyway, if half you say comes true you'll be an enormous success and I'll have done myself a good turn!'

'Please don't go on about it,' Opal begged. Edgar had arrived home shortly after Queenie's departure and she had decided it was now time to tell him what was afoot. 'Mary will be here with Daniel any minute and I don't want it mentioned then. It's Daniel I'm thinking about. He starts his new school on Tuesday and I don't want him to have anything on his mind other than that. Anyway, nothing is settled. Time enough to let everyone know when, and if, it is.'

'I suppose I'm lucky you bothered to tell me,' Edgar complained. 'Perhaps you wouldn't have if you'd not been afraid Queenie or Mark might spill the beans!'

'Don't be silly,' Opal said. 'You're my husband. I'd want to tell you. In any case how could I do anything without your knowing?'

'Easily! You managed to find the property, didn't you? See the bank manager, fix a loan with Queenie and get it approved by Mark, all without me knowing a thing!'

'It all happened so quickly,' Opal protested. 'Anyway, I knew you wouldn't approve. I wanted to take one or two steps first. If they'd all come to nothing, well, that would have been that. Please let's not quarrel, Edgar. Daniel will soon be back and you know how it upsets him when we quarrel.'

'He's going to get a good deal more upset when he learns about this. Have you actually given a single thought to me and Daniel? Do you care in the slightest what it's going to do to us? When you have your precious store, where do I fit in?'

'I'm glad you say "when" and not "if",' Opal said dryly. 'It shows you have faith in my getting it.'

'Oh I'll back you to do that,' Edgar said. 'I'll back you to get anything you set your mind on, no matter what it does to anyone else.'

'That's unfair,' Opal flared. 'I think about Daniel a very great deal, and you know it! Who is sending him to a good school, who is making sure he'll get the best possible education? And what I'm proposing now will ensure a good future for him. One day, when he's ready, it will all be there, waiting for him. As for you, it can do you nothing but good. When I get the business off the ground you can give up that job you hate so much and come in with me. I'd like that, Edgar, I really would. There's bound to be something to suit you.'

'Thank you,' Edgar said. 'I suppose it doesn't occur to you that I might not want that? I hate my job all right but it's my last bit of independence. Everything else is yours.'

Opal sighed. When he was in this kind of mood, and it happened more and more often, there was no pleasing him. All she wanted for herself and Edgar was for them to live in some degree of harmony. She had given up the high hopes of marriage she had started out with. She supposed she might even, in the end, lose her desire for physical love, though her encounter with David had shown her that it was still there in strength, just below the surface. But she would settle now for tranquillity, and just a little warmth. Everyone needed that. She tried hard, but Edgar never responded.

'Perhaps you'll find that Daniel doesn't want the future you've so carefully mapped out for him,' Edgar said bitterly. 'Perhaps he'll have ideas of his own. You won't like that will you? You like to be the one with the ideas. And another thing, when you've sold Madame Dora's and we have to leave here, where are we going to live? Have you thought of that?'

'Of course I have. I've thought of everything. We'll find somewhere, you'll see!'

It was true that she had thought of it but it had not loomed large in her mind. There had been – still were – so many other things to consider. If Miss Taylor didn't turn up trumps, then where else could she turn? But if Miss Taylor *did* agree to give her backing then there were a thousand new problems, large and small, to be settled. A place to live was just one of them. If she had only herself to think of a camp bed anywhere in the store would do for her. But Daniel, and, she supposed, Edgar, were dependent on her.

The downstairs door banged and Daniel bounded up the stairs as fast as his short legs would carry him. Mary followed close behind. He flung himself at Opal and she knelt on the floor and held him close.

'Oh, it's so good to have you back!' she cried. 'I'm not sure that I shall ever let you go away from me again, even to Aunt Mary!'

At last she let him go and he turned to his father. Edgar scooped him up in his arms and lifted him high in the air, high enough to touch the ceiling.

'You've put on weight,' he said happily. 'You weigh a ton, lad!'

'He's eaten well,' Mary admitted. 'Everything that was put before him. I can't think why you said he was finicky about his food, Opal.'

'I expect he plays me up,' Opal said indulgently. 'I must say, he does look well.'

'Grandpa taught me to milk Daisy,' Daniel said. 'And I helped to pick the apples. I've made you a picture of the apple picking, Mother. And one for you, Dad, about the sheep. Grandpa says I can go again in the Easter holidays when they've got the new lambs. Can I go, Mother?'

'Hey! You've only just got home,' Opal said. 'It's a long time to next Easter. There's Christmas to come first.'

'So you'd like to be a farmer, would you?' Edgar asked.

Daniel looked at his father in surprise.

'Oh no! I'm going to be an artist. But I might be an artist and live on a farm. That would be a good idea!'

Edgar, catching Opal's eye, raised his eyebrow. With Daniel's return home he seemed to have recovered his temper. He was usually better when Daniel was around. They both were.

'He's painted scores of pictures,' Mary said. 'I've pinned them up all over the kitchen to remind me of him when he's not there. Oh, Opal, I do envy you being married and having Daniel. If I had your lot in life I'd have nothing left to wish for!'

How unobserving Mary was! She lived in cloud-cuckoo land. But Opal doubted whether she would wish to be the one to wipe that starry-eyed look from her sister's face.

'I enjoyed meeting that nice Mr Hessle,' Mary said. 'Dad liked him too. Shall you bring him again?'

Opal gave her sister a sharp look. Surely Mary couldn't be getting ideas about David? No two people could be less suited to each other. Except – the thought stabbed her – that they were both free. But Mary, so quiet and domesticated, so naive in her approach to life, could never satisfy a man like David. He was smart, sophisticated, up-to-the-minute. Why, even a chit like Miss Browning would fit him better than Mary. The thought came, uncomfortably, that in some ways Miss Browning and David were two of a pair. Both sharp. But he would never take Miss Browning seriously because she was too common.

When Mary had left it was Daniel's bedtime. It was with great pleasure that Opal bathed him. Mostly, now that he was seven, he did it himself, but occasionally Opal indulged herself and soaped his soft child's body. When he was in bed she sat on the edge of the bed and read to him, though he was capable of doing that for himself too. 'You can have as many stories as you like tonight,' she said. 'I'll read until you fall asleep.'

He fell asleep quickly. The week on the farm and the moorland air had done him good, she thought, gazing down at him. He had a healthy colour in his usually pale cheeks. She kissed him gently and left him. Back in the living room she took a sheet of paper and, sitting at the table, headed it in bold capitals 'THINGS TO BE DONE'.

In the three years since her visit Opal had called upon Miss Taylor many times. Miss Taylor had continued one of her best customers, buying not only hats, but expensive lingerie, gloves, lace-edged handkerchiefs and the like. She had shown an interest in all Opal's ideas for getting the most out of the small business and nowadays would often call in at the shop to see what was new. But today was different. Opal was going to see Miss Taylor; and instead of a box of hats, which she would have borne with confidence, she carried her account books in an attaché case.

Should she on this occasion, she wondered, nearing 'The Oaks', present herself at the front door or the back? It was a matter for fine judgement which she was mercifully freed from making since Miss Taylor was in the garden and called out to her.

'Good-morning Mrs Carson! I'm just taking a turn around my garden while there are still flowers to see. A sad, though beautiful time of the year, the Autumn. Don't you think so?'

'I suppose that's true,' Opal said. 'Though I've never had a garden to bring it home to me.' She thought of it more as the beginning of a new season for various items of apparel.

'Well, let's go into the house,' Miss Taylor said.

Opal followed her through the front door and into the drawing room.

'Now,' Miss Taylor said briskly, 'what is it you have to tell me? It all sounded quite mysterious on the telephone.'

She sat upright in her chair while Opal, nervous at first but gaining confidence as Miss Taylor from time to time nodded her understanding, put her case.

'And I've brought my accounts for you to look at,' she said.

Miss Taylor waved them aside.

'I'll look at those later. I haven't any doubt they're all you say or you wouldn't have brought them. There are, however, one or two fundamentally important questions to be asked. For instance, you admit that the building is at the wrong end of the town. Now I'm no business-woman but it would seem to me that in a case of this sort, position was everything. What do you say to that?'

'I would say that you've put one of the most important points of all,' Opal replied. 'I don't quite agree that position is everything, but it is tremendously important and I've given a great deal of thought to overcoming this particular disadvantage.'

'So what would you do?'

'Well,' Opal said, 'in the first place I would have to make it worthwhile for the customer to come a mile out from the centre of town – which means that my quality must be good, my range wide and my prices keener. I'd need to offer more in every way than the shops in the centre of Leasfield. I would also need to make myself known – customers aren't likely to find me by chance – so I'd need to advertise. I would count money spent on advertising *well* spent. And I have several ideas for bringing customers in. Would you like to hear some of them?'

'I would.'

Opal, for the first time, put into words the notions which had been whirling around in her head since last Wednesday afternoon. It was wonderful to hear them spoken out loud and she was encouraged by the deep, sometimes amused, attention which Miss Taylor gave her.

'Most ingenious,' Miss Taylor said. 'And now another important question for you. Why come to me? Why me particularly? You can be quite frank – indeed you must be.'

Opal hesitated.

'Perhaps,' she said, 'because the first time I ever came here you treated me like a real person. It wasn't just that you gave me tea, but you asked my opinion on something not to do with trimming a hat.'

'I remember,' Miss Taylor broke in. 'Women's suffrage. Well we've got the vote now. Let's hope we know how to use it.'

'You've continued to treat me in that way,' Opal said. 'But I'm also asking you because what I want to do is the kind of thing you might have done yourself, had you been encouraged. Don't think me presumptious, Miss Taylor, for I don't mean to be – but I think that in some ways you and I are two of a kind.'

The girl was right, Miss Taylor reflected. She had spent her life doing nothing more useful than a few charitable works. She would have liked to have done so much more, and she was sure she had the talent for it. But her parents, perhaps because they had risen so quickly and successfully from trade themselves, had not wanted to see their only child soil her hands with it. How wrong they had been! Why, she might have been running her father's factory now!

'And then,' Opal continued, 'I came to you because you are a woman. I think a woman is better able to see my point of view.'

'Are those all your reasons?' Miss Taylor asked.

'Not quite. I asked you because I thought you could afford to help me. Because you are rich, and have the money I need.'

Miss Taylor nodded her approval.

'I'm glad you admit that reason. It shows a hard, practical streak, which goodness knows you'll need. And now I have something to ask you. If I were to help you, would you consider taking me as a partner?' Miss Taylor felt herself suddenly fired with enthusiasm. Perhaps it was not too late, after all, to make her mark?

Opal's spirits plummetted. It was not what she had in mind at all. 'Would that be a condition?' she asked.

'Why? Do you dislike the idea?'

'Not for any personal reasons,' Opal said. 'I wouldn't want you to think that. If I had to have a partner I think you would be a good choice. But this is something I want to do on my own. It's important to me.'

'I understand,' Miss Taylor said. She could, she supposed, hold out the partnership as a condition. But would she want to do that?

'But I would consider having you as a sleeping partner,' Opal said. 'You could be *au fait* with all I did. But . . . I have to say it . . . I would want to keep control. And I would like the option to buy you out in, say, ten years time.'

'Well,' Miss Taylor said. 'I must have a day or two to think things over. It's a big decision. And I would like to see over the premises, though that, I think, I would prefer to do on my own.'

'I would prefer that also,' Opal agreed. 'It would be better still if you didn't mention that you knew me.' She told Miss Taylor about David Hessle's visit on the previous Thursday. 'A similar one from you might work in my favour,' she said.

'Perhaps you might like me to suggest to them that they'd be wise to snap up any offer they receive?' Miss Taylor said with a gleam in her eye. 'And now before you go I think you might like a glass of sherry. I seldom drink it myself but on this occasion I think I shall join you.'

She poured sherry into thin, crystal glasses.

'Where would you live when you'd sold Madame Dora's?' she asked.

'I don't know,' Opal admitted. 'I would have to look for a small house in a suitable position. My son starts school in Leasfield tomorrow.'

'And your husband's work?'

'Is in Milton,' Opal said. 'I daresay he'd manage with the tram. And it's possible that, eventually, he might give up his job and come into the business.'

'Well,' Miss Taylor said. 'I'll be in touch with you quite soon.'

'Mr Hessle called while you were out,' Miss Browning said. 'He said he didn't have time to wait. And of course I couldn't tell him where you were because I didn't know.'

And you would dearly love to, Opal thought, but I'm not going to tell you.

Wouldn't Madame be furious if she knew who he really came to see, Miss Browning thought. Well it might be that she would have to get used to it. The way things were going it couldn't be kept hidden forever.

Two days later Miss Taylor came into the shop.

'Can we talk privately?' she asked.

'We'll go upstairs,' Opal said. 'Miss Browning, will you take over for a little while, please?'

'I won't waste time,' Miss Taylor said. 'I've thought over everything we discussed and I've been to see the premises, and you'll be pleased to hear that I've decided to help you. I will guarantee the rent, rates, heating and lighting for the first three years. At that point we'll look at the situation again. Mind you, I almost changed my mind when I actually saw the place! There's so much to be done to it. But there again I might be able to give you a little help. You see I have faith in you, Mrs Carson.'

I'm going to faint, Opal thought desperately. I know I'm going to faint! She gripped the arms of her chair and took a deep breath. She was sure that Miss Taylor must hear the loud beating of her heart.

'Oh Miss Taylor! I don't know . . . I can't find words!'

Miss Taylor put out a hand as if she would have touched Opal, but did not quite do so.

'I would like to take you up on your offer to have me as a sleeping partner,' she continued. 'I'm not making it a condition, however. I realize, after thinking about it, that I'm not young enough to be a full partner, even if you had been agreeable. But in the background I could perhaps be helpful, and it would be of great interest to me.'

'Oh Miss Taylor I'll be delighted to have you!' Opal cried. 'I really will. And now all I have to wait for is the agent's reply!'

It came the same afternoon, after the shop was closed. David Hessle had called just before closing time and, to Miss Browning's visible chagrin, had elected to stay with Opal after her assistant had left. A minute later the telephone rang.

Opal unhooked the receiver, held it to her ear and listened. 'Thank you,' she said quietly after a time, and then hung up. Then, turning to David, she rushed into his arms, burying her face in his jacket, sobbing wildly. He held her tightly until the spasm of tears had passed.

'Never mind,' he said, 'something else will turn up.'

Opal stared at him.

'Something else? But don't you understand? I've got it! They've accepted my offer. Oh David I'm so happy!'

'Then I'm happy for you,' David said quietly. 'It's what you've always wanted isn't it?'

'Yes,' Opal said. 'I think it is. And do you know what I shall call the store? I shall call it "Opal's". Nothing more. And I shall have my name plastered everywhere so that everyone will know it belongs to me!'

8

Opal gave a last look around the flat. How poky it appeared now that the furniture was out of it! Though she was not happy about the location of their new house – it was in an area of Leasfield which had been acceptable at the turn of the century but was now run down – at least they would have more room. This place, though, was quite suitable for the new owner of Madame Dora's, a woman on her own.

Opal did not think for a moment that Mrs Fletcher, an attractive woman in her thirties, would spend too much time alone. She had concluded in the first few minutes of the lady's visit that she was the mistress of the elderly man who accompanied her. Also that it was doubtful that she had the ability to run so much as a bran tub, let alone a busy shop. But that's not my business, Opal had told herself firmly. The lady wanted it, the gentleman – Opal never knew his name – was pleased to buy it for her, once he had inspected the accounts. Opal had never dreamed it could be so easy.

Connie Browning came into the room.

'I've made some tea. I thought you'd like a cup before you left. I didn't bring it up because there's nowhere to put it. Doesn't it look strange in here without so much as a table or a chair?'

Opal followed the girl downstairs. It had been good of Miss Browning to stay and help her on her half day. She had wondered, at first, whether she should offer her a position in the new store; but she knew that, good worker though Miss Browning was when the spirit moved her, she did not really want her. Opal was never quite comfortable in Miss Browning's presence – which was absurd, considering their respective positions – so it had been a relief when Mrs Fletcher had asked Miss Browning to stay on and the girl had accepted.

'Another cup?' Miss Browning asked presently. 'There's plenty in the pot.'

'I won't, thank you,' Opal said. 'There'll be a lot to do at the other end and I must get there as soon as I can.' She held out her hand. 'Well, good-bye Miss Browning. Thank you for your help over these last months. I hope you get on well with your new employer.'

She gave a last, swift look around and left. You think you've seen the last of me, Madame High-and-Mighty, Connie Browning thought, watching Opal walk with never a backward glance towards the tram shop. But you haven't, not by a long chalk. You won't be so lah-di-dah when you hear *my* bit of news!

The furniture van was at the door when Opal arrived at number seven, Alma Place. She entered the house behind one of the removal men who was carrying an inverted armchair on his head. Their possessions, seen thus, seemed meagre and shabby. She supposed the neighbours were assessing them. Edgar, standing in the narrow entrance passage, leapt out of the way as the removal man tried to pass him.

'A good thing you've arrived,' he grumbled. '*You* can try telling them where everything goes!'

'But Edgar, I wrote it all down! I made a plan of each room and indicated the positions of the furniture.'

'Oh I know you did. You gave me my instructions all right, but *they* don't want to bother with them. All they want is to get shot of the stuff. It's mostly dumped in the front room, except the bedroom stuff. That's piled in our bedroom.'

'That reminds me,' Opal said, following him into what would be the sitting room when she had had time to sort it out. 'I forgot to tell you. I've ordered a single bed from Cobley's. Has it arrived?'

'A bed?' Edgar queried. 'What's wrong with Daniel's present one? He's had it no more than four years. A bed should last a lifetime.'

'It's isn't for Daniel.' Her voice came muffled from inside a tea chest packed with curtains. 'It's for the spare room.'

'Spare room? What do we want with a spare room? No-one comes to stay.'

She straightened up, moved a step ladder to the tall window and ascended, curtain in hand.

'Well they might, now that we have three bedrooms. Mary might come, or Aunt Garnet. Also I'll be working late a lot of time over the next few months. It might be useful if I were to sleep there at such times so as not to disturb you.'

She slid the brass rings on to the pole and let the curtain drop. 'They're still going to be too short,' she said. 'I shall have to do something to lengthen them. Edgar, hand me the other one.'

There was no reply. He was not in the room. Looking out of the window she saw him walking away down the street. She sighed. She had tried to be tactful, but trust Edgar to turn awkward. How could he pretend that a shared bed meant anything any longer? And whose fault was that? Not hers, certainly. He was always the one to turn away. And it was not as if she had suggested that she should occupy the spare room permanently, though in her heart she wondered if it would come to that. Somewhere there was a limit to her feelings.

She climbed down the ladder, fetched the other curtain and hung it unaided. He had most likely gone off to find the nearest public house. Now that he had a little more money to call his own he spent more time in such places. To be fair, he seldom drank too much, and he did not usually go out until Daniel was in bed. He spent a lot of time with Daniel; taking him for walks, playing card games, talking with him. Opal wished that she could do the same.

Daniel was spending the week with Queenie. On first seeing the new house he had disliked it intensely and for this reason she wanted to have everything shipshape, his own room with his familiar possessions ready and waiting, when he came into it.

'That'll be it then, Missus,' the removal man said, coming into the room.

She paid him and he departed, leaving her in sole possession of her new home. She went from room to room, standing in the middle of each one, trying to decide what she would do with it. She had given herself no more than forty-eight hours to get everything into place. After that she must concentrate entirely on the store.

She had planned the store's opening for Saturday the twenty-third of March. The first Saturday of Spring would be an auspicious date. It was less than four months away and almost everything was still to be done. There could be no question of postponing the date since from now, until the first sale took place in the store, she would be earning no money at all. They would have to rely on Edgar's meagre earnings and – but only if it became absolutely necessary – her savings. They must economise in every possible way.

When David Hessle arrived, entering without waiting for his ring at the front door to be answered, he found her in the kitchen, putting away china in a high cupboard. Looking down at him from the top of the stepladder on which she was precariously balanced, she knew that something was wrong. His face was drawn, his eyes troubled. When he greeted her there was none of the usual pleasure in his voice. She was about to ask him what was wrong but something in her warned her not to. She must let him tell her in his own time.

'I'm sorry I couldn't get here any sooner,' he said. 'I called in at the shop but you'd already left. Connie was expecting Mrs Fletcher any minute. So what can I do to help?'

'You can hand me up all the stuff from the table,' Opal said. 'These cupboards are far too high.'

He would continue to see Connie Browning. There was no getting away from that since Mrs Fletcher intended keeping on the same wholesalers. Oh well, it wasn't important. But in that case, Opal thought uncomfortably, why did the thought niggle her?

'I was so lucky to get this house,' she said. 'I was just about at the end of my tether, with Mrs Fletcher waiting to move in on me. If Miss Taylor's tenants hadn't moved to Huddersfield and she hadn't offered me the house at next to no rent, I don't know what I'd have done.'

He was not listening. And when he dropped a willow-pattern jug he was handing to her, let it fall to the floor where it smashed into a hundred pieces, she forgot her resolve not to question him.

'What is it, David? What's wrong? I know there's something.'

'Come down here,' he said quietly. 'I have something to tell you.'

They sat on kitchen chairs, facing each other.

'Where's Edgar?' David asked.

She shrugged. 'Your guess is as good as mine. Out somewhere. So what is it?'

He sat with his head bent, shoulders drooped. He looked at his hands, examining the long fingers, the well-tended, filbert-shaped nails, as if he was seeing them for the first time. The silence seemed without end. Then he raised his head and looked at her.

'I'm going to be married,' he said.

She stared at him. She must have misheard. Who could he possibly . . . ? But before she could frame the question, she knew.

'I'm going to marry Connie.'

'No! No you can't!' She was already shouting in protest. 'Not Connie Browning! You can't!'

'It's fixed,' he said quietly. 'We're to be married in a fortnight's time.'

'But how can you? How can you, David?' The words rose in a scream. She did not understand the wild panic in her. 'She's not right for you. You know that. You'll be miserable for the rest of your life.'

But she knew inside herself that it was not David's future she was thinking of. It was her own. How could she give him up to Connie Browning?

'Come on Opal,' he said. 'She's not as bad as all that! She's a nice kid really.' He spoke without conviction. 'I know – and so do you – that she'll never be to me what you could have been. But you prefer to continue with your sham of a marriage . . .'

'I've got to,' she said quickly. 'You know that.'

'So why begrudge me someone else?'

'I don't.'

She wondered whether she spoke the truth, whether she wouldn't feel the same whoever he was marrying; her sister Mary, for example.

'It's just that . . . Connie Browning . . . David, it's not reasonable!'

'On the contrary,' he said. 'There's every reason. She's pregnant.'

Slowly, holding on to the chair back because all the strength had gone from her limbs, she rose. She wanted to say something but the words would not come. Her lips were icy cold, and stiff. Was it possible that even at the time . . . ? She choked back sick memories of his arms around her, his hands on her body. She took a deep breath, squared her shoulders, turned and began to run.

She ran along the passage and out of the house, down the flagged path. David came after her and as she reached the pavement he caught her wrist, swung her round and dragged her back into the house.

'Opal, please! Please don't turn away from me! We can't lose each other. Not you and me. We mean too much to one another.'

'I thought we did,' she said. 'I was mistaken. Let go of me!'

'You were not mistaken,' he said. 'And you know it.'

He pulled her roughly towards him and held her. His kisses, on her lips, on her closed eyes, on her throat, were fierce with longing. At first she was leaden in his embrace, her arms stiff by her side. And then the yearnings, the frustrations, the body's needs, rose up in her again and she responded to him, her hands caressing him, her mouth seeking his, willing to succumb to every demand that his body made of hers.

Then her head cleared. She shivered violently, summoned all her strength, pushed him away from her. These were the demands he had made of Connie Browning. What she herself had a moment ago been so willing to give, her former shop assistant had already given. And carried the proof within her, soon to be seen by all the world.

'No!' she cried. 'No!'

Then she heard the squeak of the gate, recognized Edgar's step on the path, and went swiftly into the kitchen, David following.

'We're here, Edgar!' she called out.

She could hardly believe that the calm voice was hers since, as she mounted the stepladder, hid her face in the china cupboard, her body was still shaking. She wondered if she might be sick. With an effort that was almost beyond her she spoke again.

'Edgar, somewhere there's a bottle of port and some glasses. Can you find them? We have to drink a toast. David is to be married – to Miss Connie Browning!'

The words were bitter in her mouth. She tasted them like poison on her tongue. But no-one would ever know her feelings.

Standing in the window, Opal saw Miss Taylor's chauffeur-driven car pull up at the gate, and went out at once. It had been Miss Taylor's idea to call for her since they were to go to the store together. Miss Taylor was interested in every detail of the alterations and could hardly wait to inspect them. In the car Opal leaned back in the thickly upholstered, leather-covered seat and wondered if, one day, she might have such a car, with a chauffeur. It was an idle dream and not something for which she longed. Its value would be as an outward sign that she had succeeded in what she'd set out to do.

'I like the date you've set for the opening,' Miss Taylor said enthusiastically. 'There's something symbolic, something hopeful about the first weekend of Spring. But shall you have everything ready in time?'

'I hope so,' Opal said. 'But I shall open in any case. I shall make certain that the whole of the ground floor is completed, and as much as possible of the first floor. If everything there is not absolutely ready I'm sure people won't mind. They might even enjoy seeing it take place over a period of time. Who knows? I intend, you see, right from the start to establish a *rapport* with my customers.'

It was a short drive only to the store. Miss Taylor instructed her chauffeur to collect her in an hour. 'But I shall stay on,' Opal said. 'I have a lot to do.'

'You see how it's taking shape,' Opal said as they entered. 'See the floor! Under all that dirt the parquet is in really good condition, and bit by bit we're getting it clean.'

Miss Taylor frowned.

'I see that,' she admitted. 'What is finished looks fine. But there's so much still to do! Acres of walls and ceiling – and this is only one floor. You need an army of people in here, not two women on the floor and a couple of men painting.'

'That's all I can afford,' Opal said. 'I've budgeted most carefully. But don't worry, Miss Taylor. It *will* be done. I myself am going to clean and polish all the old counters and shelves.'

'I'm not at all sure . . .' Miss Taylor began doubtfully.

'Come and see if you approve of my choice of colours,' Opal interrupted. 'I thought this red for the walls would make the whole place look warm and cheerful; and then the ceiling, which is rather beautiful, is to be picked out in red and white. Don't you think it will look very welcoming?'

'Perhaps so,' Miss Taylor said. 'They're not *fashionable* colours, are they? Beige, cream, green . . . they're more usual.'

'I shall *make* them fashionable,' Opal said firmly. The light fittings I shall have painted gold. There's no way for a long time that I can have them gilded, but gold paint will look pretty. A quick effect is what I have to aim for.'

'Well you seem to have it all worked out,' Miss Taylor said. 'Shall we go up to the next floor? What departments do you intend to have there?'

'To begin with, very few,' Opal admitted. 'Most of what I sell will go on the ground floor, until I can expand both the stock and the sales staff. There I'll have dress materials and paper patterns, haberdashery, hosiery, gloves, cosmetics, a sort of general gifts counter, stationery. Children's clothes as soon as I can. Toys also.'

'On this floor,' Opal said as they reached the top of the staircase, 'I shall have my millinery. There'll be a great deal of space for it – too much – but that means that women can sit down and buy a hat in comfort and at leisure. I shall also have underwear here and, as soon as possible, ladies' dresses and coats.'

'Very well then,' Miss Taylor said. 'There is one thing I insist on. This floor must be better carpeted. A nice, grey haircord. I have friends in the carpet trade in Halifax and I shall persuade them to do the whole floor and give you a year's credit!'

'That would be wonderful!' Opal said. 'Especially since here I also want to create an area, however small at first, where customers can have a cup of tea and some light refreshment – or even just a rest in a comfortable chair. If they've taken the trouble to come the extra distance to my store, then they must be rewarded. Of course I'll see to it that they have to walk through several departments to reach such an area! Hopefully they'll spend on the way.' Miss Taylor laughed. 'How many hours have you spent, working this out, I wonder?'

'It hasn't been difficult,' Opal said. 'It all seems to be there in my head, ready and waiting. If it hadn't been for you and my sister-in-law, of course, it would have had to remain in my head. I shall always be grateful to you.'

'Well you've given me a new interest,' Miss Taylor acknowledged. 'Money of itself isn't interesting. It's what one can do with it. You've shown me that. And how is Mr Hessle getting along with helping you to acquire your stock?'

She can't know the effect that even the sound of his name has on me, Opal thought. How could she. I daresay she's never experienced love, and in that case perhaps she's fortunate. Yet she remained clear-sighted enough to doubt that it was love she felt for David. Passion, yes. Jealousy, with some shame, she admitted to, could not deny. But not love as she had known it for Edgar.

'Well enough so far,' she answered levelly. 'But I'm not sure that he'll be as much help to me as I had hoped. He's getting married next week.'

'Getting married? You surprise me.' Miss Taylor looked keenly at Opal.

'He is marrying Miss Connie Browning, my assistant in Madame Dora's. You remember her?'

'Indeed I do. I always thought she was demure, yet bold. An unlikely and powerful combination. Well, we must hope that they'll be very happy together.'

'Come and see my office,' Opal said brightly. 'It's at the very top of the building, in the little square tower you can see from outside. Of course I shan't be spending much time there when the store is open. I shall be amongst the customers. That is where my place will be.

*   *   *

131

Christmas came and went. On Christmas Day Opal took time off to be with Daniel, share in his presents, but on Boxing Day she knew she must be back in the store. There was not a day, not an hour, to be wasted from now on. They had been invited to visit David and Connie Hessle but Opal had pleaded pressure of work. She had, out of duty, attended the wedding with Edgar and Daniel, and the reception afterwards in a small hotel in Leasfield. Gnawed by her own feelings she had no compassion in her heart at the unhappiness in David's eyes as he stood with his bride. Connie was radiantly pretty, inordinately pleased. She showed, as yet, no sign of her pregnancy. I shall not be able to bear it when she does, Opal thought. I shall not be able to look at her.

'You could come to the store with me,' she said to Daniel on Boxing Day. 'Perhaps you would like to come, too, Edgar?'

But Edgar had a chesty cold, a legacy of his time in the army. It was the same every winter.

'No thanks,' he said. 'I have to get right again for tomorrow.'

'Can I take my new paints?' Daniel asked.

Opal laughed. 'It's all you ever think about,' she said indulgently. 'But yes, of course you can.'

In the store she walked around with him, showing him all that had been done. 'You should be interested,' she said. 'One day it will all be yours! Think of that!'

'Can I start painting?' he asked.

'Very well,' she said. 'You can sit at this counter and I shall work nearby. Let's see if you can paint a picture of what the store will be like when it's finished!'

Perhaps, since I shall have more space than I can fill on the first floor, she thought, I could mount a children's art exhibition. Or set up a painting competition for the children of customers? It might bring people in.

Less than three months now and the people would be in this place. The counter she was now polishing with might and main would display – what? Gloves? Fine lace and ribbons? Silk or woollen materials? It was a detail she had not yet decided. What she *was* aware of, every waking moment of her life and often in her dreams, was that in such a short time, when the winter was over and the Spring came, her dream would come true.

9

Opal drew back the curtains and looked out on to the street. In the small front gardens of Alma Place a few forsythia shrubs arched their flower-laden branches against the soot-blackened stone of the house and daffodils poked their heads between the iron railings which divided each small plot from its neighbour. Nature had done well to choose yellow flowers for Spring, she thought. If, in fashion, she were to follow Nature's guide in her choice of colours for each season of the year, she would not go far wrong.

'It's a perfect Spring day,' she said. 'I knew it would be!'

'It wouldn't dare to be otherwise,' Edgar said from the bed. (She had not, after all, moved into the spare room). 'Not with you organizing everything.'

Opal could not tell whether his words were sarcastic or teasing. His face was expressionless and these days his moods were so variable that it was impossible to understand him. Yet not all that variable; more often black. His few lighter, gentler moods were saved for Daniel.

She did not take up the challenge, if challenge it was. Everything must go well today; nothing must be allowed to spoil the occasion. After all, Edgar *had* agreed to take the morning off work to be present at the opening, and she was grateful for that. In a place like Leasfield, to be seen to have the support of one's husband could do nothing but good. If she could have believed that she actually had it it would have meant a lot to her.

'I must be there really early,' she said. 'There are sure to be last-minute things to attend to.'

In fact, when she and David had left the store last

night, well after midnight, everything had been in place; everything except the cash float in the Lamson room (to which, through a network of tubes still mysterious to her money, hopefully, would speed from the counters) and her own personal flag which would be run up from the tower this morning. She had chosen a rich blue flag with her name emblazoned across it in large red letters. 'OPAL'S'. Nothing more. Nothing more was needed. From today her name would be synonymous with all that was best in department stores.

'Shouldn't you be up?' she asked Edgar. 'And I think I must go and waken Daniel. Be sure you're both there by half-past nine at the latest.'

'Stop fussing,' Edgar said. 'We'll be there on time.'

Inside the double doors of the main entrance to the store an area had been marked off by a yellow satin ribbon at waist height. The size of the area was so arranged that should a great many people attend the opening it could be enlarged by moving the ribbon, and should fewer people than hoped for turn up, the confined space was small enough to make them seem a crowd. At ten minutes to ten it was reported to Opal, in her office in the tower, that a respectable number of people had arrived and that more kept coming. It looked at though it might be necessary to adjust the ribbon.

'I'm desperate that I can't see them arriving from here,' Opal said.

Now that the moment had almost come she felt sick with apprehension, excitement, not a little fear. What if she had overestimated herself; her talents, her capacity, her potential? But she knew she had not. This was the day to which her life had been leading.

'It wouldn't do to show yourself,' Queenie said firmly. 'You're the star. You must appear at the precise moment. We shall all go down before you and set the stage for your appearance.' She put her arms around Opal and kissed her on the cheek. 'Good luck my dear!'

'Thank you,' Opal said quietly. 'Thank you for every-thing, all of you here.'

'Well I think we should go now,' Miss Taylor said briskly. 'Mr Carson, you are to escort me I believe. Then Mr and Mrs Derwent, Miss Mary Derwent, Mr Hessle and Daniel.'

Opal was still not sure whether Daniel should be there, in public. Mothers of young children who did jobs outside the home were frowned upon. But he had wanted to come and she could not deny him. She could never deny him anything.

'I'm sorry your wife couldn't be present, Mr Hessle,' Miss Taylor said. 'So unfortunate to have influenza on an occasion such as this!'

David smiled pleasantly. 'She was sorry too.'

They arranged themselves, and left by the narrow stair-case from Opal's office and then went, in a little pro-cession, down the wide staircase and towards the front entrance. Opal gave a last quick look in the mirror. Her face was pale against the grey wool dress. She would have looked better with a touch of rouge on her cheeks, but it was too late now. Her eyes, surprisingly, showed nothing of the hard work and fatigue of the last few months. They were clear and shining. She adjusted the small pink rose which David had given her to wear, and which she had accepted as a token that things were all right between them again, or as right as they ever could be. Then she smoothed down her already immaculate hair, and left.

A ripple of applause greeted her as she walked towards the respectably-sized crowd. Sensing that David was about to introduce her, she raised a hand to stop him.

'Ladies and gentleman,' she said. 'I am Opal. This is my store, and I hope from now on it will be yours. Let me introduce you to my family and friends, and to some of my staff – though I hope that before long *all* my staff will be familiar to you. This is my husband, Mr Edgar Carson . . . my son, Daniel.'

She introduced everyone in turn.

'Mr David Hessle is my Store Manager and my right hand,' she said. 'He will always be there to help you though that will not, I hope, prevent you from seeking me out whenever you wish to do so.'

Six weeks ago it had not seemed possible that David could be working for her. Up to that time she had seen little of him since his marriage, no more than business between them had made necessary. On one of his business calls he had been accompanied by Connie. 'I want to learn as much as I can about David's job,' she'd said, 'so that I can be a help to him.'

'How enterprising of you!' Opal said. 'But will you have time for that once the baby is born?'

She had forced the words out through cold lips. It was unbearable to think of this . . . this *chit* . . . with David's child. By this time – it was the only way – she had laid the blame for the whole affair at Connie Browning's door. She had been too wicked, too subtle for David. Demure and bold, as Miss Taylor had said. He had been well and truly caught.

Caught, as it turned out, was exactly what he had been. When the weeks went by with, on Connie's part, no sign of a swelling stomach, of breasts more than usually burgeoning, let alone morning sickness, fancies for strange foods or a preoccupation with baby clothes, Connie's mother began to have her doubts. When Connie admitted that she was not, and never had been, pregnant, it was her mother who insisted that he be told at once. 'If you leave it too late,' she counselled. 'If you make him a laughing stock in front of all his friends, it could be the end of your marriage! You don't want that do you?'

Connie did not, though her marriage had turned out to be much less exciting than she had expected. Boring even. So her no-longer-interesting condition was presented to David as a mistake on the part of the doctor, a wrong diagnosis for which she could not be blamed. But this time David was not deceived. His resulting anger was of a degree Connie had not thought possible, and since then it seemed that whatever she did was wrong.

Small wonder, Opal thought fleetingly, seeing David standing beside Miss Taylor, that Connie had feigned influenza. Unless obliged to do so the Hessles now went nowhere together. She believed it likely, though David had not spelt it out and it could be wishful thinking on her part, that already they no longer shared the marriage bed. 'Come and work with me,' had been her solution. 'Help me build my new store. It's something we can do together.'

Perhaps he had accepted to spite Connie? Whatever the reason, day by day they worked side by side; planning, discussing, arguing, agreeing. Life was undoubtedly enriched by David's presence, though no word passed between them which might not be heard by the whole world; and he never touched her. Their relationship was entirely platonic.

But David was not in her thoughts now as, smiling, she spoke to the people gathered around her in the store.

'I am here to serve you,' she said. 'It is as simple as that. To give you the best value for your hard-earned money. I know that we don't live in the easiest of times, so I shall always be on the lookout for bargains for you. But I also believe that when times are difficult a little variety, a little luxury, are more than ever needed. I shall run my store so that you will find these too. And if my store is not all that you want it to be, then please let me know. Never be afraid to stop me and speak to me when you see me in the store. Seek me out and tell me what you want.'

She realized, suddenly, that this was the first speech she had ever made in her life and that people were actually listening to her with interest.

'And now since you have been good enough to make the journey here,' she continued, 'there will be a cup of tea for everyone in Opal's cafe on the first floor – though when we reach our twenty-first year of trading I promise you champagne!'

'The café is small – like the rest of the store it will grow according to your needs – so we shan't be able to serve you all at the same time. May I also remind you that if you *do* make a purchase – but please don't feel obliged to do so, feel free to look around – but if you do buy you will receive a small gift to remind you of your part in this special day in my life – and I hope in the life of Leasfield.'

When the applause had died down, David stepped forward.

'Before I ask Miss Phoebe Taylor, whose family is so well known to most of us, formally to declare Opal's store open, just let me remind you of the offer in our advertisement. If you have made the journey from the centre of Leasfield by tram, then simply hand in your tram ticket at the desk by the cosmetics counter on this floor, and your fare will be refunded. But not only for today, ladies and gentlemen. This refund will be made to you for at least the next three months. It is Opal's way of saying "Thank you for coming".'

He brought Miss Taylor forward to cut the ribbon, but she beckond to Opal.

'I'm not going to make a speech,' she said. 'But in front of all of you I want to present Miss Opal with a memento of this occasion. Opals, some say, are for tears. I'm sure that this day will prove the opposite to be true!'

To Opal's surprise she slipped a pendant on a silver chain over her head. Then she cut the ribbon and the crowd surged through into the store. My store, Opal thought. My dream has come true. She watched the people fanning out this way and that into the various departments. This was her supreme moment. Nothing would ever surpass it.

She stayed near to the entrance for a few minutes, greeting new customers as they came in, introducing herself. The advertising over the last few weeks, culminating in the half-page spread in yesterday's *Leasfield Courier*, had paid off, though David had been against such extravagance.

'There's no way you can afford a half page,' he said. 'The cost is prohibitive!'

'On the contrary, there's no way I can afford not to,' she had told him. 'Not only once, but for some time to come. Advertising must be a top priority.'

The *Courier* had not been her only form of advertising. Several boys and girls in and around Leasfield had acquired unexpected riches by the payment of half-a-crown for leaflets pushed through every letter box in their neighbourhood and posters fastened to every available board. David thought it undignified. Miss Taylor had also looked doubtful.

'As yet I can't afford too much dignity,' Opal said. 'I need every ounce of publicity I can get. In fact I can tell you now that mine will never be one of those companies which goes under in dignified silence because it's too refined to seek publicity! When I need help I shall call for it.'

What she needed to know now was which way of advertising had brought people in. As she moved around the store she would ask them.

There was a short queue of women – no men amongst them – at the desk where the used tram tickets were being redeemed. The fare from the centre of Leasfield was twopence. Though she felt sure that not everyone who was entitled to it would bother to claim it, she must keep an eye on what was paid out over the next three months and make sure that the amount was offset in some other way, though not necessarily, indeed preferably not, at the customer's expense.

'Good-morning ladies!' she said. 'Welcome to Opal's! Now tell me, do the trams run often enough from the town centre, or did you have to wait?'

'They run fairly often,' a woman said. 'But they don't stop near enough. If it was a rainy day we'd get wet walking from the tram stop, wouldn't we?'

'Then there's a clear case for having the tram stop moved,' Opal said cheerfully. 'Perhaps you would sign my petition for that? Miss Conran has it right there on the desk. I'm sure all you ladies between you will be much more influential than I!'

That should do the trick, she thought. When she had approached the Tramways Department (she wished to put 'Trams stop at the door,' in her advertisements) they had laughed at her. They wouldn't laugh at a hundred or two paying customers, and a petition sent in every week until they did something about it.

She noticed that the nearby cosmetics counter was busy. That had been a good idea. She was convinced that its success would increase, especially as she aimed, by every persuasion she could think of, to encourage women to make the best of themselves. She thought of organizing demonstrations in the store. There was plenty of space for such events. Indeed, filling the space while she did not really have enough departments, or sufficient stock to put in the existing ones, was a major preoccupation with her. It must all seem to be done naturally, as if space was part of her plan. Customers must never suspect that she could not yet afford to fill it.

She saw Queenie and Miss Taylor by the glove counter, and went to join them. Queenie, already with several parcels in Opal's distinctive blue-and-white striped wrapping paper, was completing the purchase of a pair of doeskin gloves while Miss Taylor was trying on beige kid with gauntlets. Opal spoke to the assistant.

'Please see that Miss Taylor and Mrs Derwent are always given House discount on their purchases, Miss Feather.'

'I've done that, Mrs Carson,' the woman said. 'Mr Hessle gave me a list of people for House discount.'

'Good! And please remember to call me Miss Opal, won't you? Have you had many customers? What is selling best so far?'

'The doeskin at four-and-eleven are going well,' the woman said. 'But the special line in white fabric at two-and-sixpence is selling like hot cakes. We might run out!'

'Opal, everything's really splendid,' Queenie said enthusiastically. 'Just as I knew it would be. Oh I *do* wish I could help!'

'By the look of your parcels I think you have,' Opal replied. She glanced towards Miss Feather who was re-arranging her display, out of earshot, at the other end of the counter. 'Seriously, Queenie, if it hadn't been for you and Miss Taylor this day could never have happened. And Miss Taylor, my pendant is quite beautiful!'

She held the opal up to the light, admiring the ever-changing blues, the iridescent pinks, greens and purples which shot through the large, oval stone.

'There's no way I can ever thank either of you enough. I shall never forget what you've done.'

'But I mean *really* help – like selling something,' Queenie said. 'I always thought I should like to work in a shop.'

'*Store*, if you don't mind!'

'Store then. But first I was needed at home by my parents and now Mark won't let me go out to work. He says my place is with the children.'

'Opal,' Miss Taylor interrupted 'I'm suddenly rather tired. Do you think you could possibly have me a pot of tea sent to your office, and tell Gregson to bring my car around to the entrance in about twenty minutes?'

'Oh I'm so sorry, Miss Taylor,' Opal said. 'I'll take you up to my office at once.'

She really did look unwell. Was it fatigue from the excitement of the morning, or had it been coming on for some time? Am I getting so absorbed in my own affairs, Opal wondered, that I can't see anyone else?

'There's no need to go with me,' Miss Taylor said firmly. 'You have plenty to occupy you here. I'll just drink a cup of tea and then go home. Telephone me this evening if you have time.'

'Of course I will!'

As Miss Taylor walked away a tall, stout woman in a fur coat approached Opal.

'I am Mrs James Carstairs,' she announced 'And I'm taking you up on your word. About supplying what the customer wants.'

'Why certainly,' Opal said. 'What can I do for you?'

'I bought this material to make a blouse,' the woman said. 'Now I find your haberdashery department has neither ribbon nor sewing cotton to match it!'

'Dear me! May I look at the material?'

Opal took the parcel from the woman and opened it out on the counter. 'What an unusual shade of green, isn't it? But very pretty. I think green is going to be fashionable this coming summer.'

'Well, what are you going to do about it?' the woman demanded.

'Why, find you something to match, of course!' Opal said pleasantly. 'I shall try to get it today, but I might not be able to find it until Monday. However, if you'll allow me to take a small snip of the material, and give me your address, I'll see that it's delivered to you.'

'Very well,' Mrs Carstairs said. 'I want three yards of double-sided satin ribbon, three-quarters of an inch wide, and one reel of sewing silk. And I want a perfect match.'

'We'll do our very best, Mrs Carstairs,' Opal promised. 'Now if you haven't yet visited our millinery department on the first floor I think you might find the new season's straws in a shade which would go beautifully with your new blouse. If you have any difficulty, please ask the assistant to call me.'

'What an ungracious woman,' Queenie said. 'I've suddenly decided I'd never make a saleswoman. I'd have been quite rude to her.'

'*You* wouldn't be rude to anyone! But if you really want to help me, here's your chance.'

'What do you mean?'

'Would you be an absolute angel and take this pattern to try to match it with ribbon and thread. There's no-one I can ask right now. I rather think you'll get it at Miller's?'

'Why Miller's?' Queenie asked.

'Because I daresay that's where she bought the material in the first place. She certainly didn't buy it here. We don't stock this one.'

'I can't believe it!' Queenie gasped. 'I can't believe anyone would have the cheek! Why didn't you say anything?'

'Because though'll I'll start by supplying her with cotton and ribbon at no profit at all, I reckon I'll eventually make her a customer. I should say she's well-to-do. It takes a lot of pennies to buy a dyed ermine coat like that.'

'Especially in her size! Oh, Opal, can you imagine how she'll look in green satin?'

Opal pulled a face. 'But are you going to be a darling and match it for me?'

'Of course! And I'll take great pleasure in having it delivered to her by my chauffeur.'

'I shall have to think seriously about deliveries before long,' Opal said. 'All I have at present is a boy with a bicycle. But please excuse me, Queenie. I must go and see Miss Taylor before she leaves, make sure she's all right.'

Miss Taylor had finished her tea and was about to depart by the time Opal, waylaid by another customer, reached her office. She looked pale and cold, in spite of her all-enveloping fur coat.

'You really don't look too well,' Opal said anxiously. 'I do hope you haven't caught a chill. Did you feel a draught, standing in the entrance so long?'

'I never feel draughts,' Miss Taylor answered. 'But I am quite exceptionally tired. I shall go straight to bed with a hot toddy. I'll be as right as rain in the morning, you'll see!'

'I must thank you again for this beautiful pendant,' Opal said. 'I shall treasure it.'

'Well, I thought that the day ought not to go by without some memento, something tangible you could see and touch. You'll always have memories, of course.'

'Always,' Opal said. 'As long as I live.'

There was a tap on the door.

'Ah, here is Gregson!' Miss Taylor seemed glad of the interruption. 'Goodbye for now, Opal. Don't forget to telephone me.'

Opal was about to go back into the store when Edgar came in, accompanied by Daniel and Mary. She realized, guiltily, that she had seen none of them since the opening, nor had she given them a thought.

'Well then, what do you think, Edgar?' she asked.

'Very good,' he said. 'It's going to be a big success. You've done well.'

'Thank you, Edgar.' She felt genuinely pleased by his approbation. 'There's still a lot of ground to cover. But I'm on the way.'

'You certainly are,' he agreed.

'We came to tell you that we're leaving now,' Mary said. 'We thought we should get back.'

'I'm starving,' Daniel complained. 'I wish you had a proper café with meat and potato pie and jam pudding!'

'We shall have one day, I promise you,' Opal said. 'Do you know, I'd forgotten all about food. How awful of me!'

'Don't worry, Opal,' Mary said. 'I'll make a meal for Edgar and Daniel the moment we get back. Since I'm staying the night I have lots of time. And I think your store is wonderful! I bought myself some handkerchiefs and a new hairbrush.'

Mary thinks it's wonderful, Opal thought, watching them go, but she'd rather have a husband and children than all the stores in the world. Well, I shall show everyone that it's possible to be a good mother *and* a good businesswoman at the same time. I could have been a good wife to Edgar, but he wanted another sort of wife. She was not this kind any more, she thought, though she had been once.

She left the office and went downstairs, meeting David on the way.

'Satisfied?' he asked.

'More than! Very, very happy. Aren't you glad you came in with me, David?'

'I couldn't be otherwise. I still wish that you'd let me have a partnership.'

'We've discussed all that,' Opal said. 'It was never on the cards. I wanted, as I've always wanted, to go it alone.'

'I sold my business to join you,' David reminded her. 'I could have bought the partnership, put money into the store.'

'I appreciate that. But you've not done badly, have you David! Apart from my own, yours is the most important job in the store. It always will be.'

He had sold his business, she knew very well but did not choose to remind him, because having inherited it from his uncle, he had never really liked it. And when Connie started taking an interest he liked it less than ever. He had jumped at the chance of joining Opal's – so much so that she wondered if his own business had not been doing well. But she was glad to have him. She had wanted him all along.

'I must go and speak to more people,' she said. 'We both must. I'll see you at the Staff Meeting.'

The Staff Meeting took place in the café as soon as the store had closed at half-past six.

'I won't keep you long,' Opal said. 'It's Saturday and I'm sure you all have things to do. I chose to open on a Saturday because in Leasfield that's the big spending day and I wanted us to start with a bang. Well, we've done that, and I'm grateful for your part in it. I've learned several things today that will be of use to all of us, but I won't go into them now. I'll save them for the proper Staff Meeting on Tuesday. We shall meet every Tuesday at the close of business and I want you all to feel free to express yourselves, put forward your ideas on anything.

'The only thing I want to tell you right now is this.

146

As you probably know, there's a bill before Parliament to enable shop assistants to have holidays with pay. We don't know that it will ever become law, but I've decided that whether it does or not, every member of my staff is to have a paid holiday each year of at least eight days. We shall be the first store in Leasfield to do this. Mr Hessle will start next week drawing up this summer's holiday lists for each department.

'That's all for today. Again, thank you all, very, very much!'

As they filed out she called back one man.

'Mr Burton, will you see to it that what I have just announced gets into the *Leasfield Courier*? I think it might even be of interest to the *Yorkshire Post*. See what you can do!'

'I'll give you a lift home,' David said.

'Thank you, but no. It's not far to walk and the fresh air will clear my mind.'

'Are you sure?'

'Quite sure, thank you,' Opal said.

Getting ready for bed, Opal told Edgar the amount of her first day's takings.

'Do you remember,' she said, 'my first day in the house shop in Acer Street? I had one penny float in an Oxo tin.'

'I remember,' Edgar said.

They climbed into bed and lay back to back.

'That was the beginning of my success,' Opal said drowsily.

And the beginning of the end for me, Edgar thought, wide awake in the darkness. Why does every stroke of Opal's success drive us farther apart? Why aren't I capable of sharing it? He had no doubt that he loved her, admired her, looked up to her. But he could not enter into her success any more than he could now, and for many months past, enter into her body. Why? He lay awake, pondering, until another Spring day crept into the room.

10

'I don't want to go!' Daniel growled.

His voice, these days, alternated between a deep growl and a high squeak and was at times quite beyond his control. 'I shall hate it! You're cruel to send me!'

Opal faced him with all the patience she could muster. She did not want another scene, not now as they were about to set off. There had been enough of those over the last few weeks, ever since she had broken it to him that he was to go away to boarding school.

Daniel was changing fast; not only physically – he was already taller than she and would soon top his father – but in character also. As a small boy he had been so gentle, so acquiescent. She had felt him so close to her. Now, at thirteen, he was a creature of moods, one minute enthusiastic and responsive, the next dour and truculent, shutting himself up in his room, painting for hours on end. And such weird, incomprehensible paintings too.

'Don't talk nonsense Daniel!' she said firmly. 'You were just the same when you first went to Bishop Tanner's and that turned out all right, didn't it?'

'Then if it's all right, why do I have to leave?' he demanded. 'I could have stayed on until I was sixteen. Why do I have to go away from home?'

She sighed. 'We've been through all this before. Because it's best for you. Because a public school education will help you in later life. One day you'll thank me for it.'

She turned to her husband.

'Edgar, can't you talk some sense into him?'

It was foolish of her to appeal to Edgar since he disapproved of Daniel going away. But then, if their son's education had depended upon Edgar the child would still have been at the local Council school. However, Edgar would no longer argue with her in front of the boy. For Daniel's sake they had made an agreement not to do so. Their quarrels, now, took place in private. When Daniel was present they were polite to each other. They avoided controversial topics – which meant, in practice, that they spoke little.

'Father doesn't agree with you,' Daniel said. '*He* doesn't believe I should go!'

He stood squarely in front of them, looking angrily from one to the other.

'Don't think I don't know that!' he cried. 'I know what you're both like. You can't hide it from me. You . . .' he shouted fiercely at Opal, his voice rising to a treble '. . . You think you know what's best for everybody and you always get your own way. You, Father, you know she gets away with everything and you let her, even when you don't agree, you let her. You never fight for anything, not even when it's important!'

Edgar met his son's eyes, dark and angry, and was shocked at the accusation in them. He despises me, he thought. He sees me as the failure I am. He felt sick at the discovery. It did not seem so long ago that he and Daniel had been the best of friends. Always in the school holidays, when Opal was all the time tied to the Store, they went about together: to museums, to the cinema; to art galleries, for which Daniel had an insatiable appetite, where he would stand enraptured before paintings which Edgar neither liked nor understood, however hard he tried to. And in the last three years, since Opal had bought the car and he had found an unexpected pleasure in driving, they had gone farther afield. Scarborough, Manchester, once to Liverpool to see the big liners which had fascinated them both. He had thought until now that he and Daniel were friends. Was it possible that even while they were being so companionable his son had been contemptuous of him?

Daniel saw the hurt, the puzzlement in his father's eyes, and wished he had not spoken. Nowadays his anger came upon him so quickly that he could not control it, and afterwards he did not know how to make amends.

'After all, York is only forty miles away,' Opal said soothingly. 'You'll be going to Grandpa Derwent's for half-term, and then before you know it you'll be home for the Christmas holidays!'

She was pricked by his accusations against her, but determined not to show it. He did not really mean a word of it. How could he? It was all part of adolescence and she was sure he would settle down at his new school in no time at all. He was extremely fortunate that she had got him into so good a school, but now was not the time for him to appreciate that.

Come along or we shall be late,' she said. 'Daniel, you can travel in the front of the car with your father.'

She, too, had learned to drive, but she seldom did so. Edgar was so much better at it. In fact, she had some figures she wished to study on the way to York. And then she must give serious thought to how many temporary staff they must take on for the Christmas season. It must be as few as possible, yet enough not to miss any sales. She planned to start the Christmas season early this year – by mid-November at the very latest.

The journey passed in near silence, Opal in the back of the car busy with her calculations, Edgar and Daniel side by side, yet with a distance between them which neither could bridge. Arriving at the school they spoke with the Matron, were shown Daniel's dormitory, had coffee with the Housemaster. Daniel, pale and monosyllabic, trailed behind his parents. When they left, Opal with a hug and a kiss which said she had forgiven and forgotten her son's bad temper, Edgar with a formal handshake and eyes which pleaded forgiveness for his guilt, it was Edgar, even more than the abandoned Daniel, who felt that his heart must break.

'Don't run away with the idea that I don't feel

anything,' Opal said on the way back. 'I shall miss Daniel every waking moment. It's because I love him so much that I want him to have what's best.'

It was Daniel, though they had different ideas of what was best for him, who united himself and Opal, Edgar thought. But after the boy's outburst today, the revelation of what he thought of his parents if only in a moment's anger, how long could that last? He wouldn't be a child much longer, dependent upon them, needing them. The thought that Daniel saw him as a failure had come even more as a shock to Edgar since in the last few years, though he knew himself to be not much good as a husband, he had done unexpectedly well in his job. He was successful there. He liked it no better, but by hard work and a stroke or two of luck he had had several promotions. In fact he was now in a position where, given the chance, he could have kept his wife and son in reasonable comfort. Though not including expensive public schools, he thought grimly.

But he knew he could never reach Opal's heights. Her success had been phenomenal, the talk of Leasfield. And she had made it for herself, with her talents and her hard work. He was proud of her, but the gap between them was wider than ever and he could find no way of expressing his admiration. He did not know how to get near her. His sorely needed consolation was that this clever, beautiful woman – every year she grew more lovely – was his. That she was his in little more than name was something neither he nor she was likely to divulge. At least he was grateful for that.

'Drop me off at the stores,' Opal said. 'I have a busy day ahead. Shall you come in and have some lunch?'

'No thank you,' he replied. 'I have a busy day, too.'

Opal had not quite finished what she called her 'walk around' when she was asked by an assistant on lingerie to return to her office to make a telephone call. Each day she went around the whole store, not always at the same time or in the same sequence, but walking through every department. She did not pause everywhere – though she always stopped to have a word with a customer she recognized and by now there were many of those: or she would speak to someone who seemed to be in need of help. It was said by her admirers that she thought nothing of measuring out a yard of elastic, or choosing a hair-net, for a customer waiting to be served.

Usually she would make about half-a-dozen stops, enquiring about the health of a member of staff or – as at the moment when the message came – examining a line of merchandise. But though she might walk as swift as the wind through some departments, seeming to look neither to right nor to left, it was a fact that nothing escaped her. Soon after she had returned to her office a series of notes, brief but polite, would go forth. 'To Miss Butler, Blouses: Please have an assistant fasten *every* button on the white crepe-de-chine blouse on the model.' 'To Mr Simpson, Leather Goods: There is an address book upside down in your showcase.'

Her secretary, indeed most of her staff, knew that the walk-around must not be interrupted unless the matter was unusually important, so when the message came she immediately put down the cami-knickers she was examining.

'They're certainly very pretty, Miss Williams,' she said to the buyer. 'Is this new coffee shade selling well? Are we getting a good mark-up?'

'The mark-up is all right,' Miss Williams assured her. 'And at four-and-eleven for art silk with lace trimming, so is the price. But they've not taken off yet. Customers still go for white or peach shades.'

'Then if we're fairly heavily stocked perhaps we should include them in the next advertisement. The new fashion shade – something like that. I'll talk to you later.'

She left lingerie, trod the grey carpet through gowns, coats, millinery, sportswear, to the door which concealed the staircase to her office. On the other side of that door the luxury ended. The stairs were uncarpeted and her office was sparsely furnished, the only exception being a long, comfortable, chintz-covered sofa. But there was a practical reason for that. She did not sit on it during the day, nor did she encourage anyone else to do so. It was there because there were times – in the Christmas season, during the January and July sales, at the financial year-end – when she worked so late that there was no point in going home. On those occasions she slept on the sofa.

Her secretary handed her the telephone as she entered.

'It's Miss Taylor's maid. I'm afraid it's bad news.'

Opal took the receiver.

'Miss Opal here. What is it, Jenny? I see. When? What does the doctor . . . ? Yes, I'll come at once.'

'Miss Taylor has had another heart attack,' she said. 'It sounds most serious. Will you get my car around at once, please. Inform Mr Hessle. You can sign any letters which must go today. I might not be back before closing time.'

In the car her thoughts were all of Miss Taylor, dreading what she might find at Oak House. Jenny had sounded genuinely frightened, though it was by no means her mistress's only heart attack in the last few years. The first had occurred five-and-a-half-years ago, the very day after the Store's opening, and she had had three or four since then. But since each one had been less severe than the last, and the doctor had declared that if she would take things quietly she would make old bones yet, they had been lulled into security. At least I have, Opal thought. Had Miss Taylor?

The friendship between the two women, though in many ways still formal, ran strong and deep. Opal could not envisage a world without the older woman. She sometimes felt that Miss Taylor understood everything about her, even those things which were left unsaid, and that in understanding, she accepted.

She turned up Nab End Rise and into the drive of Oak House. How green I was when I first came here, she thought. A little shop assistant, delivering hats. It was a lifetime ago – yet it was only nine years, almost to the day. Jenny, who now opened the door, was the same maid who had let her in at the Tradesmen's entrance on that occasion, who had grudgingly brought tea and Barmouth biscuits. I'm not sure that she's ever approved of me, Opal thought, walking past her, going up to the bedroom.

She was shocked by Miss Taylor's appearance. It was less than a month since she had seen her last, yet from the change in her it could have been a year. Propped against the pillows she seemed small and shrunken, her skin grey, the area around her mouth darkened by pain. And on her face was the look Opal had seen long ago on that of her own mother at Queenie's wedding; the indefinable aura of death. She knelt beside the bed and took Miss Taylor's hands in her own. The bony fingers were icy cold, as if death had already taken them and waited impatiently for the rest. In spite of her resolve to remain calm, Opal cried out in anguish.

'Miss Taylor! Oh Miss Taylor! You must get better! For my sake you must get better!'

The sick woman's voice was weak. She had difficulty in summoning enough breath to speak. Opal strained to hear her whispered reply.

'Not this time . . . Everything for you, dear child. Made me so happy . . . Enjoy it all.'

As she closed her eyes for the last time the pain left her face. Opal saw her grow young again, younger than she had ever known her; her features clear, her skin unlined. When the last sigh had left her body Opal cried out and flung herself across the bed, and cried out again and again until the maid came running.

'There was no need for you to come back to the Store,' David said. 'You should have gone home. It's well after closing time anyway.'

She was sitting on the sofa in her office. David put a glass of brandy into her hand.

'Drink this,' he ordered. 'You look awful. Is there anything I can do if I go to Miss Taylor's now?'

'No. I saw to everything.'

Once she had pulled herself together she had done everything that was necessary: drawn the sheet over her dead friend's face, darkened the room, summoned the doctor, the undertaker. Then she had driven herself back to the Store. No other death, not her mother's, not Madame Dora's, so terrible in its suddenness, had left her like this. She felt herself in an unreal world, as if her own spirit had died in her.

'You shouldn't have come back here,' David repeated.

'Where else would I go? Where else?'

At his insistence she gulped down the brandy and handed back the glass. He came and sat beside her, putting his arm around her, drawing her head on to his shoulder for comfort. The touch of his hand as he stroked her hair was all she needed to free the tears which, until now unshed, had felt like a great weight inside her. He let her cry and then with gentle fingers wiped away the tears, kissed her wet cheeks.

At first they held each other with no thought except to give and receive comfort. And then the grief of the moment merged, for both of them, with the sexual longings and needs of barren months. Their lovemaking was urgent, strong, passionate. She exulted in his fierceness and met it with a ferocity of her own. How had she borne without him for so long? Was anything in life as important as to love and be loved?

When the act was over, when – murmuring endearments, kissing her body gently now – he had helped her to dress, she remembered Miss Taylor. But now, though the sorrow, the loss, the bereavement were still there, the bitter anguish, the feeling of death in herself, had gone. As if, she thought in some confusion, as if the act which could give life had exerted some sort of supremacy over death.

⋆   ⋆   ⋆

Miss Taylor's words as she lay dying, her announcement that she had left everything to Opal, did not at the time penetrate Opal's consciousness. She was too overwhelmed by her friend's death to take it in. Unlike Madame Dora's death, when to her shame her inheritance had been almost her first thought, it was not until next day that it came back to her. When it did she wept again, knowing that she would have renounced it all to have bought Miss Taylor even one more day of life.

The inheritance, however, turned out to be less than might have been supposed. Miss Taylor's investments (the lawyer said after the funeral) had not done well over the last few years.

'Then she must have made a real sacrifice in putting money into my store?' Opal said.

'I think she did. But it was what she wanted to do. Of course you will, in addition, have Oak House. You will have to decide whether you want to live in it or sell it, though I should warn you that the market for large houses is not good at the present time.'

It took Opal no time at all to decide what to do with the money. She had wanted for some time to expand her small café into a much larger restaurant. There was plenty of space for it. She envisaged a place where business men or families might come for a good lunch, whether or not they were customers of the store. Since they would have to walk through the store to reach the restaurant she felt confident they would soon become customers. It was a scheme she had discussed with Miss Taylor, one which had found her approval.

On the evening of her visit to the lawyer she drew up rough plans for the extension. She would call her architect in the morning.

'What shall I do about Oak House?' she asked Edgar.

He shrugged his shoulders.

'Do whatever you please. I don't see the need of a house that size for the three of us, but it's up to you, isn't it?'

'Well we shan't want to stay in Alma Place forever,'

Opal said. 'We've already been here longer than I intended. Of course I could sell Oak House and buy something smaller, but in a better area than Alma Place.'

They had not moved, partly because all her profits went back into the Store, partly because she was always too busy to think about it. Now she would have to make a choice.

'I'll decide later,' she said to Edgar. 'It's coming up to the Christmas season and I'm going to be very busy. Also I want to start work on the new restaurant as soon as possible.'

Opal had little doubt that she was pregnant. By the middle of November she had missed a second period, and though she told herself that there might be other causes, her body contradicted her. Already her breasts were filling out, and when, on two consecutive mornings the room spun around as she rose from the bed, and she had to rush to the bathroom to be sick, she knew she could lie to herself no longer.

It was David who had sought out the doctor, a stranger on the other side of Leasfield, in whose consulting room she now sat. On David's advice she had not given her own name. The doctor's examination had been brief, his questions few. She had dressed quickly, and awaited his verdict.

'I am pleased to inform you that you are indeed pregnant, Mrs Derwent,' he said pleasantly.

He was quite sure she was not Mrs Derwent and that he had, somewhere, seen her before. It would come back to him sooner or later. In the meantime he must be careful.

'You seem to be in good health,' he continued. 'Though perhaps you are a little too thin. From now on you must take care of yourself, eat well. Remember that you are eating for two.'

'That is not the problem,' Opal said nervously. How

157

could she tell him? How could she ask what she must? David had assured her that this man would immediately understand, but he gave no sign of doing so.

The doctor noted the way she twisted the gloves in her hands, saw the anxiety in her eyes. He knew well enough why she was here. She was not the first and would not be the last. He watched her struggling for words.

'I . . . you see, Doctor I . . . I can't have this baby! There are reasons why it's impossible.'

There always were. They were depressingly similar. He seemed to remember now that he had seen her photograph in the newspaper at some time. He was taking no chances.

'Please do something to help me!' Opal whispered.

He rose and walked towards the door.

'Mrs Derwent,' he said. 'Neither the law, nor the ethics of my profession allow me to do what I think you are asking me. And if they did I would still not do it. Also, unless you are willing to take a grave risk, to submit yourself to pain and danger, I would strongly advise you not to seek out some less skilful means of achieving what you have in mind. And now I bid you good day. Since I can be of no possible use to you there is no fee for your visit.'

He held the door open and waited for her to leave.

In the street, coughing in the damp November fog, Opal's feelings swiftly changed. She was relieved, glad almost, that he had refused her. To rid herself of the child had been David's solution, and in her panic she had agreed. But in her heart she was against it. She was not sure that she could ever have gone through with it. And now it had been decided for her. She began to walk towards the town centre. It would be more sensible in this weather to take the tram, but walking would help her to think.

She was in an impossible situation. She knew for certain, now, that she would make no further attempt to rid herself of the baby, yet it seemed equally impossible that she should have it. Everything was against it.

Edgar must be told. It could not be long before some-one or other noticed the signs and she must not risk him finding out from some other source. But only he and she (and David who already knew) could have any idea that the child was not his. In Edgar lay her only hope. She had never before been afraid of him – what was there to fear? but now she was. But it was not only fear which ate into her – of what he might do, of what he would say – but a deep aversion to the pain she must cause him.

They had given each too much pain over the last few years, not by their actions so much as by the coldness which lay between them. She did not, as Edgar seemed to think, ever want to belittle him by her own success. She would have liked to have shared it all with him, but he was unwilling. Looking back, it seemed to her that except for the first two years they had seldom made each other happy. Yet it had not been deliberate on either side. They had never been cruel to each other and she believed she would have continued to love him had he not turned away from her.

The failure of their marriage had been the slow erosion of the bonds which bound them, and in the early days the strongest of those bonds had been sex. Now she must wound Edgar in the sharpest possible way, thrust in the knife where she knew him to be most vulnerable.

By the time she reached the store, almost an hour later, the wet fog had drenched her coat, her hat, her hair. She was not aware of it and wondered why Miss Morton looked at her strangely when she came into the office.

She broke it to Edgar that evening. She was glad that Daniel was away at school, thankful that no-one in the world could witness the pain, anger, disbelief in Edgar's face.

'It happened only once,' she said. 'It will never hap-pen again. There were circumstances . . . Miss Taylor's death . . .'

'You think it makes it better that on the evening Miss

Taylor died you went straight from her to him?'

She flinched before the disgust in his voice.

'It wasn't like that. You don't understand . . .'

'You're right! I don't!'

'Edgar, I beg of you! I swear to you that if you'll stand by me now I'll be faithful to you as long as I live. I never wanted to be anything else. I will be a better wife, Edgar. I will, I will! But you must help me.'

'Why must I?' he demanded. 'Do you know what you're asking? You are asking me to take this man's child and watch it grow up in my home – perhaps looking like him, reminding me every day of your betrayal! You're asking me to accept the child in your body – a body I haven't known for a long time – as my own.'

'Who else can I ask?' Opal cried. 'Who else can I turn to?'

He was silent for a while, his head buried in his hands. She could think of nothing more to say to him. At last he looked up.

'If we'd had a loving marriage,' he said slowly. 'If we'd shown each other any warmth and affection over the last few years – if it had happened in such circumstances – I think, though I don't know, that I could have accepted it, forgiven you. But it's not like that. I happen to be the only one who can solve your problem. There's no more to it than that.'

'That's not true!' Opal protested. 'I've offered you love and affection. You've thrown it back at me. And I care deeply that I've hurt you so.'

'It's too late,' Edgar said flatly. 'And I won't do what you ask. This time I won't be your puppet on a string, dancing to your tune. I've had enough. I'm leaving!'

'You can't!' She was frantic. 'Edgar you can't leave me!'

'Oh yes I can. Quite easily.'

'But Daniel? What about Daniel? Don't you care about him?'

Edgar lunged towards her, gripped her by the shoulders

and began to shake her. She was frightened by the wild look in his eyes.

'I would like to kill you!' he shouted. 'I would really like to kill you!'

Then as suddenly as he had taken hold of her he flung her away from him and she fell to the floor.

'You know I love Daniel!' He was weeping now, deep, tearing sobs, which shocked her. 'I love him more than you've ever known how to. But I'm no use to him. You've seen to that. You're the one who can give him everything. He doesn't need me. When he finishes at his posh school he'll never need me again. But don't you ever dare to say I don't love him!'

It was Edgar who slept in the spare room that night. In the morning, by the time Opal rose, he had already gone. He had taken his clothes, and two photographs from the sideboard, one of herself and the other of Daniel. He had left behind the silver frames in which they normally stood.

Mechanically, as if she was sleep-walking, she dressed, did her hair, applied lipstick. Once she had to break off to be sick. When the time came for her to leave for the store she was ready.

'If I may say so,' Miss Morton said. 'You don't look at all well. Perhaps because you're the only one of us who hasn't had a holiday. Can I get you anything? A cup of coffee?'

Opal's inside heaved at the thought. 'No thank you,' she said.

She stood in front of the board on her office wall, which showed a plan of the whole store and the deployment of staff.

'We must move two extra people into the Toy Department today,' she said. 'And I think we must steal a little more space from Sportswear to display the new Christmas stock of board games and jigsaw puzzles. Miss Deacon's not going to like it, but games and toys sell better than sportswear at this time of the year.'

Thank God for work. It could not solve her problem, which this morning seemed less than ever soluble (where had Edgar gone to? What could she do to get him back, to get him back she must) but while there were things to attend to in the store other questions could be pushed to the back of her mind for a few hours. At least she hoped they could.

'Is Mr Hessle in?' she asked her secretary.

'I think so. Shall I ask him to come up?'

'Yes.' She must tell him about Edgar. 'No, don't bother. I think I'll do my walk-around early today. After that I'll see Mr Hessle and then I'll go through the copy orders. Will you be getting them ready, please.'

She spent a long time walking around the store, visiting almost every department, asking questions, checking sales. Christmas cards were beginning to move, though the assistant told her that no-one seemed disposed to buy the new nineteen-thirty-five calendars. 'You get the feeling that they think it's bad luck to have them beforehand,' she said.

On Toys she met David. He was talking to an assistant she had not seen before, a pretty young woman with blonde hair to her shoulders, longer than the current fashion.

'I don't know you, do I?' Opal asked.

'This is Miss Nash,' David said. 'She's with us for the Christmas season.'

That explained it. She herself always saw permanent staff before they were engaged, but staff who were to be here for a few weeks only were engaged by David.

'I'm almost through,' she told him. 'Could you meet me in my office in fifteen minutes' time?'

She moved on to a disgruntled Miss Deacon in Sportswear and was pleased to have the lady's complaints interrupted by being called to the telephone.

'You have a visitor,' Miss Morton said. 'Mrs Carson. Your mother-in-law.'

Was it her imagination, or did Miss Morton's voice sound strained?

'How long has she been waiting?'

'Just a few minutes. But I think you'd better come, Miss Opal.'

She had not seen Mrs Carson for many months. There was somehow never enough time for visiting and her mother-in-law seldom came to the store. In any case she would scarcely have recognized the woman who awaited her in her office.

Her grey hair was wild and unkempt under the old-fashioned hat; her coat unbuttoned as though she had rushed out of the house without bothering about anything. But worse than her clothes was her face – purple-red, blotched and swollen with tears, her eyes sparking anger.

'You may leave us, Miss Morton,' Opal said quickly.

'She needn't bother!' Mrs Carson shouted. 'She knows! Don't you think I won't tell everyone what you've done to my son, because I will! Don't you think you'll get away with it!'

Opal stepped forward, her hand outstretched to her mother-in-law, but the old woman pushed her away.

'My only one!' Her voice was a wail of anguish which cut into Opal. 'And now I'll never see him again! Never as long as I live! You've driven him away. Canada! Already he's on the train to Liverpool, and you drove him to it. I've seen it coming. I knew it would happen!'

She was screaming now, shaking her fist at Opal, when David entered.

'And you!' Mrs Carson yelled at him. 'You're the one! My Edgar didn't tell me that but I know. I've watched you. I've seen you look at her!'

'But it's you,' she shouted, turning back to Opal. 'It's you who've made him suffer. Don't think I haven't seen it all these years. Seen him grieving, eating his heart out because he couldn't keep up with you. May God punish you, Opal Derwent, and he will!'

She spat in Opal's face. The saliva caught her between the eyes, and ran down. The old woman collapsed in a sobbing, shaking heap on the sofa.

She's demented, Opal thought. She's gone mad. And I'm going to be sick. She felt beads of cold perspiration on her forehead.

'Miss Morton, bring Miss Opal a glass of water,' David called out. 'Quickly, please!'

He took out his handkerchief and wiped Opal's face while Mrs Carson beat her fists against the sofa.

11

Sleep evaded Opal that night. She who usually fell asleep instantly and knew nothing until the alarm sounded next morning, now stared into the darkness, waiting for the day to come, yet dreading it. If she closed her eyes she saw Mrs Carson's angry face, felt the spittle on her own face. Or she saw Edgar, white-faced and angry, his eyes bewildered by pain. She had not wanted to cause this hurt to anyone. But it was too late; all the repentance in the world could achieve nothing.

In her heart she knew that Edgar would never return. He was slow to move – how often she had been irritated by his inability to make a quick decision – but when he made up his mind he did not change it again. She flung her arms across the empty space where he should be. Why was it, when for so long his presence in their bed had meant little to her, that she could now miss him so?

Her thoughts swung around again to her mother-in-law. Mrs Carson had been so good to her when she needed help most. She had fed them, looked after Daniel to enable Opal to go to work. And now they were enemies. At least I am *her* enemy, Opal thought. I can never think of her as mine.

When she could bear the night no longer she got up and dressed, though it needed an hour or two yet to daylight. She would go to the store early. There was always work to be done and there would be other people. She, who had always valued solitude, longed for human company, could not bear the silence of this house.

She must speak with David today. He *must* help her, though she had no clear idea how. Would he leave Connie

165

and come to her? And did she want that? Perhaps Edgar meant to divorce her, and if he did then perhaps she and David might make a fresh start, if only for the sake of the baby. And then, worst of all, there was Daniel to be told. How could she possibly tell Daniel that his father had gone, let alone that she was pregnant? But he must be told.

In the store she did two hours paperwork, carefully studied the latest issue of *Vogue* to see what high fashion ideas might be translatable to Opal's, and then began her round of the store. It amazed her that with her private life shattered into pieces she could give such close attention to her work. Thank heaven she could, and thank heaven that at least everything in the store seemed to be going well. She lingered in the fashion departments – always her favourite places – trying to find solace.

'It's a lovely time for fashion, Miss Baxter,' she said to her buyer on Gowns. 'Everything's so much more feminine and graceful than it was in the 'twenties. Don't you agree?'

'Oh I do Miss Opal,' the buyer said. 'Thank heaven those short skirts and that awful close-cropped hair have gone – never to return, I should hope!'

'I like your new stock of evening gowns,' Opal said, sorting through them on the rails. 'High front, back cut lower. Backs, by the way, are going to be lower still. Nice simple lines, cut on the bias. Yes, you've bought well, Miss Baxter. But I think one or two of these might be better with, say, the addition of a flower on the shoulder, or a chiffon handkerchief to tuck into a bracelet. Have a word with Miss Tyler and see what she has on Trimmings, and try something with the models on the stands. I'll be down later to have a look.'

It was the season for evening dresses and now everyone, of every class, wore them, since everyone went to dances. Opal was quite sure that not one of her girls, however junior, would be without a floor-length evening dress. It might lack the elegance of those on sale in the store – the girl would probably have run it up herself – but to go to a dance wearing a short dress would be unthinkable.

'If I may say so, Miss Opal,' Miss Baxter remarked. 'You don't look at all well this morning. I hope you haven't got influenza or anything. It's tricky weather.'

Would to God influenza was all I had, Opal thought. She felt wretched. The sickness now seemed to stay with her until the middle of the day and she felt a deep fatigue, far beyond anything caused by her sleepless night.

'I feel a bit queasy,' she admitted. 'Something I ate, I daresay.'

Work had begun on the new restaurant, though there was no way it could be opened before the New Year since there was the matter of enlarging and re-equipping the kitchens. After the January sales had ended was the time she planned, so that the two events would not detract from each other. She tried to have new happenings in the store as often as possible; a fashion parade, a dressmaking expert, an artist to draw children's portraits, free make-up sessions. Always something new, something of interest to women. Though the store was still a place to find a bargain – she made a practice of buying good bankrupt stock and selling it in special sales at rock bottom prices – the general trend was towards more expensive goods of finer quality. She now had a comfortable, and growing, number of well-to-do account customers.

On the ground floor she met David. He looked tired and drawn, as though he, too, had not slept. He eyed her with concern.

You don't look too good!'

'So I've just been told. Don't you think, with all these women around, it can only be a short time before one or other of them guesses? I'll see you later. We've got to talk.'

Perhaps everything would seem better when she had talked with David, she thought, clutching at straws.

When she had toured the ground floor departments she walked outside to inspect the window displays. It was raining hard; ice-cold drops, dirt-laden from the smoky air. No-one but she would be mad enough to gaze into shop windows on a day like this. She went back to her office and was going through the copy orders with Miss Morton when the door crashed open and Daniel burst in. She jumped up from her chair, her stomach lurching, fear chilling the flesh on her shoulders and back.

'Why Daniel, what in the world are you doing here? Why aren't you at school? And you're absolutely soaking. Take your coat off at once!'

She turned to her secretary. 'We'll finish the orders later, Miss Morton.'

He stood there in the doorway, rain dripping from his hair, running in rivulets down his face. He made no move to take off his wet coat and she moved towards him to help him.

'Don't touch me!' he said harshly.

She stepped back. It was as though he had struck her on the face. What could he possibly know, and so soon? Mrs Carson could not . . .

'You drove him away!' he accused her. 'It's your fault! Why couldn't you be an ordinary person? Why can't you be like Auntie Queenie, or Auntie Mary?'

He looked so young, so bitterly unhappy. She wanted to take him in her arms, and could not, because he would not let her. He was no longer the small boy she could comfort. There was suddenly a wide gulf between them. He was looking at her with eyes full of misery and hate.

'How did you know?' she asked. 'Who told you?' And how much, she wanted to add.

'I had a letter from Father this morning. I ran away from school and got the train from York. I expect they'll telephone you. But I'm not going back! He wouldn't have gone if I'd been at home. It's my fault as well because I was angry with him that last time. He doesn't know I love him and now we'll never see him again!'

The words poured out of him as if he had no way of stopping them.

'Daniel, don't! I'm sure he'll come back!'

Her words sounded futile. She had no idea what to say to this child whom she loved so much. And she was afraid to speak, too, not knowing the extent of his knowledge.

'Of course he won't come back!' he cried. 'Here, read this!'

He thrust the letter into her hands. It was damp, and in places the ink ran down the page, as if he had read it and re-read it while walking in the rain.

'I'm off to Canada,' she read. 'By the time you get this I shall be on one of the liners we saw in Liverpool. There are fine chances for men in Canada. Forgive me, Son, and don't ever think I don't love you. Take care of your mother.'

She handed back the letter. So he did not know about the baby. She would not tell him yet. The burden he already carried was too heavy for him to bear. She could not add to it now – though soon she must.

'Blame me if you like,' she said quietly. 'I daresay it is largely my fault, though perhaps not entirely. Things are never as black and white as they seem. But you must not blame yourself in any way. Your father loves you dearly, you know that.'

'You don't understand, do you?' he cried. 'You never understand!' The anguish in his voice, the fact that he could not command his voice so that it wavered uncontrollably, hurt her more, even, than the words themselves.

'I *know* he loves me,' Daniel said. 'I've always known it. It's that I didn't show him how much I loved him. You have to show people or they don't know!'

He dropped down on to the sofa, as if his legs would not hold him any longer, and began to sob. Opal put out a hand and touched him and this time he did not shake her off. Let him cry, she thought. It's healing for the young to cry.

'Did you have any breakfast before you left school?' she asked presently.

'No.'

'Then you must be hungry. I'll send for some sandwiches and some hot coffee. And you *must* take off your wet coat. I don't want you to catch cold.'

'I'm not hungry,' he said. But when the food came he ate it, and immediately looked the better for it.

'Now you must go back to school,' Opal said. 'I'll drive you back myself. I'll telephone Mr Cottrell before we go and make it all right.'

It was a silent drive. Daniel had calmed down, but he was still pale, and clearly deeply troubled. She knew he did not want to return to school. It was as if however angry he was with her, he needed her presence. Well, she needed him too, but it could not be allowed.

'You could come home for half-term next week, instead of going to Highcliffe,' she suggested. 'I'll be busy in the store and you might be a help to me. What do you think?'

He made no reply.

'I'll go round by Highcliffe on my way back from York,' she said. 'I shall have to tell them about your father and these things are better said face to face. I'm glad you came to see me, Daniel, even if you did run away from school. Anyway, I'm sure . . .'

'Look out!' he yelled suddenly. 'Mother, what are you doing? Didn't you see the man? Don't you know you have to give way to pedestrians at Belisha beacons?'

She sighed. 'I'm sorry, love. I know I'm not a good driver. I don't like driving and that's the truth.'

'You're a terrible driver,' Daniel said. 'You never seem to have your mind on it.'

Opal, as she had promised, called at Highcliffe on the way back to Leasfield. Without preamble she told Mary and her father that Edgar had gone, told them about the letter he had sent to Daniel.

'I can't believe it!' Mary said, horrified. 'Not Edgar!'

She clearly blames me, Opal thought. I can hear it in her voice, see it in her face. But she was getting used to that. Even without knowing about the baby it seemed that everyone blamed her.

'It's a bad do, our Opal,' her father said. 'Nothing like this has happened in our family afore.'

What will they say when they know I'm pregnant, she wondered. She could not bring herself to tell them, not yet.

Her father was not well. He sat in front of the fire, coughing and wheezing, an old shawl of her mother's draped around his shoulders.

'He should be in bed but he won't stay there,' Mary complained. 'Which means he'll have bronchitis on and off all winter.'

When Opal left, Mary walked out to the car with her.

'He's not said anything to you yet,' she said. 'But Father's thinking of selling up. It's getting too much for him. The weather up here on the moor is no good to anyone with a bad chest, not in winter.'

'What shall you do?' Opal asked.

'I don't know. Move to something smaller where it's a bit warmer. I shall have to take a job, though goodness knows what I'm fitted for!'

You're fitted for marriage and children, Opal thought, moved by the sadness in her sister's face. Why did it come to me and not to you? You wouldn't have failed at it. You would never find yourself in the mess *I'm* in.

David was waiting in her office when she got back. 'I thought you might have gone,' Opal said. 'I'm glad you haven't.'

'Miss Morton gave me your message. How was Daniel?'

'Better, by the time I left him. Of course he blames me, and I suppose he's right about that.'

'Did you tell him . . . ?'

'That I was pregnant?' she said harshly. 'No I did not. He has enough on his plate right now. I'll break that to him in the Christmas holidays, as I will to Mary and Dad. David, what are we going to do?'

'That's what I have to talk to you about,' he said hesitantly. 'Opal, there's something I must tell you and I don't know how to begin.'

Why was he afraid? Anxious – yes – but there was something more. It came to her with absolute certainty that something was terribly wrong.

'Whatever it is,' she said, 'why don't you come straight to the point?' Yet she didn't want to hear it. She knew it must be bad.

'The fact is,' David said. 'Connie is pregnant!'

The silence seemed to go on and on, as if there was nothing left for either of them to say. And what *was* there to say?

'*Really* pregnant this time?' Opal said at last. 'Really and truly pregnant?' Her voice sounded like a stranger's. Hard, sarcastic.

'The baby is due next April. I've been meaning to tell you.'

'So she was pregnant when you and I . . . ?'

'Yes.'

'Well, you have been a busy bee haven't you?'

Why do I speak so lightly, she thought. He is killing me. He is surely killing me.

'I take it that the baby is yours? Her baby, I mean. We know mine is.'

'Of course it is!' His voice was sharp.

'Why of course?' she asked wildly. 'Not every woman in the world is bearing her own husband's baby. But perhaps Connie is finer material than I? Perhaps I'm a different kind of woman? Is that it?'

'Opal you're being ridiculous . . . !'

'. . . Perhaps I'm what my mother-in-law said I was? A whore. Is that what you think too?'

'Opal, I'm bitterly sorry . . .' he began.

'I'm sure you're sorry,' she interrupted. 'But I'd like to reserve the word "bitter" for my own feelings. And now I have something to say to you, David. Please listen carefully because I don't think I shall be able to say it twice. Only you and I – and Edgar who has gone to the other side of the world because of it – know that the baby I am carrying is yours. When she hears about it Mrs Carson might suspect, but she can't know. So from this moment on the baby is *mine*. Mine entirely; mine alone! Do you understand? You have no part of it, now and forever. If you have any feeling for this child, which I doubt, then turn it to your own child and leave me to mine. Is that clear?'

It was not her imagination that he looked relieved.

'If that's the way you want it.'

'It is. And I don't doubt that it suits you!'

She longed to punish him, yet what she was doing was setting him free. It could only be that way. She had to free herself, for once and for all, and with what little dignity was left to her.

'Do you want me to leave the store, look for another job?' David asked.

'I would certainly like that, but what good would it be to either of us? As you know perfectly well, I shall need you to take my place when I take time off to have the baby. No-one else can be trained in so short a time. And you would not find it easy to get another job as good as this, though that doesn't worry me. At the moment we're dependant on each other. I wish to God we weren't, but we are. And now will you please get out of my sight!'

When he had left the room she sat for a long time, staring at the pile of papers in front her, not seeing them. It was impossible even to think any more. She did not hear the knock on the door and was startled when it opened and the night watchman stood in the doorway.

'Just checking around, Miss Opal,' he said. 'Will you be working much later? It's gone eight o-clock.'

'I'm just going,' she said. 'Thank you, Mr Chambers.'

What was the point of going home, back to a house which was not just empty, but deserted? To another long night in which she would not be able to sleep? She realized, wearily, just how much she had been relying on

David's support, counted, somehow, on having him by her side. There was no-one left now from whom she could take strength; Edgar gone, Daniel needing strength from her, Mary against her. And then, putting on her coat, she thought of Queenie. Queenie, who knew nothing of this and must soon learn it. Queenie, who would not sit in judgement, because she judged no-one. Opal went back to her desk and picked up the telephone.

'Why, Opal, how lovely to hear you! I was coming into the store tomorrow, as a matter of fact.' Queenie's voice was like the woman herself; clear, unaffected, warm.

'Queenie, can I come and see you? I mean now? I need to talk to you.'

'Why of course! Is something wrong?'

'Yes. But I can't talk on the telephone. You don't have guests?'

'No. And Mark's in London at the Wool Sales.'

'I'll drive over now,' Opal said. 'Bless you, Queenie!'

She could not, she thought, driving through the dark streets towards Barton, tell even Queenie about David's part in this. For the sake of everyone concerned that was a secret she knew she must bear alone, and bear as long as she lived. There was no-one in the world, save Edgar, with whom she could share that burden – and he would have nothing to do with her.

Queenie must have been watching out for her. She was at the door the moment Opal rang the bell.

'Opal dear, are you frozen?' she said. 'Come in by the fire. Let me take your coat. I've poured you a glass of sherry and you can be drinking it while I say good-night to the children. I shan't be long.'

What a happy home this is, Opal thought, sitting close to the fire, sipping her drink. Why can't you be like Auntie Queenie, Daniel had said, and no wonder. But she could never be like Queenie. They were cast in different moulds. Queenie knew nothing of the ambition which drove some people so hard, and often so painfully. I didn't ask to be ambitious, Opal thought. It was born in me. And because I'm a woman, and ambition and femininity are ill-assorted, it's told against me. I shall never be what a man looks for in a woman. Yet she knew that even if it were possible she would not be without her ambition. It gave purpose to each day.

'There!' Queenie said, coming into the room. 'All tucked up for the night. Opal, can I get you something to eat? I suspect you've not had supper.'

'No thank you. I'm not hungry.'

Once begun, it was easy to talk to Queenie, so easy that the greatest effort was not to tell her everything. And Queenie was no fool. She had suspected for a long time that matters were not right between Opal and Edgar. But such was her unique gift that she could bring a positive sympathy, a deep feeling of support, to everyone. Her grief for Edgar in his lonely flight did not allow her to condemn Opal. If she wondered why a kind man who loved children, and his own son above all, should leave his newly-pregnant wife, she did not ask out loud, nor would she ever. She did not apportion blame in any direction, though this was not because she stood aside.

She accepts us, Opal thought. She accepts us all, exactly as we are. She doesn't ask us to be different or to measure up to some standard. For the first time since Miss Taylor's death Opal felt comforted. The tears which ran down her face now were tears of release.

'Opal, you must stay the night! It's a nasty wet one for you to drive home. In fact you must come here often in the next few months. I know Mark will want you to.'

Mark would want it, Opal knew, if only because his beloved Queenie did so. Whatever his wife did was good in his sight. The years which had driven herself and Edgar further and further apart had brought her brother and his wife ever closer to each other.

'And now I'm going to prepare some food,' Queenie said. 'I'm quite hungry myself. We'll have an omelette.'

Next morning Opal called Miss Morton into her office first thing. She would need her secretary's help over the next few months.

'I feel I owe you an explanation of the last day or two,' Opal said. 'You must have wondered what it was all about. Well, it's true that I'm pregnant. It is also true that my husband has gone abroad. His Company wished him to spend a few months in their Toronto office, but we both hope that he will be back long before the baby is born.'

It was a fiction she had decided upon before she fell asleep last night. Leasfield, though it might like to think otherwise, was provincial and narrow. It liked its public figures – of whom she was now undoubtedly one – to lead regular, well-ordered lives, open to public scrutiny. And especially so if they were women. It had been a slight mark against her that she attended no place of worship, professed no religion. If they bought a yard of material from her shop they liked to know that the vendor was upright and honourable.

'Of course Daniel is upset. He's not yet settled into his new school. Adolescence is a difficult time. As for my mother-in-law – well, she is elderly so we must excuse her, but I'm afraid she doesn't quite see things as they are!'

She looked Miss Morton clearly in the eye.

'You can discount anything she may have said in her distress at parting with her son. There is naturally no truth in any of it. In fact I can tell you, though I do so in confidence . . .' She took a deep breath. She could hardly bear to say the words. 'Mr Hessle's wife is happily pregnant and they are both looking forward tremendously to their baby's birth. As I am to mine.'

'Of course I don't wish anyone to know just yet that I'm pregnant. You know how people feel about pregnant women showing themselves in public – quite wrongly, I think. When I can no longer disguise my condition I shall take leave of absence until a few months after the baby is born. Mr Hessle will take over from me.'

*   *   *

The January sales had gone particularly well this year, Opal thought with satisfaction. Almost everything cleared, and at a good profit. And now the restaurant was open and beginning to do business. They could seat three hundred people for morning coffee, for a good, three course lunch, or for afternoon or high tea. The prices were right – a shilling and tenpence for the set lunch, more if one ate *à la carte* – the menus were varied and, above all, the service was efficient and friendly under the new manager, Mr Soames.

Opal had been amazed at the numbers of women of all ages who were eager to work as waitresses at the low wages paid in the catering trade. She could not pay more than the usual rate, and keep her prices down, but she saw to it that her waitresses had a good nourishing meal each day, and two breaks in the staff rest room where they could put up their feet and look at a magazine.

She had felt better in health since Christmas, less inclined to sickness and with a return of her usual energy, though she tired easily.

'You have to remember you're in your mid-thirties,' the doctor told her. 'You're not a young girl. And you work far too hard. I do think that for the sake of both yourself and the baby you should give up work at Easter.'

The doctor, a woman, came into the store once a week. A room was set aside where she could be consulted by any member of the staff, at no cost to them. Opal believed that many an illness, with its consequent loss of work, was nipped in the bud by this system, and the girls related well to the sympathetic, female physician.

'I suppose I shall have to,' Opal said. 'I'm already beginning to show, and you know what people are like. By Easter I shall be six months pregnant.'

Christmas itself, which they had spent at Highcliffe, had not been easy, though in one surprising way it had been better than she had expected. Daniel had missed his father badly. He had been both consoled and upset by the arrival of a Christmas card, posted in Toronto;

consoled because his father had thought of him, upset because he had sent no address. But about the baby he *had* been pleased, partly because he genuinely welcomed the addition to their small family but also, Opal discovered, for another reason.

'If Father could hear the news I just *know* he'd come back!' he said eagerly. 'If only we could contact him. Perhaps Grandma Carson might have had a bit more information than we have. My word, she'll be pleased about the baby! She's always on about having only one grandchild.'

His relationship with his grandmother had remained as unclouded as ever. Whatever she thinks about me, Opal realized, she hasn't passed it on to Daniel.

Her father's illness had been neither better nor worse over the Christmas holiday, but Mary had been worried about the winter still to come.

'He's had an offer for the farm,' she told Opal. 'I want him to accept it. It's really a question of where we would go, what we would do next.'

'I've been thinking about that,' Opal said. 'You know I still haven't made up my mind about Oak House? What do you say if I keep it on, and you and father come to live there? You can have your own rooms if you wish. There's plenty of space.'

Mary flushed with pleasure.

'Oh, Opal, that would be marvellous! I'm so heartily sick of being stuck in Highcliffe. And Oak House would be so much better for father. I would have to get a job, though. We couldn't live off you.'

'I've thought of that too,' Opal said. 'I shall need someone to look after the baby when I go back to the store, and Daniel in the school holidays. You're so good with children. Would you like to keep house for me and look after Daniel and the baby? I'd pay you a wage and you'd have a place to live. Besides, I'd like to have you. I know you don't always approve of me, but I'm not really difficult to live with. Anyway, most of the time I'm not there!'

Mary smiled.

'I've envied you, Opal. Perhaps I always will, a bit. But we get on well enough, so if Father agrees it's fine by me. Mind you, I'll bet Grandpa Derwent will be horrified at the thought of father selling the farm. He thinks land is sacred. He'll hang on to it until he dies – if he ever does.'

'I think Grandpa Derwent is immortal,' Opal said. 'Eighty-four and still ruling his womenfolk with a rod of iron.'

Her father had been happy enough at the thought of moving into Oak House.

'I've had enough of this lot,' he said. 'I don't know that I was ever cut out to be a farmer. It was just something my father expected me to do.'

'When *do* you move house?' the doctor asked.

'Next week.'

She would not be sorry to leave Alma Place. It had not been a happy house.

'Don't you dare to get involved in the moving,' the doctor warned.

Opal left the medical room and went down to the first floor. She was always careful, these days, not to linger on Children's and Babywear, but there were courtesies to be observed and she stopped to speak to the buyer. She had not seen Mrs James Carstairs buying rompers for her grandchild. Mrs Carstairs pounced.

'Ah! I see you're interested in this merchandise!'

'Certainly,' Opal said smoothly. 'I'm interested in everything that's sold in my store.'

'But if what I hear is correct, and my eyes don't deceive me . . .' She stared frankly at Opal's figure. '. . . In this one especially! Come now, don't be coy!'

The buyer moved away. Opal saw her speak to two assistants who were whispering together.

Anger flamed in Opal's face. She clenched her hands around the notepad she was carrying.

'When *I* was in your condition,' Mrs Carstairs said, 'I never went out in public, except perhaps for a walk after dark, and then only when accompanied by my husband. We never flaunted ourselves. But then it's a different world, isn't it?'

'Not different enough,' Opal said. 'I look forward to the day when women don't have to hide what is a perfectly natural condition. When they can go anywhere they please, freely, right up to the last moment of pregnancy.'

'Now *that* is a word we *never* used!' Mrs Carstairs said.

As Opal left the department and continued on her way around the store she felt, uncomfortably, that she was being surreptitiously looked at. She was angry with the convention that caused this, angrier still that she must bow to it. But she must do so. The feelings of her customers – and she was sure that Mrs Carstairs' reaction was the usual one – false though she thought them, were important. They were what she had built her business on.

When she returned to her office Miss Morton handed her a copy of the *Leasfield Courier*.

'I thought you should see this,' she said. 'Under "Gossip of the Day".'

Opal took it from her and read it.

'A little bird tells us that a certain well-known business lady – a jewel of a lady it might be said – is in an interesting condition. We congratulate her, and commiserate with her that her husband is not by her side.

Are we to assume that before long she will not be "Open to the Public?"'

'Get the editor of the *Courier* on the phone,' Opal said furiously. 'At once. Tell him that if he cares to send a reporter around, Miss Opal has a statement which might be of interest. And ask Mr Hessle if he can spare me a moment right away.'

She saw as little of David as possible these days, though of necessity they met to discuss business. When he came into her office she thought how fit and well he looked. His wife's pregnancy suited him. By this time next month he would be a father.

'Read this,' she said. 'And then read the statement I propose to give to the *Courier*.'

The paragraph appeared in the newspaper the next day.

'Miss Opal (in private life Mrs Edgar Carson) has informed us that she and her husband are happily expecting a child in June. "I shall take leave of absence from Easter until a few months after our baby is born" she told our reporter.

"My store will carry on exactly as usual under the expert hand of my Store Manager, Mr David Hessle."

Mr & Mrs Hessle are expecting their first child in April. A fruitful year for Opal's Store!'

She left on Easter Saturday, at the end of a record day in almost all departments. On a day in June she sent another announcement to the *Leasfield Courier*.

'To Mr and Mrs Edgar Carson (Miss Opal), the precious gift of a daughter, Emmeline.'

A bare announcement, she thought, reading it as she lay in bed. It said nothing of the heartache, of her son's unavailing desire for his father's return, or the loneliness of her future. It said nothing, also, of the love which came with the new baby, which surrounded and enfolded it. My daughter shan't be like me, Opal vowed, watching the dark-haired child in her arms. I shall teach my daughter how to love, how to *be* loved.

12

Afterwards, the summer of nineteen-thirty-five seemed like a dream; a pleasant dream, everyone moving lightly through it, until the moment when the nightmare took over.

Emmeline's birth had been straightforward and easy and from the moment she came into the world she was a good baby, sleeping and feeding well, seldom crying. Against her doctor's advice that she should go into a nursing home for the event, Opal had decided that her child should be born at Oak House. It had been the right decision. The child, though she seldom made her presence heard in the first few weeks, gave the house what it lacked; the feeling of a family home; three generations (Mary and her father were settled in) under the one roof. Not that they could ever be a complete family, Opal thought; children without father, wife without husband. But it was perhaps the nearest they would ever get.

In July, when Daniel came home for the summer holidays and the monthly nurse had departed, Opal rented a house at St Anne's for a month.

'Are you sure you're quite well enough?' Mary asked anxiously. 'It's early days. Emmeline's only six weeks old.'

Her sister had wanted the child to be named Mary. It was Jubilee summer, she pointed out, and it would be a compliment to the Queen as well as to herself. But the name 'Emmeline' had come into Opal's mind – she had no idea from whence – and she liked it above all others.

'I'm as fit as a fiddle,' Opal said. 'And I've hired the largest car imaginable. We shall be chauffeur-driven, door to door. I can rest as much as I want to in St Anne's. Do you realize that Daniel is fourteen years old and he's never had a seaside holiday?'

'I'm thirty,' Mary said, 'and I haven't had one since I was six. Do you remember that week in Morecambe? You must have been about ten. George was Daniel's age. We went with Mother and Aunt Garnet because Father couldn't leave the farm.'

'I remember,' Opal said. It had been the long, hot summer of nineteen-eleven. They had stayed in a boarding house in a side street and her mother had shopped every morning for food which the landlady cooked for them. 'We went shrimping.'

'And saw the pierrots every day,' Mary reminded her.

The House in St Anne's was on the sea front. Opal sat in the wide bay window, watching the passers by. Or joined them, pushing Emmeline in the pram, her father by her side leading Floss, the sheep dog who because she was old, her working days over, he had refused to leave with the new owners of the farm. Mary and Daniel frequently took the tram into Blackpool, where Daniel was addicted to the newly-discovered delights of the South Shore Pleasure Beach.

'It's ridiculous,' Mary said. 'He comes off the Big Wheel looking as green as grass, and then insists on going on again the next day!'

'I might go with you one day,' Benjamin Derwent said. 'This holiday is doing me good. I feel a different man from when I was up at Highcliffe.'

'I'm glad,' Opal said. 'I feel pretty good *myself*.'

In fact she felt well enough to be back at work. She found herself thinking more and more about it. The July sales would be over, the Autumn season not yet started. August was a quiet little *entre-acte*. Some of her customers would, like herself, be at the seaside. Prices, especially of food, were lower than they had been, so that for those who had jobs the standard of living was higher and a holiday could be afforded. It was more than likely that some of her customers, what she thought of (not meaning to be snobbish) as the lower end of her market, would be in nearby Blackpool. Her better class customers would be in Scarborough or Filey, or in St Annes itself. How much she looked forward to seeing them all again, even Mrs James Carstairs!

Though she had enjoyed it, she was not sorry when the month in St Anne's was over and they were back once again in Oak House. She found herself frequently opening the diary in which the date of her return to the store was marked – Tuesday the first of October – and secretly wishing that the days would pass more quickly. But she enjoyed Emmeline, cherishing especially the moments when she held her to the breast and watched her suckle. If her milk would adjust itself she might still be able to keep on the night and early morning feeds. She enjoyed the baby's bathtime, too, though that was gradually being taken over by Mary.

It was good, also, to have Daniel at home for the long school holiday, to observe his tenderness and concern for his sister, whom he adored. But in spite of his new-found happiness Daniel seemed to fret after his father more than ever.

'Why can't we at least *try* to find him?' he asked, not for the first time. 'We could advertise in a Toronto newspaper. He doesn't even know he's got a daughter. I'm sure if he knew that he'd want to come back!'

Once more Opal fended him off with excuses, but on the day she drove him back to school he took up the subject again. 'Why won't you?' he persisted. 'Why won't you give it a try?'

'If he wants to get in touch with us he knows where we are,' Opal pointed out. 'We must allow him to decide for himself. We mustn't try to force him.'

It hurt her that she must be less than honest with Daniel but honesty, in this case, was not the best policy.

'After all,' she said, 'we can't use little Emmeline as a sort of blackmail. And you must remember that it would be me he had to come back to, not just you. It was me he left.'

'And me,' Daniel said unhappily.

He was always at his most miserable when he was returning to school. He did well enough there but he did not enjoy it. He lived for the day when he would be sixteen, at which time, Opal had promised, he might leave York and start a Course at the Bradford College of Art. She would have liked him to have come straight into the store with her but it was obvious that he would first have to get art out of his system.

'Not really you,' Opal assured him. 'If anyone could have kept your father it would have been you. Perhaps sometimes we're driven to a moment when our own needs are so demanding that we have to put them first. Your father's need was to get away from me. That had to take precedence even over you.'

But Daniel was not to be comforted. It was not only his father. Going back to school he was being separated from his mother, his aunt, his grandfather, and now from Emmeline, whom he loved more than he had ever thought possible. Sitting beside Opal in the car he was sunk in gloom, and though experience told him that the gloom would lift as the days went by, that was no comfort to him. He did not believe it.

By the last week in September Opal had weaned Emmeline from all except the night and early morning feeds and Mary had taken over the daytime bottle feeding.

'I really do believe, Mary, you'll be glad to see the back of me!' Opal teased. 'You'll be glad to have Emmeline to yourself.'

Mary looked up from the child on her lap. 'I don't mean it to be like that, Opal,' she said. 'It's just wonderful to me that you let me share the children.'

On the morning of the first of October Opal was up early. She had a new dress to wear today, to celebrate her return to the store, chosen from a selection she had had sent up to her. The new autumn colours were subdued with a tendency to brown which, with her dark hair, did not suit her. But there had been one dress in Autumn Green, a lovely coppery green, dark, yet so much clearer and brighter than the old bottle green. It was perfect for her. She put on her opal pendant and took a last look at herself in the mirror. She had regained her figure quickly. She was absolutely flat.

'I shan't need a coat,' she said to Mary, walking down the stairs into the hall. 'It's quite warm.'

'I'll close the garage doors after you,' Mary said. 'Save you getting out of the car. Now remember Opal, don't work too late on your first day!'

The traffic was heavier than she had expected, as if the whole world was returning to work at the end of the summer. She was thrilled by the thought of the day ahead. She must see David first, get up to date – though she had had reports from him during her absence and all seemed to be going well. On a personal level she did not look forward to meeting him. There was a breach between them which would never be healed though, strangely, she no longer bore him malice for making her pregnant. How could she when she had Emmeline? But then she never thought of her baby as having anything whatever to do with David Hessle. Emmeline was hers and hers alone, as if she had been born of an immaculate conception.

She would do her walk-around early today, renew all her ties. And today was the day of the weekly staff meeting. She had forgotten to tell Mary that she would be a little late home because of that. When the store came in sight on her right, bright and uncommonly clean-looking in the smoky town, she tingled with excitement. She drove along the front of the store, quickly glancing in the windows, and at the far corner made a right turn towards the car park. She had no knowledge of, nor later did she ever remember, the car which came towards her on the opposite side of the road. All she knew, all she ever recalled, was the red film which came over her eyes,

186

a redness in which she seemed to drown, in the second before she lost consciousness.

The surgeon beckoned Mary over to the window, turning his back on the patient in the bed and speaking in a low voice.

'Can she hear us?' Mary asked anxiously.

'I can't be sure,' he admitted. 'We don't know how far a patient in a coma is aware of what's going on. Sometimes we think not at all. At other times it seems as though some outside stimulus, perhaps something to which the patient would, when conscious, have a positive reaction, has a marked effect. But there's so much of which we're ignorant.'

'My sister will get better, won't she?' Mary asked. 'Please be frank with me. There are children . . .'

He looked with compassion at the white-faced woman who looked as though she had not slept for a week. He so often had to answer this question, yet experience never made it any easier.

'I will be frank,' he said. 'She's had an extremely bad accident. Her head injuries are most serious. We've done all we can in theatre. Now it's up to good nursing and Nature. But I should say she's a strong young woman, in good health. If she's a fighter . . .'

'She's a fighter!'

'Then she has a chance.'

'Thank God,' Mary said.

'I would like to keep her in this private wing,' the surgeon said. 'She will need constant supervision for a long time yet, and while we do our best in the general hospital, we're always short-staffed. But it's expensive. Perhaps you would like to think about it, Miss Derwent.'

'I will. My sister isn't without money, though of course I don't know the extent of her finances. But I'm sure she must stay here for the time being.'

'I'll look in on her again later,' he said. 'And of course I'm always on call if I should be needed. I think it might help the patient if members of her family – or close friends – people to whom she relates well in life – could be here as much as possible, at least during the day.'

'Day or night, Mr Talbot,' Mary said. 'I don't suppose my sister knows the difference right now.'

As he left the room, Queenie came in. She put her arms around Mary and kissed her.

'You look all in, Mary.'

'I am rather tired. Emmeline cried a good deal in the night. It's not like her. Perhaps it's because she had to be completely weaned all of a sudden.'

'Would you like me to take her for a few days?' Queenie asked. 'Let you get some rest?'

'No thank you, Queenie. She's used to me. Besides, in a strange way she's a consolation. The same with Daniel. Thank you for fetching him home from school.'

They stood by the bed and looked at Opal, lying so still beneath the heavy bandages, intently watched by a nurse for any sign of change.

'I don't know where we're going to put all the flowers and cards which keep arriving,' the nurse said. 'As you can see, we've no more room in here, and still they come.'

Queenie sat down and took Opal's hand in her own.

'Dear Opal! She's never understood how much people admire her! In spite of all her success she never thinks well of herself as a person. She's a woman surrounded by love which she doesn't know how to accept.'

Sister came back into the room as Queenie was speaking.

'That's a pity,' she said. 'I have the feeling that if she could know of all these good wishes, this tremendous goodwill, it might help her. I've been talking with Mr Talbot. We wonder if there's anything at all you can think of which might arouse Mrs Carson? Something which might pierce an abyss, the depth of which we don't understand. What does she care for most in the world?'

Mary and Queenie looked at each other.

'Opal's Store, and her children, Daniel and Emmeline,' Queenie said.

'Well we can't bring the store to her,' Sister said. 'But the children . . . Her son, of course, has been here a great deal. But the baby . . . she's four months old isn't she? If Mrs Carson were to hear her baby cry . . . ? Oh I daresay it's fanciful, but what have we to lose? A baby's cry of need for its mother. Who knows how deep that goes?'

'Perhaps you're right,' Mary said hesitantly. 'Perhaps that's why Emmeline's cried so much these last few days. Being taken so suddenly off the breast . . . missing her mother's presence, not just food.'

'I'll contact Mr Talbot,' Sister said.

'In the meantime I shall stay here a little longer,' Queenie said. 'But, Mary, I insist you go home and get some rest.'

'Your sister-in-law is right, Miss Derwent,' Sister said gently. 'You're going to need all your strength in the next few weeks.' Whichever way it goes, she thought.

'My car's outside,' Queenie said. 'Ask Freeman to take you home. And if Mr Talbot should want you to bring Emmeline in later, I'll fetch you both.'

Later that evening Queenie returned to the hospital, accompanied by Mary, carrying Emmeline who was fast asleep. As they entered Opal's room a weary-faced Daniel walked behind them.

'Daniel wanted to come,' Mary told Sister. 'He thought he might be able to help.'

Sister looked at the boy; a lanky fourteen-year-old, badly in need of sleep and rest which he could not get; stony-faced in his effort to be brave, but unable to hide the despair and helplessness in his eyes as he looked towards the still form on the bed.

'I'm sure he will,' she said kindly. 'Perhaps it would be a good idea if Daniel were to sit by the bed and hold the baby, instead of you doing so, Miss Derwent.'

It would make no difference to the patient, she thought, but the boy might feel he was doing something. She watched as the aunt handed the baby to Daniel, noted the careful, loving way he took his sister and held her in his arms. We must fight for this patient, she told herself. We must save her for these two children.

'It's Emmeline's feed time,' Mary said. 'She should waken any time now.'

As if she knew what was expected of her the baby wakened, screwed up her face and began to cry; the lusty cry of a healthy, four-month-old baby demanding attention.

'No, don't try to soothe her, Daniel!' Sister said. 'However cruel it seems for the moment, let her cry.'

The baby's cries, raucous, angry at being ignored, rent the air in the small room. On and on. The three women and the boy watched the bruised, lacerated face of the woman on the bed. Tears streamed down Daniel's face and at last he could bear it no more. He leaned over the bed and his loud cry rang out above the noise from the baby in his arms.

'Mother! Mother, you must come back! It's Daniel! I want you!'

He collapsed, sobbing, continuing to cry out. Mary took the baby from him. Queenie knelt down and took him in her arms. Only Sister saw Opal open her eyes.

It was a slow recovery. A little each day, and there were days when she seemed to slip back, called by some dark country of the mind, then somehow rallied again. It was a month before those so carefully watching knew that she would live. Christmas came and went and the winter of nineteen-thirty-six gave way to Spring and then to early Summer before Opal left hospital.

'But she has a long way to go yet,' Mr Talbot warned. 'She needs rest and quiet for many months to come. No worries. No business affairs. You must be very strict with her.'

'I will be,' Mary promised.

'Allow me one meeting with my Store Manager,' Opal

pleaded. 'Just so that I can be assured that all is going well.'

Mr Talbot shook his head. 'It's against my better judge-ment,' he said. 'But one very short meeting to set your mind at rest, and then nothing more until I allow it.' He would have a word with Miss Derwent, get her to ensure that everything went smoothly.

On a morning in July David Hessle came to Oak House. It was a hot day. Opal was lying on a *chaise longue* in the garden, in the shade of the giant oak from which the house took its name, when Mary brought him to her. She admired his composure on seeing her. She knew how awful she looked, though Mr Talbot said the scars would fade with time. Her hair, though it was now growing well, was much too short to be fashionable. There was grey in it, too, though she was not yet thirty-six.

'I'm glad to hear you're recovering well,' David said.

'I hope to be back in the store for the Christmas season,' Opal told him.

'Well, I've been warned that we must keep our meeting short and that I mustn't overtire you.'

'As if hearing about my store could ever tire me!' Opal said scornfully. 'But if your time is to be limited please tell me everything as quickly as you can. How is the July sale going? Is the restaurant making a good profit?'

She had a hundred questions. He answered them all.

'I'm very grateful to you for taking care of things,' she said. 'I think you should get yourself an assistant, someone who'll really be of help to you over the next few months, until I return.'

'Actually,' David said, 'I did so a few months ago. As you rightly say, it's too much for one person. I took Miss Nash, from Toys. She's shaping well.'

'Miss Nash?'

'She was a temporary assistant on Toys two Christmases ago. I don't suppose you'll remember her.'

She didn't. Too much had happened.

'Here's Mary coming to see me off!' David sounded relieved, jumped to his feet.

Mary crossed the lawn hand in hand with Emmeline who, at thirteen months, was walking well. It was David's first sight of the child. If he feels any emotion, Opal thought, he is not showing it. The smile on his face remained fixed and his eyes revealed nothing. She herself felt nothing beyond the pleasure which the sight of her little daughter always gave her.

The child started to run, tottered, and overbalanced by Opal's chair.

'She is exactly like you, Opal,' David said. 'Exactly!'

Mary picked up Emmeline and set her on her feet again.

'Yes isn't she,' she said. 'There seems to be nothing of Edgar in her.'

Opal had thought often about Edgar in the long days of her convalescence, but it was not the affair with David, but the years before, which ate at her conscience. 'If it had been a loving marriage,' Edgar had said. He was right. She knew now, she had learned painfully over the last months, that it was the warmth of love and affection, given and received, which made life worth while. She knew she would have died but for the love which had surrounded her, which had refused to let her go. Well, wherever he was, perhaps Edgar had found someone who would give him the affection he needed. But she would like him to know she had come to understand, and that she was sorry.

She had thought, too, about Mrs Carson, and longed to make her peace with the woman who had been so good to her. In the end she spoke to Mary about it.

'I want you to ask Mrs Carson if she will come to see me. Try to persuade her.'

'It will only upset you,' Mary objected. 'You know the doctor says you're not to be worried.'

'I shall worry far more lying here, thinking about it,' Opal said.

Mrs Carson came, and the meeting which Opal had wanted, yet dreaded, proved easier than she (and probably her mother-in-law, she thought) had expected.

'We've a lot to forgive each other for,' Mrs Carson said. 'Let bygones be bygones.'

'I have something to tell you,' Opal said. 'I intend to try to trace Edgar. I shall put advertisements in the Canadian Press – Toronto – and deposit a letter for him at the newspaper office if they'll let me. Perhaps you could send a letter, too.'

'I can't write,' Mrs Carson said. 'Neither me nor Percy can write. Edgar knows that. But if I could just know where he was, even if I can't see him again, I'd be happy.'

Opal wrote that night – a short letter because she could not yet hold a pen well.

'Dear Edgar, (she wrote) I have been thinking of you a great deal lately, realizing what I did to you. I am writing to ask you if you can find it in yourself to forgive me.

Daniel is well. He never forgets you. I would like it if we could be friends, for his sake. I saw your mother today. She longs to know where you are, as we all do.

Please, if nothing else, let us know that.

She said nothing of Emmeline, or of her accident – which was why she signed and sealed the letter before telling Daniel what she had decided.

'Here it is,' she said. 'But you and Auntie Mary must see to the rest. I can't quite manage it.'

'I'll do *anything!*' Daniel said. 'Anything! Oh Mother, do you think he'll come back to us?'

'I doubt that,' Opal said. She was not sure that she wanted that. 'If we can establish contact with him, that's the most we should hope for.'

But as the months went by, as advertisement after advertisement appeared, with no word from Edgar, even that hope died in Opal. It never died in Daniel.

With each week that passed Opal grew stronger. But in spite of her pleas that she was as fit as a fiddle the doctor refused to let her go back to the store for the pre-Christmas season, or for the following January sales.

'If you progress as well as you are doing now, and if you behave yourself,' he promised her, 'you can start work at the beginning of February.'

With that she had to be content. Remembering a previous occasion when she had done so, she dare not mark off the days in her diary. But in her head she kept a count, and knew it would not be long now.

13

'What I want to do most of all, right away, is to walk around the store,' Opal said. 'See how everything's going, say hello to everyone. I've been looking forward to it so long.'

'Then I'll come with you,' David offered. 'Explain one or two changes and so on.'

'No. You know I've always liked to do this on my own.'

She was out of her office and hurrying down the stairs before he could reply. She made for the side door, intending to look at all the display windows before starting inside the store. She felt tremendously fit this morning, ready for anything. It was wonderful to be back.

But not ready for this, she thought, fifteen minutes later! What has happened? What has happened to my beautiful store?

At first she thought that it was just something wrong with the side windows, that they were still heaped with the sordid detritus of the January sales because the window dressers had been busy along the front. It was annoying, but she would quickly deal with it. But when she turned the corner to the windows which faced on to the main road it was exactly the same. The sale remnants – unsold skirts, jumpers, hats, teatowels, gloves, materials, china – were still unattractively on show, though the sale was over. Not a single window had been cleared and the new season's display which custom said must begin just before the sale ended had not been started. In a fashion window two naked models had been left undraped, a vulgarity undreamt of in any decent store.

Moreover, there was not a sign of a window dresser at work.

She marched swiftly into the store and made for the nearest telephone, on Haberdashery.

'Staff Office? Have someone find Mr Lambert and report to me at once! Ground floor, main entrance. Well if he's left send whoever's taken his place as Senior Window Dresser. *I* don't know where you'll find him. All I know is he's not where he should be!'

She turned from the telephone and saw a woman impatiently drumming her fingers on the counter. There was no assistant in sight.

'Could you find someone to serve me, Miss,' the woman said. 'I'll swear I've been waiting here ten minutes!'

'I'm sorry about that. I'm not quite sure what's happened but I'll be pleased to serve you myself. What can I get for you?' Opal was trying hard to control her feelings, to speak pleasantly.

'I want five yards of bias binding, navy, to match this.' She held out a piece of material.

'I'm sure we shall have that,' Opal said.

She opened the drawer marked 'bindings, bias'. True enough, there were some cards of binding in the drawer. There was also lace, tape, ribbons, and an odd card of grey darning wool. The ends of the bindings and laces had not been pinned after use and were coming adrift. She rummaged through the drawer.

'Ah! Here we are! But we seem to have only the one shade of navy at the moment. Let's see if it matches.' She placed it against the material.

'It doesn't really,' the customer said. 'It's too light. More of a French navy.'

'You're quite right,' Opal agreed. 'It won't do! Were you wanting to use it today?'

'Tomorrow at the latest. I'll try Miller's.'

'Oh, but I'm sure we can get it for you,' Opal said quickly. 'If you like to leave your name and address we'll do that today and we'll put it in the afternoon post to you. We'll enclose a bill and you can pay next time you come into the store. I daresay you come fairly often?'

'I used to,' the woman said. 'You wouldn't believe what a good store this used to be.'

As the woman was leaving the haberdashery assistant returned. She smiled happily at Opal.

'Ta! I had to go to powder my nose, so to speak. Miss Titmarsh on ribbons said she'd keep an eye open, but she seems to have disappeared.'

'You know the rules!' Opal snapped. 'No department is ever to be left untended. If Miss Titmarsh was not free to relieve you, you should have remained at your post until she was.'

'Here, I didn't know that was a rule!' the girl said. 'Come to that, I don't know who you are!'

'You soon will,' Opal said grimly. 'Where's your buyer?'

'Miss Foster? Well she had a rotten cold on Saturday so I reckon she must be tucked up in bed with a hot water bottle.'

She looked again at Opal, saw, under the make-up, the scar running down the left side on her face. 'Oh Lord,' she wailed. 'You're not Miss Opal?'

But Opal had gone, walking swiftly away towards a man in a brown overall who stood by the main entrance.

'Are you the Senior Window Dresser?' she asked sharply.

'Yes Miss. The thing is, Miss, no-one has given me the plans for the new displays. I can't dress windows until I know what's to go in them.'

'I want action, not excuses,' Opal interrupted. 'Go around to every buyer, tell them Miss Opal sent you and that they are to give you a selection of their new season's goods immediately. Tell them the theme is "Winter into Spring". We want plenty of yellow and green to brighten things up. And while you're doing that see to it that your assistants are cleaning the windows. They're filthy!

I shall expect every window in the store to be cleaned and dressed today. If it means working overtime, then you must do that. Now get going!'

At first she told herself she had simply made a bad start, picked on two inefficient employees. But it was more than that. Everywhere was the same. As she progressed, her temper rising, her footsteps quickening as she marched from department to department, she saw all around her evidence of neglect such as she could never have dreamt of. Assistants chatting in corners, dirty showcases carelessly dressed, counters cluttered and, worst of all, customers unattended. She had been away less than two years. How could her wonderful store, which had run like clockwork, which had been a bye-word far beyond Leasfield for service and efficiency – how could it have come to this? This seemingly, fourth-rate, run-down emporium?

She advanced into gowns, her high heels viciously stabbing into the carpet. An assistant sat on a chair behind a counter.

'Are you ill? Or menstruating?' Opal demanded.

'No!' The girl looked startled.

'Then stand up!' Opal ordered. 'A chair is provided in each department for any assistant who is unwell, or unduly fatigued. You are not ill, and at ten-o-clock on a Monday morning, with not a customer in sight, you can hardly be fatigued. Where is Miss Baxter?'

'Gone to coffee,' the assistant said.

Opal walked around the department, examined the dresses on the rails, looked into the fitting rooms.

'Tell Miss Baxter that Miss Opal will see her later,' she said. 'In the meantime there are several gowns hanging in the fitting rooms. Get them back on the rails where they belong. They won't sell if they're out of sight! If there is a Junior, get her to clean the mirrors. If there isn't, then do it yourself.'

In the Fabric department she ordered that bolts of cloth be replaced on the shelves where they belonged. In Glass

198

and China she demanded that the whole stock be dusted forthwith. She would have liked to have picked up the entire stock, piece by piece, and smashed it against the wall.

Last of all she went into the restaurant. By now she knew what to expect. Spotty tablecloths and messy cruets. My beautiful restaurant, she thought miserably. She sat at a table in the corner, which used to be reserved for her. She was trembling from head to foot with a mixture of rage and shock. She clenched her fists, took long, deep breaths to prevent herself breaking into angry tears.

'Why, Miss Opal! How nice to see you back! Shall I get you some coffee?'

She looked up into the bright, shining face of Kate Lewis, the waitress who always looked after her. Kate had worked in the store since opening day. At least *she* had not changed. She was as immaculate as ever in her black dress, snow-white apron, pleated cap threaded with velvet ribbon. And then, suddenly, Opal realized that nothing else around her had changed, either. The starched tablecloths were in pristine condition, there were posies of fresh flowers on each table, the cutlery and cruets gleamed. It was all exactly as it used to be, exactly as she had thought of it in the long time she had been away.

'I don't believe it,' she whispered, looking around her. 'I don't believe it. How can it be?'

The waitress looked at her with compassion.

'I can't pretend not to know what you're talking about, Miss Opal. I knew you had a shock coming to you, and as you walked into the restaurant I could see you'd had it. I just wish you'd come in here first. I'd have warned you.'

'Why *did* no-one warn me? Why did no-one say anything?'

Kate shrugged her shoulders. 'Ask me another! Of course we didn't know you were coming today, else it might not have been quite so bad.'

'No,' Opal said. 'No-one did. I'd arranged to start on Thursday but I changed my mind at the last minute, decided to come in earlier. I didn't tell anyone because I wanted it to be a surprise. Well it was that all right!'

'It's a shame,' Kate said. 'Many's the time I've said to the girls, "Miss Opal would be grieved to the heart if she could see what's happening." But you see *here* we have Mr Soames. That makes all the difference. *He* didn't change, even when the buyers' commission was cut, and his with it.'

'The buyers' commission cut?' Opal could not believe what she was hearing. It was like some bad dream.

'Well everybody's commission, right through the store. But the buyers feel it most, don't they, because they've most to lose. But Mr Soames didn't let it make any difference to him and of course we still get our tips.'

Mr Soames. She had almost forgotten him, though she herself had engaged him to manage the new restaurant when it first opened.

'Mr Soames is a bit of a martinet,' Kate said. 'A bit like yourself if you'll excuse me saying so. It's what's needed. Oh he's always fair – like you were, Miss Opal. And he looks after us like you did. He's kindness itself when necessary. You might say he's the heart of this restaurant. But the heart went out of the store when you went, Miss Opal! I hear what customers say when they sit at my tables and I've heard them use those very words, more than once. Well, let's hope you've brought it back.'

'Oh I have,' Opal said slowly. 'I have!'

In the last hour she had felt that all the world's anger was contained in her; that it choked in her throat and soured in her stomach. Now, though the fury and the rage were still in her, they were combined with a fierce, grim determination.

'Let's say that you and Mr Soames have put new heart into me! Everything's going to be all right in the end, I promise you Kate. Just you watch me!'

But to most of the people she had seen this morning it would seem, for some time to come, a heart of iron. She felt that she had a ball of iron where her heart should be and that iron ran in her veins. And David Hessle would be the first to suffer. She would gladly kill him.

'Give Mr Soames my compliments,' she said to Kate. 'Tell him I'll see him tomorrow. I'm going to be very busy the rest of today.'

Opal burst into David Hessle's office without knocking. He was comfortably seated behind his large desk. A young woman with corn-blonde hair bent over the desk beside him, their heads close together as they studied a sheet of paper. They looked up as Opal entered. David, half rising from his chair, was clearly apprehensive, disconcerted. Not so the girl. The look she gave Opal was defiant, self-satisfied. That something was going on Opal did not doubt, but it did not concern her now. All that mattered was her store, that here was the man to whom she had entrusted her most precious possession, here was the man who had wrecked it, perhaps beyond repair.

'You've not met Miss Nash,' David said nervously.

'Please leave us at once!' Opal did not look at the girl as she spoke to her.

'You'd better go,' David said.

The door closed noisily behind her. Opal had not taken her eyes off David.

'What have you done? How dare you do this to me? How dare you?' She hurled the words at him; cold, venomous, as if she would like to spit poison with them.

David sank back into his chair, raised his hands as if to fend her off.

'Opal, don't fly off the handle! Let me explain. Nothing has been easy these last two years. Business hasn't been easy!'

'Business is never easy! Do you think I found it so? You undertook the job – for which, incidentally, you were paid a higher rate than most people in the retail world – and you didn't do it! You cheated me, David, as certainly as if you'd embezzled my money.' Her voice was hoarse, trembling.

'That's a harsh judgement, Opal,' he said defensively. 'You don't know all the facts. I can explain them to you.'

'I've seen enough of the facts in front of me this morning. Filth, apathy, carelessness. An almost total lack of discipline. But worst of all, you've damaged what I hold most dear – my relationship I had with my customers, the confidence they had in me!'

'How can you possibly know that?' David demanded.

'I do know it. And you can't deny it. You've been totally incompetent. As for your dishonesty, I've yet to find out how far that has gone! But it's what you've done to my customers that I care about most.'

David leaned back in his chair. His abject air had vanished and the look he gave Opal now was insolent.

'Well now,' he sneered. 'You could never expect me to come up to Miss Opal, could you? Who could ever do that? Miss Opal, Queen of Storekeepers!'

'And I will be again!' Opal shouted. How dare he mock her! 'But not with your help! I'm giving you a month's notice from this minute. It being February it will mercifully be a short month. During that time you will have nothing whatever to do with the running of the store.'

Somewhere, deep underneath her anger, her heart ached that she should be saying these words to David Hessle. How could such a thing be? She had realized more than two years ago that in personal relationships he was weak; that the strength for which she had admired him had never been his. It was a quality with which she had endowed him because she had longed for a strong man in her life. But she had always thought, until today, that in business he was reliable, talented, trustworthy.

'You can't do that!' he objected.

'Can't I? It's my store. I can do what I like! There'll be a staff meeting tomorrow evening. You can attend if you wish, or you can leave me to announce your departure.'

'I'm sure you'll do it very well,' he said dryly. 'For the sake of your store you won't say anything cheap. Actually, you might find there are some people who quite like me, won't want me to go.'

'After you've cut their commission? Don't be absurd. You've cheated them as you've cheated me. But if anyone wants to leave with you, they're welcome. And now I'd like the Minutes of the last two years,' Staff Meetings. Have them sent up to my office at once.'

She turned to leave. She could not bear to be with him a moment longer. He called out after her as she went towards the door.

'We haven't been having staff meetings. People have better things to do after work – but you wouldn't understand that.'

Over lunch, which Kate brought on a tray to her office, Opal studied the accounts. It did not surprise her to see in the figures concrete evidence of falling sales and diminished profits, but what worried her more was the large amount of money owing to suppliers. The total was appalling. On starting the store she had been grateful for the lengthy credit many of her suppliers had allowed her, and as soon as she was established she had repaid that trust, and ensured their further good service, by paying her bills promptly. Desperately, she checked the figures again. These bills must be paid or her supplies would be cut off. Somewhere, she was dreadfully sure, she would find letters saying just that. There were going to have to be so many economies in the store, steamlining, perhaps merging of departments; cutting down of staff. It would not be popular.

She looked up as Miss Carver, who ran the Staff Department, entered.

'Ah, Miss Carver! I know Miss Morton left when she married her young man in Accounts. I can't manage without a secretary but I don't want us to take on any more staff at the moment. Is there anyone in your office, or perhaps in Accounts, who could be spared to help me?

It would mean her present job being shared out among the rest of you, but for the moment that's how it is.'

'Well,' Miss Carver said thoughtfully. 'I suppose you could borrow Mrs Sylvester. She's an older woman . . . a widow . . .'

'Has she got lots of common sense,' Opal interrupted. 'Is she a hard worker?'

'Yes to both those questions.'

'Then send her along. At once if you can. I've got several things for her to do.'

She liked the look and sound of Mrs Sylvester; plump, neat, grey-haired, with a quiet voice and a matter-of-fact manner.

'The first thing I want you to do,' Opal said, 'is to get a notice right around the store, to be read and initialled by everyone on every department, from the buyer to the Junior, about tomorrow's staff meeting. Six-o-clock in the restaurant. Make it clear that I want a full attendance.'

'And the agenda?'

'There isn't one. What I have to say won't fit into nice, neat headings. And just before you start that will you phone Mr Hessle and ask him to send Miss Nash up with the Customer Relations file? You can use this phone.'

Mrs Sylvester looked up a moment later.

'Mr Hessle says he can't lay hands on it at the minute.'

Opal took the telephone from her.

'You will lay hands on it and send Miss Nash to my office with it inside fifteen minutes!' she told him.

When Miss Nash came, carrying the file, she wore an expression which Opal, without knowing where, recognized as one she had seen before. Silently brazen, as if she had a secret which pleased her and would anger Opal. And then Opal remembered. It was the look she had seen on the face of Connie Browning a long time ago. So her impression of Miss Nash and David had been correct.

'I'd like to speak to you in private,' Miss Nash said.

'You can say anything you have to say in front of Mrs Sylvester,' Opal said. 'Make it short. I'm busy.'

'Very well then. I hear that Mr David is leaving. If that's the case I'm afraid I can't stay.'

'I quite agree,' Opal said.

'So I'm giving in my notice.'

'Wrong!' Opal said. 'I've already spoken to Staff Office. Your cards and your wages in lieu of notice are ready for you. You'll leave now and pick up what's due to you on your way out.'

'But you can't do that!' Miss Nash protested.

'As I recently told Mr Hessle,' Opal said. 'In this place I can do as I like. Good day to you!'

She stayed late that evening, working out what she would say at the staff meeting next day. By the time she arrived home Emmeline had been in bed and asleep for two hours.

'You look exhausted,' Mary said.

'I am. Why didn't you tell me about the Store, Mary?'

Mary reddened. 'I wanted to warn you,' she said. 'I didn't know what to do. I don't go into the store much, as you know, so I wasn't quite sure about things. But what I thought most important was that you shouldn't be worried. Queenie thought so too. We discussed it between us and came to that decision.

'I think it was the wrong one.'

'Perhaps it's not as bad as you think,' Mary suggested. 'You know what a perfectionist you are.'

'On the contrary, I daresay it's worse than I think,' Opal said. 'I'm pretty sure I haven't seen everything yet.'

Opal was encouraged to see that most of the staff was at the meeting. Whether they had turned up from a sense of duty or merely from curiosity hardly mattered at this stage. She was also pleased to see that David Hessle was not present.

Standing on the small platform which had been arranged for her so that, tiny of stature though she was, she could be seen by everyone, she fingered her opal pendant and waited for silence. When it came she began to speak.

'I can't tell you how glad I am to be back! I'd like you to know that I'm totally fit and in good health. I've never felt better in my life.'

There was a round of polite applause.

'I want to thank those of you who have served me loyally while I've been away. But now that I am back I think the time has come to make changes in the store. I'm sure you will agree with me.'

She looked at the rows of expressionless faces, trying to read the thoughts behind them.

'First of all,' she continued, 'I have to tell you that Mr Hessle will be leaving us at the end of the month. Mr Hessle has been of untold help to me in the past, but now he is moving on. He is sorry he could not be here this evening to tell you this himself.'

In the small movements of heads and hands, the slight shifting of bodies, she detected the signs of uneasiness.

'And now,' she said, 'I'm going to come straight to the point. This store is not what it was when I left to have my daughter two years ago. It has deteriorated sadly. In some ways it has deteriorated almost beyond belief. Those of you who were with me then – and looking around I can see many of you, though others I had hoped to see on my return are missing – you will know that what I say is true. It is now my intention, without wasting any time, to make this store what it once was! And that I can only do with the help and cooperation of each one of you, from the most Senior Buyer to the most Junior Assistant. I need to know that I can count on you. So, if there is even one amongst you who cannot give me that cooperation, then it is better that I should know. Please come and tell me tomorrow.'

A man on the back row jumped to his feet.

'*We* thought we could count on our commission,' he shouted. 'But we were let down! We're expected to work hard, give everything we've got to Opal's store, but where are the incentives?'

Heads swerved round to look at him, nodded in agreement.

It was a sign of the times, a sign that jobs were at last a little more plentiful, Opal thought, that he should dare to speak so. She did not blame him.

'If you had not mentioned that, Mr Bell, I would have. I feel bound to say that it was not with my knowledge that your commissions were cut . . .'

'Not cut – cut *out*!' someone called.

'I've gone into the question carefully,' Opal continued. 'I'm happy to tell you that it is my intention to restore your commission from the end of this month!'

She interrupted the roar of approval which went around the meeting.

'Wait! Please let me finish. I must tell you that the figures I have seen yesterday and today do not warrant me taking this step. The profit margins are far too low. But I am taking a gamble. I am gambling, as I first did when I opened this store eight years ago, on the loyalty and cooperation of my staff.

'There can be no commission without sales, no sales without customers. And it is you as well as I who must bring back the customers. People have more money to spend than when I first started in business but there is also more competition. Prospects of success are brightest when what we offer – be it goods or services – are better than those offered by anyone else in the area. That is the way it was with Opal's store – and will be again!'

She definitely had the meeting in her hand now. She could feel the power returning to her and she knew that however difficult the going was over the next few months, she would get there in the end. She held up her hand to quell the chatter which had broken out.

'I want you and our customers to feel secure, to have a sense of continuity in the very special world of a well-appointed, well-run store. Remember, where the customer is concerned, that you are not only selling the goods. Whether it is a yard of elastic or a fur stole you are handing across the counter, you are selling Opal's store.

'I told you there must be changes if we are to become strong again. What these will be, when they will take place, we shall work out together.'

She sat down. The applause now went far beyond politeness. When the meeting broke up she went and stood at the door of the restaurant, shaking hands, receiving good wishes. She hoped that the same mood would be upon everyone tomorrow when she started visiting the departments, began the work of pulling everything into shape.

She beckoned to Mrs Sylvester.

'Would you find Mr Soames and ask him if he could spare me a few minutes in my office before he goes home?'

She had it in mind, had had since yesterday's visit to the restaurant, to offer Mr Soames David Hessle's job. She hoped he would accept it.

The most worrying thing she had come across so far was not the accounts, not David Hessle, not the state of the store, even, but the contents of the Customer Relations file. After the staff meeting she had taken it home with her to study it more carefully, hoping that on a second reading it would seem less disastrous. It did not. It bulged with complaints of sub-standard goods, delays in deliveries, mistakes in almost every area, but most of all with complaints of poor service; of indifference, indolence and, occasionally, insolence on the part of her staff.

It was the most serious discovery of all because her customers were the reason for her store's existence. And because she knew that for every customer who took the trouble to write and complain, there would be a dozen who silently went elsewhere. What made it all so much worse was that, as far as she could see, not one of the complaints had been dealt with. This, she resolved, was something she must attend to personally.

'In the meantime,' she said to Mrs Sylvester on the morning after the meeting. 'I want you to write to each of these customers – just a short letter. Explain that I have only now seen their complaint, that I'm looking into it and I'll be in touch with them later. Say that if they wish they can come in and see me. I'll sign all the letters.'

One of the many good things Opal had already discovered about Mrs Sylvester was that she could write a good letter without every phrase being dictated by her boss.

'Very well,' Mrs Sylvester said. 'And before you go down into the store, Mrs David Hessle is waiting to see you. I put her in my office.'

Connie? Why? If it was to plead for her husband's job back it was no go.

'Mr Hessle isn't in this morning,' Mrs Sylvester said.

'I see. Well show her in.'

It was not only Connie who came into the office. She was accompanied by her small daughter. Opal gasped at the sight of her. The child was the image of David. The same red hair, clear skin, grey-green eyes, beautiful features. Though she never thought of Emmeline as having anything to do with David, she realized with a jolt that this was how her own daughter could have looked, instead of being a small replica of herself.

'Yes, little Dinah's the spit of her Dad, isn't she?' Connie said. 'Let's hope she doesn't take after him in character!'

'I won't beat about the bush,' she went on. 'David has hopped it. Packed up and went last night. Need I say who with?'

What have I *done*, Opal thought, what *have* I done?

'In case you're thinking of blaming yourself, don't bother,' Connie said. 'I've seen it coming. I knew he'd go sooner or later, if not with her then with someone else. I haven't come here to reproach you for sacking him. I've come to ask if there's any money due to him. I'm short.'

Opal hesitated. 'I'm not sure that I should . . .'

'Well you can't give it to him because you don't know where he is – though I happen to think he's gone to Manchester because that's where *she* comes from. So if you were to give me the cash to hand over to him – well, it's off your plate isn't it?'

'Very well,' Opal said. 'I'll give you a month's salary. Go into the restaurant and have some coffee while I have it made up for you. But how will you manage afterwards? I'd like to offer you a job here – you have some experience – but right now I'm not setting anyone on.'

'Oh don't you worry about me, love,' Connie said airily. 'What's sauce for the goose is sauce for the gander and I've got my friends, only too willing to step in when I say the word! Well, that's that then! Who would have thought it would come to this?'

As soon as Connie had left Opal rang Mr Soames and asked him to come to her office. When Kate Lewis had first mentioned George Soames yesterday morning Opal had hardly remembered what he looked like. Then, last evening, when he had come to her office she wondered how she could possibly have forgotten him. It was not that his appearance was in any way remarkable. He was a man of medium height, as dark as herself but, though a couple of years older than she, with no grey in his hair. The clear hazel eyes which looked directly into her own were kindly and honest. She felt an immediate trust in him. Kate had described him as a bit of a martinet, but it was not apparent in his manner. But then Kate had also described her as a martinet – which was absurd!

'Ah! Thank you for coming so soon,' she said. 'You already know how pleased I am that you've consented to be my Store Manager. Now I'm going to ask you if you could take over as quickly as possible. The very first minute your deputy in the restaurant can replace you. I hope it won't be long. There's so much to be done and I really do need you.'

14

'So you agree with me, now that Miss Tyler is leaving us that Miss Foster should be asked to add Hosiery, gloves and Trimmings to her present Haberdashery, Handkerchieves and Scarves?' Opal said.

George Soames, sitting on the opposite side of the desk, nodded approval.

'Absolutely. As we've said before, the more we can amalgamate several departments under the one buyer, the better. It means lower expenses on buyers' trips to London, or Manchester. And of course it saves a salary.'

'Not quite,' Opal reminded him. 'A buyer who takes on extra departments must be paid more. Also, a buyer with several departments, even if they're small ones, must have an under-buyer – though that's a job which can be combined with First Sales. Most of our First Sales will be all the better for having the added responsibility. Like you, I'm a great believer in encouraging people to do more than they think they're capable of.'

'So will you see Miss Foster, or shall I?' he asked.

'I think jointly. I've always done it myself but I think now, when it's a question of senior posts, we should do it together.'

She picked up the telephone. 'Mrs Sylvester, will you ask Miss Foster if she can spare me a few minutes right away?'

Miss Foster was the first buyer to be asked to take on extra territory. After that Opal planned that Sports Equipment should be moved to the ground floor and placed under the wing of Mr Bell, of Menswear. Ladies

Sportswear – swimsuits, hiking shorts and so on – would be amalgamated into skirts, jumpers and blouses in a department for which Opal still searched for the right name. These moves were part of a plan worked out by herself and George Soames soon after he had taken up his new post, but because of Opal's proviso that no buyer who wished to continue working for her, and was willing to work hard, should be either demoted or sacked, it was only now that the scheme could be started. When a buyer left, unless no other solution could be found, he or she was not to be replaced; at least not until better times.

Miss Foster knocked and entered. She was a large, regal-looking lady. Her black marocain dress strained over an impressive bosom. If appearance was anything to go by she should have been in charge of something very important, like fur coats or model millinery, rather than elastic and buttons. Opal put the proposition to her.

'We can't offer you any more staff,' she pointed out. 'But the departments are physically close together and I suggest that you train your staff to keep an eye on each other's counters as well as on their own. I would like them, as soon as you can manage it, to get to know the stock on each counter, so that they are really interchangeable. It's a policy we intend to follow right through the store. I'm sure you'll be an excellent person to show us the way.'

'Well I'll try,' Miss Foster said. 'But there's one thing I would like.'

'What's that?'

'I'd like to have Miss Singleton as my under-buyer.'

'Miss Singleton?' Opal said. 'Are you sure?' Miss Singleton was the young woman who had been missing from her counter on Opal's first morning back.

'Quite sure, Miss Opal. She made a somewhat frivolous start, but in the last few months she's improved enormously. She's a good saleswoman – she had experience before she came to us – she knows her stock thoroughly now, and she's particularly good with customers.'

'Well ' Opal looked at her Store Manager.

'If Miss Foster believes her to be the right person, then we should give her a chance,' he said. 'She knows the young lady better than you or I do.'

'Very well then,' Opal said.

'Do I sense, George,' Opal said when Miss Foster had left them, 'that you think our buyers should have more say in choosing their assistants – moving them around, promoting them and so on?'

'I do. I think they should have much more part in it, right from the first interview. As it is, we engage them and the first the buyer sees of the new assistant is on the Monday morning when she arrives on the department.'

'Well you could be right. But you don't mean I shouldn't see the staff we engage?'

'No. But you could take less part in it. Your job is policy, not detail. And your overriding job is Customer Relations. No-one can do that as well as you can. Look how marvellously you dealt with all those complaints.'

'Well, however you flatter me,' Opal said, smiling, 'there's one job you'll never take from me. Nothing will stop me doing my walk-around. When I do that I just pick up the whole spirit of the place. I can feel at once how everything's going, both with staff *and* customers. And I must say, over the last few months the change is unbelievable. I have a lot to thank you for, George.'

He rose, ready to leave.

'You're the one who's done it, Opal. I've been privileged to help, but you're the one who's been the inspiration to just about everyone. Not really having seen you in action before, I wouldn't have believed it possible!'

'I reckoned from the beginning that my employees would be loyal to me,' Opal said thoughtfully. 'And with a few exceptions they were. I think it helped that I decided not to look back at what had happened, but just to push forward, make a fresh start. But I couldn't have put my ideas into practice without you.'

And now, she thought as he left, he's coming up with ideas of his own, which is good. He's showing me that there's another point of view, that I'm not right all the time. She blessed the day he had taken on the job. Not only was he her right hand, he was accepted throughout the store as a manager who was firm, who would stand no nonsense, but who was fair. It was as if David Hessle had never existed.

Though not for me, Opal thought. She doubted that she would ever see him again but it was impossible that she should ever quite forget him. And there had been good times as well as bad. The last she had heard of him was that Connie was sueing him for divorce.

But however pleasing it was that matters were going so well in the store, that the place was once more its clean, attractive, efficient self, that relationships between staff and customers seemed as good as they had ever been, she knew, and so did George, that there were still serious financial problems to be overcome. She did not like to confide them to her staff, other than to exert them to make every economy, and to sell, sell, sell. It would not do for the public, for her customers, to know how difficult it was proving to pay the bills which had been run up in her absence. Sales had increased steadily over the last six months but she had needed ready money for staff commissions and, most importantly, to buy up the two bankrupt stocks which had given them a good July sale. From now until Autumn was the quietest time yet she desperately needed money to pay her suppliers so that they would let her have all the goods she needed for a bumper Christmas season. On that she depended to make her solvent for nineteen-thirty-eight.

There was a knock on her door and Daniel came in. When the school year ended she had given him a job in the Packing Department, since he needed to earn pocket money for a trip to Scotland he was taking with Queenie and her family. His cousin, Robert Derwent, was his closest friend. Almost his only friend. He was a solitary boy.

'I know I'm not supposed to invade the Big Chief's office from my humble bench in Packing, but I forgot to tell you that I won't be coming home with you this evening. I'm going to see Robert about the holiday.'

At sixteen he was taller than ever, but too thin, she thought. His voice had long ago settled down to something uncannily like Edgar's, and he had already started to shave. He was like Edgar in manner, too: quiet, reserved, and sometimes just as obstinate.

'Well give my love to Aunt Queenie and Uncle Mark,' she said. 'Don't be too late home.'

He had, with unconcealed delight, left his boarding school in July and was looking forward to taking his place in the Art school. She was sure that most of his time in Scotland would be devoted to painting and that the pittance he earned in Packing would be spent on paints and brushes. He seemed happy enough most of the time this vacation, except that he still longed for his father. It had grown to be an obsession with him and there was nothing she could do about it. As if reading her thoughts he said:

'If you were to hear from Father while I am in Scotland you would let me know right away?'

She sighed.

'My dear, of course I would. But I don't expect to hear from him. All this time – all the efforts we've made. Daniel, I hate to say it, but wouldn't it be easier for you if you resigned yourself to the facts?'

'You mean give up hope?'

The forward thrust of his chin, the way he spoke, were so like Edgar.

'Do you mean you've given up hope?' he asked.

'Almost,' Opal said quietly. Yet it seemed impossible to her, too, that they would not see Edgar again. He was more alive to her now than David Hessle would ever be.

'I'll never give up hope!' Daniel said passionately. 'And neither should you. Never! When I've finished my art training I shall go to look for him. I don't know where I'll get the money, but I'll get it somehow, and I'll go.'

'Canada is a big place,' Opal said.

'I know. It might take me a long time. But I *shall* go. Perhaps you can give me a whole year's job in Packing or somewhere, so that I can earn the money.'

'I won't condemn you to a whole year in Packing,' Opal said. 'But when you've finished Art School you can take your proper place in the store, learn all the departments.'

'Mother,' he said patiently, 'I've already told you, and I mean it – I don't want to come into the store with you. Not as a career. It isn't that I hate it. I just don't want to be caught up in it. I want to be a painter. Why can't you resign yourself to that?'

'The store's given you a great deal,' Opal pointed out. 'Almost everything.'

'I know that. I appreciate it. But please don't pretend that you've done it all for me. The store is your world, Mother. It could never be mine. Why can't you accept me for what I am?'

As, perhaps, she had never accepted Edgar. She had not wanted to shut him out but she had wanted him to be part of her world; she had never been prepared to enter his. And now she was doing the same thing with Daniel.

'I'm sorry, Mother!'

'No, don't be,' she said quickly. 'Perhaps it's I who should be sorry. Oddly enough it's the second time today I've been shown that I can't have all my own way! Well, perhaps I'm old enough to accept it now – but if I'd done so when I was younger I wouldn't have had my career. In a way you're really doing what I did then, fighting for what you want. But perhaps you won't hurt as many people on the way.'

'Perhaps I won't need to. Perhaps it will be easier for me than it was for you.'

He leaned across the desk and kissed her on the cheek. It was a rare gesture from her undemonstrative son. It gave her great pleasure.

'Get along with you,' she said. 'Or Mr Beecham will complain that you're not pulling your weight and I shall have to sack you!'

At the end of the first week in November the enlarged Toy Department, its extra territory grabbed from the reluctant buyers of other departments, was ready for the Christmas season. The Wonderland Grotto, to which it led, would in a day or two's time be fit to receive Santa Claus when he arrived, ostensibly from some far-off, cold country.

No-one would ever know, Opal thought, what effort it had cost, what juggling of accounts, what pleading with suppliers, to present this splendid display of toys, games, annuals, puzzles – everything that a child could wish for. Nor how difficult it had been to furnish the Grotto more spectacularly than ever before. Its nurseryland figures, its fairy lights and glitter, its dark, exciting corners and air of magic as well as its sacks of ninepenny parcels to be handed out to the children, had arisen only after a great effort, with small resources, by the staff of the Display Department, and much juggling of finance by Opal and George Soames. Her credit was now stretched to the limit and the bank would allow no further increase in her overdraft. Everything now depended upon the Christmas season.

It was Santa Claus himself who now presented the problem. He hailed, not from the Arctic regions but from the main entrance, where for ten-and-a-half months of the year he was the commissionaire, resplendent in uniform, with medals from the wars in South Africa and France.

'It's hopeless!' George Soames said. 'He's the worse for wear again this afternoon. He sneaks across to the Black Swan at dinnertime and people buy him drinks because he's an old soldier. Potter simply can't be Santa Claus!'

'I know,' Opal agreed miserably. 'Yet I hate to tell him. He so looks forward to it. Well, I'll see to this myself. I've known Sam a long time.'

Sam Potter, sent for, stood to attention in front of Opal's desk and saluted.

'Sit down, Sam,' Opal said. 'You know why you're here, don't you?'

'Of course I do, Miss Opal! Santa Claus time again!'

He was steady enough, but his over-careful enunciation and the powerful smell of whisky which hung around him left no doubt that he was, if only slightly, drunk.

'But not for you, I'm afraid,' Opal said. 'Sam, you must know what I'm talking about. You've been drinking again. It's by no means the first time. And now I have to tell you that you can't be Santa Claus this year. I can't have you breathing whisky all over the children. Their parents would object most strongly.'

She felt terrible, watching this man so proud in his uniform struggle for words to express his shock.

'It's only a little drop I take,' he mumbled. 'Just to keep out the cold. It's a chilly job standing in that entrance.'

'I know,' she said. 'But you can't risk warming yourself up with whisky. I can't prevent you spending your dinner hour in the Black Swan but I have to warn you, Sam, that if you don't put a stop to it then Santa Claus won't be the only job I'll have to take from you.'

He rose to his feet. He was unsteady now and swayed towards her.

'Are you threatening me with the sack?' he demanded.

'Threatening isn't a word I like,' Opal said. 'I'm advising you for your own good.'

He leaned across the desk, his face close to hers so that his drink-laden breath almost choked her.

'You'll be sorry for this,' he said thickly. 'I know all your customers, all the posh people, everyone of them. They like me. You'll be sorry for this!'

'And so will you if you don't behave yourself,' Opal said firmly. 'Now take the rest of the day off. Go home, and come back sober in the morning.'

'And if I do, can I have the Santa Claus job?'

'No,' Opal said. 'I'm sorry, I can't risk it.'

In the event a young man from the Stockroom became Santa Claus. He does it very well, Opal thought, watching him, head bent down to a small child confiding its secret wishes. She noted with satisfaction the long queue which wound, caterpillar-like, through the Grotto and out into the Toy Department. It had been like this every minute since Santa had arrived last Saturday, riding through the streets of Leasfield on the back of an elephant which had been hired from a circus in winter quarters on the outskirts of the town. He had left his sledge, he explained to clever children who asked too many questions, with the circus owner.

She walked through the grotto several times a day since the staircase to her office was at the far end of it. Apart from the business it was bringing in, she enjoyed seeing the children. She must get Mary to bring Emmeline, which would not be difficult for since George Soames had become Store Manager Mary, for one reason or another, visited the store far more often.

Sam Potter had not changed his ways. He was never very drunk but, in the afternoons, never quite sober. She had put it to him that an indoor job in the Stockroom or in Packing might suit him better but he had refused on the grounds that he would not be able to wear his uniform.

'He'll have to go,' she said to George Soames. 'But it's not something I can do before Christmas. It would be too cruel.'

Working late in her office that evening she thought again about Sam Potter, wished she could do something for him. He was too young to be pensioned off but too old to find another job. He had muttered more threats at her but that did not worry her. He was in no position to do her any harm.

She looked at her watch. Nine o-clock. She must go home. She put on her hat and coat, drew on her gloves, took the car keys out of her handbag, opened her office door and almost choked.

The narrow staircase was filled with smoke; thick, acrid. It filled her lungs and she coughed and spluttered, tried to hold her breath and could not. Beyond the bottom of the staircase, where a screen divided it from the grotto, the smoke thickened and glowed red. She was trapped!

She ran back into her office, closed the door, picked up the telephone and rang the Fire Brigade. Then she climbed on to the desk and from there she opened the high window and climbed out on to the steep, frost-covered roof. How long would it be, she wondered, shivering in the night air, trying to keep her footing on the icy slates, before the flames reached her office and licked through to the roof?

'Granted that the Grotto and most of the Toy Department is a write-off,' George Soames said 'I still say you were lucky. You were fortunate to be rescued in time!'

They were sitting in his office, which she must now share since the fire had burnt out the bottom half of the staircase leading to her own.

'Which is more than can be said for Sam Potter,' Opal said. 'Though thank goodness he *will* recover.'

'To face a charge of arson,' George said. 'There isn't any doubt that he started the fire and if the firemen hadn't come across him quickly he'd have died in it. As might you,' he added soberly, 'had you not decided to go home when you did!'

She was glad to be alive. Every hour since she had been rescued from that icy roof had been like a gift to her. But the joy of living when she might have perished did nothing to solve the problem of what she must do next.

'I'd staked everything on the Grotto and the Toy Department in these six weeks before Christmas,' she reminded George. 'You know that. Now only five weeks to go and nothing left to sell except the fairy cycles and toy motor-cars which were at the far end of the department.'

There would be the insurance, of course, when it came through, but she knew she was under-insured and had been for some time. And her credit everywhere was stretched to the limit.

'Even if we had the money,' George Soames said. 'We don't have the time.'

'You're wrong there,' Opal said vehemently. 'If we had the money quickly, we could do it in the time. I know my people. They've already proved themselves. I know they'd work night and day to put everything right. But that's no good unless we have new stock. What can we do, George? What can we do?'

She beat her hands against her head as if she would force some sort of solution from her brain.

George shook his head.

'I have a few hundred pounds, perhaps a thousand. Not being married I've been able to save a bit. It's yours if you want it but it won't go far.'

She looked up quickly, her face suddenly glowing, her eyes alight.

'George, you're a genius! You're an absolute genius!'

'I've only offered you a few hundred pounds,' he said, nonplussed. 'There's nothing especially wonderful about that.'

'Yes there is,' she cried. 'Because it's shown me what I must do! I must do exactly as I did when I needed money to start my store. I went to my richest customer, my darling Miss Taylor, and I asked her to lend me the money.'

She had also asked Queenie but it would not be fair to do that again. Queenie and Mark now had a large family to bring up and educate.

'That's what I shall do,' Opal said. She felt excited, hopeful. 'I shall write to the customers I know best, who know me and, I hope, trust me. I shall tell them the position – they know the kind of year I've had, putting the store to rights again – and I shall frankly ask each one of them for a loan – large or small, according to their means, as long as it's immediate. I shall offer them a good rate of repayment and if I must – if I absolutely must – I'll offer them a share in Opal's. I don't want to go so far, and I'd only do it for a very substantial loan, but if it's the only way then I'll take it.'

'It's impossible!' George protested. 'You can't write and ask customers to lend you money.'

'Yes I can. I'm a woman in trouble, asking for help from my fellow women. I believe I shall get it, at least in some cases. Besides, what's the alternative?'

She rang for her secretary.

'Mrs Sylvester, I have to write a number of letters. No, I don't want them typed. I shall write them in my own hand. But I don't want any interruptions. All these letters must go in today's post. And before I can begin I want the ledgers of all our account customers. It doesn't matter if Accounts Department is working on them: tell them I have to have them.'

While waiting for the ledgers to arrive she drafted out what she would say, writing and re-writing, discarding one attempt after another.

'How will this do?' she said to George at last.

'Dear Mrs So-and-so,

You will doubtless have read of the dreadful fire which destroyed the Wonderland Grotto and most of the Toy Department in Opal's store. Mercifully there was no loss of life and the one person injured is now recovering in hospital. What faces me now is the speedy restoration of those areas, partly because of the great pleasure which they give to the children of Leasfield and beyond, partly – I will be quite frank with you – for the successful continuance of my business.

As you are a regular and valued customer I need not tell you that since my return from my two-year enforced absence I have been fighting a battle to make my store what it once was. That battle was almost over. Had it not been for the fire we should have won through by Christmas. Now we cannot possibly do so without the help of our well-wishers and friends.

I am taking the bold but necessary step of asking you if you would be willing to help me, and Opal's store, by making me a loan. Large or small, it will be welcome, but I need it quickly. I have already been offered several hundred pounds but I need more, much more.

If you are able and willing to help I shall be at your disposal to discuss terms. If you cannot or do not wish to do so I hope that I shall still continue to have your much appreciated custom in my store. Yours sincerely, Opal Carson.'

'What do you think, George?'

'Fine, if you think it'll work,' George said doubtfully. 'What can I do to help?'

'Leave me alone to write. Nothing more just now.'

Two days later the replies began to arrive. There were few letters which did not contain money, sometimes in surprisingly large amounts. But even before the letters, on the very day on which they had received the appeal, the customers came in person. Of those who came thus, no-one arrived without an offering of some kind. But from first to last it was not the offer of money which moved Opal most; it was the wealth of good wishes which accompanied it. Mrs Sylvester found her sitting behind a desk spread with letters, tears streaming down her face.

'I can't help it,' she apologized. 'I just had no idea! I had no idea what people thought of us!'

'Of you,' Mrs Sylvester corrected.

'It sounds a terrible thing to say, but it was almost worth having a fire to have this happen!'

She dried her eyes and began to collect the letters together. 'I shall never part with these as long as I live,' she said. 'Now we have to show what we can do with the money. First of all, Mrs Sylvester, I want you to call a special staff meeting. I'm going to need everyone's help.'

Within ten days the Grotto had been rebuilt and the Toy Department was usable again. The display staff, joined by members of the sales staff and office workers who declared themselves handy with paint brushes, hammers and nails, buckets and brooms, had worked around the clock in shifts. Volunteer drivers collected toys from suppliers far and wide; helpers from several departments gave up their lunch hours to price and label them and put them on display.

'It's a miracle,' Opal said when it was finished. 'But no more than I expected!'

'All we want now is the customers,' George Soames said.

'They'll come,' Opal said. 'You watch. They'll come more than ever now, just to see what we've accomplished.'

She was right. When the Toy Department and the Wonderland Grotto re-opened, the smell of smoke still hanging in the air, the crowds of Christmas shoppers flocked in – and continued to do so every day until Christmas.

At closing time on Christmas Eve Opal went to every department in the store, exchanging good wishes, collecting the sales sheets. When the last late customer had left, the last cover been draped over its counter, the last assistant gone home for Christmas, she walked back through the deserted store to George Soames's office.

'You should go home, Opal,' he said. 'You look all in.'

'Not until I've checked the sales sheets,' Opal said. 'Will you give me a hand?'

Long before they had reached the last of the sheets she looked up, smiling. Her eyes were bright, in spite of the fatigue which she knew must soon overwhelm her.

'George, it's far and away the best Christmas we've ever had! We've broken all records and we still have four more departments to check!'

Not long afterwards, the job completed, she took her coat from the closet and he helped her into it.

'Don't be late for Christmas dinner tomorrow,' she said.

'I won't,' he promised. 'I'm looking forward to it. It's a long time since I spent Christmas with a family.'

15

The Christmas of nineteen-thirty-seven, as well as being the best ever in the store, was for the most part a happy one at Oak House. When Opal arrived home on Christmas Eve, coming in from the frosty darkness outside to the bright warmth of the hall, Daniel and her father were putting the last touches to the six-foot-tall Christmas tree. Benjamin Derwent stepped back to view the effect.

'I think that's a bit of all right!' he declared. 'Though I say it myself as shouldn't. What do you think, Opal love?'

'It's beautiful,' Opal agreed. 'You two have been really busy.'

She wished, with a pang of remembrance, that Miss Taylor could see her house now. She would surely approve.

'And another thing, our Opal,' her father said. 'I've sawed up enough logs to see us right through Christmas. Now if we had a great big fireplace like your Grandpa Derwent's on the farm we could have a real yule log, big enough to last until New Year.'

Opal shook her head. 'You do too much, Dad. You know you shouldn't overtire yourself.'

'Nay lass, I haven't,' he assured her. 'I'm a very fit man, nowadays, for my age.'

Opal laid a hand on his arm. 'I know you are, love. And now I'll just go up to Emmeline. I wanted to be home before she fell asleep.'

'You are,' Daniel said. 'The little monkey's too excited to sleep.'

As Opal entered the bedroom Emmeline darted back

under the bedclothes, bright eyes wide open, determined not to miss a moment of this exciting day. On either side of her a teddy bear, a stuffed elephant and two dolls shared the bed.

'Hey, Miss! You're supposed to be asleep!' Opal said. 'Do you know what time it is?'

'I'm not a bit tired!' Emmeline protested. 'Will it soon be Christmas Day, Mummy?'

'After you've been to sleep. Now you lie still and I'll tell you the Christmas story again, and then you must try to sleep. What if Santa Claus came and found you awake?'

Sitting beside the bed, Opal had hardly begun the story before Emmeline's eyes closed and she was fast asleep. Opal tucked the blankets around the child's shoulders and went back downstairs.

'She was worn out,' she said, laughing. 'But quite determined to stay awake. She'll sleep until morning now.'

On Christmas Day Emmeline delighted, and was delighted by, everyone. In her wonder at the tall tree with its glass baubles, tinsel and fairy lights, in her excited cries as she tore the wrapping from her presents, revealing the spinning top, the toy piano, the dolls, the sweets, they all took pleasure. Benjamin, in particular, watched her with loving eyes.

'Little 'uns are what make Christmas,' he said.

Though he tried not to show it and would never have admitted it, Opal was sure that Emmeline was her father's favourite grandchild.

'Well I must get on,' Mary said, picking up the wrapping paper, smoothing it out to be used again. 'What time do you suppose George will arrive?'

'He said he'd be here at twelve noon,' Opal answered. 'Mary can't you slow down? You've hardly given yourself time to look at your presents!' Her sister was flushed this morning, though whether it was from the heat of the kitchen or from the thought of George Soames's presence at such an intimate family gathering, Opal was not certain.

'Nonsense! I'm thrilled by my presents,' Mary said. 'But I've still got lots to do. The dinner won't cook itself. And I want everything to be just right.'

'I'll help you,' Opal offered.

'Indeed you won't!' Mary retorted. 'If anyone needs a rest it's you!'

In the event, George Soames arrived early, laden with presents.

'I thought if I came in good time I could give a hand,' he said.

'Well if you really mean it you can help me with the table,' Mary said. 'Come along. I'll show you what's to be done.'

With mixed feelings Opal watched the two of them disappear into the dining room. In the last few months she had sometimes caught herself wondering whether she and George might not come together, make a go of it. In spite of her success in the store she felt herself incomplete, felt, from time to time, an indefinable sadness, an inner loneliness, especially when the day's work was over.

She admired and respected George and she was confident that he was fond of her. It was a good basis for marriage and more might be added to it. But when she observed the meeting between George and her sister on that Christmas morning she knew it was not to be. Mary lit a flame in him so bright and clear that no-one, seeing them together, could miss it. It was a flame she could never have kindled.

After the huge Christmas dinner, when they had pushed back their chairs and George and Mary had gone into the kitchen to make coffee, Opal said, 'I'm going to put Emmeline to bed for a while. She's tired out.'

'I think I'll have a lie down,' her father said. 'I don't want any coffee.'

When Opal came down again Daniel was on his own. Sitting at the table, his head in his hands, he did not hear her enter. She put an arm around his shoulders, stroked his hair.

'I know,' she whispered. 'I know!'

'If there'd only been a word from him,' he said. 'I thought at Christmas there'd be a word.'

On Boxing Day the word came. Opal and Daniel drove over to Mr and Mrs Carson's to take presents.

'But are you otherwise happier, now?' Opal asked as they sat in the car.

'Of course I am,' he replied. 'I've had a great term at College, doing what I actually want to do. And the new easel you've given me for Christmas is perfect. I'm going to feel really professional using it. I think I shall paint your portrait.' He hesitated. 'It's just . . . well, you know!'

'Let's go by way of Acer Street,' Opal said on an impulse.

It was the first time she had been near the street since they had left to go to Madame Dora's. It was narrower than she remembered it, the houses even smaller. The stonework was still soot black but the net curtains which hung at every window had been newly laundered for Christmas and all along the street the front doors had been painted and glossily varnished in a light oak colour. The mill was doing better now. Most of the families in Acer Street would be in work.

'Do you remember this, Daniel?' she asked.

'Of course I do,' he said. 'I was five when we left here. I didn't want to go.'

She drove slowly down the street. She had passionately wanted to leave it, never to see the place again, but now she could admit that not every day in Acer Street had been a bad one. The first year with Edgar, when Daniel was a small baby, had been happy enough. It was poverty which had changed everything. Though had it not been for poverty, which had relentlessly compelled her to find something better, she would not now be driving along the street (too ostentatiously she thought) in this expensive car.

At the end of the street she turned right into William

Street. Her parents-in-law no longer ran the bakery. Percy Carson had been ailing for some years and they had sold the business and moved into a small terraced house nearby. By the time Opal stopped the car Mrs Carson was at the front door, waving an envelope.

'It's for you, Daniel love!' she cried. 'It was delivered to the bakery in the Christmas post and they brought it down here this morning. One for me as well. From Montreal!'

'Montreal?'

Daniel tore open the envelope, took out the card, read it while his mother and grandmother watched.

'What does he say?' the old lady asked impatiently. 'Does he give an address?'

Opal knew the answer, read it in the sick disappointment in her son's face.

'I'm afraid not,' he said slowly. 'He just says "Merry Christmas, Son. Merry Christmas to your mother." Nothing more.'

'Aye, that's about all mine says, except that he's well. I hope he might have let us know where he is.'

Mrs Carson's voice was flat with dejection. Daniel put an arm around her shoulders. Opal looked at the two of them and could hardly bear the sadness in their eyes.

Daniel handed her the Christmas card. The familiarity of the angular handwriting was like a presence. She had not seen it since before she was married, in the days when, between visits, Edgar used to write surprisingly fluent letters to her at Highcliffe. The Christmas card was the first time in three years that he had mentioned her. Did it mean she was forgiven? Perhaps that was reading too much into it, but she would like to think they were no longer enemies.

'Come and see me more often, lad,' Mrs Carson said to Daniel when they were leaving. 'It does me good to see you.'

'I will,' Daniel promised.

The first half of nineteen-thirty-eight brought so much

work with it that Opal, except occasionally, had no time for the loneliness she had felt at Christmas. Daniel, though she noticed that he visited his grandmother more often, worked hard and said little. No word came from Edgar.

In the store it was the busiest time Opal had ever known. New housing estates were going up in and around Leasfield – semi-detached houses for a few hundred pounds. As young couples paid the deposit and moved into them, so the demand came for furniture; three-piece suites, kitchen cabinets, curtains – everything (especially if it could be had on hire purchase) to make the new home a palace. Opal quickly had the cellars under the store cleared out and decorated, bright lighting installed, and opened up a basement entirely devoted to everything which could possibly be needed to furnish a home in the latest style.

'Do you realize,' she said to George Soames as the store closed on Easter Saturday, 'that we've done so well this Spring, not only with the new departments but with fashion too, that we're now on an even keel with our suppliers? It even looks as though by the end of the year I'll have repaid most of the loans to my customers.'

'I do realize,' George answered. 'I've sometimes felt this last few weeks that the whole of Leasfield is putting up new curtains and refurnishing! But you deserve the success, Opal. Once again you were quick off the mark.'

And now it was June, and Emmeline's third birthday, and since it was a perfect summer Sunday she and the children were in the garden. George had taken Mary and her father for a drive to Ilkley, promising to be back in time for the birthday tea. Daniel was gently pushing his sister on the swing. From the seat where she watched them Opal smelt the spicy clove scent of the border pinks and the more heady perfume of the roses. The rose, old-fashioned ones which bloomed profusely now and by next month would be gone, had been planted by Miss Taylor.

She watched Daniel. He was so good with Emmeline,

so caring; as if, at seventeen years old, knowing his own loss, he was trying to be the father the little girl did not have. How very much she loved her children! They were the mainspring of her life, more to her than anything in the world, and she wanted the world to be perfect for them.

But people were saying that war would come, that it was inevitable. When she went to the cinema, as she sometimes did with Daniel or her father, the films were full of music and romance but the news reels showed uniformed men marching across Europe. If war came, what about Daniel? The thought came unbidden and unwelcome into her mind, as it did all too often these days. She pushed it away. It had no place in this perfect June day.

From time to time she closed her eyes, trying to banish all thought, letting the heat soak into her body; sliding towards sleep, so that when the man came towards her she did not see him, or hear his footsteps on the grass. It was only when his shadow blocked out the sun that she opened her eyes and looked up – and believed that she must, in fact, have fallen asleep and be dreaming.

'Edgar!' She managed no more than a whisper.

At the same time as she jumped to her feet, Daniel saw his father. He cried out, and bounded across the lawn, leaving Emmeline to fend for herself. The two men – automatically Opal noticed that Daniel was taller than his father – were locked in an embrace. She stood awkwardly by, not knowing how to act, confused thoughts crowding in on her. It was too sudden. Why had he not warned them?

Emmeline climbed down from the swing, ran across the lawn and took her mother's hand, examining the strange man with a quizzical look. Edgar and Daniel turned to face Opal and she felt herself deeply moved by the luminous joy in her son's face. Edgar made no move towards her, not even holding out his hand. He looked at her with a hard, direct gaze and then from her to the little girl at her side.

'So this is Emmeline,' he said quietly. 'I've seen my

mother and she told me about Emmeline. Well, she's a beautiful child, Opal. And the image of you.'

'I was never beautiful,' Opal said nervously. How stupid she sounded, but she could not think of the right words, if there were any for an occasion like this.

'You don't appear to have changed much,' he said.

She could not say that Edgar had not changed. It was not only that he looked older; he was thinner; held himself straighter, like a man who could face the world and take it on. Perhaps the greatest visible change in him was the air of strength, which had nothing to do with physique. It was in his eyes, clear and unafraid; in the firmer line of his mouth, in the confident way he held himself. Here was a man who was in charge of himself and of his life, Opal thought. He had not returned to her cap in hand, she was sure of that. He was as strong as she was.

'I'm sure I *have* changed,' she replied. 'Though perhaps not in looks.' And then she remembered, as she still occasionally did, and lifted her hand to touch the scar which ran down her cheek.

'I heard about your accident from my mother today,' Edgar said. 'I'm sorry. I'd have come back if I'd known.'

'I'm completely recovered,' Opal said. 'What brought you . . . ?' She was interrupted by Daniel.

'This is your new daddy, Emmeline,' he said happily. 'Say hello to your new daddy!'

Opal's eyes, meeting Edgar's, flashed a warning. Don't spoil it for him. For his sake, not yours or mine, don't spoil this moment. She tried to will him to understand but his eyes gave nothing away. She was terrified of what he would say. It seemed an age before he spoke, turning to Emmeline, holding out his hand.

'Would you like me to push you on the swing?' he asked.

The evening, it seemed to Opal, went on forever, the long northern daylight lingering in the summer sky. She was ill at ease, wanting to be alone with Edgar, knowing that there were things which must be said – yet not wanting to be. She was glad of Daniel's presence long after Emmeline had gone to bed, yet uneasy because of it. Mary and her father, embarrassingly tactful, had gone off to their rooms early, as soon as George had left. In the end Daniel, too, had wished his parents a reluctant 'goodnight'.

'But you'll be staying, won't you?' he asked his father anxiously.

'I have to go back to your grandmother's,' Edgar said. 'I daresay I'll have to stay there quite a while. Grandad's very ill, you know. But I'll see you tomorrow.'

Opal was grateful for his tact. She felt herself surrounded by people who now saw her future miraculously bright, all problems solved. Daniel saw it that way from ignorance; Mary and her father, she supposed, because they wanted a happy ending. Mary, in the throes of a love which had come suddenly and late, wanted everyone else as amicably settled as she herself would soon be. But it was not so simple, Opal thought. The future was not at all clear to her. It was all too soon. Even if she could sort out her own feelings – which she could not – she had no idea of Edgar's.

One thing was certain, he was not the man who had left her. He was a new man. It seemed impossible that in three years he could have changed so much, but the evidence was there before her and had been constantly reaffirmed in the hours since his arrival. Was it possible that but for the years of unemployment, followed by the third-rate job which he had hated, he would in any case have emerged like this? What part had her own success, at the very time when he saw himself as a failure, played in keeping down this man? She didn't know the answer to that one.

But the success he had won for himself, without help from anyone, had made him into a different person. Whether she would like this new person or not she didn't yet know. Nor could she guess at his feelings for her. The talk over the last few hours, in the presence of the rest of the family, had been general. He had treated her with no more familiarity than he had shown to Mary, and he had shown no eagerness to be alone with her.

When Daniel had finally gone to bed Edgar said, 'Let's go outside again. We don't get midsummer nights like this in Canada. It's one of the things I've dreamed about.'

They walked around the garden. With the setting of the sun the scents of the garden had intensified. The flowers seemed all one pale shade of cream, starkly outlined in the dusk. It was a romantic atmosphere, the last thing she wanted.

'You haven't *really* said what made you decide to come back. I know you never had my letter.'

'No. But then as I've told you, I was never in Toronto after the first year.'

Once in Canada he had quickly found a job, in a new insurance company just starting up. He had done well, grown with the company, until in three years he had become a senior manager. It had meant, though, that he must move about the country, finding new business, opening new branches.

Was it possible, Opal wondered suddenly, that he had met someone in Canada? A woman he wanted to marry. Had he come to ask her for a divorce?

'I came back because there's going to be a war,' Edgar said. 'I didn't want to talk about it in front of your family, not today. But I reckon it's a certainty. I couldn't stay in Canada with my family in England when there was a war on. At Daniel's age he'll soon be called up. Apart from anything I can do in the war, I had to be here to see Daniel!'

Why must everyone be so sure about war, Opal thought? Did men make war inevitable by accepting it as inevitable? But could she, by refusing to think of it, make it go away?

'You're thirty-nine,' she said. 'Won't you be too old to fight?'

'I didn't come back just to fight,' Edgar said. 'And I have a job here if I want one. My company are only too eager for me to start up here. I may have to fight, of course, though I shall hate it. That's been my trouble. Even for something that meant most in the world to me – you, Daniel – I wouldn't fight. I gave in, ran away. It's not a mistake I shall make again. *You* fought for what you wanted.'

'Is that why you fought for your new company?' Opal asked, 'for your place with them?'

'I didn't fight for the company. I fought for me. For my own self respect. I had something to prove and I proved it. I assure you, the world looks a very different place to me now! But I also discovered you usually wound someone. I hurt Daniel.'

'Yes you did,' Opal agreed. 'As much by your silence as by your leaving. But Daniel will be all right. He's never doubted that he'd find you again one day, and now he has. Right now, Daniel's world is complete!'

How long it would stay complete if she and Edgar were not to come together was another matter. But Daniel was almost grown up and she must give him credit for understanding. His parents could not build their future on what would please him. Not even Emmeline, she thought, can claim that from me – though my debt to her is greater and will take longer to discharge.

'And you and me?' Edgar asked. 'What did I do to us?'

'We did it to each other. But it appears not to have been all loss for either of us. You found strength and independence. You found that you could survive without me.'

'And what did you find?' he asked.

'Oh quite a lot. Including my weaknesses. I'd been arrogant enough to think that I could run my world single-handed, needing no-one. I was wrong. I've needed – and been given – the help of so many people. I couldn't have survived otherwise.'

It was dark now. The last vestige of colour had faded from the garden and a breeze was beginning to blow.

'I love Emmeline dearly,' Opal said, apropos, it seemed, of nothing.

'And her father?'

'David? I never think of him as Emmeline's father. He's only set eyes on her once, for a few minutes – far less time than you have. He never will again.'

'Where is he?'

'Who knows? Wherever he is I doubt if he'll stay there long. He, at least, is someone I don't have to think about. But Emmeline is another matter.'

They were silent for a while. Then Edgar said, 'She's your child. More important, she's a person in her own right. Emmeline shouldn't be punished.'

'And never will be,' Opal said fiercely. 'I wouldn't allow it. As I've told you, I love her dearly.'

'If war comes,' she said after a while, 'Daniel will be involved in no time at all. He'll join the Air Force or something silly like that.'

'We shall all be involved,' Edgar said. 'It will be that kind of war. But Daniel will make out. He has his own strengths. I can see that.'

Opal shivered. 'It's getting quite cool,' she said.

'Yes. And I must be leaving.'

'Would you like a nightcap before you go?'

They went into the house. Watching him as he sipped his drink Opal thought that he was an attractive man. He always had been, but now the bitterness of those years in the 'twenties had left him. He was a man at peace with himself. At peace, but not necessarily acquiescent.

He raised his head, caught her watching him.

'There is the question of you and me, Opal.'

'Not now . . .' she began.

'I agree,' he said. 'It's early days. That was what I was going to say.'

'Unless,' Opal said quickly, 'there is someone else involved. Someone I don't know about.'

'There's no-one else. There was, but it's over. But you and I are two different people, Opal. We have to get to

237

know each other again. It won't be like it was before.'

'I know.' She knew, too, that if there was to be a relationship between them it would not be on her terms alone. 'We have to be certain,' she said.

'Nothing is certain,' Edgar said. 'But at least let's try to be honest with each other.'

By mutual, unspoken consent, they dropped the subject. It would come up again in its own good time. Neither of them would force it.

'What shall *I* do if war comes?' Opal speculated, turning the conversation. 'Though I refuse to take it for granted that it will. I suppose I'll go on as usual. They say there'd be conscription for women as well as for men so I expect half my staff would be taken. There'd be shortages, rules, regulations – goodness knows what other difficulties. I'd have my battles all right. But the country can't do without retailers so I suppose I'd come through!'

'Oh I know you would,' Edgar assured her. 'I can't see Opal's Store going under! I can't see you ever giving up!'

He stood up, ready to leave.

'I'll see you tomorrow, then?' he said.

'Yes,' Opal replied. She was surprised how the thought pleased her.

Doctor Rose

To Harry, with my love

I acknowledge with gratitude the help of
Dr R.A. Leake, who checked all the medical
details in this book.

PART ONE

I

Rose sat upright in the high-backed, leather-covered chair. She was small, slightly built, and if she leaned back at all she thought it would engulf her. Clearly it was not a woman's chair. It was a chair built for the kind of men who faced her in a semi-circle across the polished table; solid-looking men with dark suits of best Yorkshire worsted; with high, stiff, gleaming white collars – and with gold alberts slung across ample stomachs; men whose shapes and appearances befitted them for their roles as Town Councillors of Akersfield.

It was not so much that they faced her as that she must face them. She was the sole object of attention of all seven members of the Health Committee. On these men depended whether she did, or did not, get the job. And she wanted the job. She wanted it badly.

'Have any of your family been doctors, then? Does it run in the family?'

The questioner, sitting on the Chairman's right, was different from his colleagues; younger looking, with no sign of grey in his dark hair, his face lively and alert. Up to now he had seemed to be the one most in her favour. But better not take anything for granted, Rose thought.

'No Sir. I'm the first of my family to qualify.'

'Speak up Doctor Stanton. You young people all mumble nowadays. There's no need to be nervous, you know. Just answer the questions in a nice clear voice.'

The speaker this time was an elderly man whom the Chairman had earlier addressed as Councillor Patterson. Rose had already diagnosed that he needed his ears syringing – that or a deaf aid, poor man. From the irritated looks his remarks drew from the others she guessed that he made this complaint at every meeting.

'I'm sorry,' she said, raising her voice. 'I said I'm the first of my family to train as a doctor.'

'What does your father do?'

'What made you want to do it?'

'Don't you reckon it's a rum job for a woman?'

The questions now came from all sides, as if they wanted to shoot her down with rapid fire. The last speaker seemed especially hostile. It wasn't his first antagonistic question. She manifestly found no favour with him and she wondered how much influence he had with the rest of the Committee.

'My parents keep an inn in the Dales,' she said. 'In Faverwell. It's been in my father's family for four generations. Just a small inn.'

Too small, she thought, to bear the expense, of her training. And yet it had. Her parents had never made enough money to save much and it was only by mortgaging the inn to the bank that they'd been able to send her to Medical School. It was a measure of her father's love for her that he, who had never owed a penny in his life and couldn't bear the thought of debt, had steeled himself to go cap in hand to the bank and to put all he owned at risk for her career. That was one of the reasons she needed this job, so that she could begin to repay her parents.

'As for what made me want to do it,' she said. 'It's difficult to tell. I just know I've never wanted to do anything else ever since I can remember, ever since I was a child.'

That was true. She recalled her mother complaining to a neighbour 'Our Rose doesn't play with her dolls properly. Not like Emily does. She paints measles spots all over 'em and puts 'em to bed. Or puts their arm in slings and their legs in splints. It's not natural in a little girl.'

The tetchy-sounding man was repeating his question.

'I said don't you think it's a rum job for a woman?'

2

She met his disagreeable look with her own direct one, schooling herself to speak calmly, hoping her irritation didn't show in her face. It wasn't the first time she'd been asked that particular question and it was too much to hope that it would be the last.

'I agree that there still aren't many women doctors,' she said. 'Though there are more now than before the war. But in this case I think being a woman gives me a real advantage. Whoever works in your Welfare Centre will be dealing all the time with women and children, mothers and babies. I like to think I understand them.'

'I reckon Doctor Stanton has a point of view there,' the man on the Chairman's right said. 'A very good point.' He had a pleasantly deep voice with slightly drawn-out north country vowels. It was a reassuring voice.

'But she knows nothing of the married state,' another man objected. 'Now some of our other applicants are family men, with wives and children.'

'Doctor Stanton – if she were to be appointed – wouldn't be without a man's guidance,' the Chairman said. 'She'd be working under a male doctor.' He looked towards Rose. 'The Medical Officer for our welfare services is a man, a Doctor John Stanton as it happens. Now there's something that could cause confusion, I'm afraid. Two doctors with the same name!' He shook his head as if he had suddenly found an insuperable problem.

'Which I'm sure could be sorted out,' the man on his right put in. 'She could be Doctor Rose, I daresay.' His eyes twinkled and he lengthened the sound of her name, rolling it off his tongue slowly as if he was reluctant to let it go.

I like the sound of that, Rose thought.

'Yes, well, there's a lot more to be settled than that,' the Chairman said hastily. 'Now I suppose you're not engaged to be married or anything like that, are you? You're not courting?'

'No, nothing like that.'

Just as well, she thought, that Gerald, busy in his veterinary practice up in the Dales, couldn't hear her decisive reply. It wouldn't please him.

'Good! As you know, we don't employ married women.'

And that's something I'm prepared to argue about, Rose thought, but not just now.

The Chairman shuffled through his papers, scanning them as if he sought fresh inspiration.

'Well then Doctor Stanton,' he said, not finding it, 'I think that's about all. There's nothing wrong with your training. Leeds is a highly-respected Medical School. It's turned out some good doctors. I see you won a scholarship. And then you've had a couple of years on the wards of our own Akersfield hospital and they speak well of you. I think also we've fully explained what the job is.' He glanced around the rest of the Committee. 'Have any of you gentlemen any more questions for the young lady?'

A man raised his hand.

'I'd just like to ask Doctor Stanton why she isn't considering going into private practice?'

Rose hesitated before replying.

'Naturally I have considered it. I suppose most doctors do. In the first place I have to admit that I couldn't afford to buy into a practice. But if I put up a plate on my own I might have to wait a long time for patients to come to me. I couldn't afford that either.'

'You mean people don't trust women doctors like they do men? Well I'm sure that's true enough!'

The speaker was the awkward man. I've played right into his hands, Rose thought angrily.

'But more important,' she continued firmly, ignoring his interruption, 'is that I know I'd like working in the Infant Welfare Centre. And it would be good experience for me too, especially here. I know how go-ahead you are in Akersfield in these matters.'

A wide, satisfied smile spread over the Chairman's face. I've hit the target, Rose thought.

'We pride ourselves on it,' he admitted. 'We pride ourselves on it. Oh, there are those in the West Riding who are bigger than us, have the advantage of having started out sooner. We can't expect to compete with Bradford, though we've learnt from them. But we do our best, and our best is pretty good, eh gentlemen?'

He looked around for approval, which came in the shape of nods and grunts and murmurs of 'hear, hear' from the other members of the Committee. But Rose knew he spoke the truth. Akersfield's reputation in health matters was way ahead of most other towns of its size.

'But . . .' The Chairman was well into his stride now. '. . . In common with the rest of this land of ours, four years of bitter war have diverted our resources into other channels, like that of defending our shores, defeating the enemy. But that's all over now, praise God. It's nineteen twenty, and from now on things are going to get better and better. Me and my fellow Councillors will be proud to march ahead, leading Akersfield into a new and more prosperous age . . .'

His rhetoric was interrupted by the awkward man.

'I still say it's a waste of time and money, training women to be doctors! All they do is get married and have children. Money down the drain!'

But my father's money, not yours, Rose wanted to say. And he believes in me.

The Chairman, coming down to earth, took a gold hunter from his waistcoat pocket and looked at the time.

'Well, Doctor Stanton,' he said. 'As I'm sure you know, we still have one more applicant to interview. So now we'd like you to wait outside and we'll call you in again – if need be, that is. If need be.'

As Rose stood up the man on the Chairman's right gave her an encouraging smile. Leaving the room she tried to take the thought of that with her rather than the bland, non-committal, or downright discouraging expressions on the faces of the other six members of the Committee.

*   *   *

5

The waiting room offered no comfort. It was a narrow room with a door at each end, and on one wall a high window which looked as if it had remained firmly closed since the town hall was erected. The window was glazed with opaque glass so that it was impossible to see the sky, even if that had not been obliterated by the November fog. Ugly yellow wooden chairs stood against two longer walls. Brown linoleum, scarred with cigarette burns, covered the floor. The room could have been specially designed, Rose thought, to subdue the spirits of whoever had to use it.

The other five candidates had ranged themselves around the room, leaving at least two chairs between themselves and the next person so that there would be no need to speak to each other. As Rose came in from the Committee room five pairs of eyes fixed themselves on her. She couldn't help but smile.

'No decision, gentlemen! I'm to wait until called for, like the rest of you.'

A young man of about her own age returned her smile. The rest, when the last one to be interviewed had gone into the Committee room, lowered their heads again. But they can't be worried about me, Rose told herself. I'm no threat. They're simply in competition with each other. The cards are stacked against me all right. How many of *them* have been told it's a rum occupation for them to follow? And if they happen to be married it's in their favour. She took a seat two empty chairs away from the man who had smiled at her. He leaned towards her and spoke.

'Would you like to look at my newspaper while we're waiting?' he asked. 'I've read it.'

'I'd be grateful,' Rose said.

The Akersfield *Record*. She unfolded it and looked at the first page. Sugar rationing was to end next Monday. Butter was still in short supply and likely to continue expensive. She turned the pages. The weather would be unsettled and foggy and, of more immediate interest, they were advertising fur-trimmed velour cloth coats at four pounds ten shillings, which wasn't bad. If she got a job she would buy one. She had not had a new winter coat since the middle of the war.

But she couldn't think about that now. She couldn't concentrate. Her thoughts were all on the other side of that door. What would she do if she didn't get the job? Her hospital appointment finished at Christmas. All she had been offered so far was an assistant's job to a doctor in the better-class area of Akersfield, for three days a week. It was not residential and the money wouldn't be enough to keep her in food and lodgings, however meagre. Also, she didn't fancy it. Knowing the doctor – she had met him in the hospital – she was well aware that she'd be used as a dogsbody, as cheap labour, rolling pills, dispensing potions, kept well away from all the interesting cases which the doctor would claim as his own. In any case, she really wanted this job in the Welfare Centre. She was drawn to it. It was in the kind of neighbourhood – far from well-to-do – in which she wanted to work. She was sure she could make something of it.

She folded the newspaper and handed it back. 'Thank you,' she said. 'I'm afraid I can't take anything in just now. Too nervous, I expect!'

He grinned sympathetically. 'Aren't we all?'

She liked the look of him. If she didn't get the job herself then she hoped he would. She wondered about him. He looked too young, too untouched to have served in the war. The men who had been in France had the experience written in their faces, as if they saw life through different eyes. If she was not to work with women, then she would have liked to have used her skills as a doctor to help some of the men she saw around her all the time; in the streets, in the hospitals, everywhere. There were many who would need help for a long time to come. They had a sickness of the heart and mind which was often worse than the wounds they had brought back in their bodies. But it was an area of medicine which was closed to her. As a woman she could not be expected to understand men.

All heads were raised as the door to the Committee room opened and the last candidate emerged. His expression was non-committal. No-one spoke as he sat down. Twenty minutes passed, each one of them an eternity, before the door opened again and a man came out. He looked around at the candidates and consulted the piece of paper he held. Rose felt her heart thumping so strongly in her chest that she was sure the others must hear it. She gripped her handbag tightly. Please God! Please God!

The man approached the candidates in turn, speaking quietly to each one. As she sat farthest away from him she would obviously be the last to know. She watched the others as, one after the other when the man had spoken to them, they rose to their feet and left. He was with the young man next to her now and she heard his words.

'Would you please go back into the Committee room, Doctor Cartwright.'

Disappointment engulfed Rose like a wave seeking to drown her. And as they said happened to a drowning person, all the hopes, fears, trials, difficulties she had gone through to reach this point came together before her. But she managed to smile at her neighbour as he set off for the Committee room.

'Congratulations!'

'Thanks,' he said.

She started to rise to her feet but the man with the list stood in front of her.

'No, you're not to go, Doctor Stanton. Will you wait for a moment or two and then go into the Committee room when Doctor Cartwright comes out?'

Oh well, it was something to have come second, she supposed. Not that it was any use to her. She wondered, in fact, whether she should bother to wait to receive the

Committee's condolences. But she'd better do so in case she ever had to come before them again. There was the future to think about, however bleak it looked at the moment.

She didn't have to wait long. Doctor Cartwright soon emerged, still smiling, but not stopping to speak on his way out. A minute later she was back in the Committee room, sitting on the edge of the same large chair, waiting for the members to stop whispering to each other. Come on, she thought impatiently, get it over with!

'Thank you, gentlemen,' the Chairman said, bringing them to order. Then he looked at Rose.

'Well then, Doctor Stanton, we've all discussed your application very thoroughly, very carefully. It hasn't been easy. It's an important matter for us and, if I may say so, for Akersfield itself. The health of our Mothers and Children . . .'

Oh no, Rose thought! Spare me the speech! She couldn't bear it. Not now. She looked towards the man on the Chairman's right and as she did so he carefully lowered one eyelid in what amounted to a wink.

'. . . and the citizens of the future upon whom our town, nay, our country, will depend in the future as they have in the past . . .'

She stopped listening – and when the words came, the words which changed the world for her, it was as if she heard them from a great distance.

'. . . And so, Doctor Stanton – Doctor Rose Stanton as I suppose we shall have to learn to call you – we are pleased to offer you the post of Assistant Medical Officer in our Welfare Centre at a salary of three-hundred-and-seventy-five pounds per annum.'

She must pull herself together, quickly! She was going to faint, or burst into tears – and she mustn't because that was exactly what the beast of a man who didn't approve of woman doctors was waiting for her to do! She looked at him and saw it in his face.

She took a deep breath. 'Thank you, gentlemen. Thank you very much. I'm grateful. I shall try to serve you well.'

'Not only us,' the Chairman said sententiously. 'Not only us, but Akersfield.'

This time she would have been prepared to listen to him, to let him have his fling, but it seemed he had almost finished.

'See the clerk before you go,' he said. 'There are one or two things for you to sign. And your appointment starts on the first of January 1921.'

'Thank you,' Rose said again. 'Thank you very much.'

As the Councillors gathered their papers together, preparing to leave, the clerk came towards her. While she was still answering his questions the nice man on the Chairman's right passed on his way out.

'Congratulations, Doctor Rose,' he said, and was gone. She hoped that wasn't the last she would see of him. She felt he'd been especially kind to her, that all along he'd been on her side.

The man standing by the far door of the waiting room watched Rose as she left the Committee room. He saw a small, slender woman, whom he supposed must be in her mid-twenties though she looked younger. She had a country complexion: clear, flawless skin tinged with pink, and a deeper flush of pink on her cheeks. The severity of her straight-brimmed felt hat fought – and lost – against the deep auburn hair which escaped in tendrils from under it: against the short, tilted nose, the gently-curving mouth which looked as though it had just finished smiling and might start again any minute. The tailored lines of her coat and skirt, which ended decorously a few inches above neat ankles, were softened by the red scarf she wore at her neck. The fact that its colour shrieked against the auburn of her hair only added to the vibrancy which was exuded by her whole being.

She had not seen him as she crossed the room, her head held high, her face alight with happiness, but when he stepped in front of her, barring her way, she raised wide-set, slightly-puzzled green eyes to his. But the puzzlement could not hide the joy in her eyes.

Rose saw a man so tall that she had to tilt her head back to look at him. He must be more than six feet. He raised a fawn trilby, revealing crisp, fair hair. He had a thin, pale face and blue eyes which, meeting hers, were at one and the same time, humorous and serious. There was also, if she was not mistaken, a hint of admiration in them.

'I'm sorry,' she apologized. 'I wasn't looking where I was going.'

She had a pleasant voice too, he thought; clear and soft; a north country voice with its short vowels, but not from the West Riding.

'Don't apologize,' he said. 'I can see you have other things on your mind. Pleasant things, too, if I'm not mistaken.'

'Does it show so much? But you're quite right as it happens. It's turned out to be a special day for me.'

'I know,' he said. 'That's what I want to talk to you about.'

'You know? How can you? You weren't on the Committee were you?' He couldn't have been. She had studied the face of every single member. She would not have forgotten him.

'Were you one of the candidates?' she asked. 'If so . . .'

He took a card from his pocket and handed it to her. 'As it says there, Alex Bairstow, Akersfield *Record*. I'd be grateful for a few minutes of your time, Doctor Stanton.'

She looked genuinely puzzled now.

'How do you know?'

'I knew the interviews were taking place,' he said. 'I also knew there was a woman on the short list. It's my job to know things like that. Then I met Councillor Worthing, the Deputy Chairman, as he was leaving, and he gave me the news. He seemed very pleased about it. Allow me to congratulate you, Doctor Stanton.'

Councillor Worthing? So he must be the man on the Chairman's right, the one she had known all along was on her side.

'I see,' she said. 'So you've come to cover me – like Births, Marriages and Deaths?'

He smiled. He had a particularly nice smile. It widened his already generous mouth and brightened his eyes.

'Not quite! I used to do that when I was a cub reporter, before the war. At this time of the year I attended funerals most days of the week. Since I returned I've been promoted. No more Hatches, Matches and Despatches, not even chapel bunfights. I go after stories. You know the kind of thing? Local boy makes good, or preferably, for our readers, goes to the bad! The human element, especially if it's controversial.'

There was a sharp edge to his voice, as if he didn't quite take himself seriously. And yet he does, Rose thought. I'm sure he does.

'And I'm controversial?' she queried.

'I'm sure you know you are. But you were at the interview, I wasn't. I'd be delighted to hear that it was one hundred per cent in your favour but I'm not sure that I'd believe you.'

The clerk came and interrupted them.

'I'm sorry, Doctor Stanton, Mr Bairstow. I have to lock up these rooms now.'

'Right, Tom, we're moving,' Alex Bairstow said.

Rose walked with him down the wide staircase into the lobby of the town hall.

'We can't break off the conversation at this point,' Alex Bairstow said. 'And I'm sure you don't want to continue it in the town hall entrance. Will you let me buy you a cup of tea? To celebrate. There's a café quite close by.'

'Honestly,' Rose said, laughing, 'there's not much to know about me. I'd be taking your tea under false pretences.'

'I'll be the judge of that,' he said. 'Let's go.'

Outside the town hall's impressively pillared entrance he tucked his hand under her elbow and guided her across Market Street and through a labyrinth of narrow back streets to a small basement cafe, halfway up a steep hill. He walked with long, easy strides and Rose had difficulty in keeping up with him.

'I always have toasted currant teacake with my cup of tea,' he said when they were seated. 'Would you like one?'

'I'm really not sure what I'm doing here,' Rose said. 'But since I *am* here – yes please. I miss my mother's teacakes.'

'But these are very good,' she admitted a few moments later.

'You were trying to tell me you weren't controversial,' Alex Bairstow said. 'Well maybe *you* aren't – I haven't decided about that – but you must know your appointment is. Five men short-listed and they pick a woman! The first woman doctor we've had in the town, let alone working for the Council. So tell me, how did the interview go?'

'I don't propose to tell you that,' Rose said sharply. 'The interview was confidential, as you must very well know.'

'All right I'll tell you,' he said. 'I've sat in on enough Council meetings to know. Councillor Worthing would be for you. He's a fair-minded, enlightened sort of chap, and what's more he likes women, especially pretty ones. Councillor Thwaites – he's the Chairman – would sound off about the glories of Akersfield and his part in its making. Councillor Patterson wouldn't hear half that went on and Councillor Rogers would be against you. I daresay he told you that a woman's place is in the home?'

'More or less,' Rose admitted. 'It's what most men say. I'm used to it. I daresay it's what you tell your wife.'

'I haven't got a wife,' he said. 'I suppose I haven't really got a home. I live in digs. And I know you're not married or you'd never have got as far as the interview.'

'The Chairman said, "Are you courting?"' Rose giggled at the memory.

'And are you?'

'Not really.'

'Ah! Then there's someone?'

'Yes and no,' she said thoughtfully. 'And please don't write that down and use it.'

'I won't,' he assured her. 'It isn't part of my plan to make things more difficult for you. Besides, you don't sound very sure, and I like to get my facts right. When do you start the job?'

'In the New Year.'

'And what are you going to do between now and then?'

'Well,' Rose said, 'I shall be working in hospital up to Christmas. Also I'll have to look for lodgings. You can put that in your paragraph if you like. Someone might make me an offer. I'll probably go home for Christmas. Home is Faverwell. My parents keep a pub there and they can always do with extra help at Christmas. Anyway, you've no idea how beautiful the Dales can be at Christmas.'

'Oh yes I have,' he contradicted. 'Before we went to France my Company was stationed in Swaledale. I'd have been glad to have stayed there.'

'Did you have a bad war?'

'Are there any good ones, then? But mine was better than some. As you see, I'm here, and all in one piece. And I've got a job, which is more than can be said for some. Was your friend about whom you're not sure in the Army?'

'No,' Rose answered. 'He's a vet. The only one for miles around so he was needed on the farms. But he looked after army horses sometimes, when they were stationed nearby.'

'I see. Well, Doctor Stanton – by the way, has anyone told you that your boss's name is Stanton?'

'Yes,' she said. 'I've settled for Doctor Rose.'

'Doctor Rose. Nice. Can I quote that? The human touch that endears itself to our readers.' His voice was mocking. 'Now if I could also say that you're fond of animals that would go down really well.'

Rose flushed.

'It's your idea to write something about me, not mine. It makes no difference to me.'

'Ah but it could, you know. Never underestimate the power of the press, Doctor Rose, either for you or against. But don't worry, the editor won't give this item undue importance. It's not front page stuff.'

'I'm sorry,' Rose said. 'But if I decide to rob a bank or murder Councillor Rogers, I'll be sure to let you know.'

She had thought at first that she quite liked Mr Bairstow. Now she was not so sure. He was too cocky by half, too full of his own importance. But what did he matter anyway? She'd got the job. That was all that mattered. Everything would be good from now on.

Alex Bairstow was grinning at her.

'Thanks,' he said. 'I'd appreciate that.'

2

When the train drew into Grassington station Rose's brother-in-law, Christopher, was there to meet her. As she stepped down from the carriage he took her case from her.

'Whatever have you got in it?' he asked. 'It feels heavy enough for gold brick. How long are you here for?'

'Would it were gold bricks,' Rose replied. 'Warm clothes and Christmas presents mostly. And I'm here until almost the end of December. How are you?'

To her eyes Christopher always looked the same. No different now, at thirty, from ten years ago when he had married her sister. But since they had all known each other since they were children he had never changed in her eyes and she supposed he never would. He was tall, broad-shouldered, with the ruddy complexion of someone who had spent most of his life out of doors. His features were well put together but unremarkable.

'Can't complain,' he replied. 'And you? We were pleased to hear about the job.'

'Isn't it wonderful,' Rose said. 'I was so lucky.'

She followed him out of the station to where his Morris car stood by the kerb.

'It's good of you to meet me,' she said. 'I wasn't at all sure there'd be a bus and I didn't fancy walking all those miles. I've done it often enough, goodness knows; but Christmas Eve isn't the time.'

It was raining as they left the station; a thin, mean sleetish rain. Outside the village Christopher turned the car down the hill towards the river, then north on to the narrow road which led to Faverwell, seven miles up the dale. In an hour or so it would be dark, but as yet there was still some light in the cold, grey sky. It was a sky which promised snow to come. And true to its promise, after two miles or so of the twisting road, which followed closely the bends and curves of the river, the rain turned to snow, falling in soft, thick flakes.

Rose, not speaking – one of the nice things about Christopher was that you could enjoy a comfortable silence with him – watched it settle on the high green fells which rose on each side of them. It began to mark out the tops of the grey limestone walls, walls which climbed to the summits, now going straight, now diverting to form fields of strange geometrical shapes. When, in Leeds or Akersfield, Rose thought of home, it was the whitish-grey walls running up the hillsides which she pictured.

'I'd hoped it was going to be a white Christmas,' she said. 'It seems so right.'

'Shows you're not a farmer,' Christopher said.

'I know. Still I *am* a daleswoman, so I should know better. But it does look so very beautiful.'

'Well we've got all the sheep down from the tops, so I'm not too worried,' Christopher said. 'At least there's no wind to speak of, so it won't drift.'

'How's the farm been this year?' Rose enquired.

'Not too good. Sheep are fetching a poor price. I wish I knew some other way of making a living but farming's in my blood. The Bishops have been at Fellside as long as the Stantons have kept the Ewe Lamb. It takes someone like you to break away.'

'But I'm not breaking away,' Rose protested. 'It's simply that I can't do my job here. But however far away I go I shall always come back. I'm sure of that.'

'Anyway it's good to have you back for Christmas,' Christopher said. 'Emily will enjoy it, not to mention your Ma and Pa. She gets a bit down, Emily does. And when she's down she gets to thinking about Robert. Not that I don't think about him as well, you understand; but having the farm to think about helps me.'

Robert was their only son. He had died two years ago, aged five, from diphtheria; by coincidence at a time when Rose was doing her stint in the fever hospital, so that every small diphtheria patient she saw there reminded her sharply of her nephew. Christopher and Emily had two other children, Helen, who was nine years old and four-year-old Kitty; but Rose suspected that Robert had always been the most deeply loved.

'I understand,' Rose said. 'Or at least I try to. But some members of the Health Committee, when I had my interview, seemed to think it was impossible to understand something if you hadn't experienced it.'

'I daresay someone like you can understand a lot,' Christopher said thoughtfully. 'And you can sympathize. But you can't know what it feels like unless you've gone through it.'

'Do you think that applies to something like marriage, or giving birth?' Rose asked.

'I think so,' Christopher said.

They could see Faverwell now. The winter afternoon was closing in and the lights were showing in the cottages and on the farms.

'I'll drop you at the Ewe Lamb,' Christopher said. 'I'll not come in. I've got jobs to do, and being Christmas Eve Emily'll want to get the children off to bed in good time.'

'When shall we see you?' Rose asked.

'Tomorrow for dinner. After the Ewe's closed. Your Ma and Pa aren't opening up in the evening.'

'I know,' Rose said. 'It's about the only evening they have off together in the year. Well I'll see what help Mother needs, and if there's time tell Emily I'll walk over in the morning.'

When Christopher drove away, it being not yet opening time and the front door of the Ewe Lamb being locked, Rose went around to the back. Before she could raise a hand to the door knob her father was there, his eyes bright with welcome, his thin face creased in a smile.

'My word, lass, it's good to see thee! Tha's a sight for sore eyes, an' no mistake!'

It was a measure of his excitement that he spoke in the dialect. It was not his usual way, though he could speak it with the best of them, and did so when the occasion called for it, and always when he was moved or excited.

'It's good to see you, Father,' Rose said.

They embraced warmly. He was alight with happiness, Rose thought, and marvelled that once again her home-coming could do this to him.

'Where's Mother?' she asked.

'She's around at the church, giving a hand with the decorations. You'd think she had enough to do without that, wouldn't you? She's been up since five this morning. She'd have been here, only we didn't expect you quite so soon.'

'It was kind of Christopher to meet me,' Rose said.

The kitchen door opened and her mother, bringing a flurry of snow with her, entered.

'Coming down fast now,' she said. 'Somebody'll have to clear that path up to the church or it'll be real slippy for early service.'

It was her mother's way, Rose knew, not to show outward emotion. She was quite unlike her husband in that. She took off her gloves, scarf, coat and hat, placed the gloves in the dresser drawer, put the pins from her hat in a small vase on the mantelpiece, hung her coat behind the door and put her hat on the dresser before she turned to speak directly to Rose.

'Well then, Our Rose?'

'Well then, Mother. How are you?' Rose leaned forward to kiss her mother but Clara Stanton, as if by accident, turned away, so that the kiss landed only lightly on the edge of her cheek. She seemed unable to show affection, though Rose knew that it was in her. As a child she had longed to have a mother who would kiss and cuddle her, like the mothers of her friends. She had determined at an early age that when she grew up and had children she would hug and kiss them a lot. They would never have to wonder about her love for them.

'Have you put the kettle on, then, George?' Mrs Stanton asked. 'I daresay we could all do with a cup of tea.'

'Meanwhile,' Rose said, 'I'll take my case upstairs and unpack. After that I'm ready to give a hand with anything you want me to do.'

'No call for you to start working. You haven't come back to work,' Mrs Stanton said. She was getting out cups and saucers. The best china, Rose noted; delicately thin, gilt-handled, decorated with pink roses. She should have felt complimented but she was not. The sight of the flowery china on the embroidered linen cloth saddened her.

'I've come because it's my home. I wanted to come. I wanted to be with you and Father and the rest of the family.'

She put out a hand and touched the back of her mother's hand as she arranged the cups. 'I'm not a visitor, Mother. Please don't treat me like one. The kitchen cups are good enough for me.'

'Well . . .' Mrs Stanton hesitated. 'Well you *are* a doctor!'

'I'm your daughter, same as I always was. But all right, just this once to celebrate we're together. After that don't you dare!'

She went upstairs to unpack. She had slept in this room, with its small window overlooking the beck which ran down to join the river, ever since she could remember, sharing it with Emily until her sister left home to marry. Every night of her childhood she had fallen asleep to the sound of rushing water, for even in the hottest summer the beck never ran dry. When she had first gone to Medical School she had returned home every weekend that she could find the return fare from Leeds, but a few months later she had become so involved in this and that society in the university, in weekends spent walking or cycling with new friends, or in rather pleasurable and not too strenuous efforts to raise comforts for the troops, that she had come back less and less often. If she was now regarded as a visitor she supposed it was partly her own fault.

When she went downstairs again her mother was pouring the tea and there was buttered currant teacake on the table.

'I had a fair currant teacake in Akersfield,' she said. 'Not as good as yours, though.'

She had seen Alex Bairstow a couple of times since that first occasion. Once, meeting him in the street by chance, he had taken her to the same cafe; once he had taken her to the cinema to see 'Beyond the dreams of Avarice'.

'You said in your letter you were pleased with your new lodgings,' her father said.

'I think I'm going to be. Anyway, they're cheap, which is important.'

'And clean too, I hope?' her mother said sharply.

'They looked fine to me. Of course I don't start living there until after Christmas.'

'How did you come by them?' her father wanted to know.

'Through a friend. Well, an acquaintance, really. His name is Alex Bairstow. He's a reporter on the Akersfield *Record.* He has digs in the same house.'

In the act of refilling her husband's cup Clara Stanton paused, her body tensing.

'You'll be living in *the same house?*'

Rose laughed. 'Really, Mother, don't look so shocked! It's all right. Wherever I'd gone into digs there might have been young men. Alex is quite respectable, I assure you.

If it's any comfort to you we're not on the same floor.'

Mrs Stanton finished pouring her husband's tea, spooned in more sugar, added water to the teapot, fetched hot mince pies from the oven.

'Gerald's coming over in the morning, barring emergencies.'

She was trying to sound casual, but Rose was not deceived. Her mother never lost hope that her daughter would make a go of it with Gerald. To be a vet's wife would be a good position and, more important, it would keep Rose within the world Clara Stanton knew and understood; the country world of farms and animals, of villages and small market towns. Just once, when Rose had qualified, Clara had visited Leeds. She hadn't liked it at all, had been glad to get home to Faverwell and didn't care if she never saw a city again.

'On Christmas Day?' Rose queried.

'He reckoned it might be his quietest time, though you never can tell with a veterinary.'

'Well it won't be *our* quietest time in the Ewe Lamb,' Rose said. 'And before you say another word, you're not doing me out of helping in the bar for a bit. You know I enjoy that. I also told Christopher I might go over there for an hour. And then there's the Christmas dinner. What about that?'

'I can manage,' her mother said firmly. 'Gerald will want to have a bit of time with you, coming over from Wensleydale. It's only natural.'

George Stanton looked at his watch and stood up. It was time to open the bar and it would be a busy night in spite of the snow. Passing his wife, he pressed his hand on her shoulder.

'Leave it be, Clara! Leave it be!'

'I'll be with you in a minute or two,' Rose called after him. 'Give you a hand.'

She turned to her mother.

'It's no use, Mother. I'm not going to marry Gerald. I've made up my mind.'

'But he's always been that fond of you,' her mother protested.

'I know. And I'm fond of him. But I don't have plans for marrying anyone. I've got a job to do and I'm looking forward to it. Can't you understand that?'

'If you *had* to be a doctor,' Mrs Stanton said, 'then I don't see why it couldn't be in the dales. There's sick folk here as well as in the towns.'

'But not so many. Anyway there's no place here for a doctor. Doctor Harper is good for a long time yet.'

'He might take you as an assistant,' her mother said.

Rose sighed. 'Mother, of course he wouldn't. He couldn't afford to pay me enough. Anyway, no-one in the dales would take me seriously as a doctor. I'd always be Clara Stanton's little lass. And what I'm interested in right now is working with mothers and babies.'

'Plenty to do if you had your own babies,' Mrs Stanton said sharply. 'You ask our Emily!'

It was clear to Rose that her mother wouldn't mind her throwing up her entire training, for which she and her husband had made so many sacrifices, if only her daughter would marry Gerald – or someone like him – and settle down near to hand and raise a family. She left the kitchen and joined her father in the bar.

'Don't you worry about your mother,' George Stanton said. 'Deep down she's as pleased as Punch, as proud as Lucifer of you. It's just that it's a new pattern and she can't get used to it. You see, lass, you're the first woman in the family ever to work away from home.'

'What about Great-grandmother, Mother's own ancestor?' Rose reminded him. 'She went off to America. Perhaps I've got it from her, though I've never thought of going so far.'

Her great-grandmother had lived further up the dale, leaving as a poor emigrant in the middle of the last century. Many years later her daughter, Aurora, had returned, married an Englishman, and given birth to Clara.

'That was a long time ago,' George Stanton said. 'Anyway it's time to open up.'

On Christmas Day the fells were magnificently clothed in pristine white and on the road through the dale there were three inches of crisp, hard snow underfoot. But it had stopped snowing and the sky was clear and blue.

Gerald arrived at half-past ten. George Stanton, tidying up in the bar, saw his Rover draw up in front of the inn and unlocked the door to him.

'Merry Christmas, Mr Stanton,' Gerald said.

'Merry Christmas. What was the road like coming over?'

'Not too bad.'

'The womenfolk are in the kitchen. Go through. I have to finish in here.'

Mrs Stanton gave him the welcoming smile she reserved for a few, favoured people.

'Our Rose will give you a cup of tea,' she said. 'And perhaps something in it – a drop of rum – against the cold. If you'll excuse me I have a few things in the bar to attend to.'

Rose grinned at Gerald as her mother left them. If she and Gerald had not been such good friends her mother's heavy-handed tact would have been embarrassing. As it was they were amused by it.

'All the same,' Gerald said, taking off his overcoat, sitting beside Rose on the horsehair-covered sofa, 'all the same I'm glad of a minute or two alone with you. If this Christmas follows the usual pattern there won't be many of them.'

Rose's first thought when Gerald had entered the kitchen was how attractive he looked, more so, even, than she had remembered. His face was tanned, his hazel eyes bright and kind. Now, guessing what he was going to say as he sat down beside her, she thought what a pity it was that she didn't love him – or didn't love him enough, for she had always been fond of him. If things had

24

been different she could have done worse than to marry Gerald. But things were not different.

'Gerald,' she said quietly, 'please don't say what I think you're going to say.'

'Is it so obvious?'

'I'm right, aren't I?'

He nodded.

'It's no use, Gerald,' Rose said. 'It's not just that I won't marry *you*. I don't want to marry anyone.'

'No-one? Ever?'

Rose hesitated. 'Ever is a long time. I can't say that. But it isn't part of my plans. Do you realize, for instance, that if I were to marry I'd lose my job? Have you heard about my new job?'

'I have. Congratulations. And I realize you'd lose that particular job. But that needn't be the end of your career. You could put up your plate in Wensleydale. Married to me, you wouldn't starve while you waited for patients.'

'Oh Gerald, you know you have a perfectly good doctor there already. Who would come to me? But even if they would, it's not what I want. When I was in Medical School we talked a lot about conditions in towns, about people who didn't have much, lived in terrible houses, were often sick. It's places like that where I want to practise. Places where I'm really needed. Does that make me sound self-righteous?'

'No,' he said. 'I know you too well for that. So I suppose until you get this out of your system . . .'

She felt her anger flare, clenched her fists to control her temper.

'It's not something I intend to get out of my system. Why can't any of you understand that? I'm sick of being treated as if I were simply playing at being a doctor, as if it's all a childish game!'

He had risen now and was standing in front of her. Before she could say more he had taken her in his arms. She struggled to free herself but he was too strong for her. He was kissing her, his lips hard, sweet and strong on hers. She could not escape, and for a few seconds she did not want to. He had never kissed her like this before. This was not the kind, patient Gerald she was used to.

He let her go.

'Perhaps that'll convince you I'm not playing either,' he said sharply. 'You don't give either of us a chance. If you let yourself go you might find you could love me. I wouldn't keep you from the job you've taken,' he said more quietly. 'I understand about that and I'm willing to wait a year or two – but not forever, Rose.'

'I'm sorry,' Rose said. 'I don't love you like that. Not enough to give up what I'm doing, even in a year or two's time. Selfish of me, I daresay. And I'm sorry. But there it is, and you must believe me.'

'You've made it quite plain,' Gerald said. 'If you'll excuse me, I won't stay. Anyway, I've got some visits to make. Animals don't stop being sick because it's Christmas Day. You'll find it's the same with people.'

'I already have,' Rose said. 'I spent last Christmas Day delivering awkward twins. I was on midwifery duty and I'd been out on a case all night. I know what it's about.'

'I'll let myself out the back way,' Gerald said. 'Make my excuses to your parents.' Then he smiled. He never showed himself out of humour for long. 'Your mother's going to be awfully disappointed, you realize?'

'In me, not in you,' Rose said.

How quickly men recover, or seem to, she thought. She was still shaking inside, still surprised by his kiss. He had aroused feelings in her, not for himself but for his sex, which she had thought she had well under control, feelings which she must learn to deal with. The world, certainly the world of Akersfield, would have to change a great deal before she could order her life as she wanted it; before she could marry, have children, and keep her job. It was an impossible combination.

She did not, in the end, walk over to Emily's house. There was no time. They were extra busy in the bar and she was kept hard at it, serving drinks, washing glasses, and in between chatting to old friends and acquaintances. It was four o-clock before her father could lock the door on the last customer and they could make final preparations for the Christmas dinner. Emily, who had arrived an hour earlier with Christopher and the two little girls, helped Rose to lay the big walnut table in the dining room, a room only used for meals on ceremonial occasions.

'You look tired, Emily,' Rose said. 'Are you all right? It must be hard going with the work on the farm and two lively children to look after.'

'I can assure you it is,' Emily retorted. 'There never seems to be a minute to spare. You'll find that out for yourself if ever you marry and have a family!'

Rose was surprised by the edge in her sister's voice. Emily, always the more gentle, always – in her fair-haired, rosy-cheeked way, the prettier – had been the placid one, taking life as it came, making none of the demands on it her younger sister made. All she had ever wanted was to be married to Christopher, to have his children. But now, Rose thought, looking at her more closely, she had a drawn, discontented look. Of course she had never been quite the same since her small son's death. Who could expect it? But why is she so sharp with me? Rose wondered.

'But you're such a good wife and mother,' Rose said. 'Everyone admires you for it. You wouldn't have wanted anything else, would you?'

'As well I didn't,' Emily cried. 'There wouldn't have been enough for two in the family to be doctors. It took Father all his time for you.'

Rose felt suddenly sick to the stomach, not only at her sister's words but at the venom with which she expressed them. She was shocked by the jealousy she saw in the blue eyes which met hers. How long had Emily been nursing this grudge against her? She had never before suspected such a thing.

'You were the first,' she said quietly. 'You're the elder. If you'd said you wanted to be a doctor, Father would have found the money for you instead of for me. You never said anything that I remember.'

'Even if I didn't want to be a doctor, I might have wanted to go to university,' Emily said stubbornly. 'I don't remember that I was asked. And if I didn't say anything it was because I knew how hard it would be for Father. You never thought of that did you? All that mattered to you, all that has ever mattered to you, was your ambition! Anyway, I never came first with Father.'

'But Emily that's not true!' Rose protested. 'He treated us equally well. And I was well aware what he was doing for me, the sacrifices he was making. I told him I'd pay him back when I could. And I shall – every penny. You'll see.'

She was angry, but underneath her anger a cold little thought clawed at her mind. Was what Emily said true? Had her ambition made her selfish, blind to anyone else's needs, taking everything she could get?

Emily sighed. 'I'm sorry Rose. I didn't mean it. I seem to flare up for nothing these days.'

But you did mean it, Rose thought. Every word. How long have you felt like this about me?

'The farm isn't doing too well,' Emily went on. 'Christopher works hard, far too hard, but in spite of that things don't get any better. We need more capital investment. I worry about him – about all of us. I worry all the time about the children's health. I never used to, but since Robert . . . well, things happen so quickly, don't they?'

Rose put out a hand and touched her sister.

'I do understand,' she said gently. 'And I'm sorry. Perhaps the farm will pick up this year.'

'I hope so,' Emily said.

'As for the children,' Rose said. 'I assure you I never saw two healthier looking girls. They're lovely!'

Emily's face brightened.

28

'They are, aren't they? And would you believe it, Helen, at nine years old, wants to be a doctor like her Aunt Rose!'

'Well I must have a word with her,' Rose said. 'And Kitty? What about Kitty?'

'Kitty? Oh she's like I was. Content to play with her dolls.'

'I think this table looks quite pretty now, don't you?' Rose said, changing the subject. 'Shall we see if we can give Ma a hand with the goose?'

Matters seemed all right again between them, but in Rose's heart there was a small, persistent doubt. She had seen feelings in her sister which she had not realized existed there. She was by no means sure that they had been laid to rest or that things would ever be quite the same again. She hoped she was wrong, and in the happy meal which followed, the exchanging of presents, the carol singing, the childish games they all played until the children were exhausted and had to be put to bed in the spare room, she managed to persuade herself that she was.

On the twenty-seventh of December, a day earlier than she had intended, she left Faverwell. Her mother bade her a brusque farewell while pressing into her hands a parcel of home-made teacakes, spice cake, and a Wensleydale cheese. Her father went with her on the bus to Grassington station – Christopher had an emergency on the farm and could not take her in the car. He embraced her before she climbed into the carriage and as the train moved out of the station she watched him standing there, a slight, thin figure, his coat collar turned up, his rounded shoulders hunched against the wind. She loved him so much. One day she would make up to him for all he had done for her.

Apart from her father, she thought, it had not been the happiest of Christmases. She had not fitted in as she once did. As the train drew away, steaming towards Akersfield, she realized that she was not entirely sorry to be leaving. She hoped that Akersfield would be more welcoming.

29

3

On the doorstep of number fifteen Victoria Street Rose put down her suitcase and reached up to the bell, but before she could press it the door opened and Mrs Crabtree stood there, smiling a welcome.

'No need to ring, love! Number fifteen is Open House – except of course after ten-thirty in the evening when I like to lock the door because you never know who's about do you? Not since the war. Have you had a nice Christmas then? I think it's turning colder.'

Mrs Crabtree did not pause for breath. It was as if her speaking and breathing arrangements worked on separate circuits.

'Very nice, thank you,' Rose said. 'And yes, it is turning colder.'

The entrance hall of number fifteen was like many others Rose had seen. A door on the right of the narrow passage led to a small, bay-windowed sitting room where Mrs Crabtree liked to think (though she was wrong) that her boarders gathered for civilized conversation after meals. A door further along the same side led to the dining room where breakfast was served between eight and nine and a sort of high tea – which Mrs Crabtree referred to as supper because it sounded better class – at six-thirty every evening except Sunday, when there was a cooked dinner in the middle of the day. At the far end of the passage a door, kept closed, led to Mrs Crabtree's own quarters.

The stairs rose steeply on the left, the red-and-blue Axminster carpet – the pride of Mrs Crabtree's heart – held in place by stair rods of highly-polished brass. Rose's only desire was to mount those stairs to her own room on the second floor, but Mrs Crabtree stood in her way.

'Mr Bairstow's gone to Manchester to visit a friend,' Mrs Crabtree informed her. 'He left a note for you. I'll bring it up presently. Would you like a nice cup of cocoa? I'm afraid you've missed supper.'

'Don't bother, Mrs Crabtree,' Rose said. 'I'll take the note now if you'll give it to me. Save you climbing the stairs.'

'No trouble, love. I'm used to stairs. I'll fetch the note and I'll bring you a cup of something at the same time. You look perished.'

That means she's going to stand in my room chatting, Rose thought. It had taken no more than the first meeting with Mrs Crabtree, when she'd called to inspect the room, to discover that her landlady liked to talk. Rose didn't feel like it now. She was tired, and a bit depressed. She wanted to make herself a cup of tea – there were gas rings in the bedrooms and the boarders were allowed to boil a kettle, even to make toast in front of the gas fire, though that was the extent of permissible cooking and woe betide any from whose room the smell of soup wafted down the stairs.

Her room looked smaller than she remembered it, more crowded but still pleasant. The chintz curtains at the window matched the cover of the one armchair. A well-polished chest of drawers, with a mirror on top, was reflected in the shining dark-green linoleum which covered the floor and was itself obscured in the middle of the room by a floral-patterned carpet square. Against the far wall the narrow bed was spread with a honeycomb quilt of dazzling whiteness and the small table by the window boasted a hand-crocheted cloth. Yes, her mother would have found it clean all right.

Rose crossed to the window, but before drawing the curtains she stood there for a moment, watching the lights of Akersfield. Starting from a denser patch of light in what must be the centre of the town, they were strung out like pale jewels – not bright enough for diamonds, more like milky opals – until somewhere on the outskirts they faded into the darkness. There was a street lamp right outside her window, its gas light flickering, yet managing to pierce the thin December mist which hovered and swirled around it. She hoped its light would not keep her awake. The winter nights were long and it would be morning before the lamplighter came to put it out.

She looked down the length of Victoria Street; a long, respectable road of houses built in the eighteen-seventies. It was about a hilly mile from the centre of the town, near enough for her to walk to the Clinic every day, just far enough out to miss the once-decent, now near-decrepit and multi-occupied houses closer to the town. There were no mills on the east side of the town, but the rest of Akersfield had mills in plenty. Here and there, where there was enough light from the gas-lit streets, she could see the outlines of the tall chimneys against the sky, not emitting smoke now, for the boiler fires were damped down for the night.

When she had closed the curtains she took two pennies from her purse, put them in the meter, and lit both panels of the gas fire. The room needed warming up. Then she hurried to the door as Mrs Crabtree's knock came, but the landlady had a foot in the door before Rose could stop her.

'I brought you tea, not cocoa. There was some in the pot and it's still quite hot.' She advanced and placed the cup and saucer on the table.

'A cosy little room I always think this is,' she re-marked, looking around. 'I see you've got your own bits and pieces out.' She nodded in the direction of the photographs on the top of the chest and the small Corot print which Rose had hung by the side of the fireplace. 'Makes it feel more like home, I daresay. I like my ladies and gentlemen to feel at home.'

Anything less like the Ewe Lamb, with its spacious living kitchen, her bedroom overlooking the beck, Rose could hardly imagine. But Mrs Crabtree meant well.

Anyway since she had not felt wholly comfortable at the Ewe Lamb on this last visit, it would be sensible to get used to this.

'I'm sure I'll be very comfortable, Mrs Crabtree,' she said politely.

'That is my aim,' Mrs Crabtree said. 'Home comforts. I made that my motto when I started this business. Of course I'd never kept a boarding house before and I wouldn't now if Mr Crabtree hadn't been taken so sudden. Appendicitis, they said – which is not what they called it before the late King Edward had it. Stoppage of the bowels it was then, and a fancy name didn't cure my husband . . .'

'Thank you for the tea,' Rose interrupted. 'Did you say there was a note for me?'

'Yes. Of course Mr Crabtree was well insured. Insurance and sanitation were the two things he was most careful about. Ah yes, the note!'

She handed it to Rose and waited for her to open it. When Rose put it on the table without any sign of doing so she said, 'Well I'd best leave you in peace. It's been nice having a little chat, getting to know you. Everybody else is out, by the way.'

At eight o-clock on a Wednesday evening they would be. It was half-day closing in Akersfield; an evening for visiting friends, or going to the pictures or the pub. Rose felt suddenly lonely. At Medical School she had had lots of friends and in the hospital there had always been someone to talk to.

When Mrs Crabtree had left she opened the note. 'Taking you to a New Year's Eve party on Friday. Will give you a knock 9 p.m. Be ready. A.B.' Nothing else. No polite 'would you like to go' or 'if you're not already engaged'. It would serve him right if she refused. But she wouldn't. Invitations for New Year's Eve weren't likely to come pouring in. Beside, she liked parties and she quite liked Alex Bairstow.

She cut herself a slice of spice cake and a wedge of

cheese, unpacked a book, and settled down in front of the gently-hissing fire.

At nine o-clock on New Year's Eve Rose was ready, waiting to be called for. She had not seen Alex in the meantime. Mrs Crabtree said he had not yet returned from Manchester.

'Well, I'm sure he will,' Rose said. 'He's taking me to a party.'

Mrs Crabtree beamed. 'Just what you need, if you don't mind me saying so. You've been looking a bit peaked. You need to get out more.'

Rose had gone out the morning after her arrival back, to buy material to make herself something new to wear to the party. She had nothing in her wardrobe which would do. After much deliberation she had chosen a deep green crepe material, and a paper pattern of a dress with a low round neck, short sleeves, 'falls' from the waist down each side of the skirt, and the Turkish hemline, very much in favour at the moment. It had all cost more than she could afford and she would have to pull in her horns until she received her first month's salary. Thursday afternoon and all day Friday had been spent in a frenzy of cutting and stitching. It had taken hours to stitch on the sequins around the neckline and at the hem of the dress.

Now, surveying her upper parts in the inadequate mirror – she had to stand on a chair to see, separately, her lower half – it seemed worth it. The deep green colour, more subtle than emerald, suited her. She had pulled her hair back from her face into a soft chignon at the back of her neck. Tomorrow, for work, she would plait it and twist it into two businesslike 'earphones'. But what she really desired was the short, swinging 'bob' which was now so fashionable. As soon as ever she could afford it she intended to have her hair cut off. Long hair had really gone out with the war.

By the small clock on her mantelpiece it was already ten past nine and there was neither sight nor sound of

Alex. It was too bad of him. She had been promised a party and had gone to a lot of expense and trouble. She picked up a newspaper to scan while she waited.

'Good riddance to 1920,' she read. 'It has reduced our money, stolen our trade, given us unemployment. We were promised a new world, homes fit for heroes. But where are they?'

Perhaps she should knock on Alex's door, if she could do so without Mrs Crabtree hearing her. Then while she was making up her mind she heard him running up the stairs. He beat a sharp tattoo on her door.

'Sorry to be late,' he said breezily. 'Blame the train. We had to stop to take on water. Anyway, a quick wash and brush up and I'm yours. Say in about fifteen minutes.'

He was gone before she could reply but in fifteen minutes he was back again, standing in the doorway of her room. He wore a dark suit with a stiff white collar and shirt. His hair was sleeked back with a liberal application of brilliantine. She had never seen him look so respectable.

His gaze swept her from the top of her red head to the Louis heels and pointed toes of her black kid shoes.

'Doctor Rose, you look lovely,' he said. 'I've never seen you dressed for a party before. You come up a treat. I doubt if your patients would know you!'

'Thank you for the double-edged compliment,' Rose said. 'And speaking of patients, I start work tomorrow. I mustn't stay out too late or I'll be good for nothing.'

'I'll bear it in mind,' he promised. 'But we can't leave until we've seen the New Year in.'

'How do we get back into the house?' Rose asked. 'I gather the drawbridge is raised at ten-thirty every night.'

'So it is. But Yours Truly has wheedled a key out of our landlady.'

'Good,' Rose said. 'All the same, I wouldn't put it past her to be waiting up for us when we get back, no matter what the time.'

'Mrs C leads a vicarious life,' Alex said. 'Our parties

are her parties, our friendships are her concern and, you'll find out if you ever need to, our troubles are her troubles. Don't underestimate Mrs C.'

The party venue, a double-fronted house in Picton Square, was within walking distance of Victoria Street, in a road which seemed to have retained its exclusivity in spite of its proximity to the town. It seemed, as they approached the house, that the party must be taking place in every room, since from every window light showed behind the drawn curtains.

'Who do you know who lives here?' Rose asked.

'A solicitor. Name of Peter Benford. You'll like him.'

She did, too, from the first moment of introduction. He was smallish, fiftyish, with blue eyes behind gold-rimmed spectacles and a handshake so strong that it made her wince.

'Glad you could come,' he said. 'Alex has told me a lot about you. What will you have to drink? There's sherry – or one of those new-fangled cocktails if you like.'

'Sherry please,' she said. She had never drunk a cocktail, wasn't sure what its effect would be.

He supplied her with a drink and then, after a few polite sentences, left her with Alex. She watched him as he moved among his guests in the large, crowded room and was impressed by his skill as a host.

'Here, let me fetch you another drink,' Alex said.

'I've hardly started this one,' Rose protested.

'Then I'll fetch one for myself. Stay right where you are. I'll be back in a jiffy.'

She had noted before that he drank swiftly, usually whisky, downing three to everyone else's one. But he seemed to hold his drink and, as far as she could tell, it had little effect on him.

Standing waiting – there was nowhere left to sit – she appraised the gowns of the other women. They were unexpectedly smart; well made, in beautiful materials and expertly cut. But she did not feel too out of place in hers. It was smart, yet inconspicuous enough to pass muster.

And she had been right to choose the Turkish skirt. There was not a gown here which did not curve in towards the hemline. She would have expected the women of Akersfield to have lagged behind fashion, to be provincial in their taste, but it was not so. These ladies of Akersfield, she thought, could have held their own anywhere.

She was observing the scene with interest when her host approached her, accompanied by another man.

'Here is someone who insists on meeting you – and I can't say I blame him,' he said. 'How Alex can risk leaving you, even for a minute, I really don't know! But let me introduce Councillor John Worthing.'

'We've met, after a fashion,' Rose said. 'Good-evening Councillor.'

'Good-evening Doctor Rose.'

He had the same teasing look in his eyes, an air of not taking her quite seriously, of mocking in a kindly way. Standing close to her he was more attractive than he had been with a large table between them. He exuded an air of intimacy which was at once fascinating and slightly alarming. She wished Alex would return – and then almost immediately hoped he would not.

Councillor Worthing noticed her quick glance around.

'Let's move from here before young Bairstow comes back to reclaim you,' he said. 'The party's going on in the room across the hall also, and it's a bit less crowded there.' He took her elbow and began to lead her across the room.

'But I promised Alex I'd stay put,' she protested. 'When he comes back . . .'

'He'll see how foolish he was to leave you. Anyway, he knows his way around. He'll find you again. But not too soon, I hope.'

The room across the hall was identical in size and shape but, as he had promised, less crowded than the first. In the wide hall which separated the rooms a gramophone was playing and some couples were dancing.

'Do you do this stuff?' Councillor Worthing asked, weaving a way through the dancers.

37

'Given the chance,' Rose replied. 'We danced a lot when I was in Medical School. Sometimes in the hospital also.'

'I'm no dancer,' he said. 'Perhaps you should teach me? Anyway, I don't think you'll find much dancing in Akersfield's Infant Welfare Centre.'

'I don't expect to,' Rose said. 'But I shan't be living there, you know! I do expect to have a life apart from work.'

He would make a good dancer, she thought. He moved well, with good coordination. But dancing was more than doing the right steps and moving well; it required something in the soul. She was in no position to know whether Councillor Worthing possessed that.

'So you start tomorrow,' he said. 'Silly day to start, Saturday. You're not nervous are you?'

'As a matter of fact, I am,' Rose admitted.

'No need to be. You'll be all right. I knew that as soon as I set eyes on you in the Committee room.'

'Well, not everyone agreed with you!'

He shrugged. 'More fools they. Though the majority *did*, or you wouldn't have got the job. You don't need to bother about the others. And don't be too worried about John Stanton.'

Rose looked up sharply. 'Why should I be? Is he alarming? I haven't met him yet.'

'Which is part of the trouble,' Councillor Worthing said. 'He feels – perhaps he's right – that he should have had some say in the choice of his assistant.'

'And if he had, he wouldn't have chosen me?'

'Who knows? But he wasn't consulted. And then . . .'

He left the sentence in mid-air. Rose finished it for him.

'And then he doesn't want a woman?'

'Well, don't let him worry you,' Worthing said. 'You'll get used to each other. And I don't think you'd really find any man alarming, would you?' The look he gave her was bold, direct. She felt as though he was touching her, though he was not.

38

'You're wrong, Councillor Worthing. In fact I think I find you a little alarming!'

It was a silly thing to say and she was immediately annoyed with herself, but he threw back his head and laughed. He had a splendid, deep-throated laugh. It seemed, without being the least bit raucous, to involve his whole body. It made him seem years younger, not a day older than herself, though Rose judged him to be forty.

'That I don't believe,' he said. 'And by the way, you can keep the Councillor Worthing stuff for official meetings and the like. Otherwise I'm John and you're Rose.'

She liked this man. There was a directness in him which reached out to her, moved her. There was an intimacy which she had sensed even at the interview. Now it stirred her feelings so that she felt that they had known each other from a long way back, while at the same time promising more, much more, for both of them to discover. It was with a sense of disappointment that she saw Alex come into the room. He was in the company of a pretty young girl of about eighteen.

'Good-evening, John,' he said, joining them. 'So it was you who pinched my girl? I might have known!'

'You shouldn't leave valuable property around,' John Worthing said. 'It's too tempting.'

'I'm not anyone's property,' Rose said sharply.

'In the meantime, John, your daughter's been searching for you.' Alex turned to the girl. 'I told you we'd find him with some attractive lady.'

The girl smiled affectionately at her father, coolly at Rose.

'I came to remind you that we promised Mummy we'd be home early, to see the New Year in with her.'

Rose felt suddenly foolish, ashamed of the thoughts which had been in her mind only a few minutes ago. How could she be so naïve? He was like a dozen others she had met. And yet, meeting his eye as he stood behind his daughter, seeing the way he looked at her, she found herself hoping he wasn't. Somehow, it mattered.

'Come and dance, Rose. It's a one-step,' Alex said.

With a cool nod to John Worthing she took Alex's hand and followed him.

They left not long after midnight, staying just long enough for the 'first footing', when the darkest young man at the party went outside into the street, and was re-admitted as midnight struck, carrying a piece of coal to bring good luck to the household.

'It's too soon to go!' Alex protested. 'We're just beginning to enjoy ourselves.'

'I'm sorry,' Rose said. 'I really am tired – and I have to be up early.'

There was no sign of John Worthing. She supposed he had done his daughter's bidding and gone home to his wife.

When they left the house the night was fine and cold with a clear, starlit sky. Rose shivered a little and Alex drew her arm through his own, entwining his fingers in hers. When she tentatively tried to draw away he looked at her in surprise, so she let her hand lie in his as they walked through the quiet streets.

'Why wasn't Councillor Worthing's wife with him?' She asked the question carelessly, as if the answer was unimportant.

'She's an invalid,' Alex said. 'She's seldom well enough to attend parties.'

'Have you met her?'

'Briefly. They give a garden party each year for some charity. If she's well enough she puts in an appearance. She's a pretty woman – beautiful, I should think, before she was ill.'

'What's wrong with her?' Rose asked.

'I honestly don't know. I've heard that when John married her – they were both very young – she was the life and soul of any party. Linda was born a year after they were married and it appears Mrs Worthing has never been the same since.'

'Poor woman!' Rose said. Then 'poor man', she added softly.

'I'm sorry for both of them,' Alex said. 'Though John doesn't let it cramp his style too much.'

At the gate of fifteen Victoria Street he paused, then turned Rose around to face him, drew her into his arms and bent his head to kiss her. She had known, even before the evening started, that this would happen. A few hours ago the prospect had been pleasurable, her body already alive to the prospect. Now, her heart and mind full of that brief encounter with John Worthing, though she knew nothing could come of it, she could not respond to Alex. She wanted to, she tried to, offering her lips to his in submission. He kissed her once, then released her. She was sure he had sensed the submission.

'Happy New Year to you, Alex,' Rose said before he could speak. 'How do we know Mrs Crabtree isn't watching through a chink in the curtains?'

'We don't. Does it matter?' He sounded surprised.

'I wouldn't want to give her any wrong ideas,' Rose said. 'They *would* be wrong, you know.'

The Baby Clinic – that being the name by which everyone referred to the Maternity and Child Welfare Clinic – was in Beech Grove, occupying the first floor of a narrow-fronted, eighteenth-century house in a short street of similar houses. All were in a state of genteel decay, like so many elderly ladies, once beautiful but now gone to seed. None of them was in private occupation, most of them being divided up and taken over by lesser-known insurance companies, moneylenders (grandiosely named financial consultants) and the like.

Rose pushed open the front door and went in. The hall was untidy, with cartons, full and empty, sharing the space with a row of dark wooden cupboards and a wheelchair. A printed notice at the foot of the elegantly-curving staircase said, 'Maternity & Child Welfare Clinic First Floor, Dental Clinic Second Floor'. In a small room off the first floor landing, marked 'Enquiries', she found a young woman.

'Good-morning,' Rose said. 'I'm Doctor Rose Stanton. I start work here today. You are . . . ?'

'Miss Mabel Pearlman. I'm the clerk. Pleased to meet you, I'm sure.' Her voice was hoarse and nasal. She was clearly in the grip of a nasty cold and Rose hoped she wouldn't pass it on to too many babies. But the girl's smile was welcoming.

'We've been looking forward to seeing you, Doctor Stanton. Doctor Stanton should be here any minute . . . Oh dear!'

'Doctor Rose! To avoid confusion.'

'Doctor Rose. That's nice. Well I'll show you to your room. I've put out a white coat. I'm afraid it'll be miles too big for you,' she said, appraising Rose's figure. 'Oh, here's Nurse Butterworth!'

Nurse Butterworth filled the doorway with her comfortable shape. She held out a hand.

'You must be our new doctor!'

'Doctor Rose, we're to call her,' Miss Pearlman said.

'You're very welcome here,' Nurse Butterworth said. 'We can certainly do with an extra pair of hands.'

'I was just going to show Doctor Rose her room.'

'You do that, love. Then how about a cup of tea all round. Doctor Stanton should be here in about a quarter of an hour. I'll see you later, Doctor Rose.'

Rose's room was small, partitioned off from a bigger room, but the sash window uncurtained, was a fair size, so the room was light. She put on the white coat which, as promised, was a mile too big for her and, sitting on the chair behind the heavy oak desk, looked around. This was where most of her waking life was to be spent for goodness knew how long.

There was not much to look at: two chairs, an examination couch, a hatstand, a wooden filing cabinet. The floor was covered in brown linoleum, the walls were dark brown at the bottom, fawn above, the ceiling had once been white. Then she saw the calendar. Someone had hung it on the wall facing her: a country scene with a village, as it might be Faverwell itself, and a tear-off pad with today's date showing in large red letters. January first, nineteen-twenty-one.

'I put it there,' Miss Pearlman said, entering with a cup of tea. 'Doctor Stanton's arrived. He'd like to see you in ten minutes. Just give you time to drink your tea. His room's across the landing.'

He was sitting, white-coated, behind his desk when Rose entered. He had greying hair, and *pince-nez* set on top of a sharp nose, under which he had a dark moustache. He looked at her from cold grey eyes set in a pale face. Everyone in Akersfield looks pale, Rose thought.

'Good-morning,' he said. 'I understand we're to call you Doctor Rose. I find it a little frivolous, but in the circumstances . . .' His voice trailed off.

He doesn't like me, Rose thought swiftly. He doesn't like me and he doesn't want me here. Councillor Worthing was right.

'Nurse Butterworth will inform you about the routine,' he said. 'After that I suppose you had better sit in on my surgery. Naturally, I have no idea of your capabilities.'

'But my references, my application . . .' Rose ventured. 'My experience is written down there. I'm properly qualified and I've spent more than a year since qualification on the women's ward of Akersfield hospital.'

'While I, my dear lady, have been a doctor for twenty-five years, and my father and grandfather before me. I'm afraid I can't possibly turn you loose on my patients just yet.'

His voice was cold, his face stony. Was this his usual manner or was it reserved especially for her? Well whatever the case, he wasn't going to beat her. She wouldn't let him. She braced herself to speak as pleasantly as possible.

'I quite understand. Of course I'll be happy to sit in on your surgery. I'm sure it will be valuable to me. And then

43

I hope it won't be too long before I can be of real help to you. Doctor Stanton. I understand there's enough work in the clinic for at least two doctors. I'd like to take my share.'

His head was bent over a sheaf of notes he had started to read. She might never have spoken. She wanted to take him by his narrow shoulders and shake him until his silly, prissy spectacles fell off.

'See Nurse Butterworth,' he said curtly, not looking up.

4

Eva never liked to admit it, and she never would out loud, but she had quite enjoyed the war. Well, not enjoyed it exactly. That was a word which made her feel guilty. And you couldn't help but be sad even now, when it had been over, going on three years, about all those men killed or wounded; on the Somme, in Gallipoli, at Passchendaele. Some of them were boys she'd gone to school with, boys who'd joined up under age, so eager were they to be up and at 'em. All the same, there were bits of the war, things she'd done, which gave her satisfaction. Her present life did not offer that.

'You'd be better off on munitions,' her mother had said from the minute Eva left school. 'Nice clean work and well paid.' But she hadn't wanted to go on munitions. She preferred her work in the hospital, even if she didn't earn much. She had liked the idea of looking after the wounded, helping them to get on their feet again.

Not that she'd actually looked after them. Not as if she was a nurse, which was what she really wanted to be, what she dreamed about. As a domestic she had washed up, cleaned the sluices, polished the ward floors until you could see yourself in them. Sometimes she shook up a patient's pillow if no nurse was around to restrain her. And on the side, unofficially, she'd run messages for the men; posted letters, placed sixpenny bets with Bert Sugden, the bookie. Once or twice she'd been persuaded into smuggling in a packet of Woodbines, which was how she'd got to know Jim.

'You know I shouldn't,' she told him. 'If there's a no smoking rule it's for your own good.' But he was so

45

handsome, so persuasive – and with a bullet in his leg from Amiens what could a strong young man like Jim Denby do but smoke? He always seemed to have money and he was generous with it. 'Keep the change,' he'd say. 'Buy yourself some chocolate.' He didn't seem to know you couldn't get it.

When Jim was discharged from hospital and came out of the army at the beginning of 1919 it had taken him less than a month of courtship to get Eva pregnant.

'He'll have to marry you,' her mother said. 'We're having no bastards in this family. I'm saying nowt about you getting caught; that's easy done, as we all know. But since you are, it's marriage – and preferably in church!'

By this time Eva had not wanted to marry Jim, couldn't imagine what she had seen in him in the first place, but she knew she'd have to. So her dreams of being a nurse vanished. Not that they could ever have come true. For someone of her class it was impossible. She knew of no-one who had stayed at school after the age of fourteen and when she'd been there some of the children were still half-timers: half-time in school, half-time in the mill.

But dreams cost nothing and they kept you going. As she pushed the pram along Babcock Street, the new baby tucked in under the hood and eighteen-month-old Dorothy propped up at the other end, she was at it again. Then, right in the middle of saving the life of a desperately sick man by her devoted nursing, she heard this voice. It could only belong to Mrs Harris. No-one else had a voice so loud.

'What are you calling the new bairn then? Have you picked a name?'

There being no gardens to the back-to-back houses in Babcock Street, Mrs Harris, plump, slatternly, was sitting on the step outside her door, enjoying the afternoon sunshine while keeping an eye on everything that went on in the street and supposedly guarding her several small children who were playing in the gutter. How *could* she sit out on the street like that? Eva wondered. It was so common. Though her own family had never been anything other than hopelessly poor, she had been brought up to dread anything common.

'We haven't quite decided, Mrs Harris,' she replied. 'I thought perhaps Meg, short for Margaret – or Mary is always nice, don't you think?'

Mrs Harris's fruity sniff showed what she thought. 'I like something a bit different myself. Something special. Gloria or Pearl or Angela. Give a child a nice name and you set it up for life.'

Three less suitable names for Mrs Harris's runny-nosed female offspring Eva couldn't imagine, unless it was the ones she knew they already bore; Hyacinth, Miranda and Selina.

'I get them out of novels,' Mrs Harris confided. 'Whenever I see a name I fancy I jot it down, just in case it might come in handy.' She chuckled. 'It usually does!'

She got up from the step and peered into the pram, touching the sleeping baby with a grubby fat finger.

'Well you'll have to think of something soon, love. You'll have to get her registered. Going on six weeks, isn't she?'

'That's right.'

'I thought so. What does Jim say?'

'He doesn't mind. He leaves it to me,' Eva said.

As he left most things. He didn't go much on babies anyway, regarding them as inevitable and inconvenient results of what a man must have as his right. He probably wouldn't care if she gave them numbers instead of names.

'Quite a posh pram you've got there,' Mrs Harris said. 'That didn't come off a Christmas tree!'

'Mam had it given by a lady she does for,' Eva informed her. 'She told Mam she kept it in the attic for years, waiting till she was past having any more. She reckoned the minute you gave the pram away you fell for another.'

Mrs Harris nodded wisely. 'She's right at that. And it happens to the rich as well as the poor.'

47

But not as often, Eva thought. Families of nine, ten, even twelve children were not at all uncommon here in the Ridgetron area of Akersfield, but you didn't see anything like that in the Park Moor district where the better-off lived. In Ridgetron when a woman couldn't stand the thought of another birth tearing at her, or despaired of feeding another mouth, she might pay a visit to old Ma Radlett who did mysterious things with a mucky darning needle. You didn't see many Park Moor women knocking on Ma Radlett's door and Eva doubted if they had her equivalent on Park Moor. So how? And why, and what? Perhaps the men were different there?

'I must push on,' she said. 'Mam's expecting me.'

When she reached her mother's house she manoeuvred the pram into the already overcrowded living room. 'I'm not leaving the baby outside,' she said. 'Too many cats and kids. And I don't want to pick her up. She's only just gone off.'

'Been keeping you awake, has she?' Mrs Foster asked sympathetically.

'Half the night. She doesn't seem to need sleep. And I don't think my milk's satisfying her. I don't think she gets enough.'

Mrs Foster snorted. 'How can she when *you* don't get enough? Now you sit down at that table and you're going to get a good plateful of sheep's head broth inside you. A nursing mother needs good food.'

'It's not that easy,' Eva said.

She sat to the table and started avidly on the food her mother put before her. The broth was steaming hot and thick with vegetables, the dumplings floating, light as feathers, on the surface. It was a strange dish for a summer's day but to Eva it was perfection. Her mother watched her with satisfaction.

'I know it's not easy, but I daresay Jim doesn't go short. He fathers these kids on you – bless their little hearts – and it's you has to bear the burden! Well next time I see him he's going to get a piece of my mind!'

Eva had heard it all before. And it was true. But Jim wouldn't get a piece of her mother's mind because he never came here and her mother didn't visit them. She had been once to the room where they lived, ate, slept – and decided that it was better for Eva to visit her. At least it got her out of that dump and she could see to it that she got a decent meal, and sometimes give her a copper or two that Jim needn't know about.

Eva scraped her plate clean, then wiped it round with a piece of bread. She felt better now, not so weak.

'Why did you push me into marrying him, Ma?' she asked. 'We'd have been better on our own, me and Dorothy.'

Her mother poked the fire, which had to be lit, though it was hot in the small room, or how else could she cook or heat the water?

'That's dirty talk, Our Eva,' she said. 'I'm surprised at you. A baby needs to be born in wedlock.'

'What about *my* needs?' Eva said. 'Don't I have any? Don't my needs count?'

'You should have thought of that sooner. You made your bed and you must lie on it,' Mrs Foster said sharply.

It had not been a time for thinking. Nor had there been a bed. Jim had been waiting for her at the hospital gate when she came off duty. Less than quarter-of-an-hour later he had taken her, on an uncomfortable bit of spare ground behind the hospital, both of them shedding the minimum of clothing because of the cold March wind. It was almost unbelievable that that single, swift, urgent – and for her painful – action could so have changed her life.

'I'm sorry for you right enough,' Mrs Foster said more gently. 'You know I'll do anything I can to help. And after all, you wouldn't have wanted to be without little Dorothy, would you?'

The baby started to cry, a thin little wailing sound, as though it was too tired to make the effort but knew it must. Eva took it out of the pram and held it close, unbuttoning her blouse to give it the breast. The child turned its head from side to side, reluctant to take the nipple which Eva tried to push into its mouth.

'She's always like this,' she said despairingly. 'She won't feed and I'm sure she's not gaining weight.'

The two women looked with concern at the baby, noting the pallor of its complexion, its pursed-up mouth, its delicate, bluish eyelids, the way the skin stretched tightly over the skull.

'Why don't you take her to the Baby Clinic, Our Eva?' Mrs Foster said in a worried voice. 'See what they think.'

'Jim doesn't go much on baby clinics,' Eva said. 'He reckons women should know what to do with their own babies.'

'Damn Jim!' Mrs Foster said.

Eva stared at her mother. She was seldom so vehement and she never swore.

'Perhaps I will take her,' she said. 'They say there's a new lady doctor at the clinic. I've heard tell she's ever so good.'

Mrs Foster looked doubtful. 'I'm not so sure about a *lady* doctor. After all, she won't be married, won't have bairns of her own.'

'Well I might go tomorrow,' Eva said.

The baby in her arms relaxed, stopped fighting and began to suck greedily. Eva leaned back and gave herself up to the moment. She was so tired. Perhaps the doctor would sort everything out. Perhaps she could tell the doctor her other worry. It had been present with her now for several days and it was something she dare not tell her mother.

Miss Pearlman watched Rose climb the stairs, and stopped her on the landing.

'You look hot, Doctor Rose.'

'I am, Mabel. It's stifling outside. Worse than in here.'

She had been down into the town in her lunch hour

to buy some stockings. Whenever she could afford it she bought silk ones, rather than the more servicable lisle, but there was no doubt that they snagged and laddered very easily. But – she admitted it – she was vain about her shapely legs and slender ankles. In any case, Alex was taking her out this evening so she had to wear decent stockings.

There had been no air in the town with its narrow cobbled streets, stone-flagged pavements and high buildings – and every chimney belching out smoke. Not for the first time in the last six months she asked herself why she had chosen to work in Akersfield. It was the kind of day to be walking the fell tops, or discarding her shoes to dip her feet into Faverwell's fast-flowing river.

'Don't forget there's the Committee inspection this afternoon,' Mabel said. 'I was worried in case you were going to be late back. They could arrive any minute.'

It would have been another black mark against me, Rose thought, going into her room, donning her white coat. Goodness knows I can do without that.

Doctor Stanton had ceased being openly rude to her, and sheer pressure of work meant that he had to allow her to deal with cases, both in the baby clinic and in the ante-natal clinic: but he gave her no encouragement, showed no confidence in her. He would not allow her to see any new cases until he himself had dealt with them, decided all the treatments, given Rose her orders. He passed on the routine cases, keeping the more interesting and unusual ones to himself. There were no discussions between them about how to help particular patients. Rose could go to him with a question if she wished, though he would never mention any of his cases to her. But he was a good doctor, Rose allowed him that.

'He's one of the best,' Nurse Butterworth frequently said. 'We're lucky to have him.' Which was true. Nurse Butterworth was Doctor Stanton's strong ally, but she was never less than fair to Rose, never made her feel, as he did, that she was not part of the team.

She had been at her desk a few minutes, reading the case sheets which Mabel Pearlman had put out for the afternoon clinic, when Nurse Butterworth entered.

'Doctor Stanton would like you to see one or two of his cases this afternoon,' she said. 'He'll be busy with the Committee. There's nothing you can't handle. He's put off all the tricky ones until tomorrow or Friday.'

Trust him, Rose thought – but said nothing out loud. Where the others were concerned she refused to give any sign that all was not sweetness and light between herself and the Medical Officer. But unless they were fools, which they were not, they must know.

'This Committee is a damned nuisance,' Nurse Butterworth said. 'What do they know, anyway?'

'Which members of the Committee are coming?' Rose asked. 'Do you know?' It was the first Committee visit since she had joined the clinic. All she knew was that three or four members came, talked to Doctor Stanton, to Nurse Butterworth and – as a token courtesy – for about two minutes to Mabel Pearlman. So Rose presumed they would also want to see her.

'Councillor Thwaites – he's the Chairman – Councillor Rogers and Councillor Worthing,' Nurse Butterworth said.

At the mention of John Worthing's name Rose felt a tensing of her body, a sharpening of her breath. She bent her head over a file, afraid of what she might show in her face. She had fought against her feelings for this man, reminded herself that he was married, that most likely he was only amusing himself with her; also that she hardly knew him. She had had neither sight nor sound of him since the party on New Year's Eve.

'The other two are all right but Councillor Rogers is a bit of a tartar, doesn't approve of much,' Nurse Butterworth said.

'I know. I've met him. He certainly didn't approve of me! Well, if there are any new cases this afternoon I'll see them,' Rose said. 'If one doesn't see new people the first time they come, then they tend not to return.'

Nurse Butterworth looked doubtful.

'I suppose you're right,' she said reluctantly. 'I suppose you can take down the particulars and then arrange for them to come back to see Doctor Stanton.'

I shall do nothing of the kind, Rose decided.

It was very much a routine clinic that afternoon. Miss Pearlman admitted the mothers and babies; Nurse Butterworth weighed the babies and gave them a quick inspection before their mothers took them in to see the doctor, in this case Rose. The babies were too often underweight, their limbs less than straight; they had muddy skins and nappy rashes. The similarity of so many cases was depressing to Rose.

But the mothers were often in a worse state than their babies: undernourished, badly dressed, dull-eyed and tired-looking, though most of them were younger than she was. She had the feeling that life was one long struggle for most of these mothers. As well as the newest baby they were often accompanied by a toddler, even two, whom they struggled to discipline at the same time as trying to keep the baby quiet. Rose kept a small supply of jelly babies in her drawer to quieten awkward toddlers, though she knew the dentist on the floor above would be furious with her if he knew.

She would have liked to have taken all these tired-looking mothers, separated them from their children for a whole day, given them a *charabanc* outing to some beautiful place, with a great big meal at the end of it.

It was almost the end of the afternoon when Eva Denby came in. Whatever the Committee members were up to they had not troubled Rose. Mabel Pearlman, bringing in the card for the new patient, said they were all in Doctor Stanton's room.

'There's a Mrs Denby here. She hasn't been before though she's got a little girl of eighteen months as well as the baby. Would you like a cup of tea, Doctor Rose?'

'Yes please. Tell Mrs Denby to come in.'

A timid knock on the door announced Mrs Denby's arrival.

'Come in,' Rose called. 'Come and sit down,' she said when Eva Denby hesitantly entered.

Just like all the rest, Rose thought. Tired. Anaemic without a doubt. Yet somehow she felt that there was a spark here. Mrs Denby was pretty – even allowing for the fact that she was too pale, wore a dress totally unsuited to the heat of the day, and that her dark hair hung lankly around her face. She had a Pre-Raphaelite appearance, with large eyes and sensuously-curved lips in an oval face.

'It's the baby,' she said. 'She doesn't seem to be thriving. And now the nurse says she's underweight.'

'Are you feeding her yourself?' Rose asked.

'As well as I can. She doesn't seem to take to it. Yet I had no trouble with this one.' She indicated Dorothy, who stood quietly beside her.

'Give the baby to me, let me have a look at her,' Rose said.

She laid the baby gently on the examination couch, talking meanwhile to the mother. The child lacked the plumpness, the creases in the flesh, the pink-tinged skin and vigorous movement of a thriving baby. It lay still, not kicking. It was clearly undernourished and weak.

'Well,' Rose said. 'There's nothing here that can't be put right, Mrs Denby. We shall just have to work on it. I'm sure she needs some supplementary feeding, which we can arrange. You see you can't feed your baby well if *you* are undernourished, and I think perhaps you are. Is your husband in work?'

'No,' Eva said. 'Not for the last six months. He has this war wound, you see. It plays him up in the winter and he gets laid off. Then he can't get back again.'

So she's probably been underfed right through pregnancy, Rose thought, handing back the baby. It was common enough.

'I wish you had come to see us when you were expecting,' she said. 'We could have helped. There's a free milk scheme for which you would have qualified, and free dinners at one of our centres. Still, it's not too late. As a nursing mother you can still have those. Your name would have to go before the Committee but I'm sure they would agree.'

It was one of the bugbears of the system; it annoyed Rose intensely, that in a case such as this not even Doctor Stanton could order free milk and dinners. Everything had to go to the Committee for a decision, even when it was a clear-cut case and certain to be agreed.

'I see you live in Paradine Street,' she said. 'Once it's agreed, we can arrange to have the milk delivered daily. Could you come to the centre in Slater Road for dinners?'

'I don't know,' Eva said doubtfully. 'I don't know that my husband would like it.'

'But it's for the sake of the baby,' Rose protested. 'Once you're eating properly you'll get your milk back and then the baby will thrive. It will be better for all of you.'

There was a hesitation, a fear in the woman's attitude which puzzled Rose. Surely no man . . . ?

'There's something else,' Eva blurted out. 'There's something else! I think I've been caught again! I think I'm expecting.' Her tone was a mixture of fear and despair.

Rose sat back, squared her shoulders, looked into the worried face of the mother. Not another one, she thought. Not another one. What could she do?

Mabel Pearlman came in with a cup of tea.

'Will you bring Mrs Denby a cup, please?' Rose asked.

'Rightho!' Mabel looked surprised. It was not the usual practice but Doctor Rose had her own little ways. 'As soon as you're through with Mrs Denby you're wanted in Doctor Stanton's room,' she said.

'You could be wrong, Mrs Denby,' Rose said gently when Mabel had closed the door behind her. 'The body takes time to settle down after a birth. It's sometimes difficult to know just what is happening. And your baby is only six weeks old.'

'I'm not wrong,' Eva said stubbornly. 'A woman knows these things. You feel it in your insides.'

'I suppose neither you nor your husband took any precautions?' Rose asked.

'Precautions?' There was scorn in Eva's voice. 'You don't know my husband when he's had a pint or two. Anyway, he reckons that's a woman's job, though how and why I really don't know. But I thought you couldn't get caught when you were breastfeeding.'

'That's not true,' Rose said. She had lost count of how many women had said that to her. Yet they had only to look around. It was the triumph of hope over experience.

'But it's not a good idea to get pregnant when you're nursing. And perhaps you're not. We'll have to wait a week or two and see. In the meantime it's more important than ever that we build up your strength, just in case. So will you agree to the free milk and dinners? I'll try to hurry the Committee.'

'All right,' Eva said reluctantly. 'But isn't there anything you can do for me . . . ? I mean . . .'

'If you mean can I get rid of the baby, the answer is "No". It's against the law, even if I were agreeable. What you really need is advice on how not to have babies so close together. But now isn't the time.'

'It's men that need the advice,' Eva said sharply.

'Men and women both,' Rose said. 'It's a partnership. In the meantime I'll give you a chit to collect some baby food from the clerk – and I'll ask the Health Visitor to drop in and see you in a couple of days, see if you're having any problems with it. You will come and see me again next week, Mrs Denby? I'm sure I can help you.'

But to what extent, she wondered sadly, when Eva Denby had left the room. If she *is* pregnant – and she's as likely to be right as not – how much can *I* do? She felt tired and helpless and wished the long, hot afternoon would end. But now she must face Doctor Stanton and the Committee. She wondered what they wanted of her.

Doctor Stanton sat behind his desk. Rose took the chair he indicated and found herself sitting directly opposite John Worthing, who was flanked on either side by the other two Committee members.

'Good afternoon, Doctor Rose,' the Chairman said. 'We've had a full and interesting report of the work of the clinic in the last six months – and of course your part in it – but we just wondered if you had anything you wanted to bring up? Any little matter?'

So what has he said about me? Rose asked herself. Do I need to defend myself? But against what?

'There is one thing,' she said. 'Could it not be made possible for the clinic doctors to sign the orders for free milk and dinners without having to wait for the Committee? It would make such a difference to the mothers.'

'I have naturally raised that point myself,' Doctor Stanton said stiffly. 'It's not new . . .'

'Then I underline everything I imagine you've said about it.'

'We have to remember it's the ratepayers' money we're squandering,' Councillor Rogers said disagreeably. 'They won't thank us for throwing it about.'

Rose looked at his waistcoat straining over his plump body, at his round, red face and heavy jowls. She doubted that he had ever been hungry.

'Come on, Albert, it's scarcely squandering,' John Worthing said. 'And it's not a king's ransom we're talking about.'

'We are the guardians of the rates,' Councillor Rogers said pompously.

'I think the doctors have a point,' the Chairman said. 'I'm agreeable to putting it to the full Committee. Of course we couldn't have just anyone signing the orders. It would have to be done by the Medical Officer.'

Which means I'll have to argue every case with him, Rose thought impatiently. But never mind, it was a forward step. And to give Doctor Stanton his due, he was reasonably fair-minded on that question.

'Anything else, Doctor Rose?' the Chairman asked. 'If not, then we won't keep you. Time we were off, gentlemen!'

She was back in her room, bringing the records up to date, when the door opened. She raised her head and saw John Worthing, his height and breadth filling the doorway.

'May I come in?'

Not waiting for an answer, he entered, and closed the door behind him. His physical presence, the air of cool arrogance which fitted him like a second skin, filled the room with an almost tangible excitement. Rose could not find her voice.

'I'm here to offer you a lift home,' he said. 'I'm dropping Doctor Stanton so it's on my way.'

She knew that she must excuse herself. Here and now was the moment to stop something which, if she allowed it, might overwhelm her. It would never do that to him, she judged. She felt sure he was always totally in control.

'I rather wanted to finish . . .'

He stretched across the desk and closed the file she was working on. 'Come on now,' he said. 'Everyone else has left. And you look whacked!' His lips curved in an amused smile, as if he read the reason behind her refusal. 'I'm only offering you a lift home!'

So he was. She was making too much of it. And she was hot and tired, disinclined to walk through the stuffy streets.

'Thank you,' she said. 'I accept.'

She put away her papers, doffed her white coat, took down her hat from its peg. It was a cream straw hat, narrow brimmed and trimmed with brown petersham ribbon. She pulled it down over her springy hair, stuck a hatpin through, and was ready.

In the car Doctor Stanton sat in front beside John Worthing while Rose sat in the back. She was not included in what little conversation there was, but that did not worry her. She was glad of a chance to relax. She was surprised when they arrived at Doctor Stanton's house first.

'I thought he lived further away from the clinic than I do,' Rose said when they had dropped him.

'So he does. I came a different way round. I'm going to drive out of the town and up on to the top of the moor beyond Barnswick, to get some fresh air. I hoped you might like to come with me.' His tone was casual. He kept his eyes on the road, not turning to look at her as he made the invitation.

'Oh but I don't think . . .' But her spirits rose sky high, even as she protested.

'I'm not forcing you. We shan't be long. Fifteen minutes there, ten minutes out of the car, fifteen minutes back. Do you the world of good.'

It would too. A breath of moorland air would be the next best thing to Faverwell. But ought she . . . ?

His dark eyes, creased at the corners with amusement, met hers in the driving mirror.

'I don't plan to kidnap you,' he said.

He's mocking me and I deserve it, Rose thought. How silly I'm being!

'I'd love it!' she said quickly.

She thought he might have invited her to sit in the front seat, but he did not do so, nor did he speak again. As they drove through the centre of Akersfield and took the road for Barnswick she studied him from behind. His hair was thick and dark, his shoulders broad. She wondered how men coped with worsted suits and stiff collars in weather like this, then wondered how he would look when he was not formally dressed. His hands on the wheel were as shapely as a woman's, out of character with the rest of his strong, squarish appearance.

They had left Akersfield behind now and were climbing the long, narrow hill which led to the moorland village of Barnswick and then, half a mile further on, to the moor. When they reached the crest of the hill he drew his car into the side of the road and stopped.

'Out you get,' he said. 'We'll walk a bit and do some deep breathing. Fill our lungs with decent air.'

He took her hand to help her out of the car. She freed herself as quickly as good manners allowed her to, afraid of the feelings which ran through her at his touch. They walked forward to the high point of the moor, the ground dipping away in front of them to the wide valley. It was a West Riding scene; softer, and with more trees than in her native dale. The hills were rounded, not as high, and the farms and clustered cottages across the valley were of dark millstone grit instead of the pale limestone of Faverwell. But the air was clear and bright and there was a breeze moving here on the tops.

'It's heavenly!' Rose said. 'Good to be away from chimneys.'

He made no answer and she searched for words to break the silence.

'Were you satisfied with this afternoon's meeting?' she asked.

'Quite. Incidentally, since I daresay you're wondering, Stanton didn't speak at all badly of you. But we're not here to talk about work, Rose – and that's enough.'

She looked up at him, surprised by the abrupt change in his voice.

'I wasn't entirely honest with you, Rose,' he said. 'I brought you here for something more than the view.'

She questioned him with her look.

'Rose, will you come and have supper with me? There's a place Ilkley way, only a few miles across the moors . . .'

There was an invitation in his eyes which said more than his words. With everything in her she wanted to accept it. And why should she not? she asked herself. But she knew the answer, and she must make it quickly if she was not to weaken.

'John, I can't. You know I can't.' The words were almost inaudible. She felt as if all her strength had gone into forming them.

'Why can't you, Rose? I'm only asking you to have supper.'

'When we started out you were only asking me to come up to the moor. And you know why I can't.'

'Tell me! Tell me why you can't have a meal with me. It's a little thing.'

'It might . . . lead on,' she said quietly.

'And you wouldn't want that?'

Why was he forcing her into making these admissions? And why did she not simply refuse to answer him? But already there was something in their relationship which ruled out dishonesty, even insincerity, between them. Or was that feeling only on her side? She had no way of knowing.

'I . . . couldn't allow it.' She sounded so prim, so cold. It was not how she felt. She wanted to take whatever this man offered, and to give to him in her turn.

'I've thought about you a great deal since New Year's Eve,' he said. 'There are things I want to tell you. If the opportunity hadn't arisen today, I would have made it anyway.'

What things? she wondered. But she would not allow herself to hear them. She must not let him weaken what little resolve she had left.

'Please don't say any more, John,' she begged. 'You have your marriage, I have my job. There's nothing more to be done.'

Hearing her own voice, she thought how calm she sounded – but inside she was weeping with longing.

'I shan't give up,' he said. 'Not yet.'

But he would in the end. She faced that. He would tire of her refusals and turn to someone else.

He took her hand, raising it to his lips, gently kissing the tips of her fingers. She wanted him to take her in his arms but he made no move to do so. How strong he was, she thought, how totally in command of himself.

'I must go,' she said presently, 'I have to go out this evening. If we don't leave soon I shall be late.'

'You're going out with Bairstow?'

'Yes.'

For one instant she saw jealousy flash in his eyes.

'He's not right for you, Rose!'

'We're going to the theatre,' she said. 'He's a good friend. I know what I'm doing.'

He smiled his sardonic smile. 'At least you had the sense not to offer me friendship,' he said as they walked back to the car.

In the front of the car, when they took the bends on the curving road, she felt her shoulder against his, and closed her eyes against the thrill which went through her body at the contact. She must not put herself in this situation again. It was more than she could bear – and dangerous.

'Promise me something,' he said as they turned into Victoria Street. 'Oh, it's nothing you can't do! Promise me that if you ever want anything – any kind of help – you'll come to me.'

'I promise,' Rose said.

There was no harm in it since she could not imagine such a thing ever happening.

5

The weather continued hot. Doris Chalmers, the Health Visitor, came into Rose's room in the clinic fanning herself with the sheaf of papers she carried. Her round face was suffused with colour and there were beads of perspiration on her downy upper lip.

'It's too much in my job,' she complained. 'Walking up and down these hills all day. Anyway, I popped in to tell you I visited Mrs Denby yesterday.'

'How was she?' Rose said quickly. 'She hasn't been back to the clinic since her first visit three weeks ago.'

Doris Chalmers shook her head.

'Not good, I'm afraid.'

'The baby . . . ?'

'Baby Meg is much better. She's taking the supplementary feeding well and she's put on a bit of weight. It's Mrs Denby I'm worried about. It's pretty certain she's pregnant again. She's suffering morning sickness, which she tells me started early with her other two pregnancies.'

'I was afraid of this,' Rose said.

'She'll have to be persuaded to wean Baby Meg. But she's reluctant. And that slob of a husband is no help. He seems to work on the lines that if the one inside her is ignored it'll go away! But if she's going to carry this baby and keep herself going she'll need a sight better food and more rest than she's getting. She could do with a holiday, too. Fat chance of any of it!'

'We've got permission through for the free milk and dinners,' Rose told her. 'Could you call and tell her that and try to persuade her to come and see me?'

Doris Chalmers looked doubtful. 'I will when I can but

I'm rushed off my feet. New babies everywhere. The fewer they can afford, the more they have!'

'Then I'll go myself,' Rose said.

Doris Chalmers pursed her lips, shook her head. 'Not allowed, Doctor. Not your province. Not that *I'd* mind, of course. Anyway you wouldn't like it much when you got there. Paradine Street stinks in this weather. Privies and middens; and dirty water and the Lord alone knows what else tipped into the drains right outside the houses. And the insides of the houses infested with bugs. Those houses were condemned before the war. It's time they were all pulled down.'

'It sounds as if it's a miracle they don't have an outbreak of typhus,' Rose said.

'That could be a blessing in disguise. Might make the authorities do something. Well, I'd best get going. I just thought you'd like to know about Mrs Denby.'

'Thank you, Doris,' Rose said. 'I wish I could do something. Does Mrs Denby have relatives nearby?'

'Her mother lives in Babcock Street. Mrs Foster's a decent woman but I gather she doesn't visit Eva. Can't stand the husband.'

'Perhaps you could ask her mother to persuade Eva to come back to the clinic,' Rose suggested.

'Not unless I was to meet her in the street,' Doris Chalmers said. 'I can't call on her.'

Throughout the afternoon Rose dealt with a succession of pregnant women, most of them young, but a few in their late thirties and early forties. Two of the women were carrying their tenth child and in appearance, she thought, they looked years older than her own mother.

They were a surprisingly cheerful lot. Every time the door opened she could hear the chatter from the landing where they waited. But talking to each one of them in the privacy of her room she found that close underneath the cheerful surface lay apprehension and worry, fear of how they would make out. Their lives – with few exceptions, for there were no better-class women amongst them – were close-patterned with unemployment, poverty, fatigue, bad housing. There was scarcely one who was not undernourished and she was constantly reminded of the girl from Paradine Street.

In between examining babies, advising mothers, pacifying fractious toddlers with jelly babies, vague thoughts flitted around in Rose's mind about what she could and could not do for Eva and the rest.

She would like to set up some sort of fund – she had no idea how – from which such women could be sent for a few days' holiday. Akersfield had its own convalescent home at Morecambe Bay, but that was for people who had recently come out of hospital. Rose saw in her mind some place where these women could have a change of atmosphere, a short freedom from work and worry when they most needed it. But it was a dream and she was in no position to make it come true. In the meantime she must get permission from Doctor Stanton to visit Mrs Denby, get her back to the clinic.

When the afternoon session was over she knocked on his door, and entered. He did not look up from his papers.

'Yes, what is it?'

'It's about Mrs Denby.'

'Mrs Denby? Do I know her?'

'She came on the afternoon of the Committee visit. A new patient. I saw her because you weren't available. She hasn't been back since.'

'So?'

'I'm rather worried about her. She has a child of eighteen months, another of about nine weeks, and it seems she's pregnant again. And she's not a very fit woman.'

'I imagine not. What do you expect me to do about it? I remember now that free milk and dinners were agreed.'

'That's the point. I'm worried that she won't take them up. And I think we ought to keep an eye on her through this pregnancy.'

'I'm sure that would be wise,' Doctor Stanton agreed.

'But if she doesn't wish to come to us we can hardly drag her here by the hair of her head.'

'I thought if I went to see her . . . I thought I might persuade her . . .'

'That is not your job,' Doctor Stanton said coldly. 'I explained the rules to you on your first day with us. That, you will remember, is the job of the Health Visitor. Why have you not asked her to do this?'

'I have. I put the baby on supplementary feeding and Nurse Chalmers has visited twice. She's advised Mrs Denby to come back to the clinic, but to no avail.'

'Then I see little we can do. If this lady needs a home visit from a doctor then she should call in her own.'

'I doubt she's even got one,' Rose said. She matched his quiet tones with her own, trying not to lose her temper. 'Her husband has been out of work for some time now. It's likely she's not in benefit.'

'Do you know this for certain?'

'Not for certain. But I'm sure it will be true. Please, Doctor Stanton, all I want is to pay one quick visit – not to give any treatment in the home; just to persuade her for her own sake and the children's to attend the clinic. If she doesn't get good ante-natal care I'm afraid of what might happen to her.'

She recalled Eva's pale prettiness, and her own feeling when she had seen her that somewhere under the drab and worried exterior there was a person of character. She felt a deep pity for, and a sense of rapport with, Eva. She was determined to fight for her.

'I'm sure if you could see her you'd agree with me,' she pleaded.

'I daresay I would. I don't need to see her to believe you. It's a story all too common among our patients and I deplore it as much as you do, Doctor. But visiting them is out of the question.' He met Rose's troubled look with an expression so calm that she wanted to hit him. With great difficulty she controlled herself.

'If it's common,' she said, 'then isn't it time something

66

was done about it? We're just patching up trouble instead of trying to prevent it. I know we can't do much about the bad housing and the drains and such, but as doctors there is some advice we could give them.'

And then suddenly she could contain herself no longer. Her voice rose and she spoke with passion.

'You know as well as I do that the infant mortality rate in Akersfield is a disgrace, in spite of anything we do here in the clinic. Isn't that partly because too many babies are born to women not strong enough to bear them? Women who breed like rabbits until they're worn out and prematurely old. Why doesn't someone *do* something? Why doesn't someone give these women some advice?'

She hated him because he remained unmoved in the face of her anger. She hated him for the reasonable tone of his voice as he replied.

'And who is this someone you're thinking of, Doctor? Are you setting yourself up, perhaps, as knowing what's best for everyone?'

'You know I'm not!' she retorted.

'We are not here to interfere in people's marriages. You in particular, since you are not married, can hardly have the answers. Nor are we here to run people's lives for them. We are doctors. Our role is to help the sick.'

'It would make sense to try to prevent sickness when we could,' Rose said sharply.

'And what do you think our ante-natal clinic is doing?'

'It's not enough,' Rose said stubbornly. 'There should be something, someone, so that women don't get pregnant when they don't want to.'

'Even if that is true,' he said, 'I repeat that it is not our job. It is a matter between man and wife. And now, Doctor, if there is nothing else . . .'

'There is one other thing.' In fact she had only just thought of it. 'I want to suggest to Mrs Denby that she goes and stays with my mother in the country for a couple of weeks. I'm sure my mother would have her. There will be no expense for anyone in the clinic . . .'

He interrupted her.

'Doctor, that is nonsense. Such an action is well beyond the scope of your job and if you persist in such a thing you could get yourself, and this clinic, into difficulties. Your job, let me remind you, is as Assistant Medical Officer to this centre. You are here to treat patients who present themselves, within the resources of the clinic. Your job does not go beyond that. Do you understand me?'

'Perfectly,' Rose said. 'But outside my job, as a private person . . . ?'

He sighed. 'I cannot govern what you do as a private person.' But he would like to, Rose thought. 'I strongly advise against such activities. Such actions can border on the political. As doctors, especially in the public service, we must never to be seen to have anything to do with politics.'

'Politics!' Rose protested. 'I'm talking about giving a woman who's not well a couple of weeks' holiday.'

'There is no knowing where things end,' Doctor Stanton said.

He walked to the door and held it open for her to leave. How right you are, Rose thought, walking past him with her head in the air. How very right you are! And he would never know that it was his calmness in the face of other people's troubles which suddenly fired her resolve.

In the first place, she decided, as soon as she was finished in the clinic and before she went back to her lodgings, she would visit Eva Denby.

She found Paradine Street without difficulty and a small child, playing on the street, informed her that Mrs Denby lived at number seventeen. Nurse Chalmers had not exaggerated. Rose doubted if anyone could exaggerate the awfulness of the place. The street was narrow, the paving stones broken. On each side of the street was a long row of mean little houses, with every so often an entry which led to the houses at the rear, for they were built back-to-back.

Rose walked through a dark passageway and found

herself in a cobbled courtyard, down the middle of which a drain ran. On one side of the courtyard the three privies which served twelve houses stood next to the middens which spilled out rubbish, attracting a cloud of flies and bluebottles. On the other side the house doors mostly stood open. The privies and middens stank in the summer heat and Rose tried to hold her breath against the putrid smell. Children played on the cobblestones and two small boys, naked except for short, dirty cotton vests, sailed paper boats in the pool of water around the grating. One of them broke off to pee into the pool to make his boat sail faster.

Dodging the lines of washing slung between the houses and the privies, smiling at a group of women who stopped their conversation to stare at her, Rose knocked on the door of number seventeen. It was Eva Denby herself who answered the door, holding it open no more than an inch or two. Rose was shocked by the change in her appearance since she had seen her three weeks ago. Her face was chalk white, her fine eyes deeply and darkly circled, her lips colourless. There was a film of sweat over her forehead which Rose doubted had anything to do with the surrounding temperature, and she was as thin as a stick. She carried the baby on one bony hip and Dorothy clung to her skirt on the other side.

'Good afternoon, Mrs Denby!' Rose said. 'Perhaps you remember me? I'm Doctor Rose, from the clinic.'

'Oh yes.' She spoke in a dull, disinterested whisper.

'May I come in?'

Eva Denby did not move. 'My husband's in,' she said.

'Fine!' Rose said. 'I'd be glad to meet him. I'd like to come in if I may.' She had no wish to conduct a conversation on the doorstep, within sight and sound of several clearly interested onlookers. Also, she did rather want to meet Mr Denby.

Reluctantly Eva moved aside and Rose followed her into the house. She recognized the smell as soon as it assailed her nostrils. It was the characteristic odour of

69

bug infestation and it pervaded the little room. She had met it often enough on midwifery training, visiting houses where at night the wallpaper could be seen to move and where nurses kept their hats on for fear of bugs dropping in their hair.

Rose's second thought was that Mr Denby, who rose slowly from his chair as she came into the room, was an extremely handsome and physically attractive man, not at all as she had expected him to be. He was tall, blond, with the looks of a Viking warrior and a physique to match. It was clear who was first in line for food in this house.

'Good afternoon,' Rose said to him. 'I'm Doctor Rose Stanton, from the clinic. I was around this way and I thought I'd drop in, see how your wife was. Quite unofficially, of course!'

'You were around this way, Doctor? Paradine Street?' He was sharp. He didn't believe a word she said.

'So how are you, Mrs Denby?' Rose asked.

'The Health Visitor came,' Eva Denby said defensively. 'She said the baby was doing all right.'

'I know. She told me.' She must somehow assure the girl that she was not here to accuse her of something. 'Nurse Chalmers was pleased with the baby. She said she was a bit concerned about you, though.'

'Did you say you were here unofficially, Doctor?' Jim Denby looked her straight in the face as he asked the question. 'Not on behalf of the clinic?'

'That's right.' He was a slippery customer, this one. She didn't trust him. but that was unimportant as long as her visit didn't make trouble between husband and wife. 'But I would like to persuade your wife to come to the ante-natal clinic and that's why I'm glad to meet you. I'm sure you can persuade her.' She turned to Eva. 'I take it you were right about being pregnant?'

Eva Denby nodded.

Jim Denby smiled. 'Well now, Doctor, I wouldn't stand in the way of Eva attending the clinic if that's what she wants to do.'

'I was sure you would agree,' Rose said pleasantly. 'Just as I'm sure you'd want her to have the milk and dinners which the Committee have agreed she's entitled to.'

His face clouded at that. 'I don't like charity. I've never taken it and never will.'

'Oh but it's not charity,' Rose said swiftly. 'You've paid for it in the rates. It's nothing more than your due. I understand you fought in the war. What did you fight for if not for better things for your family. It's certainly not charity.'

'Well if you put it like that,' he said truculently.

'I do, Mr Denby.' It was her guess that he would take anything that was offered, providing his pride could be saved.

Rose turned to Mrs Denby. 'You could do with a bit of a holiday. How long is it since you had one?'

Jim Denby burst out laughing; a strong, uninhibited laugh which reminded Rose sharply of the way John Worthing had laughed on New Year's Eve. Strangely, this man had some of the same strong, masculine attraction which was also John Worthing's; an almost animal sexuality. She could understand why Eva had first fallen for him. Apart from that, of course, he was nothing like John Worthing.

'Holiday, did you say? The likes of us don't have holidays, Doctor! Some say being unemployed is one long holiday, but I suppose that isn't what you meant?'

'Not at all. But I thought it would do your wife a world of good to get away for a week or two's rest and change. You want this new baby, perhaps a son, to be strong and healthy, I'm sure?'

'If he's anything like his Dad, he will be!' He drew himself up to his full height, thrust out his chin and his chest. 'There's nothing weak about his Dad, I can assure you Doctor Rose!'

His eyes challenged her. He had used her first name deliberately, she knew that. He was thrusting his sexuality at her, lacking the sensitivity to know how he revolted her.

71

'We once went on a half-day *charabanc* trip to Knaresborough,' Eva Denby said. Her face was alight, her voice suddenly and astonishingly animated. 'Afore we were married. Do you remember, Jim? It was lovely! All those trees and the river and everything!' Then she stopped speaking as suddenly as she had started, and turned away.

'Where would *we* get the money for a holiday?' Jim Denby asked.

'I don't know. I'd think about it. But it would be nothing to do with the clinic.'

'I understand, Doctor. Quite unofficial, as we said before!' He closed one eye in a wink. I can't stand him another minute, Rose decided. She turned to Eva.

'So you'll come to the ante-natal clinic next Monday?'

'I'll see that she does, Doctor,' Jim Denby said. 'Have no fear.'

Well if she comes it will have been worth it, Rose thought, taking her leave. She could put up with the husband for the sake of his wife. Also, she would write to her mother this evening, see what could be done about a holiday. She should have a reply before next Monday's clinic.

Rose slipped into the dining room and took her place at the supper table. The other boarders, including Alex, were already seated. Aside from Alex she knew none of them well. They were friendly, but seemingly had their own pursuits. They included two schoolteachers, a man who worked in the Surveyors' department in the town hall, a buyer from one of Akersfield's department stores. Mrs Crabtree was delighted with the standing of her boarders and to capture a doctor, albeit a woman doctor, had been the final accolade.

'You look as though you've been hurrying,' Laura Browning, one of the schoolteachers, said.

'Yes. I had a call to make after work.'

Rose met Alex's questioning look, but this was not the

time to tell him what she had been up to. After supper they walked upstairs together.

'I'll give you a cup of coffee,' she said.

They had long given up the habit of standing chatting on the threshold of each other's rooms and several times a week she either gave him coffee or took it in his room. If Mrs Crabtree had any thoughts about this she kept them to herself.

'I have something to tell you,' Alex said.

'And I have something to ask you!'

'Go and put the kettle on. I'll join you in a minute,' he said.

When he came he was bearing an unopened bottle of whisky.

'A celebration!' he said.

'Really? What this time?'

He was one for celebrations, always finding something worth commemorating.

'No really, I mean it. It's really special this time. I've been promoted, Rose! Standing before you, you see the new Assistant Editor of the Akersfield *Record*!'

'Oh Alex, I'm so glad!' Rose's pleasure was genuine. He was good at his job; keen and ambitious. It pleased her to see him so obviously happy.

He poured generous glasses of malt whisky.

'I knew you'd be glad,' he said. 'Let's drink to it!'

'It's a big step up, isn't it?' Rose asked.

'More money, more responsibility – and next in line for the Editor's job when the old man goes – though that won't be for a long time yet.'

'Is that what you really want – to be Editor?'

'I suppose it is,' he said. 'Eventually. To run the whole shoot. But what were you going to ask? I'd say it was a pretty good evening for asking.'

'It's an idea I have. I don't know whether it would work. I'd like your opinion.'

She told him about Eva Denby, about her visit to Paradine Street.

73

'A holiday wouldn't solve her problems,' she concluded. 'But it would give her a bit more strength to face them. I think I can do something for her if only her husband lets me.'

'Wait a bit,' Alex said. 'Something rings a bell. What's her husband's name?'

'She called him Jim.'

'James Denby, Paradine Street. I remember now. I've come across him in court. He's a petty criminal, but clever with it. I'd steer clear of him if I were you, Rose.'

'Then I'd say she needs help all the more,' Rose said. 'The thing is, she's only one of many. I see them all the time. I thought if I could get a scheme going, some sort of fund to send these women for a few days into the country or to the seaside, give them some good food and a taste of pleasure, it might make a world of difference to them.'

'They'll still have to come back to the Paradine Streets of this town,' Alex said thoughtfully. 'That could make life seem worse than before.'

'But you're wrong,' Rose contradicted. 'They'd have something to look back on. You should have seen Mrs Denby's face when she talked about the half day in Knaresborough. She was transported.'

Alex shrugged. 'So how would you set about it?'

'The trouble is, *I* couldn't. Doctor Stanton made it quite clear that I mustn't put a foot wrong. I don't agree with him, but he's my boss and he could make things awkward. So I have to find someone else who likes the idea and will undertake to get it off the ground. I thought of you, Alex!'

She smiled up at him as though she was handing him a precious gift.

'Me? You can't be serious, Rose! I can't do that any more than you can. However much I might sympathize with your mothers, in my job I can't take sides.'

She was astonished by his reaction.

'You mean now that you're Assistant Editor,' she said bitingly. 'Does your new job mean you're going to sit on the fence for the rest of your life?'

'Don't be silly, Rose! It has nothing to do with me being Assistant Editor. It would still be the same if I was the most junior reporter. On a newspaper we publish the news. We don't make it.'

She felt suddenly deflated. It had seemed a wonderful idea and she had felt so sure of Alex's cooperation.

'Then you won't help?'

'I didn't say that, Rose. Of course I'll help. When you find someone to take up the idea I'll get the *Record* to give it plenty of space. That'll be a tremendous help.'

'But I don't know anyone,' Rose objected.

She stood up, walked across to the window, looked out on to the street. 'Oh well, I suppose I'd better do what I can to fix up Mrs Denby with my mother. That seems to be about my limit. So if you'll excuse me, Alex, I'd like to write my letter. I could catch the late post.'

'Rose Stanton, you amaze me!' Alex said. 'I never thought you'd give up so easily. We'll think of something. Write your letter. We'll take it to the post and then go for a walk.'

'I'm sorry,' Rose said. 'I'm too tired to walk any further than the post box. It's been a long, hot day.' But longer and hotter in Paradine Street, she thought. 'But I am really pleased about your promotion, Alex,' she added.

He left her, taking the whisky with him, but when later she walked downstairs on her way out to post the letter he came out of his room. 'I'm coming with you,' he said. 'I've thought of someone. I can't imagine why I didn't think of him right away!'

Out in the street it was cooler, and there was a slight but refreshing breeze.

'Who?' Rose asked.

'John Worthing.'

'I couldn't possibly ask John Worthing,' Rose said quickly.

'Why ever not?' Alex looked at her in astonishment.

'It's the kind of thing he could do. And he likes you so you're halfway there.'

There was no way she could explain. She tried to push away the feelings which even the mention of his name had stirred in her.

'He's a generous bloke,' Alex persisted. 'And he can afford to start it off with a bang. He's rich. He manufactured khaki cloth for uniforms right through the war. Made a packet.'

'Why wasn't he in the army?'

'He has a foot injury from when he was a kid. He could never have marched.'

'So he's a war profiteer?' Why did she speak as though she wanted to hear something bad about him?

'Not the way you mean it,' Alex said. 'Yes, he made a lot of money, but he made it fairly. His cloth was good stuff. Some of the cloth which went into uniforms was so bad that it fell to bits in the rain and the mud in France. There was nothing like that about John Worthing's product. And he was generous with his money, gave a lot of it away. He'd probably start you off with a good donation and lend his name to the fund.'

'I don't want to take money from him,' Rose said stubbornly.

'I don't understand you. The money would be for the fund. But if you want to give up the idea . . .'

She couldn't. She thought of Eva Denby in Paradine Street, thought of the women she had seen that afternoon, and knew she couldn't. She would approach John Worthing. 'Promise to come to me if you need anything,' he'd said.

She telephoned his home next day. A woman answered. 'Who is speaking?' she asked. She had a gentle, slightly petulant, cultured voice. Mrs Worthing, Rose had little doubt. She wondered what the other woman looked like, there at the end of the telephone. She sounded tall, slender and elegant.

'Doctor Rose Stanton.'

'Just a minute.'

The silence seemed to last forever but in the end John Worthing came to the phone.

'I'd like to see you,' Rose said hesitantly. 'Whenever it suits you. It won't take long.'

His reply was terse, almost as if she was a stranger.

'Saturday. Twelve-thirty. I'll pick you up at Victoria Street.' He rang off without another word.

At twelve twenty-five she was looking out of her window, watching for his Daimler to turn the corner into Victoria Street. She wished she had arranged to meet him away from Mrs Crabtree's prying eyes, but his manner on the phone had given her no chance to do so. The Saturday morning clinic had dragged on until noon, so that she had had to take the tram back home and had had time only to wash her face and change into her best dress of striped Macclesfield silk. Thank heaven she had now had her hair cut. The style suited her, with the sides curving forward on to her cheekbones and a fringe showing under the same straw hat which must see her through this summer. Yesterday evening had been spent in re-trimming it with pink Petersham ribbon to match her dress. She was annoyed with herself that she cared so much how she looked for this occasion, but there was no denying the truth of it. She wanted John Worthing to find her attractive – though she intended, all the same, that it should be no more than a business meeting.

At half-past twelve exactly the long, black limousine rounded the corner. She was downstairs and waiting on the pavement by the time it stopped outside number fifteen. John looked serious and unsmiling as he held open the door for her. As she took the seat beside him her heart thumped so loudly that she thought he must hear it. In less than a minute they were away. As on the previous occasion, he drove through the centre of Akersfield, though now it was thronged with Saturday shoppers, and took the road towards the moors. He drove in silence, his eyes fixed on the road ahead. Rose wondered why he did not ask her what it was she wanted. She felt that she was sitting here under false pretences.

'Where are we going?' She had to break the silence. Was he angry with her because she had telephoned him at home?

'Ilkley way. I haven't waited for your agreement this time. Since you asked to see me I've taken it that whatever it was about didn't preclude you eating. I've booked a table at the Heifer.'

He sounded neither angry nor pleased. His concentration seemed to be on his driving, which was fast and skilful. When it seemed that he had nothing more to say to her, Rose studied his profile, noted his aquiline nose and strong jawline, the curves of his full, yet firm, mouth, his strongly-marked dark eyebrows and uncommonly thick lashes. It was not a Yorkshire face. Somewhere in the past, she wondered, was there Middle Eastern blood? And everything worked together in his appearance. What he wore enhanced his strong good looks. The worsted of his dark suit was the finest, the velour of his grey trilby hat the smoothest, but a silk tie in reds and blues lifted the conventionality of his appearance, gave him the touch of flamboyance which suited him, added to his slightly foreign air. He took off his hat and handed it to her.

'Chuck it on to the back seat!'

She held it on her lap, finding a strange comfort in the feel of it, surreptitiously stroking the underside of the brim with the hand furthest away from him. It was almost as though she was stroking his own, dark hair.

He drove up through Barnswick and out again on the moorland road, travelling fast, not another car in sight.

'Don't you want to know what I want to see you about?' Rose asked him at last.

'Yes,' he said. 'But not until we've eaten.'

The Heifer Inn was on the bank of the river, close to the bridge. As they sat at their table, in an alcove by the window, they could see the clear brown, peaty water rippling over the pebbles. They ate fresh, local-caught trout, new lamb, strawberries, meanwhile making desultory conversation about matters of no importance, as if they were polite strangers. It was unbearable. Is this what I wanted? Rose asked herself. Had he absolutely ceased to care about her? Had he already – the thought stabbed her – found someone else who was prepared to be more generous than she was? But why bring her here at all? He could easily have summoned her to his office.

'We'll take coffee in the garden,' John Worthing told the waiter.

Not until they were seated in the shade of a tree and the waiter had served them and left them, did he say, 'And now what's it all about?'

It was a relief to be able to speak something other than pleasantries. Rose told him of the scheme she had in mind. She thought for a moment, just at first, that he looked disappointed, and she wondered what he had been expecting from her. But the look passed and as she unfolded her ideas with mounting enthusiasm he listened intently.

'I'm sure it would work,' Rose said. 'And it would make such a difference to the women I'm thinking of.'

'I like the idea,' he said. 'Of course there are details to be gone into – like do you want to buy a house in the country or at the seaside, or do you want to use existing boarding houses and have the mothers stay there. That kind of thing.'

'If we wait until we have enough money to buy a house, then we might have to wait a long time,' Rose said. 'We could work towards that, but it would be best in the first place to send the mothers to established boarding houses. That way we could make the money work right from the beginning . . .'

She broke off, conscious that for the first time that day he was smiling at her. She was glad to have lightened his mood, though she had no idea how.

'It's your enthusiasm,' he explained. 'It's a pity you can't run this thing yourself. Your enthusiasm would have people bending over backwards to help you.'

'Well I can't,' Rose said. 'You know my job won't allow it.'

'I do know. So I will. At least I'll start it off. I'll make a donation of a hundred pounds. It's not a fortune, but it's enough to do a bit of good, and not too much to arouse curiosity.'

His eyes met hers, and with relief she saw in them, for the first time that day, the admiration which he had been so quick to show on previous occasions.

'I'll have a word with the editor of the *Record*,' he said. 'He can publish the idea and start a subscription list.'

'What about the Health Committee?' Rose asked. 'Will they be awkward?'

'It's nothing to do with the Committee. They don't employ me. In fact I'll wager they'll chip in, especially if they can do it publicly. But don't worry, your name won't be mentioned.'

'I don't know how to thank you,' Rose said.

'Yes you do. But I'm not looking for thanks.'

There was a silence between them, which he was the first to break.

'Let's go for a walk,' he said suddenly. 'There's a path along the river bank, on the other side of the bridge.'

The path was stony, and so narrow and overhung by trees, that most of the time they had to walk in single file. When, about half a mile along the bank, they came to a gate which led into a field, John held it open and motioned Rose through, into the meadow which lay on the other side.

'I didn't bring you along here to walk behind you, conversing with the back of your neck,' he said. 'The grass is as dry as tinder here, so we can sit down. I want to talk to you.'

He sat down first, in the shelter of the wall, then took her hand and pulled her down beside him. She landed off balance, so that she fell against him. At once his arms were around her, holding her fast.

'Please John . . .'

He stopped her words with his kisses; searching, passionate, demanding kisses. After her first protest she gave in to him. But it was more than that, much more: she responded with a passion to match his own, her demands were no less than his. She had never known, until now, the feelings he released in her. It was as if she had suddenly been born; a new person, eager, aware, wanting to receive, longing to give. It was she who wanted no boundaries, he who suddenly pushed her from him and sat up. Rose lay outstretched on the ground, looking up at him, not understanding the abrupt change in his manner.

'I can't do this!' he said roughly. 'I didn't intend it. I didn't bring you here for a quick roll in the grass. I brought you here to talk to you. I told you on that evening three weeks ago that there were things I wanted to say to you. I brought you here to make you listen.'

Rose sat up. Her hands shook as she fastened the buttons of her dress. She was trembling from head to foot and she felt ashamed, not so much from what she had done as from what he might think of her. I didn't come for a roll in the grass, either, she wanted to say. It was the first and last time with him. It had to be. But the agony of that decision, swiftly taken, was almost more than she could bear. If he came back to her now, only touched her with one finger, would she be able to keep to it?

'Please listen to me, Rose,' he said.

She didn't want to listen. She was afraid that what he had to say might take away her resolve. She opened her mouth to protest, but no words came.

'You know my situation, Rose. My wife is ill. She's been an invalid since our daughter was born. I married her when she was eighteen and I was twenty. I knew almost at once that it was no good, but by then the baby was on the way. It was my fault. I was wrong for her from the start, but I'd persuaded her into marrying me. I can't ever give her what she wants from me but I owe her a debt.'

'John, you mustn't say this to me,' Rose interrupted. 'You can't want me to hear it.' Her heart ached for him; it hurt her to see this strong man shedding his pride.

'I do want you to hear it, Rose,' he insisted. 'I want you to know where we stand. I'm serious about you. There's no way I could ever leave Diana, not while she needs me. She depends on me totally. But you must know how I feel about you, Rose. It began the minute I saw you in the Committee room. I went away thinking about you. When I met you at the party on New Year's Eve you'd scarcely been out of my thoughts.'

It can't be happening, Rose thought. This green meadow, the sound of the river, the peace of the afternoon – and in her heart a turmoil which shattered everything. He was saying the things which with all her heart she wanted to hear, but could not take.

'I'm certain you feel the same way about me,' he said. 'Don't deny it.'

'I don't deny it,' she said softly. 'How could I? But there's no future in it.'

'Not the future we both want. I know that, Rose. Not what I would give you if I could. But something, surely? Something worth having. I love you, Rose.'

He pleaded with her as she could not have believed so arrogant a man could plead.

'That is infinitely worth having,' Rose said. 'I'm proud that you do. But I can't agree to the kind of relationship I know we both want, I as much as you. You know this has to be the start and the finish.'

He gave her a long look. She saw the hardness come back into his eyes, saw the proud lift of his head, wanted to take back everything she had said and to be in his arms again. She felt herself to be utterly defeated.

'Very well, I believe you, Rose – for the moment. But you'll find I don't give up easily. You'll change your mind. You will be mine in the end, you know!'

'We mustn't see each other again,' Rose said helplessly. It sounded trite, banal.

'Don't be ridiculous! That's impossible in Akersfield.'

'Then we must do the best we can.' She felt lifeless, as if nothing mattered any more. 'In the circumstances we must scrap my holiday scheme.'

'So you're willing to sacrifice these women for your own comfort? I don't believe that.'

'I wish I hadn't asked you,' she said. She wished she had never thought of it.

'I'm glad you did. There's nothing I wouldn't do for you, Rose. I mean that, in spite of everything.'

Except break up your marriage, she thought. But if he offered to do that, would she let him?

Once again he read her thoughts as if he was inside her head.

'If my wife were as strong as you are, I would leave her. As it is, she can't manage without me.'

But I must, Rose thought. For the rest of my life I must live without you. She wondered how she would bear it.

He held out a hand, pulled her to her feet. When she was standing before him he kissed her gently, no passion. Her lips were cold.

'It's you I love,' he said.

A shiver ran through her as they walked back along the river bank towards the car.

6

On Monday morning the postman brought Rose a letter from her mother. 'Your lass and her bairns will be welcome,' Mrs Stanton wrote. 'Emily will lend her a pram and she's looking out some baby clothes. I am sending you a parcel with some oatmeal parkin and a nice cheese.'

Rose smiled. She had been the recipient of such parcels all the time she had been in Medical School. Her mother constantly feared that, away from home, she would not eat enough. An unfounded fear, Rose thought, getting up from Mrs Crabtree's breakfast of bacon, eggs, sausages, bread and marmalade and lashings of hot, strong tea.

She was pleased, but not the least bit surprised, by the reply to her request. Her mother, in spite of her taciturn ways, would always give help where it was needed, and with the minimum of fuss and palaver. Rose knew that at the Ewe Lamb Eve Denby would be cared for by both her parents, cosseted even, in a quiet way which would not embarrass her. Now she must persuade the wretched husband to let his wife go, and that might not be so easy.

Rose wanted to give Alex the good news but for the last two days he had been visiting his aunt, in Manchester. She wouldn't see him until tonight. She had been surprised by how much she had missed him over the weekend. It had taken his absence to show her how close they had grown, what good friends they had become since she had come to live at Mrs Crabtree's. They were always there for each other to turn to. She suspected that on Alex's side the feeling was one of more than friendship, but it was not so for her. Her feeling for John Worthing – a feeling she did not want, which she passionately desired to tear out of herself – made that impossible.

She had wanted to see Alex when she returned from lunching with John Worthing on Saturday, her mind in turmoil, her spirits low. She badly needed his everyday sanity, the calmness of their friendship, but he had already left.

Unable to bear her own thoughts she had taken herself off to the cinema on Saturday evening, watched a film of which she afterwards remembered nothing, and on Sunday she had taken an early tram to Saltaire and walked vigorously over Shipley Glen. The outing had refreshed her body but it had done nothing to quieten her mind. She was glad when the weekend was over and she could get back to work.

On Monday afternoon it was the ante-natal clinic again.

'It's going to be a busy one,' Nurse Butterworth said. 'It's amazing how this clinic has grown.'

'It's good that more women are catching on to the idea of ante-natal care,' Rose said. 'The trouble is that most of these women ought to have been taking more care years ago, not just in the few months before they have the baby. Look at the state of their teeth, for instance!'

'Terrible!' Nurse Butterworth agreed.

It was a sad fact that there was always a procession of women from the ante-natal clinic to the dentist on the floor above, where most of the treatment was wholesale extractions. 'A tooth for every child,' Nurse Butterworth continued. 'But some of 'em lose the lot! But what can you expect? They've been badly fed from the cradle.'

Halfway through the afternoon Mabel Pearlman brought in another file.

'Mrs Denby is here,' she said. 'I told her she wanted the Infants' clinic, but she said not. I just can't believe it!'

'You should,' Rose said. 'You've seen it all before.'

'I've seen too much,' Mabel said. 'I'm never going to get married. I can tell you that for certain!'

Rose laughed. 'You'll change your mind. Most women do.'

'Even you, Doctor Rose?' Mabel asked cheekily.

The words went deeper than the girl could know. In her heart Rose knew that with part of her she envied every one of these women who came with their swelling bellies, and she coveted the tiny infants she so carefully tended. But such thoughts were an indulgence she did not often allow herself.

'I couldn't do my job if I were married,' she replied.

It was not quite true. She couldn't stay in this job but, married or not, she would always be a doctor. She had won that for herself and no-one could take it away from her. There was nothing against her setting up in practice if she could afford to do so. She recalled Gerald's words, that married to him she wouldn't starve while waiting for patients. It was the first time she had thought of Gerald in months. She knew now that whatever she did in the future, Gerald would not be part of it.

'So Mrs Denby will have to be seen by Doctor Stanton,' Mabel said. 'Seeing she's new to this clinic.'

'I suppose so,' Rose said.

But if luck was with her Doctor Stanton would pass Mrs Denby back as she had already treated her in the Infants' clinic. Would she unwittingly mention that she had been visited by Rose? Oh well, if it happens I'll simply have to deal with it, Rose thought. She hated her fights with Doctor Stanton. And now, she realized, she would have to visit the Denbys again to make arrangements for the visit to Faverwell.

She was pleasantly relieved when, towards the end of the afternoon, Mabel Pearlman showed Eva Denby into her room. 'Doctor Stanton has seen Mrs Denby,' she said. 'He said you should take over.' It seemed there were to be no repercussions.

'Sit down, Mrs Denby. How are you?' Rose said.

'I'm all right.'

It was the standard reply from most of the mothers. It

meant that they were surviving, that they had learned to take whatever came. To find out more she had to question them closely

She examined Eva. Her chest was not too good and she had the all-too-common pallor of skin and fingernails and the slight breathlessness of anaemia. She was also far too thin, each rib clear enough to be counted, her hip bones prominent under the inadequate covering of flesh.

'We'll have to try to build you up,' Rose said. 'By the way, I've had a letter from my mother. It's all right about the holiday!'

She had expected the girl to be pleased but she was taken aback by the sudden glow in Eva Denby's face. It was as if someone had lit a torch inside her.

'I'm glad you're happy about it,' Rose said. 'I can't discuss it here. It's not clinic business. I was thinking of visiting you tomorrow evening but perhaps you and your husband would like to come to see me instead?'

The light went out of Eva's face as suddenly as it appeared. 'It's no good, Doctor,' she said. 'He won't let me go.'

'Not let you go? You mean not let you come to see me?'

'Not let me go on holiday. He says he can't manage.'

'Can't manage? But you'll be taking both children with you. I've arranged that.'

'It's his dinners. There'll be nobody to make his dinners. And do his washing.'

There is no point in losing my temper, Rose told herself quickly. It won't help this poor, silly girl. *I* shall have to tackle that pig of a husband.

'Well, anyway, ask him to bring you to see me tomorrow evening. At about seven-thirty. Fifteen Victoria Street. Do you know where that is?'

'Yes I know it,' Eva Denby said.

'Will your mother look after the children while you come?'

Eva nodded.

'Very well then. And if you don't turn up I shall come to Paradine Street on Wednesday after clinic. Now this is what you are to do about the free milk and dinners . . .'

Rose had been home no more than a few minutes when there was a tap on the door and Alex entered.

'How did your weekend go?' she asked.

'Fine. And what about yours? What did he say?'

For one moment she was bewildered. The events of the day, her meeting with Eva Denby, had momentarily driven John Worthing out of her thoughts. But not really out of her mind. He was never quite that, only waiting in the wings; and now he came on stage again, as dominant as ever. She saw the dark, lively eyes, which sparked with passion when he looked at her, saw the full-lipped, sensual mouth, the shapely hands, heard the deepness of his voice – as if he was standing there before her.

'What did he say?' Alex repeated the question. 'About the fund?'

'Oh, the fund! He liked the idea. He said he'd back it; establish a fund and start it off with a hundred pounds.'

'Why, that's wonderful, Rose! You'll have the whole scheme going in no time. You could even fit in some holidays this summer.'

'I suppose so.'

'What do you mean, you suppose so? What's wrong? You don't look all that pleased.'

'Of course I'm pleased,' Rose said.

'You surely haven't gone off the idea? You were so keen.' Puzzled, he sought her face for an answer.

'Of course I haven't. Why would I do that?'

'I can't imagine.'

'There are several details to be settled,' Rose said. 'Where the mothers are to go not being the least of them. But I don't suppose I'll be involved in that.'

'I expect you will be,' Alex said. 'Once the fund's been set up I don't see that Doctor Stanton or anyone else can prevent you supporting it in your spare time. It's a good scheme.'

Providing it went ahead successfully it would be better not to be involved, Rose thought. If she was to know any peace of mind she must avoid John Worthing.

'My mother says she'll have Eva Denby and her children,' she said, changing the subject. 'But Mrs Denby now says she thinks that husband of hers won't let her go. I've asked them to come and see me here tomorrow evening. I thought I might do better with him on my own ground.'

'If he should come alone, call me in,' Alex said. 'I don't trust him as far as I can throw him.'

'I can deal with him,' Rose said firmly. 'He might scare the living daylights out of his wife but he doesn't frighten me.'

Until she heard the ring on the doorbell at half-past seven, followed by Mrs Crabtree's loud voice, with its overlay of refinement, and Jim Denby's rough, but somehow attractive tones, in reply, Rose had doubted whether the Denbys would come. She had warned her landlady of the impending visit, said that she would have to see them in her own room since other boarders were using the sitting room. Now Mrs Crabtree stood in her doorway, the Denbys behind her.

'Two *persons* to see you,' she said frostily. She did not like this kind of visitor and she hoped that Doctor Rose wasn't going to encourage such people often.

'Thank you Mrs Crabtree,' Rose said. 'Mr and Mrs Denby, please come in.'

Against the comparative comfort of her room they looked so shabby. It had not been as noticeable in Paradine Street, where everything was dilapidated and seedy, but here they looked dreadful. Mrs Denby's navy serge dress, clearly a hand-me-down and a poor one at that, fitted where it touched. It was hot and cumbersome for the summer evening and seemed to weigh her down. Her shoes were trodden over at the sides, scuffed at the toes. I must look out a summer dress or two, Rose thought.

Jim Denby was equally shabby, his jacket and shirt frayed, his trousers thin at the knees; but somehow his personality rose above his appearance. How splendid he would look, properly dressed, Rose found herself thinking. And how she disliked him. He stood there, cap in hand, but there was arrogance in his attitude.

'So what's all this our Eva's been telling me, Doctor,' he asked, taking the offensive.

'Well I expect she's been telling you that my mother has invited her to Faverwell for a fortnight's holiday. My parents keep an inn there. Naturally I wanted to see you about it also, though I knew you'd want her to go.'

It was humbug, but she had discovered on her visit to Paradine Street that it was the way to deal with this man. She was sure he could take no end of flattery. She saw the quizzical look Eva Denby gave her. She knows what I'm up to, Rose thought.

'So who's paying for all this?' he asked. 'Train fares, board and lodgings?'

'That will all be taken care of. You don't need to worry about that. All we have to think about is getting your wife well again. Once you're in work, if you want to repay the train fare you can do so.'

'Oh I should want to do that, Doctor,' he said swiftly. 'Naturally I'd want to do that!'

Never in this world, Rose thought.

'A pub,' Denby continued. 'Now that sounds very nice. Not that I'd want my wife going into a pub, not unless I was with her, you understand.'

'I understand perfectly,' Rose said. 'But I'm afraid that wouldn't be possible. Your wife would have my room. It has only a single bed. My mother will borrow a cot for the baby and perhaps Dorothy will have to share her mother's bed. But Mrs Denby won't be in the bar at all. I assure you my mother will look after her very well indeed.'

'Well I don't know . . .'

'You realize your wife is far from well, Mr Denby?' She spoke forcefully, looking him straight in the eye.

She sensed at once that she had touched a nerve. She saw the beginning of fear in the eyes which had been so bold in meeting her. It was the fear of someone who knew that death was no stranger to Paradine Street, and that it did not always wait for people to grow old.

He really is worried, Rose thought. Though most likely he was worried about what *he* would do if his wife were to be really ill. She pressed home her advantage, hating herself for playing on his fear. But after all, there was substance in it. The sanatoria were full of young men and women who would die from tuberculosis because they had lived in places like Paradine Street, where germs grew and multiplied, and they themselves were too run-down and weak to resist the infection. Eva Denby had no more immunity than some of those, and she was far from fit.

'It would be difficult for you, with Dorothy and the baby, if your wife were to be ill,' she said. 'It's not easy for a man, looking after things.'

She hated herself for the sympathy in her voice which this man took to himself. But if it was the only way . . .

'She could go on Saturday week. I'd make all the arrangements, get the train ticket and so on. So that's all right then, is it?'

She spoke as though he had already agreed. He gave in.

'I want whatever's best for my wife. Whatever's best.'

'Good! I knew you would!' She tried not to show her relief.

'And you say this has nothing to do with the clinic? It's all off your own bat?' he said.

'Quite!' But remembering Doctor Stanton she did not feel as confident as she sounded.

'Very well then,' she continued. 'I'll call and see you in a few days' time when I've made all the arrangements. I'll get the train ticket.'

'Now if you give me the money, there's something I could do for you,' Jim Denby offered quickly. 'No trouble at all and save you the time.'

And no chance at all, Rose thought. He'd never get as far as the booking office.

Eva, from first to last, had not spoken, but as Rose showed them out she turned to her with a smile of singular sweetness. a smile which reached to her beautiful eyes.

'Thank you, Doctor!' she said.

On the following Saturday afternoon Rose went again to Paradine Street. She passed the same women sitting in their doorways, the same small children playing by the drain. It took her all her time not to say something to the mothers but she doubted whether it would do any good. In any case, where else were the children to play?

Jim Denby opened the door of Number Seventeen.

'Come in, Doctor,' he invited.

It was dark, coming from the bright sunlight into the room – such a shabby little room with its stone-flagged floor with one meagre, rag rug in front of the fireplace. It was not until she stood in the room that she realized that Eva was not there.

'I had hoped to see your wife, Mr Denby. There are one or two arrangements . . .'

He had somehow manoeuvred her into the middle of the room and placed himself between her and the doorway. With his great physique he towered above her, so close that the aggressive masculine smell of his body filled her nostrils. She was not afraid, she told herself. It was his way of imposing himself on her simply because she was a woman. He wouldn't dare to try anything on, not with all those women outside who had seen her come in.

'Eva's gone to her mother's,' he said amicably. 'But that's all right, you can tell me.'

'It's nothing important,' Rose said quickly. 'Mrs Denby's mother lives in Babcock Street doesn't she?

I can walk that way and perhaps catch your wife there.'

'Hot weather to be walking the streets, Doctor. And not really your kind of streets at all. Not what you're used to. You should be careful coming into these parts on your own. Why, even the police only come in pairs!' His voice mocked her. 'It could be . . . awkward for the likes of you.'

'I'm sure I'm quite safe,' Rose said firmly. 'Doctors go anywhere.'

'Lady doctors?'

'Even lady doctors. And I assure you, I'm not in the least afraid.'

She challenged him deliberately with her boldness, with the direct look she gave him. He was not to know that her knees were trembling, her throat dry. He took a step towards her, raised his hand and touched her shoulder. She tried not to shudder as she felt the strength and heat of his hand through her thin blouse.

'You're really much too pretty to be a doctor!' The sudden, soft intimacy of his voice was more alarming than any of his blustering. 'That pretty red hair! I daresay you're a fiery one, given the right place!' It was clear to her what he thought the right place was.

Rose took a deep breath, managed to speak normally, ignoring his words.

'Well, I'll be off then, Mr Denby. I'll see your wife another time.'

She tried to side-step him but now his hand gripped her shoulder and she could not pass.

'Please let me go,' she said. 'This is rather silly.'

'Silly is it?' he said. 'You're the one who's silly, Doctor. Poking your nose into other people's business, coming down here with your posh ways. My Lady Bountiful throwing us a few scraps. What difference do you think you can make in the end? What can you do about this stinking, rotten existence? You'd draw the line at sharing it wouldn't you? When you leave here you'll be glad enough to go back to your fine room, your well-filled table.'

He spoke quickly, the words running together in a long, low growl. He was too intent to hear the door open and see the woman standing there.

'Could your Eva let us have a cup o' sugar?' she said.

Jim Denby turned at the sound of her voice and Rose slipped past him.

'Oh, I didn't know you had company!' the woman said.

Yes you did, Rose thought. You watched me come in. But thank heaven for your curiosity.

'Pardon me, but aren't you the lady doctor from the clinic?' the woman asked.

'That's right. And I'm just on my way.'

She'd like to know why I'm here, what my business is – and no doubt she'll somehow find out. It was impossible to do anything by stealth.

Rose decided to walk to Babcock Street. She had no wish to make a return visit to Paradine Street.

The whole area through which she now made her way was broken down and nasty: mean, rubbish-strewn streets, cracked pavements, houses which if they were not soon pulled down must surely fall down. There was nothing green. Not even grass or weeds would grow between the cobblestones here. Jim Denby's words rang in her ears. She shuddered at the remembrance of his touch but his words ate into her. 'What can you do about this stinking, rotten existence?'

In Babcock Street a woman told her where she could find Mrs Foster. The door was open and, standing on the step, Rose could see into the house. The room was basically like the one in Paradine Street, but altogether brighter, cleaner. And since there was no bed in view Rose assumed that Mrs Foster also had the bedroom upstairs, whereas in the case of the Denbys, the Health Visitor had informed her, the upper room was occupied by an old man who scarcely ever left it.

She knocked and called out, 'May I come in?'

Mrs Foster came to the door, Eva behind her.

'Why, it's Doctor Rose from the clinic!' Eva said.

'Step inside, Doctor,' Mrs Foster said. 'Pleased to meet you, I'm sure. Our Eva's told me about you.'

Rose was surprised and heartened to see that in these surroundings Eva Denby was different; still thin, pale, worried, but with more life and without the dumb despair which darkened her face when she was with her husband.

'I've been to Paradine Street,' Rose said. 'Your husband told me you were here.' At the mention of Jim Denby, Rose saw the hunted look come back into Eva's eyes.

'I came to say, would you be at the railway station next Saturday at two o'clock? I'll have your ticket for you and see you on to the train. Can you manage that?'

'She'll manage it all right. I'll see to that!' Mrs Foster promised. 'It's very good of you, Doctor. Very good indeed of you to take all this trouble.'

I guess *she* knows why I'm not parting with the ticket until the last minute, Rose thought. She knows as well as I do that if Jim Denby gets his hands on it he'll as likely as not sell it back and get the money.

'It's just what our Eva needs,' Mrs Foster went on. 'A couple of weeks away from everything. What she's going to do with three bairns and only the dole, I'm sure I don't know.'

'The dole's run out, Mam,' Eva said. 'We've been on relief for a month now.'

The three women stood silently for a minute. There were no words for their feelings. 'Well, there it is,' Mrs Foster said at last. 'As I said to Eva, I'd have been glad to take little Dorothy while Eva went away, to make things easier. But he wouldn't let me.'

'The fresh air will do Dorothy good,' Rose said.

She turned to Eva.

'All you have to do, Mrs Denby, is get off the train at Grassington and someone will be there to meet you.

95

Either my father or my brother-in-law. Oh! I've brought you a couple of summer dresses and a few other bits. I hope you don't mind.'

Eva took the parcel from Rose and opened it on the table.

'Oh Mam, just look here! Two lovely dresses – and a petticoat and a bodice! And look at this!' She held up a string of pink coral beads which Rose had included in the parcel. She turned to the small square of mirror on the mantelpiece, holding the beads against her neck, then turned again to Rose. 'Oh Doctor, they're beautiful! Aren't they beautiful, Mam?' Her eyes shone, her face was animated. This is how she used to look, Rose thought. No wonder that awful man wanted her, though how could she have fallen for him? But she remembered his good looks and his powerful masculinity. He had no doubt swept Eva off her feet.

'What size shoes do you take?' Rose asked.

'Fives.'

'A pity. Mine would be too small.'

'I'll see our Eva has a decent pair of shoes to go in,' Mrs Foster said. 'Don't you fret, Doctor. I'll manage it somehow. The Insurance man can wait, for one!'

That evening Alex came into Rose's room waving a copy of the Akersfield *Record*. 'Look at this, Rose!' She took it from him and read:

MOTHERS' HOLIDAY FUND
ENTERPRISING MOVE BY LOCAL COUNCILLOR

Councillor John Worthing, a well-known local bene-
factor, today deposited the sum of one hundred
pounds with the Penny Bank to launch a fund whose
aim will be to send young mothers, especially those
whose husbands are unemployed, on holiday.

'We shall not have to look far to find these needy
mothers,' Councillor Worthing declared. 'In these

days there are far too many of them, in Akersfield and elsewhere.'

The Councillor, ever ready to help a good cause, appealed to the people of Akersfield to support this fund by sending donations, large or small, either to the Penny Bank or to the Akersfield *Record* itself.

'The *Record* has done him proud,' Alex said. 'That'll set the fund off to a good start.'

'Councillor Worthing has done Akersfield proud,' Rose said quietly.

She had neither seen nor heard from John Worthing since their lunch together. It was better that way, she told herself. Better just to read about him in the newspaper.

'If I'm to be ready by seven-thirty I must make a start,' she said. Alex was taking her to a tennis club dance.

He looked at her keenly. There was something not quite right.

'You don't sound yourself, Rose. Promise me you're not getting too involved. The Denbys . . . the Fund . . . all those women you worry about in the clinic.'

'Do you expect me to be indifferent?' Rose asked. 'Shall I tell you what that awful Jim Denby said to me? He said "You'd draw the line at sharing it, wouldn't you?" I can't bear the man, but he was right.'

'I should hope so,' Alex said. 'You can't afford to get in too deep. You have realized that since the moment you started to train as a doctor. You have to keep your distance from these things. It's the same with me. I have to report no end of things I dislike, I come across injustices all the time, but I can't let myself get entangled in them or I'd not do my job properly. That applies to you, Rose.'

Rose shook her head. 'I don't see it like that.'

He took her hands in his, drew her towards him.

'I really do want your happiness, Rose. I'd do anything for you. You know that, don't you?'

'Yes. And it means a lot to me.'

'I wish you felt about me as I do about you.'

'I wish I did, dear Alex,' Rose said. And it was true.

Eva Denby, carrying the baby and accompanied by her mother, who had Dorothy by the hand, was at the station early. She was relieved that Jim had decided not to come, but not surprised. He hated his mother-in-law and on this occasion Mrs Foster flatly refused to be left out of the party. She would not feel secure about this holiday until she had seen Eva safely in the train and the train pulling out of the station, without Jim Denby. She prayed to God that he would make no attempt to visit Eva in Faverwell.

The two women sat on a bench in the station forecourt. It was exciting just to be here, to watch the luckier citizens of Akersfield, those who had somehow managed to hold on to jobs in spite of everything, the straw-hatted men and women with their large suitcases and carpet bags, the children with their buckets and spades, on their way to or from the seaside. Mrs Foster felt that she could have spent the day in the station, happy simply to be part of the scene. Eva was more intent on watching for Doctor Rose and felt a great relief when she saw her walk into the station, accompanied by a tall, fair man. She waved her hand and Doctor Rose spotted her through the crowd and came across.

'This is Mr Bairstow,' she said.

Alex had insisted on accompanying her in case, he said, Jim Denby turned up and started any awkward business.

'A lovely day for the start of your holiday,' Rose said. 'Now here is your ticket. And this is something for the journey; sandwiches, and some fruit and chocolate.'

Eva took the paper bag from Doctor Rose. She would have liked to have started on it there and then but for the sake of politeness she put it in the top of the carpet bag which contained her clothes and the children's for the holiday. Although her mother had given her some dinner before they left Babcock Street, she was still hungry. She was always hungry, as though she had some ravenous beast inside her, waiting to be fed. But it was not a wild beast, it was a baby, which, try as she might, she did not want. She was ashamed of the fact that she could offer it no welcome.

She was also ashamed of the carpet bag, which had a hole in one corner. How wonderful it would have been to have carried a suitcase, even a cardboard one; but no-one she knew had such a thing because very few of her acquaintances had ever been on holiday for more than a day.

'Thank you, Doctor Rose,' she said.

'I think the train will be in,' Rose said. 'Platform three. Why don't we get you settled?'

They all four, plus the children, trooped on to the platform. It was all excitement, all marvellous, even the snorting engine which let off steam just as they passed, frightening little Dorothy half to death so that her cries and the engine's noise echoed together against the station's high glass roof. Eva breathed in the steamy smell and vowed that she would never forget it. When, some minutes later, she waved good-bye to everyone, felt the bump as the train moved, watched the party on the platform getting smaller and smaller as they receded into the distance, it was with the most tremendous sense of adventure, all her troubles for the moment forgotten.

Mr Bairstow seemed a nice fellow. He had pushed a brand new copy of *Peg's Paper* into her hand before the train left. Was he Doctor Rose's Young Man? She doubted if anyone in the world was good enough for Doctor Rose.

When the figures on the platform were no longer visible and the train was steaming its way through the suburbs of Akersfield, she took out the paper bag and began to eat, spreading her handkerchief over her lap so that no crumbs should soil the pretty, pink-flowered dress which Doctor Rose had given her. From time to time her hand strayed towards the coral necklace around her throat.

7

Heaven must be something like Faverwell, Eva thought. Her mother reckoned heaven was a big garden with lots of lawns and with the Black Dyke Mills Band somewhere in the background, playing 'The Lost Chord' and selections from 'The Gondoliers': three nice meals a day waiting for you when you went in from the garden, and an occasional glass of Guinness in the evenings.

Eva, pushing the pram slowly along the road which ran by the river, could now disagree. The baby, propped against Mrs Stanton's snowy-white pillow; Dorothy, who was forward at walking but did not yet talk, tottering beside the pram; Bess, the Stantons' ancient sheepdog who had taken upon herself the guardianship of this new family, walking at the same easy pace: the high green hills, and the river itself, rushing over the stones here, but dark and still down by the bridge – what better combination could heaven offer? And there was no mill smoke to blacken everything it touched, no coal carts, no rubbish spilling in the road.

The only thing was that once you got to heaven you presumably stayed there, but in her case she would have to go back to Paradine Street. And to Jim. Not only that, but the child she was carrying would inevitably make its appearance, bringing more trouble with it. She had almost stopped being sick in the mornings now and after ten days in Faverwell felt better in her body, but nothing stilled, completely, the fear and apprehension in her mind.

'We'd best turn back now,' she said to Dorothy. 'We mustn't be late for dinner. Would you like a ride on the pram then?'

Although Dorothy seldom spoke, she understood every word that was said to her. Now she stood in the road, holding out her arms to be lifted up.

'I wonder what's for dinner?' Eva said.

Every day it was something delicious. Ham and new potatoes; a meat-and-potato pie running with gravy; a forerib of beef with Yorkshire pudding, and potatoes roasted around the joint. And to follow, treacle tarts, gooseberry pies, apple charlottes, jam rolls. And then later in the day the teas! Ox tongue, tinned salmon, potted meat, currant pasty, stewed fruit, sponge cakes: the kind of food you got only at funeral teas in Akersfield. Eva's mouth watered in anticipation and remembrance. She swung Dorothy into the pram and stepped up her pace along the road back to the Ewe Lamb.

'Just in nice time!' Mrs Stanton said, opening the door to them. 'It's shepherd's pie.'

'I wondered if you'd like to give me a hand with the church brasses this afternoon,' she said when they were sitting down to heaped plates. 'The little lass can have her nap and Mr Stanton'll keep an ear open. We'll take the babby along wi' us.'

'I'd be more than willing,' Eva said.

She had done whatever she could to help Mrs Stanton but she had not been allowed to do any heavy work; nothing more strenuous than dusting, mending, polishing the glasses in the bar – that sort of thing.

Eva had seldom been inside a church except for one or two christenings and, even rarer, weddings. It was cool and dim quiet and still, smelling of summer flowers. Through the clear glass windows she could see the green fells and the blue sky behind.

'Now,' Mrs Stanton said briskly, 'Candlesticks or lectern, which is it to be for you?'

The lectern, it appeared, was the big, brass eagle on which the Bible stood.

'I'll tackle the lectern,' Eva said.

Her mother would have enjoyed this, she thought, setting to work. Mrs Foster's favourite household task was blacking the grate and the fireirons and polishing the brass rail and knobs on the fender. But Babcock Street seemed a long way away. Eva rubbed hard at the massive bird, giving extra strength to the breast feathers, and the sun streamed in through the window, changing the brass to pure gold.

'You're making a real good job of that,' Mrs Stanton said. 'It was about the only job I could get our Rose to do when she was a little girl.'

It was pleasant to think of Doctor Rose doing this. None of the other mothers in the clinic would know that much about her. It made her seem, just for the minute, almost a friend.

When she had finished the lectern, the eagle shining gloriously, reflecting her own face – and Mrs Stanton was still at work in the vestry on what she called the plate – Eva sat at the back of the church, Baby Meg asleep in a basket in the pew beside her. She desired so much to pray, but the words would not come. And she knew that the reason they would not come was that what she wanted to pray for was not right. Dear God, she wanted to say, please take away the baby in my body. But she was afraid to say it. Supposing her request angered him and he punished her by striking at Baby Meg or Dorothy? Vengeance is mine, saith the Lord. I will repay. She could not put the children at risk.

If only there was something she *could* do! But she had no idea what. If she had mixed more with the women in Paradine Street, shown herself readier to join in the gossip, they would have advised her what to do in such circumstances. Eat a pound of parsley, some said; but that must be a pillowcase full – and where would she get hold of it anyway? And if it didn't work, then what about the baby? That much parsley could turn the blood green!

'There! All done and dusted,' Mrs Stanton said, emerging from the vestry, taking off her pinafore. 'I was just

thinking that you'd said you'd like to walk up Faver
Fell. If you want to do that tomorrow I'll look after the
bairns. Mind you, you mustn't expect to climb to the
top, not in your condition. It's quite a hill. But lovely
views, even from halfway up.'

It was something Eva had wanted to do from the day
she had arrived in Faverwell and seen the green hillside
rising up behind the village. 'Thank you. I'd like that,'
she said.

The following day she set off after breakfast, Mrs
Stanton pressing a packet of sandwiches into her hand.

'For biting on,' she said. 'It's hungry work, walking.
Keep to the path. I'll expect you back for dinnertime and
if you're a bit late I'll keep your dinner in the oven.'

The track was clearly defined. Around Eva as she
walked the black-faced sheep cropped the grass to a green
sward. Some of these sheep would be Mr Bishop's. He
and his wife, Doctor Rose's sister, had been very kind to
her. Everyone in Faverwell was kind.

At first the slopes were gentle, short grass underfoot,
but then they became steeper, with rocky outcrops and
areas of scree over which she had to scramble as best she
could. In her mind she had determined to reach the top,
but it was hard going. Up and up she climbed, keeping
her eyes firmly on the summit, not allowing herself to look
back. But in the end, though she was no more than a few
hundred yards from the summit, her heart pounding and
no breath left in her, she knew she had to stop. She would
sit awhile, eat her sandwiches, and then try again.

The view from this height was stupendous. The river
wound its way up the dale, here and there disappearing
under a bank of trees. The cattle in the fields looked like
toy farmyard animals and the village itself like a child's
plaything. A rare motor car moved like a small, black
beetle along the twisting road. In all her life she had never
seen a view like this. Also the sandwiches, homecured
ham spread with Colman's mustard, were first class.

She had just eaten the last crumb, licked her fingers,

when the pain started; too soon and too fierce to be indigestion. She knew at once that she would never reach the top of the fell and, seeing the long hillside which stretched down before her, her disappointment was mingled with worry as to how she would get to the bottom. Then the pain went away as suddenly as it had come and she set off at once down the slope.

But within minutes it was back again. Sweat broke out in great beads on her forehead and ran down her face. The pain came and went, though never leaving her for long. Sometimes it tore at her so badly that she had to lie down on the grass, biting her knuckles so as not to scream. Whenever it eased she went forward a few yards. Nothing more than blind instinct and an overwhelming desire to reach some haven, got her back eventually to the Ewe Lamb. As she went in the door she felt the blood trickle down her thighs.

'George, get Doctor Harper at once!' she heard Mrs Stanton say. And then she was in Doctor Rose's bed, with the deep blackness of the pain and the sound of the rushing beck coming together to drown her. Mrs Stanton's voice, a long way away and perhaps some time after, for it was dusk in the room, said, 'I'm afraid she's lost the baby.'

Rose was getting ready to leave the clinic after what had been a busy day when the telephone message came through.

'I'm speaking from the post office,' her mother said, shouting because she was not used to the telephone and could not believe that anything other than the full use of her lungs could carry her voice as far as Akersfield. 'Can you hear me?'

'Perfectly! Is everything all right?'

'No it isn't,' Mrs Stanton said. 'Well, I suppose it is now, in a sort of way . . .'

'What do you mean, Mother?'

'It's Eva. She's had a miscarriage. She won't be able

to travel back to Akersfield on Saturday. You'll have to tell her husband.'

Shall I ask Alex to go with me? Rose wondered when the brief conversation was over. She did not fancy another encounter with Jim Denby. But it was her responsibility; why should she involve Alex? She would go to Paradine Street right away and get it over with.

In one way she could not feel too unhappy about the miscarriage. Nature had, not for the first time in Rose's experience, found her own solution. But she abominated the worry which had gone before, the unfruitful pain, the waste of a life, though hardly formed. Women who had suffered miscarriages had told her that they were affected in mind and spirit as much as in their bodies, and for a long time after the event. Some even said that the pain was worse than that of giving birth. Eva would recover, but she was not in a condition to do so easily. She needed to take things quietly for a while, to be built up again. That much she must, at all costs, get across to Jim Denby. But at least she didn't expect him to be unduly upset at the loss of the baby.

She was wrong about that. Facing him across the table, which was littered with the dirty pots and pans and detritus of what looked like every meal since Eva had left, she saw the quick anger flare in his face as she broke the news.

'This is your doing!' he shouted. 'I hold you responsible for this! I never wanted my wife to go away. I knew she wasn't fit.'

'I'm sorry,' Rose said. 'I truly am. I'm sorry Eva has had to go through this. But going to Faverwell wasn't the cause. On the contrary, it might well have prevented it. But she was clearly not strong enough to carry the baby. Nature has its own way of dealing with some situations, you know.'

'That's a load of rubbish! She carried the other two, didn't she? She had no trouble at all until you started interfering. *If* she'd stayed at home, *if* she'd never gone near your bloody clinic, this would never have happened. I don't . . .'

'Mr Denby,' Rose interrupted. 'It could have, I assure you. It was always on the cards.'

He was not listening to her. He had stopped shouting and was looking at her intently, a sharp, calculating expression on his face. There was a moment of charged silence as they looked at each other. Rose felt a *frisson* of apprehension. When he spoke his voice was quiet and incisive.

'As I remember it, Doctor, you did all this off your own bat? Nothing to do with the clinic, didn't you say?'

'That's right.'

'Aye, I thought so. So I should think your employers'll be none too pleased. You might get into a deal o' trouble – sending a patient away, causing her to lose her baby!'

'I've told you, it is not at all like that . . .'

'It's exactly like that, Doctor. And it doesn't sound too good, does it? After all, you didn't know my wife, except through the clinic. You'd never have met her otherwise. Now our Eva said there was another doctor up there, a man who was the boss . . .'

'Doctor Stanton is head of the clinic.'

'That's it. Doctor Stanton. But of course he doesn't have to know . . . well, not your part in it anyway.' Jim Denby's voice was silky smooth. 'She could have had the miscarriage right here in this place.'

'Which is exactly what I've been saying!' But thank heaven for Eva's sake that she hadn't. It was a hell-hole.

'But she didn't, did she, Doctor? She had it right in your mother's house. Well now, I can see I'm going to be put to a lot of expense over this. There's the question of money to go and visit my wife. I can't leave her alone in her hour of trouble, can I? And I can't go empty handed. Flowers, chocolates . . . And then when I bring her home there'll be extra foods, little comforts . . . Yes, a lot of expense. It could easily come to fifty pounds. Oh yes, quite easily. But worth it, wouldn't you say?'

Disbelief and fierce anger struggled in Rose. She could have leaned across the table and struck him, wiped the leer from his slack mouth, the cunning from his eyes. But she forced herself to speak calmly.

'That's blackmail, Mr Denby. I could go to the police, you realize that?'

'But you won't, will you, Doctor?' he said softly. 'It wouldn't be very nice for my Eva, wouldn't do her any good at all if you was to go to the police. We have to think of her, don't we?'

He was clever all right. But Rose had no intention of letting the slimy creature get the better of her.

'For the sake of your wife I shall not go to the police,' she said. 'Not this time. But if blackmail is your game you've picked the wrong person. I don't respond to threats, Mr Denby. I shall give you enough money to visit your wife in Faverwell, and to take something to cheer her up. That is all, and not a penny more.'

She opened her purse, took out a pound note and a ten shilling note and laid them on the table.

He stared at her defiantly.

'Thirty bob for the life of a bairn! So you reckon that's all it's worth?'

'I reckon it's all you're getting,' Rose retorted. 'Your wife lost the baby because she wasn't fit to carry it, because she should never have been made pregnant. I hope you see to it that she's not made pregnant again, not until she's fit and ready.'

His fair skin flushed scarlet, his blue eyes bulged and blazed with anger. He raised his hand as if he would strike her and she was glad of the width of the table between them. But it would never do to let this man see that she was afraid.

'You interfering bitch!' he shouted. 'You foul-mouthed virgin! What do you know about anything?'

'Enough to see the results!' Rose cried. 'It's men like you . . .'

'Men like me,' he broke in scornfully. 'You know nowt

about men like me – nor any others for that matter. I knew that when I first clapped eyes on you. I know when a woman's never had a man. You live through other people. You know nowt yersen. I could give you a lesson you wouldn't forget in a hurry!'

'If you dare to lay one finger on me I *shall* go to the police!' Rose threatened. She was sick with fear. She felt powerless against him. But something . . . perhaps it was her refusal to show fear, she would never know – changed his attitude.

'Get out then,' he said savagely. 'Get out! And don't think you've heard the last of this. You haven't, not by a long chalk!'

She left quickly, head held high, looking neither to left nor to right as she passed the inevitable group of women. She knew she ought to go and break the news to Eva's mother but as yet she didn't feel able to. She was trembling from head to toe, as much from anger as from fear. Foul-mouthed virgin he had called her. Her anger lasted all the way to Victoria Street, where she met Alex, also on his way in.

'What's wrong?' he asked.

A few minutes later he brought a tot of whisky up to her room.

'Get this down you,' he ordered. 'You look all in. Why didn't you let me go with you? I'd have dealt with him!'

'I *did* deal with him,' Rose pointed out. 'And really, I don't need whisky.' But she sipped it gratefully all the same. Inside herself she knew that it was not Jim Denby's threats – frightening though they had been at the time – which had upset her most. It was the other things he had said. He had said out loud things she preferred to bury in her own heart.

Though Denby meant it as an insult, to be called a virgin was, to Rose, the least of his taunts. In his eyes it denoted a woman who was of no worth at all; sexless, too sterile ever to flower. That was not true of her. It *was not true*! The feelings John Worthing had so quickly aroused in her were the proof of that. She knew herself to be as able to love, as capable of sexual passion, as any other woman. But even had the man she loved been free, her job at the Welfare Centre precluded marriage. In accepting it she had knowingly relinquished her chance of wifehood, motherhood. She complied with the rules, unwillingly, since there was little she could do about them. Yet Doctor John Stanton was doubtless considered a better doctor because he had a wife and five children.

But it was the other things John Denby had said which had given her a jolt. 'You live through other people. You know nothing for yourself.' Could that be true? Would it always be so?

That was the way it was for a vast number of women. The war had robbed them in their thousands of husbands, lovers, the possibility of bearing children. Since there were not enough men to go around they would go through life dry virgins, denied the experience which most people thought made a true woman. They would seek fulfilment in work, suppress their sexual emotions, expend their maternal feelings on other people's children. Could she be content with that? In spite of herself, the blatant masculinity of that lout of a man had challenged her afresh.

'Anyway,' Alex said. 'Put him out of your mind. I've got – pleasanter news.'

It was more easily said than done. Jim Denby had made her face more than she wished to.

'Do you want to hear it?' Alex asked.

'Of course! I'm sorry.'

'John Worthing's giving a garden party. He does it every year for some charity or other. And I've been sent two tickets. But that's not all. Guess what the profits are going to?'

'Not the Mothers' Holiday Fund?'

'Right first time!'

She wondered, for a moment, why John Worthing had not sent an invitation to her. Perhaps he had assumed, correctly as it happened, that she would not attend alone, but that the sending of two tickets to Alex Bairstow would bring her.

'Where's it to be?'

'At his own home. He lives on the outskirts of Akersfield. A house called Moorgate – well you know that, you telephoned him there. It's a big place. Standing – as the advertisements say – in its own grounds. You'll like it.'

'I'm not sure I want to go,' Rose said.

She wanted to with all her heart. She wanted to see him again; she wanted to see him in his own setting. But could she bear it, this glimpse of intimacy?

'You must go,' Alex said. 'No question about it. If only because it's for your project. Besides, anyone who is anyone will be there. It's your chance to meet Akersfield society. Also, if it means anything to you, it would give me the greatest pleasure in the world to take you there.'

'Thank you, Alex. I appreciate that. And I'll think about it,' she promised.

'In the meantime,' he said. 'If we don't go down to supper it'll be all over. I'm not allowing you to miss a meal just because you feel a bit down.'

The ante-natal clinic was in full swing, the waiting benches on the landing crowded. It seemed to Rose that half the women in Akersfield were pregnant. She was busy examining a patient when she heard the unmistakeable voice of Jim Denby, loud and strong, in full spate.

'Right, Mrs Fletcher,' Rose said. 'You can get dressed now. Please excuse me. I'll be back in a minute.'

He was standing on the landing, shouting, a flustered Miss Pearlman trying unsuccessfully to quieten him.

'I demand to see the Chief Doctor,' he yelled. 'I know my rights. l demand to see him at once!'

As Rose came out of her room he swung around and pointed an accusing finger at her.

'She's the one!' he shouted. 'Doctor Lah-di-dah Rose! She's the one who lost my wife her baby!'

He turned towards the waiting mothers, who had at once ceased their conversations, not wishing to miss such a promising diversion.

'Don't let her near you, any of you! Don't you take the risk! Otherwise that little lot you're carrying . . .' His eyes swept their burgeoning figures '. . . might never live to know you.'

He was unsteady on his feet, lurching a little as he spoke, and his words were too carefully enunciated. Also, Rose doubted not at all, this was how he had used the money she had given him to visit Eva in Faverwell. What a fool she had been to put the cash in his hand.

'You're drunk, Jim Denby!' one of the mothers called out. 'I know you.'

'I've had a drink,' he said carefully. 'Which I don't deny. I had it to console myself. This woman . . . this woman who calls herself a doctor . . . has robbed me of my bairn. She's an interfering bitch! Don't you let her come near you!'

Two dozen pairs of eyes swung around to Rose. They half believe him, she thought. They're wondering what I've done. They're wondering if I've given her some terrible treatment which I'm about to force on them! She could see the apprehension beginning in their eyes.

'Mr Denby, you must calm yourself,' she said firmly. 'You can't come in here upsetting everyone like this. You know you're talking nonsense.'

'Nonsense is it? Well I'll see your boss and we'll see if *he* thinks it's nonsense.'

'Shall I tell Doctor Stanton?' Miss Pearlman asked. 'What shall I do?'

At that moment Nurse Butterworth came out of Doctor Stanton's room. She positioned herself squarely in front of Jim Denby, arms akimbo. He swayed a little towards her.

'Now my man, what's all this about?' she demanded. 'You can't come in here making this sort of noise!'

'Oh yes I can,' he said belligerently. 'And I don't want

any truck with you. I want to see the doctor. The real doctor, not this one.' He pointed at Rose. 'She's the one who lost my wife her baby. She's the one . . .'

Nurse Butterworth cut him off. 'We've heard all that rubbish. Anyone can hear you a mile off. You can go in to Doctor Stanton now and he'll give you ten minutes. Not a second longer. And I wouldn't stand too close to him if I were you. He doesn't care for the smell of drink.'

All eyes followed him as he went with Nurse Butterworth – and then turned to look with curiosity at Rose.

'I'm sorry about that, ladies,' she said. 'Don't let it worry you. The explanation is quite simple. I'll be ready for my next patient in five minutes.'

Back in her room she sat behind her desk, her head in her hands, taking deep breaths to try to calm herself. It was all nonsense, of course. No-one was going to take much notice of a drunken oaf. She pulled herself together, stepped out on to the landing and called for the next patient . . .

'Mrs Porter!'

There was an uncomfortable silence and then a woman said, 'She's left, Doctor. She went home.'

Rose discovered, going through the list, that six of the women had left. It was unbelievable! Was her reputation as a doctor so slight that a drunk in a rage could undermine it like this?

Her next patient in was the woman who had recognized Jim Denby.

'I know him for what he is, Doctor,' she said. 'A bastard if ever there was one – if you'll pardon the language. All wind and water, but a nasty piece of work. I've tried telling that lot out there but some of 'em only take notice of whoever shouts loudest. And of course they're worried about their babies,' she added frankly.

Miss Pearlman knocked and popped her head around the door. 'Doctor Stanton would like to see you as soon as you've finished with this patient.'

It might have been her imagination, but it seemed to Rose, as she crossed the landing to Doctor Stanton's room, that the benches were even emptier. When she went in Jim Denby was seated opposite to her boss.

'This is her,' he began. There was triumph in his face and in his voice.

'Thank you Mr Denby,' Doctor Stanton said. 'I have noted all you've said.' He turned to Rose.

'Mr Denby has made certain accusations, Doctor. To get matters into perspective I would be grateful if you would answer one or two questions in his presence.'

'Certainly Doctor.' But why did he not see her alone? Why was she not allowed to present her side, as Denby had his? Also, she badly wanted to sit down. Her knees were trembling. Jim Denby occupied the only visitor's chair and she was obliged to stand.

'Quite simply,' Doctor Stanton said, 'is it true, as Mr Denby states, that you arranged for his wife to go away to your parents' home, that you paid for her to do so?'

'Yes but . . .'

'We won't go into the reasons just now. And is it true that while there, Mrs Denby has suffered a miscarriage?'

'Quite true. But in my opinion . . .'

Doctor Stanton held up a hand, silencing her.

'We will discuss all that later, Doctor. I wanted to verify, or otherwise, Mr Denby's statements. I won't keep you any longer, Doctor. I'll see you later this afternoon. Just now we have a busy clinic.'

Less busy than you believe, Rose thought. Why would the man not allow her to put her side? But perhaps he had a point. There could be no reasoning in Jim Denby's presence.

Denby followed her out, a yard or two behind her as she crossed the landing. 'You'll not get away with it!' he shouted. 'I'll make you pay for this, Madam! I'll see the papers get hold of this!'

Yet it is not the loss of the baby he is making me pay for, Rose thought. She was to pay in another way because she had refused to succumb to his blackmail; and because, somehow, she had interfered with his masculinity, had dared to suggest that he went easy on his wife.

At the end of the clinic she presented herself to Doctor Stanton again. He faced her with a stern, cold expression.

'It is true, is it not, that you knew Mrs Denby only as a patient in the clinic? You were not acquainted with her otherwise?'

'Quite true,' Rose agreed. 'What I did was a private thing.'

'I must differ with you about that,' he said. 'However, allow me to continue. I wish first of all to know why I was not informed of Mrs Denby's miscarriage. I understand you yourself were acquainted with the fact twenty-four hours ago.'

'You were not here,' Rose pointed out. 'You left to attend a meeting before my mother telephoned with the news. And you were not on duty this morning. Of course I would have told you at the first opportunity. How could I do otherwise?'

'But in your own good time, I imagine. While I, together with everyone in the clinic, I am sure, have to hear it from her husband. The fact that he is an odious creature does not alter the fact that he would seem to have right on his side.'

'It is not as clear cut as that, Doctor . . .'

'On the contrary . . .' He was getting into his stride now, really enjoying himself, Rose thought. He's been waiting all these months for an opportunity like this. He's not going to let me down lightly.

'. . . On the contrary, it seems particularly clear cut to me. In the first place, had I been consulted, which I was not, I would have cautioned against Mrs Denby going away from home at a time like this. I would have said she was not in a fit state to travel. In fact – reluctant though I am to agree with Mr Denby – I have to say that I believe that if Mrs Denby had stayed at home in

Akersfield she would not have lost her child. You can see for yourself the gravity of this position.'

'But it's not true!' Rose cried. 'It's a hundred to one that Mrs Denby miscarried because she was too weak to bear another child so soon after the last one. She conceived when her baby was only three weeks old and her elder child eighteen months. Perhaps it's just as well she did miscarry.'

'How dare you say such a thing?' Doctor Stanton demanded. 'It is not for us . . .'

'I dare more,' Rose interrupted. 'I dare to say that as doctors we evade our responsibility by not advising women in Mrs Denby's position how to avoid having too many children. I say we have a duty to do just that.'

'Then you are in the wrong profession. Birth control is not, and never has been, part of any doctor's training. It does not lie within our orbit.' His voice was cold, measured. The flat calm of his statements goaded Rose more than a display of feeling could ever have done.

'That's false reasoning!' she cried passionately. 'It's not long ago that most doctors thought anaesthetics were wrong, that patients were meant to bear pain. That didn't mean doctors were right – and most of them now think differently. It will be the same with contraception.'

'Not in my clinic,' Doctor Stanton said. 'And may I remind you, Doctor, that you are working in my clinic. You are not independent, though I daresay you would like to be. You are responsible to me for any actions which affect our patients. So far I have to say that, although I do not question your medical skill, you have been a disruptive influence. One could hardly describe today's incident as other than disruptive!'

It was no use. She would never get through to him. She wished, for a moment, that he *had* been allowed a say in the choosing of his assistant. None of this would have happened, and half-a-dozen pregnant women who needed medical care would not have walked out and abandoned it. He had yet to learn about that.

'What do you propose to do?' she asked quietly.

His answer surprised her.

'Nothing. Unless the husband takes this further I shall do nothing. If more unpleasantness occurs, why then, I shall have no option but to place the matter before the Committee. By the way, I gave the man a pound to go to see his wife. I consider we owe him that much. And it might be that that will serve to quieten him. You may reimburse me or not, as you wish.'

She could not help it. In spite of the deep disturbance within her, Rose smiled a wide smile.

'Of course I will reimburse you, Doctor. But don't think the money will take Jim Denby to see his wife. His concern doesn't stretch that far. It will go straight into the till of the nearest pub, where the thirty shillings I gave him obviously went!'

8

Three days later, when Rose returned in the late afternoon from the clinic, Mrs Crabtree stood in the hall, waving a copy of the Akersfield *Record*.

'There's a bit in here about your clinic!' she said, her voice high with excitement. 'Have you seen it? "Akersfield Mother Loses Baby" . . .'

'Could I borrow that for a moment?' Rose said abruptly. Without waiting for a reply she snatched the paper from her landlady's hand and ran up the stairs.

Mrs Crabtree was disappointed. She had hoped to relate the story and have a nice discussion about it with her favourite boarder. Not that Doctor Rose's name was mentioned, but Mrs Crabtree distinctly remembered that a Mr and Mrs Denby had called a few weeks back. She hadn't liked the look of them at the time and she flattered herself that she was seldom wrong about people.

In her own room, not stopping to take off her hat and gloves, Rose began to read; and as she did so the sick feeling which Mrs Crabtree's words had given her increased. It seemed incredible that this could be happening. The report had a prominent position in the 'Letters to the Editor' section – a part of the paper which, Alex had told her, people sometimes read more avidly than the news because it was a better source of local gossip.

Dear Sir, (she read)

In view of the recently launched Holiday Fund for Mothers, readers of the *Record* will be concerned to hear that a young mother, recently despatched on just such a holiday (though not by the fund), suffered a miscarriage and lost the child she was expecting. 'She is too ill to return home,' her distraught and grieving husband told me. 'I am convinced that this would never have happened if my wife had not been sent away. She was clearly not fit to travel.'

If this is to be the result of sending mothers on holiday we should think twice about the Mothers' Holiday Fund. Leave well alone, I say.

Mrs Denby, at the time she was sent away, was attending Akersfield's Infant Welfare Clinic.

Yours faithfully,
P. Blamires, Esq.

It was unbelievable! Rose had dismissed Jim Denby's threat that he would go to the newspaper as an idle one, or in the remote chance that he did so, that the *Record* wouldn't entertain him. So who was this P. Blamires who had taken up the cudgels on his behalf?

She was so unutterably tired of it. Since their stormy interview Doctor Stanton had scarcely spoken to her and he had made a point of seeing as many patients as possible himself, handing next to no-one over to her. Of the six women who had walked out, only one had returned, and two more had left since. There was clearly no doubt in Doctor Stanton's mind as to where the blame lay, and it seemed that Nurse Butterworth shared his view. She was professionally polite, but no longer friendly. Only Mabel Pearlman seemed to be on Rose's side. In the last few days Rose had been grateful for the encouraging smiles she had received from Mabel and had forced herself to drink all the extra cups of tea which the girl, it being her way of giving comfort, had sneaked in to her.

She took off her hat and gloves and threw them on the table. She picked up the paper again and was re-reading the letter when she heard Alex's knock. When he came in she realized by the look on his face that he knew all about it.

'Why didn't you warn me?' she demanded. 'You could at least have warned me. Or you could have stopped it.'

'I didn't know,' Alex said. 'The Old Man keeps "Letters to the Editor" close to his chest. But in any case it's not something I could have stopped.'

'Not stopped? Why ever not? It's ridiculous. It's not even true!'

'But the facts stated in the letter *are* true,' Alex said gently. 'Mrs Denby *did* lose the baby. She *had* been attending the clinic. The opinions are those of the writer . . .'

'And Jim Denby – though he knows they're false.'

'And of Denby. But people are allowed to express opinions. That's the whole basis of the column. That's why people read it.'

'So who is P. Blamires, Esquire?' Rose asked. 'Aside, that is, from being a mouthpiece for Denby?'

'He's the mouthpiece for a good many people in Akersfield,' Alex told her. 'He's a respectable citizen who is more than willing to write letters to the paper for those he reckons can't do it for themselves – especially if the letters are going to stir things up. But what he writes is usually interesting to the reader so more often than not it gets published.'

'And never mind the harm done!'

'There won't be much harm done, Rose,' Alex assured her. 'It'll all blow over quickly. In a day or two there'll be a letter about something different and all this will be forgotten.'

'But already some of the women have decided not to come to the clinic,' Rose pointed out. 'This will make it worse. And they're women who need to come. They'll miss more than the medical care. They'll miss the free milk and dinners they desperately need.'

'It doesn't say the clinic sent her.'

'The inference is clear enough. Though of course no-one sent her. She went of her own free will, and glad to go.'

Alex took both her hands in his. 'I can see you've

had a bad day. I'm sorry, Rose. Let's go out somewhere after supper. We could make the second house
at the Empress. Cheer you up.'

Rose pulled her hands away from his, though in her
heart she wanted nothing as much as to lay her head on
his broad shoulder and have a good cry. She was sick of
it all.

'Every day's a bad day now. I'm doing no good to
anyone. I doubt if I've done any good to Eva. Perhaps
you were right when you warned me that she'd have to
go back to Paradine Street. By the way,' she said, 'I've
decided to go to Faverwell to see her on Saturday. I doubt
if her husband will be going.'

A thought struck her. 'I wonder,' she mused, 'if
P. Blamires also gave him some money to visit?'

'Let me take you there,' Alex said quickly. 'I can
borrow a car and we'll drive up.'

'If you like.'

'And the second house at the Empress tonight? Florrie
Forde?'

'I'm sorry,' Rose said, 'I'm not in the mood.'

It would be hellish in the clinic tomorrow. She couldn't
hope that Doctor Stanton wouldn't have seen the letter.
She wondered if John Worthing had seen it, and what his
reaction would be.

She was at the clinic early next day but Doctor Stanton
was there before her. So was Mabel Pearlman, her face
troubled as she greeted Rose.

'He says will you go into his room right away, Doctor
Rose.'

'I will.'

'I saw the letter in the paper,' Mabel said. 'If you want
to know, I think it's rubbish.'

'Thank you, Mabel,' Rose said.

She went into her room, took off her hat, put on her
white coat and went to face Doctor Stanton.

'I need hardly tell you why I want to see you,' he said

tersely. He did not look at her as he spoke, but fixed his pale eyes on a point somewhere behind her left shoulder. 'I have had both the Chairman and Councillor Rogers on the telephone. They are considerably disturbed and distressed, as am I. There is no doubt that your ill-considered action, private though you might have meant it to be, will harm the welfare service which the Health Committee and myself have built up with such care and patience and which was at last beginning to bear fruit.'

'But that's not fair!' Rose cried indignantly. 'I don't like it any more than you do when a woman loses her baby, but you know it's not uncommon, especially among our kind of patients. It's incredible to me that so much is being made of it.'

'It may seem incredible to you, but it is happening, and in the glare of the press. With the agreement of the Chairman I have composed a letter, which Miss Pearlman will take at once to the offices of the *Record*, stating categorically that the clinic had no part in sending Mrs Denby away. For the sake of the clinic the letter does not mention you in any way, and for the same reason it has been decided that nothing else shall be done in the matter. You are fortunate this time that you will not be asked to appear before the Committee, but you are specifically requested not to grant an interview to any reporter who might approach you from the *Record*. That will be all, Doctor. We have a busy morning ahead.'

He bent his head over the papers on his desk. She was dismissed.

She had a patient with her, was examining a baby whose legs were thin and rickety, whose buttocks and groin were covered in an angry rash, when the telephone rang.

'I'm going to give you some cream,' she told the mother. 'Apply it every single time you change the baby, and change him often. Don't leave him in a wet nappy. This rash is very irritating to the child.'

The telephone rang again and she picked it up, speaking

sharply into it. She disliked being interrupted when she was busy with patients.

'Yes?'

'John Worthing. Are you busy?'

She caught her breath at the sound of his voice, felt the heat in her face, the trembling of her hands; hoped the woman with the baby, who was listening with undisguised interest, would not notice.

'I have a patient with me.' She tried to keep her voice steady.

'I won't keep you.' His voice was sharp, businesslike. 'I've heard all about your bit of trouble. I just wanted to say "Don't worry". It will pass.'

'Thank you.'

'Are you coming to my garden party?'

She had not, until now, made up her mind; but hearing him she knew she could not keep away.

'Yes,' she said.

'Good!' He rang off. She turned back to the baby's mother. 'I think we might try some cod liver oil,' she said with an effort. 'It will help your baby's limbs grow straight and strong.'

Saturday morning was free, since once every six weeks she did not have to assist in the clinic on that day. Immediately after breakfast they set off in the car Alex had borrowed – a small, navy-blue Morris two-seater with an open top and dicky seat.

'I'm thinking of buying it,' Alex said. 'I can get it for twenty pounds. What do you say?'

'If that's what you want.'

To buy, or not to buy, a secondhand car was of no moment. She was too dispirited to care. Doctor Stanton's letter had been published in the *Record* and there had been no repercussions so far, but the atmosphere between herself and Doctor Stanton was icy. He had stepped up his policy of keeping as many patients as possible to himself, so that all week she had been left with not enough work to do and with too much time to think. It was the subtlest and most efficient way of punishing her and she was sure he knew that.

'I'm hoping a trip to Faverwell will cheer you up,' Alex said, driving out of the town. 'You've been a bag of misery this week.'

'I'm sorry,' Rose apologized. 'And I daresay Faverwell will do the trick. Anyway, I'll try to be more cheerful.'

'You don't have to be for me,' Alex said. 'You don't have to put on a show.'

It was true. He was understanding and accepting, and she was grateful for it. She wondered if, sometimes, she did not take advantage of his good nature.

It was another warm, sunny day. She was glad to have the car hood down, to feel the breeze as they drove through the dale. The limestone walls glistened in the sun. The long, hot summer had all but dried the river in parts, exposing its pebbly bed. The river meadows were golden with what would be a good second crop of hay. A second crop, not possible every summer, made all the difference to winter feeding the stock. Between Grassington and Faverwell Alex slowed down, driving leisurely on the traffic-free road. Rose breathed in the country air and felt better for the sights and smells of the dale.

The Ewe Lamb looked busy. Since the war cycling had flourished and at this moment there were a dozen or more bicycles propped against the walls of the inn while their owners drank beer in the bar parlour and ate the packed lunches which they had brought with them.

'You're a sight for sore eyes, and no mistake!' George Stanton said, breaking off serving to greet his daughter and to shake hands with Alex. 'Your mother's been looking forward to seeing you. Go through to the back. I'll bring you a pint in a minute or two, Mr Bairstow.'

Mrs Stanton's greeting was less effusive but Rose, knowing her mother's ways, could tell that she was glad to see them and that she took to Alex.

'Eva's gone into Grassington with our Emily and Christopher and the children,' she said. 'They thought it might make a change for her. She should be back any time now.'

'How is Eva?' Rose asked.

'Much better. Almost well enough for home. But I'm feared you'll find she doesn't want to go.'

'You'd understand that, Ma, if you saw where she lived.'

Mrs Stanton frowned. 'I do understand, Rose, but there's nothing for her here. You know that. Besides, she's a married woman.

'Has her unspeakable husband showed up?' Rose enquired.

'No. Nor written. But I think she's written to him.'

'So much for his concern,' Rose said.

Ten minutes later the party from Grassington returned. Eva's face lit with pleasure at the sight of Rose.

'You're looking well,' Rose told her. In spite of her recent miscarriage, Eva looked a little plumper, rounder in the face, and her skin had a degree of the clear healthiness which characterized Rose's own complexion. But she had a worried look.

'While you, on the other hand,' Emily put in, 'don't look all that blooming. It seems to me the city air doesn't agree with you.'

Rose shrugged. It was not the city air which got her down but she had no intention of going into that. 'I'm all right,' she said. 'A bit tired, that's all.'

After lunch Rose took Alex on one side. 'I'm going to take Eva for a walk,' she said. 'Find out what's on her mind.'

Emily and Christopher had taken their daughters back to the farm for the midday meal. Rose thought Emily looked a little more cheerful, but then farmers and their wives usually felt better when the summer was good.

'Let's go for a walk, Eva,' Rose said.

'Leave the bairns with me,' Mrs Stanton said quickly.

They walked down to the river.

'We can cross by the stepping stones when the water's low,' Rose said. 'In the winter you can't even see them. The winter here is long, cold and wet.'

They climbed up from the river bed on to the far bank and began to walk along the path towards the dale head. At first Rose talked of general things – the weather, Eva's children, her own two nieces. She liked Eva Denby; she wished they were just two women, friends, taking a country walk. But there was more to it and the subject had to be broached.

'Eva,' Rose said, 'You really are much better, aren't you?'

'Oh I am, Doctor Rose. I am! You're mother's been ever so kind to me. Everyone in Faverwell has been kind to me. I've never been so happy in my life.'

'I'm glad,' Rose said. 'Look, let's sit here for a while. I hate to say it,' she said when they were seated, 'but it is time you were thinking about going back home, Eva. No-one wants to rush you, of course, but . . .'

She saw the instant fright in Eva's eyes, saw the girl's hand clench until the knuckles showed white, heard the entreaty in her voice as she interrupted.

'Oh no, Doctor Rose, I can't go home! Please don't make me!'

'I'm not . . .'

'I've thought it all out. I know I can't stay and be a burden on Mrs Stanton, but I could take a job in service, somewhere where I could take the children with me. They're ever such good children!'

Rose shook her head. 'There isn't anywhere, Eva. Unemployment in the dales is as bad as it is in the towns. No-one has the money to take on extra help. And with a small child and a baby, however well-behaved . . .'

'Then I'll get a job in Grassington!' Eva cried. 'There's more jobs there.'

'I'm afraid you'll find it quite impossible,' Rose said sadly.

'Well I'm not going back to him! I'm never going back to him. You don't know what it's like, Doctor!'

'I can imagine,' Rose sympathized.

'You can't really,' Eva said. 'Begging your pardon, and I don't mean to be cheeky, Doctor, but you can't imagine what it's like. You have to go through it to know.'

Tears welled in her eyes, rolled down her face. She lowered her head and sobs tore at her body. Rose put an arm around her, felt the thin shoulders shaking.

'I'm sorry, Eva. I'm truly sorry. Perhaps it was wrong of me ever to suggest you coming here. Perhaps I've only made things more difficult for you?'

Eva raised her head.

'Oh no, Doctor Rose, don't ever think that! I've had the happiest time of my whole life here. And if I have to go back I'll never forget it.'

'Perhaps you could come here next year,' Rose suggested. 'I'm sure my mother would welcome you.'

'Oh no I couldn't.' Eva spoke with hopeless conviction. 'He won't ever let me come again. You see I haven't told you everything.'

'What do you mean?'

'I haven't told you I've already written to him to tell him I'm not going back, not ever. He'll have had the letter this morning. If I have to go back to him now he'll make me pay for that.'

She started to cry again. 'What am I going to do, Doctor?

'I don't know, Eva,' Rose confessed. 'I don't know.'

She felt herself to be the last person in the world to help in any situation which involved Jim Denby, though Eva did not know that she had no intention of adding to her troubles by telling her what had happened while she had been away.

'Cheer up,' she said. 'We'll think of something.'

But of what, she had no idea.

'Perhaps we should be getting back now,' she said. She got to her feet and held out a hand to Eva. As they walked back along the river bank Rose put an arm around Eva's shoulders, trying to comfort her.

When she and Alex drove away from the Ewe Lamb on Saturday evening Rose's spirits had not improved. Remembering last Christmas she realized that this was the second time Faverwell had failed to work its magic on her. But the fault was in herself and the thought troubled her. Faverwell had not changed and her family were as supportive as ever.

'A good place,' Alex said. 'A loving family. I envy you your background.' His own parents had died when he was still at school. His only relative was his aunt in Manchester.

'I am to be envied that,' Rose acknowledged.

But the thought of Eva Denby's troubled face would not leave her. She had put the girl in a situation which was worse than the one from which she had tried to rescue her, and she could think of no way out of it.

'I feel helpless,' she told Alex. 'With part of me I wish I'd never started it. And yet I suppose I'd do the same thing again.'

'And you will,' he said. 'But you won't always come up against a Jim Denby.'

'What do you suppose he'll do about Eva's letter? She's got to face him.'

'He'll make her pay,' Alex said. 'My guess is by making her pregnant again. And I doubt if he'll stop at making his wife pay.'

'You mean he'll be after my blood?' Rose said.

They drove in silence for a while and then, just short of Grassington, Alex, without warning, pulled into the side of the road and turned off the engine.

'Is something wrong?' Rose asked quickly, unused to the ways of cars.

'No,' he said. 'I simply want to talk to you. Not about the Denbys, or anyone else. This time it's just you and me.'

There was an air of suppressed excitement about him. She knew at once what he was going to say and she did not want to hear it.

'Alex. I don't think now is . . .'

He interrupted her.

'Please listen to me, Rose!' The determined look on his face, the force in his voice, were new to her.

'Rose, will you marry me? I love you and I want you. I want you for my wife. Give me the chance and I swear I'll make you happy.'

He took both her hands in his own firm grasp, as if he was afraid she might somehow escape him. She was moved by the excitement and longing in his eyes, the eagerness in his voice.

'I can't,' she said, faltering, not because she was unsure, but because she did not want to hurt him.

He was not in a mood to accept refusal.

'Yes you can,' he said eagerly. 'All you have to do is say "Yes". Oh, I know what it will mean! Don't think I haven't considered it. I understand that it will mean giving up the clinic, and I know how much that means to you. But there are other things you can do. We can rent a house. You can set up a private practice . . .'

'That's not what I want . . .'

'Wait!' he commanded. 'Let me finish. I know the usual kind of private practice isn't all that you want, and I understand the difficulty, in any case, of waiting for patients to come to you. But you could also open up a surgery, say a couple of days a week, in the area where you want to work – Babcock Street for instance. You could rent a room, work right among the women you want to treat. You'd no longer be tied to the clinic, subject to Stanton. You'd be a free agent. I'd help you in every way, Rose. I'd deny you nothing!'

He was alight with enthusiasm, gripping her wrists so tightly that she was sure he must leave marks on them. She hated herself for she knew she was going to kill his fervour.

She shook her head. 'I truly appreciate everything you offer me. I wish I could accept. But it won't do, Alex. It all sounds tempting, and professionally it's what I'd like – especially the women's clinic. But I can't return your love, Alex, and I can't marry you as a business proposition. It wouldn't be fair. What would you get out of it?'

'I'd get you,' he said. 'I want you.'

'But I don't love you,' Rose repeated. 'Not in the way you love me. I can't pretend I do.'

'I know that, I'm willing to take the gamble. You do care something for me?'

'Of course I do. A great deal. You know that. You're the best friend I have – the one I turn to.'

With all her heart she wished she could love this man. With an equal love on her side, marriage to him could be a pleasant thing. They were in so many ways compatible. And to the pleasure of marriage and children, which she had always known she desired, she would be able to add the satisfaction of a job which she wanted with all her heart to do; to practise among working women without the restrictions which at the clinic seemed constantly to tie her down.

But Alex Bairstow, for all the liking she had for him, could not raise in her one hundredth part of the excitement, the longing, the soaring of the spirit which even the sound of John Worthing's voice over the telephone aroused in her. The spark was missing; there would be no fire in such a marriage. While John Worthing existed she was trapped by him. She did not want to be, but that was the way it was.

'Then I'd settle for that,' Alex said. 'Friendship is a pretty good foundation. So is need. I need you; you need someone – so why not me?'

She leaned forward and kissed him on the cheek.

'It's still "No", Alex. I'm honoured and I'm grateful, but I can't take so much and give so little.'

He shook his head. 'Let me be the one to worry about that!'

'No,' Rose said. 'I can't.'

Still holding her wrists, he looked at her steadily, searching for a sign of hope in her face. But there was none. He let go of her and got out of the car. He cranked the engine with the starting handle and when the engine leapt to life he got back in again.

'Promise you'll tell me when you change your mind,' he said.

Rose could think of no circumstances under which she would do so.

On the following Monday Rose was met once again by a wide-eyed Mabel Pearlman, bursting with news.

'That Mr Denby was here again on Saturday. Shouting and bawling something awful, he was, and in front of all the mothers. You should have heard the things he said Doctor Rose.'

'I'm quite pleased I didn't,' Rose said shortly. 'Could I have this morning's case files, please, Mabel?'

Mabel bit her lip, looked away.

'I can't. That is, I've been told . . .'

'What do you mean, Mabel?'

'It's just that . . . well, Nurse Butterworth said that Doctor Stanton said that I wasn't to hand out any files until later, until you've seen him. It's not me, Doctor,' she added quickly. 'It's just what I was told.'

'I see,' Rose said. 'Is Doctor Stanton in yet?'

'He's been here the past hour.'

So it was to be a near repetition of last week's scene Rose thought. But when, a few minutes later, she stood in front of him, she realized that it was to be much worse Afterwards she could not remember everything he said in his cold, cutting voice; but some words stood out, echoed round and round in her head.

'We are accused – you are accused, by your unwarrantable interference, not only of being the cause of his wife losing her unborn child, but of breaking Mr Denby's marriage to the extent that he has now lost his wife and his other two children. He lays this directly at your door.'

'That I did not do,' Rose said vehemently. 'He has driven his wife away himself, by his own intolerable behaviour! Ask her!'

'She is unfortunately not available,' Doctor Stanton said dryly. 'But he is. He has shown me the letter he received from his wife. He has said that unless I report you to the Health Committee he will take that letter to the editor of the Akersfield *Record*. And he makes it quite plain that he will have no compunction in involving this clinic as well as yourself. He will state – and he will do it through the man Blamires who knows how to use words – that you and this clinic have used undue influence over his wife.'

'How dare he!' Rose cried. 'And how can you believe him? Surely you cannot allow him to dictate what you must do?'

'He dares because he is in a strong position,' Doctor Stanton said. 'He speaks of damages, though whether that will hold water one cannot tell. What is quite certain is that he can damage this clinic, and that I am not prepared to risk. I have therefore no alternative but to report the whole matter to the Chairman of the Committee. You will be summoned to appear before them in due course.'

'I see. So it's to be my word against his?'

'There is little need of his word. His wife has lost the baby, and now he has her letter. She goes so far as to say that but for you, but for the time she has spent away from Paradine Street, she would never have had the courage to leave him.'

'She has not left him,' Rose said. 'I know for a fact that she will be returning – more's the pity! And now may I have my files for this morning's patients? Miss Pearlman informs me that you are holding them.'

'Ah yes.' he said smoothly. 'In fact, Doctor, you will not need them. The Chairman has agreed with me that until this matter is cleared up – he hopes to arrange an emergency meeting of the Committee in two or three days' time – it would be best for all concerned if you did not see patients.'

Rose was summoned to appear before the Committee on Wednesday afternoon. The intervening hours were the longest of her life. The town hall clock was striking three as she walked into the room where nine months earlier she had been so delighted to receive her appointment. John Worthing, sitting as before to the right of the Chairman, raised his head and looked long and directly at her as she seated herself in the big chair. Longing to hear from him, wondering why he had not communicated with her, she had this morning succumbed to temptation and telephoned his office. He was in London, his secretary said. He would be back in time for this afternoon's meeting. In the look he gave her now, though his face was stern, she felt sympathy. But in the long faces of the rest of the Committee she could detect none at all.

The meeting began as predictably as she had expected. After all, she had been through it all with Doctor Stanton, though she hoped that the Committee would be less chilly than her immediate boss.

'Why did you take this action without consulting your superior officer?' Councillor Rogers barked. He treated her as though he was conducting a court martial. She disliked him more than ever.

'I've already explained that I considered there was no need to do so . . .

'You considered there was no need to inform the Head of the clinic?'

'None,' Rose said. 'I had mentioned to him that I wanted to visit Mrs Denby, mainly to get her to come to the clinic. I thought she badly needed the help we could give. I understood from Doctor Stanton that such a visit could not be made as part of my duties and for that reason I visited her in my own time. The idea of offering her a holiday was a secondary one and every part of that was a private matter. The clinic was not involved.'

John Worthing spoke for the first time.

'I find that a reasonable explanation.' His tone was mild. He's trying to play it down, Rose thought. She wondered if he knew what she was going through.

It was too good an opportunity for the Chairman to miss. He cleared his throat, sat upright, clasped his small, fat hands in front of him and spoke.

'All of us who have the privilege of serving the public, of serving Akersfield, realize that we can have no private lives. Our deeds can never remain hidden. What we do, we do in the full light of day, the glare of the footlights!' He leaned towards Rose, shaking his head regretfully. 'We belong to Akersfield, Doctor Rose!'

She wanted to laugh at the absurdity of it all. She wanted to scream. She couldn't believe it was happening to her.

'You mean I've been bought, body and soul, for three-hundred-and-seventy-five pounds a year?' she blurted out. 'Is that what you're saying, Mr Chairman? Because if it is I want to tell you here and now that in my case it's just not true! I was engaged to do a job. I've done it. Even Doctor Stanton can't deny that. But neither this Committee nor anyone else is going to buy my private life!'

The Chairman flushed puce. He seemed likely to suffer a stroke at any second. There was a swelling murmur of disapproval, disbelief, among the men around the table. Only John Worthing remained silent, his eyes never leaving Rose.

'How dare you, young woman!' Councillor Rogers demanded.

'I dare all right!' Rose flared. 'I'm being pilloried because you – this committee – can't stand up to a man you know to be wrong. I'm your scapegoat because you're afraid of the newspapers. You'll all feel better when you can say you've chastised me. Why don't you just tell Jim Denby to go to hell?'

The Chairman struggled to speak.

'My dear young lady . . . I had hoped that a few words

from the Committee . . . there is no need whatever . . .'

'I understand perfectly,' Rose interrupted. 'I can see that you've already decided against me. If Denby can be told, officially, that I've been reprimanded, then everything will be settled. Well you can go further, gentlemen.

You can tell Mr Denby, and anyone else you wish, that I've resigned my job! I'm giving my notice here and now. And if I hear the slightest suggestion that I've been dismissed, or have in any way harmed the clinic, then I shall fight. I'm not afraid of Denby, or of a dozen like him!'

She could not believe her own ears. How could she be saying these things? How could she be throwing away her job like this? But she knew, as clearly as she had ever known anything in her life, that she could not continue to work with Doctor Stanton.

'Doctor Rose, are you sure you know what you're saying?'

John Worthing's voice, clear and incisive, cut through the buzz of astonishment which ran around the meeting. Rose looked directly at him, no longer seeing anyone else in the room.

'I'm quite sure. Councillor Worthing.'

It was with a great effort that she kept her voice steady. She was terrified that she would break down.

'Then you're a little fool!' he snapped. It was as if for him also there were only the two of them. No-one else mattered.

For a second, which seemed an eternity, they held each other with their eyes, across the width of the table. But it was no use. He could not help her, and suddenly she could stand no more. She picked up her handbag, pushed back the chair, and ran out of the room. She ran through the empty waiting room, down the long flight of stairs, and was running across the lobby when John Worthing caught at her from behind, jerking her to a standstill, swinging her around to face him.

'Stop it! What in the world do you think you're doing, Rose? There's no need for this!'

They faced each other angrily.

'Let me go!' Rose shouted.

'I've told you,' he said. 'It will all blow over! Now go right back in there and make your peace. I promise you it will be all right. They had no intention of doing anything very terrible, you know.'

His tone was quieter, but she was not to be mollified.

'I'll do no such thing,' she said, pulling away from him. 'I'll die first!'

His anger flared again.

'Don't be such an exasperating little fool!'

She was stung by his sharpness when what she craved was sympathy. Had he no understanding at all?

'What will you do?' he demanded. 'Where will you get another job?'

'I don't know. Most likely not in Akersfield if they have anything to do with it. I don't know and I don't care!'

'Rose, don't do this,' John Worthing pleaded.

She was aware that other members of the Committee were now walking past them in the lobby, that she was attracting attention. The glances they gave her were not so much hostile as curious, wondering if there was something further to be learned about this young woman who had flown off the handle so unexpectedly, so divertingly.

'I'm going, John,' she said. 'Please don't follow me.'

For the rest of the week she went in to the clinic but was given no work to do. She was quite sure that her resignation had pleased Doctor Stanton, but they did not discuss it. She felt numb, unable to decide what she should do next. She felt certain that there was no work for her in Akersfield and that she would have to leave the town. It surprised her that the thought of leaving Akersfield was so painful to her. She had known it such a short time. But in her heart she knew it was not Akersfield, much though she had grown to like it, but those whom it held which bound her so closely.

Saturday was the day of John Worthing's garden party, to which she now no longer wished to go.

'There'll be all the wretched Committee there,' she said to Alex. 'I never want to see them again.'

'Face them,' Alex said. 'It's the best thing. In any case they'll be lost in the crowd. Anyone who's anyone in Akersfield will be there. Apart from all that, you promised me.'

'Very well, I'll go for you,' Rose said in the end. And she would see John Worthing again, perhaps for the last time if she was to leave Akersfield.

Saturday was also the day fixed for Eva's homecoming. Rose had been to see Eva's mother, who had told her that she intended to meet Eva at the station.

'She can come back with me to begin with, but she can't stay here,' Mrs Foster said. 'We've only got the one small bedroom. I don't know what's to become of her, I'm sure!'

'I'll come to the station, too,' Rose said. 'I want to tell her myself that I'm leaving the clinic. I'd rather you didn't tell her why, Mrs Foster.'

'I won't,' Mrs Foster promised. 'Though I daresay *he* will! It's a sin and a shame you're going. You're just what we need here. Not just young mothers with babies, but lots of women around here could do with someone like you to turn to.'

It was a chastened and apprehensive Eva the two women welcomed at the railway station. though physically she seemed stronger and the children were blooming with health. She was clearly upset at the news of Rose's departure from the clinic. 'I shan't go if you're not there,' she said.

'You must, Eva,' Rose urged her. 'It's important for the baby.'

They parted outside the station, Eva to go with her mother, Rose to get ready for the garden party.

In spite of her protestations that she did not want to

attend the garden party, Rose had purchased a new dress – flowered voile, with floating panels around the skirt, which was a daring eight inches above the ankle. Skirts were getting shorter all the time. And, going the whole hog, with money she could now ill afford to spend, she had also bought a new hat of Bangkok straw, trimmed with a large, squashy pink rose. She rubbed a *papier poudre* leaf over her nose and chin to take off the shine, pinched her cheeks and bit her lips to bring the colour into them, and was ready when Alex arrived.

'You look wonderful!' he said.

'You don't look so bad yourself,' Rose told him.

He was wearing a pearl-grey suit and, in keeping with the occasion, a straw boater with a coloured band.

She was surprised by the size of John Worthing's house – a many-gabled, mid-Victorian building – and by the extent and beauty of the grounds around it. There were close-mown, undulating lawns, flower beds and pergolas, trees and shrubberies, even a small lake.

'I had no idea it would be like this,' she said to Alex.

'I told you, he's a rich man. And a man of taste.'

Alex seemed proud to have her on his arm as they moved around, taking pleasure in introducing her to people. He seemed to know everyone. Rose acknowledged greetings, exchanged pleasantries, conscious that all the time her eyes were scanning the throng for a sight of John Worthing. They had been at the party almost an hour when, rounding a corner, she came face to face with him – she on Alex's arm, he with his wife on his.

'So there you are!' John Worthing said. 'I was beginning to wonder if you hadn't come.' Rose met his look, saw the admiration in his eyes, followed quickly by a look of enquiry. There had been no word between them since the afternoon of the committee meeting and she wondered if, after all, he did not care that she was going out of his life.

Then she realized that Mrs Worthing was looking at her. 'Allow me to present my wife,' John said. 'Diana, my dear, this is Doctor Rose Stanton.'

137

'My husband has spoken of you,' Mrs Worthing said.

Her voice was cool, clear, light; no trace there of local accent, only the very best education. Rose wondered what John had said about her. There was a polite reserve in Mrs Worthing's manner which gave nothing away.

'You have a lovely garden here,' Rose said.

'Yes, it is nice, isn't it? It was a wilderness when we came here. My husband and I made it – or, rather, planned it – together. It was great fun, wasn't it darling? It still is. There's always something to be done.'

Mrs Worthing was, as Rose had pictured her, tall and elegant. She was too thin, even for the current fashion, and there was a nervousness about her which showed in the restless movements of her slender hands and the unquiet expression on her fine-featured face. Behind the flimsy curtain of her impeccable manners, Rose sensed a turbulence of emotion. Though it was impossible to judge on so short an acquaintance it seemed to her that Mrs Worthing's invalidism might be more nervous or mental than physical. But she was beautiful, charming, and quite clearly in love with her husband.

'Do go and have something to eat,' Mrs Worthing urged. 'They're serving refreshments in the marquee. Perhaps we shall see you both later.'

With a quick pressure on her husband's arm she bore him away. Rose, her arm still through Alex's, watched them until they were out of sight.

'She's attractive,' she acknowledged.

'They say she was a beauty when John married her,' Alex said. 'I must say, she's looking in better health than I expected. Let's hope it lasts. But John, nice fellow though he is, doesn't help her.'

'What do you mean?'

'Women! You'd think with a lovely woman like that he'd never stray. In fact he's well known for it. Of course he always returns to her in the end. I daresay, underneath, he's as much in love with her as she is with him.'

STOP! Rose wanted to shout. Stop, stop, stop! He

was driving knives into her. Suddenly she saw so many things, saw what must be the truth of it all. She had been a silly, romantic fool! She was no doubt one in a long procession of John Worthing's spare women. Of course it wouldn't matter if she left Akersfield. Someone else would take her place. Did he take them all to the Heifer for lunch? Has he a *penchant* for redheads, she wondered bitterly, or am I at least different in that respect? But in no other, she thought.

'I don't know what women see in him,' Alex said. 'Perhaps as a woman you could tell me?'

He was not being consciously cruel. That was not in Alex.

I could tell you all right, Rose thought. I could tell you that he moves the heart, lifts the spirits, stirs the senses, as no other man has ever done for me – or ever will: that the sight of him and the sound of his voice make me tremble.

'I haven't the slightest idea!' she said brightly. 'Shall we go and find some food? I'm starving!'

After they had eaten, though she scarcely tasted the delicious food, or the pale, China tea in delicate cups, they walked around again, patronizing the sideshows; knocking down coconuts, dipping into the bran tub, guessing the weight of a cake. It was fun. In spite of herself she began to enjoy it. Alex was a good person to be with.

'You realize all this money's going into your fund?'

That was something else she would have to abandon when she left Akersfield. Although she was not known as the instigator, she recognized that she would always have been closely connected with the project, would have done everything she could for its success. She felt that in abandoning the fund she was somehow casting aside all those mothers who needed it.

'I'm sorry I shan't see it in action,' she said. 'I feel almost more guilty about that than about anything.'

She had still not the slightest idea where she might be, even in a month from now. She had started at once to look for jobs, but so far there was nothing. Perhaps she would have to go back to Faverwell – but what would she do there?

'You could be here,' Alex said. He took her arm, drawing her close to him as they walked. They were exploring the perimeter of the garden now, away from the stalls, the tents, the sideshows. When they came to a bench, set under an oak tree, they sat down.

'Rose,' Alex said quickly, 'I'm asking you again. Will you marry me? In spite of all you've said before, I know we could make it work. Look how much we've enjoyed this afternoon. A large part of marriage must be like that – I don't mean garden parties, but liking the same things, enjoying being together.'

She turned towards him. He was so good, so sincere. How much simpler life would be if she could fall in love with Alex, marry him and live happily ever after. But it was not simple.

'I would be afraid, Alex,' she said. 'I would be afraid that I'd take so much more than I could give. I do care for you – but not in the way I'd want to if I were your wife.'

Not in the way that she would care if it were John Worthing sitting beside her. For a brief moment she hated John; that he had ever encouraged her, caused her to love him more than she might have, bound her to him by enticing him into admitting it. But, she told herself firmly, there were no bonds which she could not and would not break if she made up her mind to it.

'I understand all that,' Alex was saying. 'You've never been less than honest about it.'

Oh yes I have, she thought. But she had no intention of telling him the whole truth, risking further hurt to him.

'I'm prepared for that,' he said. 'I won't expect from you what you can't give. I promise that, Rose.'

They fell silent. Into Rose's mind came all the advantages of marrying Alex. She would stay in

Akersfield. She would set up her own practice and – more important – be free to open a clinic where she could, among other things, help women to plan their families. She would be able to continue with the Mothers' Holiday Fund. But none of these things, important to her though they were, mattered if she could not also make Alex happy. She tried to put it into words to him.

'. . . I would *have* to believe that there was a chance, a good chance, that we could be happy together, before I gave way to the other temptations,' she said. 'If that sounds somewhat cold-blooded, then I'm putting it hadly. It's because I care for you as much as I do – and respect you utterly – that I would have to feel that there was a likelihood that we'd make a go of it.'

'But there is, Rose!' Alex said eagerly. 'I'm sure of it! Rose, say you will! I love you so very much.'

She hesitated – but not for long.

'I will marry you, Alex,' she said.

Held closely in his arms, returning his kisses, she vowed to herself that she would be a good wife to Alex. She would learn to love him as he loved her. She would forget her feelings for John Worthing as though they had never existed.

After a while, Alex's arm still around her, they went back to the big lawn. Through the crowd Rose saw the Worthings moving towards them. They were still arm-in-arm, she looking up at him with a proprietary air, he smiling down at his wife. Alex spotted them at the same time.

'Let's tell our host and hostess,' he said quickly. 'It's their party. They should be the first to know.'

As a jubilant Alex broke the news, his arm possessively about her, Rose looked at John Worthing. The eyes which met hers were as black as coal, as hard as flint.

'And when is the wedding to be?' Mrs Worthing asked pleasantly.

Rose turned away from John Worthing's icy regard and looked up at Alex. She was glad she had promised to marry him. It was going to be all right. They would be happy together.

'Quite soon,' she said. 'As soon as possible.'

PART TWO

9

When Rose walked into the Babcock Street surgery at nine o-clock in the morning Mrs Foster was still there, hard at work scrubbing the lino-covered floor. She sat back on her heels, surprised to see her employer.

'Good-morning, Doctor. I didn't expect you this early, otherwise I'd have finished.'

'It's all right, Mrs Foster,' Rose said. 'I know surgery isn't until ten, but if I'm going to be absent for a week or two there are a few things I must see to.'

'If you'll pardon me saying so, you shouldn't be here at all today. You should be at home, resting. That's what you'd tell your patients to do.' Mrs Foster's voice oozed disapproval. She plunged her hands into the bucket of water, wrung out the floorcloth, mopped the suds from a square of floor so that Rose could get by.

Rose contradicted her. 'It isn't what I tell my patients, Mrs Foster. I tell them to keep going normally until labour starts – but not to get overtired. It helps to be occupied.'

Mrs Foster grunted. 'Well mind how you walk over this wet floor, Doctor. We don't want any accidents, do we?' She stood aside while Rose picked her way to the back room.

'I know you don't approve of me working right through my pregnancy,' Rose said, 'but I assure you it's quite all right. I'm as fit as a flea.'

'It's not for me to approve or disapprove,' Mrs Foster said primly. 'But after what you've been through . . .'

'Don't worry, everything's going to be all right this time,' Rose assured her. 'I feel pretty good.'

But in fact she felt tired, her body heavy and awkward now that her time was near. She was thankful that the hot summer had given way to a cool September. That, at least, made things easier.

'You've waited a long time for this baby,' Mrs Foster said.

Rose did not need the reminder. So much had changed since that October day, almost two years ago now, when she had gone into the church in Faverwell on her father's arm and come out on Alex's, irrevocably, and a little frighteningly, bound to him.

She had wanted the quietest possible wedding; no fuss, preferably in a registry office. In spite of the honesty of her intentions, she had this uneasiness about making her vows in church, feeling that her forthcoming marriage was somehow not real, afraid that she might thereby mock God. Surprisingly, Alex had strongly backed her parents' desire for a church wedding.

'Why disappoint them?' he said. 'Anyway, I want to turn around and see you walking down the aisle in all your glory!'

She gave in. Since from the first moment of their engagement she had known there were things she could not give Alex, whenever she could she gave freely, and with all the affection she could command.

They were married in a church packed with relatives, friends, customers of the Ewe Lamb – and with her two small nieces as bridesmaids. She wore a dress of pale cream chiffon, trimmed with silver lace on the skirt, embroidered with seed pearls at the neck and on the short sleeves, which fell like petals from the shoulders. Alex's eyes shone with love and admiration at the sight of her, but there were tears in her own. The wedding dress hung at the back of the wardrobe now, draped with a piece of sheeting. She never looked at it.

'All done and dusted,' Mrs Foster said, standing in the doorway, drying her hands on her apron. 'I'll be off then, Doctor.' She adjusted the round, black hat which she wore all the time, even when she was scrubbing the floor.

Rose took a half-crown from her purse and handed it to Mrs Foster. It was more than the going rate for cleaning the two tiny rooms, plus a lavatory at the back, but Mrs Foster's need was great. Also, Rose felt certain that a little of the money found its way to Eva Denby in the form of food.

'So you won't be wanting me for the next week or two,' Mrs Foster said. 'What with the surgery being closed.'

Rose laughed. 'It's not as cut and dried as that! The baby's due today, but you know what first babies are. It could be another fortnight before it decides to appear. I shall keep on here as long as I can and get back as quickly as possible. In the meantime I'd be grateful if you'd pop in here and keep an eye on things. If there's any post, for instance, you could bring it to my home.'

Mrs Foster's face brightened. 'That I'll do with pleasure, Doctor. Only don't you be coming back to work too soon, now!'

'Dear Mrs Foster,' Rose said. 'How many of the mothers you know around here have the luxury of two whole weeks' rest, with a nurse in attendance, after their babies? Did Eva, for instance?'

'That she did not!' Mrs Foster replied. 'Two days, more like! Thank God she's never got in the family way again. No thanks to Jim Denby, you can be sure of that!'

Rose herself thought it strange that in the last two years Eva had not conceived. She had not been to the Babcock Street surgery for the birth control advice which Rose gave to other local women. She was doubtless too afraid of her husband to defy him on that, though from time to time she surreptitiously set foot in the surgery with the children, simply in order to see Rose. Perhaps the miscarriage Eva had suffered in Faverwell had left her unable to conceive, but Rose had had no opportunity to examine her and she knew she had not been back to the clinic.

'Well I daresay Mr Bairstow'll be glad when it's all over,' Mrs Foster said, lingering, wanting to chat. 'Men aren't a mite of good at times like this – begging his pardon of course!

'I suppose he will,' Rose agreed.

'They like to get back to . . . well, you know what I mean, Doctor. The married bit. It's not much cop for them, the last few weeks, is it?'

It wasn't much cop for the wife, Rose thought; but that wasn't true for her, and she knew it. In spite of being so big and awkward, she had felt a freedom in these last few weeks such as she had not known since her wedding night. It seemed to her that everything that was wrong in their marriage had started then, from the moment the uniformed page boy had shown them to their room in the hotel in Scarborough, where they were to spend a three-day honeymoon.

While the boy deposited their suitcases and received a generous tip from Alex, Rose had stood there, seeing nothing but the large double bed which, with its deep, frilled valance, its rose-coloured bedspread, its rails and knobs of gleaming brass, dominated the room. There was scarcely space for the other bits of furniture, which seemed to have been added as afterthoughts. The bed was everything.

She had wanted, instantly, to run and run and run: out of the room, down the wide stairs, out of the hotel, across the dark cliff tops; anywhere to escape that voluptuous, threatening bed.

She did not do so, of course. She remained where she was, seemingly rooted to the thick, crimson carpet. She heard the page boy leave and then she heard Alex turn the key in the lock. Only her utter stillness, her rigidity as he came behind her and put his arms around her, betrayed her feelings – but he did not even notice. He swivelled her around towards him and kissed her long and tenderly. Then with equal gentleness – she could not complain on that score – he took off her hat and tossed it on to the dressing table, removed her jacket, letting it fall to the floor, and began to unfasten the buttons of her dress.

She moved, twisting her body out of his embrace.

'Not now, Alex!' she protested. 'It's after seven o'clock. We have to go down to dinner.'

'We don't have to go down to dinner,' Alex said. 'We can skip it.'

'But I don't want to skip it!' She managed a smile. 'I'm really quite hungry!'

'So am I,' he said. 'But not for food! Rose, we've waited a long time for this.' He picked her up and lifted her on to the bed. 'You're a wee bit of a thing,' he remarked. 'You weigh next to nothing!'

It was true that he had waited patiently to possess her. Throughout their short engagement he had been loving but restrained, kissing her often, declaring his love in words, but not fondling her even as much as John Worthing had done on that afternoon which now belonged to another world. It had seemed to her that Alex was not a sexually demanding man, that he knew nothing of the kind of passion which showed in John Worthing's every glance, sounded in his voice.

She was wrong; utterly mistaken. From the moment Alex laid her on that soft, wide bed, removed the last of her satin underwear, he was caught up in a passion which knew no bounds; his hands on her breasts, his tongue probing her mouth, then his face, bristly because he needed a shave, buried in the softness of her belly; and all the time the endearments pouring out of him in a frenzied, incoherent stream.

When he started to enter her, he said, 'I won't hurt you, Rose. I promise I won't hurt you!'

'Let him hurt me!' she found herself praying. 'Let him hurt me so that I can pay for the wrong!' She drew in a long breath, arched her neck in sharp pain as he pierced her, but she did not cry out. When his climax came she turned her face away from him and the tears ran down her cheeks on to the pillow.

She should not have married him. She should have listened to the voice which had told her over and over again that there was only one man she should ever marry. And now it was too late, there was nothing she could do. But at least Alex must never know. She would see to it that he did not. In their daily lives it would not be too difficult. They were good friends, compatible. It was this which had deceived her into thinking that marriage with him could work. In bed she would be acquiescent, she would give him all the affection she had for him, and more. He need never know.

They had missed dinner.

'There's no point in dressing,' Alex teased her. 'It would be a waste of time! I'll order a tray to be brought up – and a bottle of wine.'

It embarrassed her that the waiter saw them both in their dressing gowns so early in the evening, but Alex was nonchalant about it.

'I daresay he knows we're on honeymoon,' he said. 'They won't really expect to see much of us downstairs.'

After the meal he had made love to her again, with as much ardour as if it was the first time. It was physically less painful to her, but she could not respond. She lay quiescent and let him do what he wanted. Caught up in his own mounting desire, he seemed not to notice her, and when it was over he fell quickly asleep, his head uncomfortably heavy on her breast. When she felt sure, by the depth of his breathing, that he would not easily waken, she moved from under him and turned away, occupying a narrow space on the edge of the bed. She faced the fact that from now on it was the furthest she would ever be from him. She would never sleep alone, never again be free.

Sleep did not come. After an hour or two she got quietly out of the big bed and went to the window, drawing back the curtains a little. The night was dark.

She could hear the strength of the sea, but it was not visible. She stood there a long time, listening to the waves beating against the cliffs. Eventually the first streaks of a hesitant grey dawn broke over the sea. Another day. Perhaps it would be better. She would think of a way. She began to shiver with cold, and crept back into bed, moving carefully so as not to waken Alex.

And then as she lay there, straight as a lamp post, the tears came, racking her whole body with deep sobs, so that Alex stirred in his sleep, and then awakened. At once his arms were around her and he was holding her to him.

'What is it, my darling? What's wrong?' He held her against him. stroking her hair.

'I'm sorry,' she said. 'It's just that . . . well, I couldn't sleep. I don't know what came over me. I'm sorry, Alex.'

'I'm sorry,' he said. 'I've been selfish. I didn't realize you hadn't been satisfied. I'll do better, I promise. You're so wonderful. Rose. Everything's going to be marvellous. You'll see!'

His hands were moving over her body, caressing her breasts, stroking the curves of her buttocks, the length of her thighs. And then he was on top of her and inside her again. It was growing daylight now and she closed her eyes against the sight of the room, which she hated, and knew she would never forget.

As her husband's passion mounted, his arms gripping her in a frenzy, the face she saw before her closed eyes was that other face; that dark, foreign-looking face with the aquiline nose, the sensual mouth, the eyes dark with desire. The hands moving over her body were John Worthing's hands. It was then that her own passion was stirred.

'Was that better?' Alex asked when it was all over.

I have just committed adultery, she wanted to cry out! She felt that the sin must be visible on her, like a brand; that in the now full light of day Alex must see it on her face and in her eyes.

'Don't look so worried, my dear one,' he said. 'It *will* come all right. We must give ourselves time, that's all.'

It would never come right. She knew that for certain. But for his sake she must hide the knowledge. The pretence that everything was fine was the least she could offer him. In trepidation, she wondered how long it would be before he saw through her pretence.

Within weeks of their honeymoon she found herself pregnant. In her own mind she was convinced that the child had been conceived in that first early morning when in spirit she had been in John Worthing's arms. She was a stranger to herself in those first few weeks of pregnancy: wretched, constantly sick; torn by a guilt which turned into an obsession that the child would look like John Worthing. She knew that it was a totally foolish thought but she could not shake it off.

'I hate to see you like this,' Alex said. 'You're clearly not suited to having children. Perhaps we shouldn't have any more?'

'Do we want an only child?' Rose asked.

'I don't mind if we don't have any,' Alex admitted. 'I just hate to see you like this. And there's another thing.'

She knew what he was going to say. It had been inevitable from the beginning. But she did not want it put into words. While it was not mentioned, it could somehow be glossed over.

'Please, Alex!'

'No, Rose. It has to be said. I know you don't want me to make love to you. It's become quite clear to me, though I know you try to hide it. I'm assuming it's because you're pregnant . . .'

'Of course it is!' Rose broke in quickly.

'. . . But it's not easy for me, Rose. I try not to bother you, I try to be gentle . . .'

'But you are. Alex,' she protested. 'Please don't blame yourself. Sometimes it happens to women when they're pregnant. It will pass.'

Once she had had the baby, she promised herself, she would really try harder. She would make it up to him. But for the present she seized gratefully on the excuse he had given her.

The excuse was short lasting. At three months exhausted by nausea and vomiting, she miscarried. At once all her apprehensions about the baby were swallowed up in a deep disappointment as she realized how much she had wanted this child. And as the weeks passed and the winter gave way to spring it became clear that there was to be no improvement in her relations with Alex. She became adept at refusing him. She was ashamed of the dozens of ways she found to say 'No'. When she was too ashamed to say it yet again, she gave in to him. But now there was more than apathy on her part. As Alex assuaged himself at her body she felt an aversion to his nearness: She tried to dissemble her feelings, but more and more often she failed to deceive him. In the end he turned on her.

'What is it about me?' he cried. 'Am I so loathsome that you have to turn away in disgust? Am I so cruel that you have to weep every time I make love to you – which God knows isn't often? Tell me what it is!'

'It isn't you, Alex. It's me. And I don't know why!'

But she did know why, though there would never be any way she could tell him of this other man who came between them whenever Alex took her in his arms.

'How long is it to go on?' Alex demanded. 'You're over the baby. What's the excuse now?'

'I haven't one,' Rose said. 'I do try, Alex. I really do try!'

He turned round on her angrily.

'Do you think it pleases me to know that my wife has to *try* to bear it when I make love to her? That she *tries* not to find me repellent?'

For ten days after that occasion he had not come near her. They had slept in the same bed, not touching. It was during that time that she found she was pregnant again.

'Perhaps it will be better when we have the baby,' she said to Alex.

But that was not to be, either. In August she miscarried for the second time. Afterwards she lay weak and desolate, convinced that the loss of her babies was a judgement on her. Though he tried, Alex found it impossible to comfort her; nor could he find solace for himself in her. It was then that he started to drink.

Rose tried to tell herself – and it was true – that he had always drunk a lot. But that had been a different kind of drinking. Then it had been part of being happy – a few drinks to celebrate. Now he was driven by unhappiness and frustration, and she knew that it was her fault.

Except for one occasion, he did not get drunk, nor did he ever drink much in the daytime, and never enough to affect his work. He sat at home in the evenings with the whisky bottle to hand, morosely sipping. Or he went out to drink, which was worse because she was not there to try to stop him when she thought he had had enough.

It was on a night early in January that he came home drunk. She had gone to bed and, hearing him come upstairs, pretended to be asleep. He had pulled the bedclothes off her and shaken her shoulder.

'Wake up! he shouted. 'If you're asleep. which I doubt!'

She sat up immediately.

'I'll go and make some coffee.' She made to get out of bed but he pushed her down again.

'I don't want coffee!' he said. 'I want you! I want my wife! And why do I want my wife? Because I'm celebrating!'

'Celebrating?'

'Bloody well celebrating! I've been made Editor! Editor of the *Record*. The Old Man's going to Sheffield. and from now on it's all mine. So lie down in that bloody bed and I'll show you just how a normal man celebrates with a normal wife – which you're not, and never have been – but I'll show you just the same!'

'Please Alex!'

She had seen him in drink before, muddled, over-amorous, but always amiable. This time he was a different man. The gentleness and consideration which. though less in evidence over the last year, had always been part of the real Alex, were gone.

'Please Alex!' he mimicked her. 'Please Alex, not to-night! Well I'm going to show you, Madam!'

His eyes were tormented, as if something against his will was driving him to hurt her. He tore back the bedclothes and came on to her, violent, demanding; making love with the vengeance of a man who had been frustrated beyond endurance. There was no thought in her mind this time of that other man. Her thoughts were on her own pain, and the shame that they must both feel when this was over.

It was thus that the child she was carrying now, had carried this time to full term, had been conceived.

In spite of its beginnings, she wanted this child. She had kept fit and well through most of her pregnancy and now she looked forward to its birth.

With Alex there had been no repetition of that drunken scene. He had been ashamed, but his shame had put an even greater distance between them.

'What can I say, Rose?' he apologized. 'I was drunk. It's inadequate to say I'm sorry.'

'I understand,' Rose said. 'It's best that we forget it.'

But she never would, and for him her pregnancy, the sight of her swelling body, was a daily taunt.

If her salvation was in the child she longed for, Alex's, Rose thought, was in his work. His job as editor of the *Record* brought him new responsibilities in which he immersed himself. She thought that perhaps his increased work load absorbed his sexual energy, in the way that her own work, and her pregnancy, filled her mind. He was drinking – she knew the signs; but steadily, not to excess. And in his new job, encountering more people, meeting deadlines, it was part of the everyday scene.

'I'll be off then, Doctor,' Mrs Foster repeated. 'All the best, I'm sure.'

'Thank you. Of course you never know. I might still be here when you look in on Thursday!'

As Mrs Foster left, Rose unlocked her desk drawer and took out a small card index file. She kept the minimum of paperwork on the patients who came here since she had sensed early on that they did not like having things written down about them. She had also simplified every routine so that on the three mornings a week when she was there, patients could walk in off the street and be sure of seeing her. They paid a minimum of a shilling a visit, more if they could afford it. When she thought it might cause hardship, she took no fee.

She quite expected a rush of patients this morning since it was known in the district that her baby was due and that she would soon be unavailable for a week or two. She did not have to wait long. Five minutes after the door had closed noisily behind Mrs Foster it opened again, clanging the bell which made her premises sound like the corner shop they had once been.

'Come straight through!' Rose called.

The visitor was Eva Denby.

'Why, Eva! Your mother left not five minutes ago!'

'I know. I met her. She's taken the children. I wanted to see you.'

Two more years of Paradine Street, of unemployment and near starvation, of Jim Denby's hectoring and bullying, had added ten years to Eva's appearance. She was twenty-three, and in her pale, drawn listlessness, looked thirty-five. Rose guessed that, like many a mother who came in here, she lived largely on tea with skimmed condensed milk, and bread-and-margarine.

'How are you?' Rose asked.

'I'm all right.' The usual reply. She was quite clearly anaemic, too thin, and her pretty face was spotty. But her eyes were alive, questioning; anxious and hopeful at one and the same time.

'What do you want to see me about?' Rose asked. 'Won't you sit down?'

Eva perched on the edge of a chair as if ready at any second to take flight.

'I don't like to ask you,' she said. 'You've been good to me. I don't like to keep on . . .'

She paused, not knowing what to say.

'Are you . . . not well?' Rose asked tentatively. 'Are you pregnant?' was what she meant. Eva shook her head.

'It's not that. Though the Lord alone knows why. He uses me every night of the week, so why don't I get pregnant? Sometimes I think God has made me barren because I wanted to lose that child. I get so afraid that I'd almost like to find myself expecting again.'

'Then what . . . ?'

Eva took a deep breath and suddenly the words rushed out.

'They're building some new houses Marton Green way. Council houses, to rent. They have three bedrooms and a bathroom, and a lavatory by the back door, one to each house. And a garden where you can grow things and the children can play. They say they have electric light, which is a bit frightening, but I daresay you could get used to it . . .' Her voice trailed off. She looked apprehensively at Rose. 'I've never slept in a bedroom since I was married,' she said. 'Just in the living room, me and the kids and him. I'd like to have a bedroom.'

She didn't add that she had never lived where there was a bathroom, or a lavatory not shared. There was nothing unusual about that.

'It sounds wonderful,' Rose said. 'Do you think, then, that you might get one of these houses?'

'That's just the trouble,' Eva said. 'There aren't enough. And some people have six children; we only have the two. They take notice of that. But if you was to put in a word . . . you know a lot of people . . . Oh, I wouldn't ask, Doctor Rose, I wouldn't trouble you, only I can't bear to go on

157

living in Paradine Street for the rest of my life. If only we lived somewhere decent I'm sure Jim would be better! I'm sure he'd change!'

Fat chance, Rose thought. But presumably miracles could happen.

'I don't know what I could do, Eva,' she said. 'Has your husband been to the town hall?'

Eva's face shadowed.

'He says it's no good. He says you have to know someone.'

'He wouldn't thank *me* for interfering.'

'He wouldn't know it was you,' Eva said swiftly. 'If you was to put his case to the town hall . . . if someone was to come and see where we live. If only someone *saw* it, *smelt* it!'

Rose nodded. 'I agree. Though I can't imagine that the Housing Committee doesn't know about Paradine Street.' She knew, while she was speaking, whom she could ask. But from loyalty to Alex, from a true desire to make their marriage work, she never saw or spoke to John Worthing unless she had to. The only occasions she could not avoid were the meetings of the Committee of the now thriving Mothers' Holiday Fund, of which she had been a member for more than a year. Even there she kept a polite distance from him.

'I'll think about it, Eva,' she promised. 'I'm not sure what I can do. Could you afford the rent with Jim still out of work?'

'The rent is . . . what do you call it if the Council helps . . . if you're out of work?'

'Subsidised.'

'That's right. For a little while. And they say Marton Green is a lovely place. Right on the edge of Akersfield. Almost in the country. Ever so clean.'

'It's a long way from most jobs,' Rose pointed out.

Eva shrugged. 'What does that matter if you haven't got a job? All Jim has to do is to walk to the Labour Exchange. He has plenty of time to do that.'

'Well, I'll try to speak to someone,' Eva promised. 'But don't build on it, will you?'

Eva's face flushed with pleasure.

'I can't thank you enough, Doctor! I'm sure if you do it, it'll all turn out all right. And I hope everything goes well with the baby. I truly hadn't forgotten that.'

Rose, getting up to see Eva to the door, suddenly thought, 'My baby will be born today.' The doorbell clanged as she stood up. 'Ask whoever it is to come straight in, will you, Eva?'

Yes, though there was no sign of it yet, she was quite sure that the child would be born today.

IO

Though at the moment her shape made driving uncomfortable, Rose drove herself home in the little
two-seater which Alex had given her for a wedding
present. It was the same car in which he had taken
her up to Faverwell when Eva Denby was there. She
had quickly learnt to drive and after two or three
lessons from Alex drove herself everywhere, at what he
complained was far too high a speed.

'Home' was now number fifteen, Beechcroft Road, not
very far from Mrs Crabtree's. They had stayed with Mrs
Crabtree for a few weeks after the wedding, until Alex had
found the house in Beechcroft Road at a rent they could
afford. Drawing up at the gate she saw, as always, Alex's
other and most wonderful present. It was attached to the
iron gate, a highly-polished rectangle of brass, the September sun glinting on the engraved letters which never
failed to delight her. 'Dr Rose Bairstow, MB, ChB.'

Her afternoon surgery was due to start at two o-clock,
though even now, nearly two years after she had put up
her plate, it was still not certain that anyone would attend.
She had a modest number of regular patients, almost all
of them women and children, but while some days she
waited in vain for a patient to ring her bell, she guessed
that they were streaming into Doctor Henry Lewthwaite's
surgery at the other end of the road. Only Doctor Patel,
with his plate in the next road, would have fewer patients
than she; but he was an Indian practitioner which was
worse, even, than being a woman.

Since she could not afford to engage a locum for the
period of her lying-in she would have liked to have

made an arrangement with Doctor Patel to deal with her patients then, but she knew that there were those to whom he would not be acceptable. Reluctantly, she had asked Doctor Lewthwaite to help her out, and he had willingly agreed. How many patients, she wondered gloomily, might stay with him permanently?

Annie, the little maid-of-all-work, met her in the hall.

'There's a lady in the sitting-room, Doctor. She's just arrived.'

'Then will you tell her I'll be free in about ten minutes? And could you get me a quick cup of tea and a sandwich? I haven't eaten.'

'A cup of tea and a sandwich is no sort of meal,' Annie said disapprovingly. She prided herself on speaking her mind.

'I know,' Rose apologized. She often found herself apologizing to Annie. 'I'll have something more substantial later.'

She ate the sandwich and drank the tea quickly, then asked Annie to show in the patient. On the whole, the patients who made up her private practice were as predictable as those in Babcock Street, though the underlying causes of whatever ailed them were different. She did not deal here with women who lived in hovels, could not afford to eat properly, and had too many children. Her patients in Beechcroft Road were mostly middle class. More often than not she saw them in their homes, because that was how they liked it, especially if there were children to be treated. She sent them quarterly bills and hoped they would not make her wait too long for payment. It was this money, because Alex refused to take it for household bills, which paid for the rent of Babcock Street and also went towards paying off what remained of the debt to her father.

The patient Annie showed in was a new one. She was tall, slender to the point of thinness, expensively dressed in the new autumn shades of russet brown and forest green, with a fringe of pale gold hair showing beneath her velour hat. Rose judged her to be about her own age. As she sat down she peeled off immaculate beige kid gloves to reveal delicate hands, the manicured nails buffed and polished to a rosy pinkness. Rose pushed out of her mind the sudden memory of Eva Denby's swollen hands as she had stood before her this morning, twisting them in embarrassment. If the woman before her was ill, she had as much right to her help as any of the Babcock Street women.

'Good-afternoon, Doctor.' The woman's voice was low, well-modulated, would have been attractive but for a note of discontentment. 'My name is Gwen Mayfield. Mrs Gwen Mayfield.'

'Good-afternoon,' Rose said. 'What can I do for you?'

Mrs Mayfield sighed. 'I don't know that you can do anything. No-one else has. And now that I'm here I'm not sure why I bothered to come. Maybe I'm not ill. I only know I feel awful.'

It was not an unusual opening nor, as Rose skilfully persuaded the woman to talk, was her story an uncommon one. Mrs Mayfield was a widow, her husband, a Major in the West Yorkshire Regiment, having been killed in November nineteen-eighteen, less than a week before the war ended.

'He was killed at Amiens,' Mrs Mayfield said. 'The thing is, he should have been on leave. If he hadn't volunteered to put it off . . .'

She shrugged. There was no hint of self-pity in her. It was just one of those things.

'Have you any children?' Rose asked.

'No. We'd been married only a few months. I suppose we would have had children later.'

And maybe you wouldn't have been sitting here now, Rose thought. You'd have been enjoying a full life, too busy to include me. She suspected that she was not the first doctor this patient had been to. Women like Mrs Mayfield, with time and money to spare, went the rounds.

When Rose had asked all the questions, she examined Mrs Mayfield. She could find nothing wrong with her except that she was far too thin, her lace-trimmed, *crepe-de-chine* underwear hanging loosely on her.

'Have you been losing weight?'

'Oh yes, I've tried to. One can't look at all decent nowadays if one is fat. I've been banting.'

It was really too stupid. Her Babcock Street patients were emaciated because they couldn't afford food, while in her home surgery she was constantly up against patients who starved themselves in pursuit of the breastless, hipless, boyish figure which was currently fashionable.

'That won't do,' Rose said firmly. 'That way you'll continue to be listless, tired, not able to sleep or concentrate.'

'I hope you're not going to lecture me, Doctor,' Mrs Mayfield said. 'I'd hoped you'd simply give me some magic tonic, or a bottle of pills . . .' She made languid gestures with her hands, as if conjuring something out of the air.

'I shan't give you anything of the kind,' Rose said. 'I believe you when you say you feel awful, but the remedy's in your own hands. You must eat properly and, in my opinion, you should try to find something interesting to do with your life. That's where your cure is.'

The woman was suffering from acute boredom, Rose reckoned, which brought depression in its wake. But she would not thank her for saying so.

'There *isn't* anything interesting,' Mrs Mayfield said. 'All these interminable tea parties, charity concerts. It's so tedious. I've practically stopped going to anything.'

'You don't think of taking a job?' Rose asked.

Mrs Mayfield stared at her.

'Take a job? What in the world could I do? I'm not trained for anything. I'm a married woman . . . well, I was. I don't actually *know* anyone who goes out to work. Except of course . . . well, you're different, aren't you?

163

And then there are clerks and shopgirls. You don't mean that, surely?'

'No,' Rose said. She couldn't imagine it. Besides, there were not enough of those jobs for the people who really needed them. 'What about voluntary work?'

'You mean . . . flag days? Or visiting old ladies?' She sounded doubtful.

'Something more demanding,' Rose suggested. 'More regular.'

'Like what?'

'On the spur of the moment I'm not sure,' Rose admitted. 'But there must be something. For instance, I've just recently formed a Club for working-class mothers. Somewhere where they'll meet and talk, learn how to cook nourishing meals out of next to nothing, how to sew, how to look after their children's health. That sort of thing.'

How terribly dull she made it sound! How worthy! It was not at all how she intended it to be.

Mrs Mayfield looked at her in astonishment.

'I could never do that! I can't boil an egg!'

'You wouldn't need to. We can get experts to do all that. What we need is a person of intelligence to organize it, to contact speakers, look after the accounts.'

She felt quite sure that underneath her airy manner Mrs Mayfield was intelligent. At the moment what she lacked was drive and purpose.

'Anyway, you could teach them how to look nice, how to make the best of themselves. I think that's important.'

For the first time since she had walked into the room a glimmer of interest showed in Mrs Mayfield's face. 'I daresay I could,' she said thoughtfully.

'Well, there it is, Mrs Mayfield,' Rose said. 'I'm by no means suggesting that this particular job is for you. I don't know you well enough for that. But think along those lines; start to eat properly and find an interest in life. And don't think that I don't sympathize with you, because I do. But no-one else can do these things for you.'

Mrs Mayfield stood up. drew on her gloves, smoothing

164

down each finger. 'I'll think about it,' she said. 'Well, he said you'd sort me out, and you did!'

'He?'

'John Worthing. Councillor John Worthing. Didn't I tell you it was he who suggested I should come to you?'

The questions raced around in Rose's mind. What was Mrs Mayfield to John Worthing? Was she one of his reputedly many women? Perhaps a special one? She was a young widow, undeniably attractive. But he would not, could not be so cruel as to flaunt her if that was the case. He was simply sending her a patient because he thought she needed them. It was nothing more.

'No, you didn't say.'

'I thought I had,' Mrs Mayfield said. 'He spoke highly of you.'

'Thank you.'

Rose showed her to the door.

'When are you having your baby?' Mrs Mayfield asked.

'Today,' Rose said firmly. 'I'm having it today.'

As Mrs Mayfield was about to leave, Alex came in, almost bumping into them in the small hall. The three of them stood there, so that Rose had to make polite introductions. She was taken by the quick interest in Alex's face as Mrs Mayfield held out her hand to him. A pang of jealousy like a small pain shot through her, but the jealousy was not to do with Alex. If this woman has an effect on Alex, who is not susceptible, a cold voice inside her asked. what does she do to John Worthing?

'I'll see you again, Doctor,' Mrs Mayfield said.

As Rose closed the door on her she wondered which was preferable, that she should not set eyes on Mrs Mayfield again, or that she should know where she was, what she was doing? In any case, the choice was not hers to make.

'I have to go out again,' Alex said, following Rose into the sitting room. 'An editorial meeting.'

She was used to that. They spent more time apart than together, but because she was fully occupied with her work she did not mind.

'Alex,' she said. 'Do you know anything about new Council houses being built at Marton Green?'

'Yes. They've started on them. Why do you ask?'

'Eva Denby came in today. She's desperate to get one. It certainly would be a new life for her if she could.'

'She'd still have Jim Denby,' Alex said. 'Strange, though, how he's kept out of trouble these last two or three years. It must be his longest clear run since he was in Borstal, aged fifteen.'

'Do we know anyone? Eva's quite right in thinking it's who you know that counts.'

'Well I can't do anything,' Alex said. 'Not in my position.'

'Ah yes! I keep forgetting how high the editor sits above we ordinary mortals?' Rose said.

A fleeting look of annoyance crossed Alex's face. He sometimes wondered if Rose took his position seriously.

'Ask John Worthing,' he suggested. 'You're bound to be seeing him at the Holiday Fund meeting.'

'Perhaps I will.' Alex had echoed her own earlier thoughts. She had no wish to ask a favour of John Worthing, but Eva needed all the help she could get.

'Try not to be too late. And don't drink too much,' she said to Alex. 'I'm having the baby today.'

He looked at her in surprise. 'Or the next day or the next. How can you know?'

'I just do,' Rose said. 'I feel it in my bones.'

'I'll be back as soon as I can,' he promised. 'But you know how these things go on.'

She was sitting quietly by the first fire of the autumn, skilfully darning the toes of her silk stockings. She watched the coal glow and spark and the flames lick against the fire back. And as the flames leapt, suddenly the pain leapt in her body; sharp, insistent, consuming.

When her daughter was born, a few minutes before midnight, Alex was not yet home. She was glad that he was not, for in the hours of her labour, at the times when the pain had been the greatest, it was not Alex she had wanted to hold her hand, to give her comfort; it was not his name she had wanted to cry out. She had been unfaithful to him even in the fact of giving birth to his child.

When he did come, she by this time lying tidily in bed, the baby in its crib by her bedside, she saw that he had been drinking – and knew that it was because here was the situation he could not face. The child in the cot was the living reminder of that night nine months ago. The torment was in his eyes as he forced himself to look at his daughter. Would he be reminded every time he saw her? Rose wondered. And what would it do to the child?

As Alex bent to kiss Rose, his breath smelling of whisky, they were two people racked by their differing shame, crying out to each other, though not aloud, for forgiveness.

Rose lay flat on her back in bed, her abdomen tightly bound. She had been ordered to stay in this position by Nurse Dobson, who at this moment was tiptoeing around the bedroom in the most irritating fashion. She steadfastly refused to let Rose sit up, except on necessary occasions like feeding the baby, or washing her own hands and face in the enamelled bowl set on the bed table.

'At all other times, Doctor, you must lie flat!' Nurse said. 'I'm sure you know that as well as I do. We want everything to go back into place, don't we? And we don't want to lose our figure!'

Rose sighed. 'It's so difficult to read, lying down like this. Especially the newspaper.'

'But we shouldn't be reading, should we?' Nurse Dobson said brightly. 'We should be having a little nap, building up our strength. And concentrating on *pleasant* thoughts when we're making milk for our baby! Not strikes and politics and murders which, with all due respect to your husband, is all we get in the newspapers these days.'

'Sometimes my husband complains that there isn't enough news,' Rose said. 'A nice juicy murder is meat and drink to the *Record*. Better still if it's a local one.'

Nurse Dobson tut-tutted her disapproval. 'I blame the war for all this unrest. Nothing's been the same since. Except babies, of course!' Her expression lightened as she surveyed the sleeping infant.

'What a little darling she is! Is she going to have her mother's red hair, I wonder? Of course it's usually dark when they're born.'

'Can't I hold her?' Rose pleaded. 'Just for a few minutes?' She longed to cradle her daughter in her arms, to examine yet again the tiny hands and feet, the rosebud mouth. the miracle of the pearl-like fingernails. each one perfect.

Nurse Dobson looked shocked.

'My dear Doctor, we can't have that! There's at least an hour to go before it's time for you to hold her. We must keep to the routine. Babies know, you know!'

Does my daughter know that I long to cuddle her? Rose wondered. Does she know that she's the most beautiful, the most wonderful, the most loved . . . ?

'We must begin as we mean to go on,' Nurse Dobson said firmly. 'As a doctor you must know that.'

Little did Nurse Dobson know that this was not how Rose meant to go on. She could hardly wait for the nurse to depart, which she was to do at the end of a fortnight instead of the usual month because Rose had flatly refused to keep a nurse for so long. When the child was a little older she knew she might have to hire some help to look after her, but for now, and for as long as she could, she intended to keep her daughter close. When she went back to the Babcock Street surgery she meant to take the baby with her. It would lie there in a Moses basket while she attended to her patients. She had it all worked out.

'Now I'm going to leave you,' Nurse Dobson said. 'You're to be a good girl and lie still and try to sleep.'

When the nurse had left the room Rose raised herself on one elbow and began to read the *Record*. The woman was quite right, of course. It *was* full of politics and crime:

the likelihood of another General Election, the threat (as the *Record* saw it) of the Labour Party, the utterances of Trade Union leaders, the fear of the new Russia. A jeweller in Bradford had been robbed; an Akersfield woman had been knocked down by a car travelling at the disgraceful speed of forty miles an hour.

She turned the page and learned that skirts and hair were even shorter and that Oxford undergraduates were wearing trousers measuring as much as thirty-two inches around the bottom of the legs. Also that a greengrocery chain was selling a rabbit, plus four potatoes, two carrots and an onion, for tenpence. 'Ways with Rabbits' might be a good subject for the Mothers' Club.

She almost missed the 'Letters to the Editor' – she was uncomfortable in this half-sitting posture and afraid that Nurse Dobson might return at any minute – until her own name leapt out at her from the page.

It is with pleasure that all readers of the *Record*,' (she read) 'will wish to congratulate the editor and his wife, Doctor Rose Bairstow, on the recent birth of their daughter. It is good to know that Doctor Rose does not follow the advice she so freely hands out on "How Not to have Babies". May we hope that, having now experienced the delights of motherhood herself, we shall hear no more of the opinions which are a threat to family life and abhorrent to all decent people.'

She sat bolt upright, flinging the newspaper to the floor – then went dizzy and had to lie down again. The effrontery of people! The letter was signed M.B. Taylor, so there was no telling whether it was from a man or a woman. But it was not, by a long way, the first brickbat she had received, and as her dizziness passed, so did the sharp edge of her fury. At Babcock Street, and occasionally here in her own home, she had a steady stream of abusive letters, some signed, many anonymous; many of them grounds for libel

169

if she had chosen to go so far. 'Destroyer of homes', 'Dirty beast', 'Disgrace to Womanhood', 'Purveyor of Filth', were among the milder epithets which had been hurled at her. At first she had been shaken by so much animosity but now, on a personal level, it did no more than niggle her. What surprised her most was that there was always a fair sprinkling of letters from women.

It did not surprise her in the least that Alex had allowed the publication of this latest letter. He could well have suppressed it but he would have thought that quite wrong, even though the subject of the abuse was his own wife. It had not taken her long to learn that he was an editor first and a husband second. Well, now she would approach him as an editor and he would have to publish her reply.

Nurse Dobson came back into the room. She stood by the bed, straightening the counterpane, mitreing the corners, tucking it in tightly at the foot.

'There now, have we had a nice little sleep?' she asked. Not waiting for a reply, she picked up the newspaper, re-folded it, and put it on a table. 'We just have time for a lovely bed bath and a nice beaker of Benger's Food before it's time to feed baby!'

'I don't want a bed bath,' Rose said. 'I want a pencil and a sheet of writing paper.'

Nurse Dobson looked at Rose in shocked disbelief. She was not an easy patient, but then doctors never were, and being a lady doctor she was worse. But this was too much – unless it was the onset of puerperal fever!

'A pencil and paper,' Rose repeated, sitting upright. 'I'll have my bed bath some other time. Better still, I'll get up and have a proper bath. Right now I have to write an important letter.'

Nurse Dobson was bereft of speech. She did what her training told her to do, which was to advance on Rose, push a thermometer in her mouth, take hold of her by the wrist and, consulting the watch which hung from her starched bosom, take her patient's pulse.

Rose removed the thermometer from her mouth and

handed it back. 'I don't have a temperature, Nurse. I'm perfectly well. Now if you don't fetch me a pencil and paper I shall get up and find them for myself!'

Nurse Dobson knew the answer to that. Keep the patient calm, keep her in bed. Without another word she left the room, and returned five minutes later with pencil and paper.

Alex came home earlier than usual. He greeted Rose, and then bent over the cot, gently touching the baby's cheek with one finger. Rose could not conceal her surprise. It was the first sign of interest he had shown in the child.

'I intend to try, Rose,' he said quietly, answering the question on her face.

Rose put out her hand and touched him. 'I'm glad, Alex. She needs a father as well as a mother. She's just going to be bathed. Stay and watch.'

Annie had built up the bedroom fire for Nurse Dobson until the room was like a hothouse. Nurse had allowed her to bring in jugs of hot and cold water, though she herself mixed the contents in the baby's bath, testing the temperature with her elbow.

'That will be all, Annie,' she said. She suffered the presence of mothers and fathers because that was the cross she had to bear, but little maidservants were another matter.

'You can stay and see her bathed if you want to,' Rose said, seeing Annie's disappointed face.

Alex sat beside the fire, silently watching Nurse Dobson's ministrations. From the bed, Rose tried to see the expression on his face, but his back was to her and he did not turn around.

When the baby was clean and fresh again, liberally sprinkled with talcum powder on what Nurse Dobson referred to as 'all her little parts', tightly bandaged around the abdomen in a clean binder and swathed in a long flannel petticoat and a nightie, with a matinee coat on top, Nurse Dobson handed her to Rose.

It was the moment Rose had been waiting for. She

wanted to hold the child close, crush her in an embrace, never let her go. It might be true that her baby needed a father, but not just now, not at this moment. Now she's mine, Rose exulted. She's all mine!

'Have you decided what we're going to call her,' Alex asked, coming over to the bed, reminding Rose of his presence. 'Is it to be Heather or Jenny?'

'Jenny, I think. It has a warm sound.'

'I agree.'

Rose unfastened the front of her nightgown, eased out a breast swollen and veined with milk, and offered it to the baby. It was accepted greedily. It was, Rose thought, watching the baby suckle, the most exquisite sensation she had ever known. Alex, bending over the two of them, reached up a hand and tentatively touched Rose's breast. She tried not to flinch. She wanted to be alone with the baby.

'I have to go back to work,' Alex said.

'Before you go, there's something I want you to read,' Rose told him. 'Only not just now.' She wanted nothing to interfere with this moment.

'We're going to banish Daddy now!' Nurse Dobson said playfully. 'Only Mummies and Babies allowed at feed times!'

An hour later Alex returned to the bedroom. Rose handed him the letter she had pencilled. When he came to the end, he handed it back to her.

'I can't publish it, of course.'

'Not publish it? Why ever not?'

'You know perfectly well why not.'

'You published the one today. I understand why you did even if I don't agree with you. In a way, I suppose I don't mind. It's all publicity. But why can't I reply to it?'

'Because you're my wife,' Alex said. 'I would be abusing my position if I let my own wife have the last word. I'm sorry.'

'Your position?' Rose cried. She was incensed by the

steady reasonableness of his tone. 'Do you ever think of anything except your position? What about my position?'

'You knew what you were letting yourself in for when you started all this. I don't mind that if it's what you want to do – I never did. I don't even mind the publicity . . .'

'It's all news, I suppose!'

'Quite.' He seemed unaware of her sarcasm. 'But I can't publish my wife's letters on so controversial a subject. It would smack of favouritism.'

'So I'm to go undefended? Is that it? The Royal Family and the wives of newspaper editors must never answer back?'

'Someone else might write in your defence,' Alex said. 'If they do I'll publish it.'

'Pigs might fly!' Rose said scornfully. 'The people who would defend me hardly know how to write. If they could they'd tell you I don't threaten family life. I try to improve it. I don't persuade women not to have babies. I teach them how to have them at reasonable intervals, not to have more than they can cope with – for the sake of the baby as well as the mother. And I don't work for wives against husbands. I try to make things better for both of them. I thank God every time – rare though it is – that a man comes with his wife to my surgery . . .'

'All right,' Alex said. 'Calm down!'

'I will not calm down,' Rose cried. 'These people know what I'm trying to do! How is it the so-called better classes can't understand? Everyone knows that the middle classes practise birth control, one way or another, so why do they want to deny it to the poor, who have far more need of it?'

She was suddenly weak and shaking, all her strength gone. Why did she always have to fight for things? Nothing came easily. It was not fair. It was not fair! She burst into noisy tears, which immediately brought Nurse Dobson from where she lurked on the other side of the bedroom door.

'Dear me, dear me, we can't have this!' she cried. 'We'll

turn our milk sour, and then where will poor baby be? I knew all this activity would end in tears! Mr Bairstow, call me interfering if you will, but I really must ask you not to upset my patient like this!'

Rose lifted her head, accepted the handkerchief Alex offered her to dry her eyes. 'Don't blame my husband. Nurse,' she said wearily. 'It's my own fault. I shouldn't have got so worked up.'

'Indeed you should not!' Nurse Dobson straightened the counterpane, shook up Rose's pillow, and shooed Alex from the room.

At the end of a fortnight Rose parted thankfully from Nurse Dobson. She felt guilty that she was so pleased to see her go. The woman was a good nurse and had done her duty as she saw it. Because of her guilt, Rose gave her a large box of expensive chocolates and two pairs of fine silk stockings on top of her fee.

Tomorrow she would open her surgery here, and in a week or two's time, perhaps sooner, she would be back in Babcock Street.

11

Rose glanced around the sitting-room, checking that everything was in order; chairs more or less in a circle, ashtrays to hand. It was the afternoon of the Mothers' Holiday Fund Committee meeting and it had been agreed, in view of Rose's present circumstances, to hold it here. She turned to speak to Annie, who came into the room carrying a vase of bronze chrysanthemums.

'Put them on the small table there, I think.'

'Right-ho, Doctor,' Annie said.

'Jenny went straight to sleep after her two-o-clock feed. With luck there won't be a sound from her for two or three hours. But if she should cry you'll go to her, won't you?'

'She'll be all right with me, the little pet,' Annie promised. 'Don't you worry!'

Rose viewed herself in the mirror over the mantelpiece and wondered if the members of the Committee would see any difference in her. Physically she looked well now. She had benefited from the enforced rest and her hair, which had not been at its best when she was pregnant, had regained its bounce and bright colour. She was as slender as ever, except that her breasts were rounder and fuller, which was an improvement.

It was the way she felt which was so different. Since Jenny's birth everything in life seemed bigger, brighter, more significant. Far from being discouraged about her work in Babcock Street, as she had momentarily been on the evening of that silly outburst, she felt more than ever fitted for it and knew that nothing, least of all stupid letters in the *Record,* would stand in her way.

She wished that her marriage ran as well as her job. She

and Alex, though now amiable enough on the surface, seemed to have less and less to say to each other. His interest in the baby seemed already to have abated, though in any case Jenny was usually asleep long before he arrived home. If he was around when she was having her late evening feed he would glance at her, perhaps touch her on the cheek. That was the sum of his physical contact with her. He never picked her up, never held her.

'I'll ring for tea at about a quarter-to-four,' she said to Annie. 'There'll be seven of us.'

'I know,' Annie said. 'You told me.'

So she had. Everything was catered for. There was no reason at all for the nervousness she was feeling. So she told herself, but it was not true. She was apprehensive about meeting John Worthing, whom she had not seen for so long, he having missed the last meeting. Would he find her different? It should not matter, but it did, and she faced the fact that it always would. Though nothing could ever come of it, she wanted always to be desirable in his sight.

Rose answered the ring at the door herself. Miss Nesfield, matron of a home for unmarried mothers and, with Rose, one of the two women on the Committee, stood on the doorstep with the Reverend Thomas Francis, a Wesleyan minister and Chairman of the Committee. Behind them, inches taller, stood John Worthing. His eyes, serious, lacking their usual glint of humour, met and held Rose's until her attention was claimed by the Reverend Francis.

'Councillor Worthing kindly gave us a lift,' he said. 'Such a help!'

Before they were in the house the other members arrived, with the punctuality of busy people. The Reverend Francis settled himself in the most comfortable chair and made a start.

'The main business this afternoon, as we all know, is to decide where we shall have our second holiday home. We have two proposals. One is that we should use the money we've accumulated, plus the substantial sum we inherited under the will of the late Mrs Sebastian Preston, to enlarge our existing home in Ilkley; the other is that we should acquire a house at the seaside – Blackpool has been mentioned. If, as we said at the previous meeting, we want to open the house next Spring, then we must make our decision today.'

'I've brought details of one or two properties in Blackpool,' one of the members said. 'Good, sound places; not too expensive.'

'We're fortunate in having an estate agent on our committee,' the Reverend Francis said. 'Thank you, Mr Mortimer. But perhaps we should decide in principle where we're to go – Ilkley or Blackpool – before we begin to look at properties.'

That, as Rose and everyone present knew, was the bone of contention.

'I vote for Blackpool every time,' she said decisively. 'Nothing against our house in Ilkley, but Blackpool would be such fun for the mothers. It's lively – always something happening.'

'Too lively by half!' one of the men said. 'And is fun the object of our exercise? Remember that these ladies would be in Blackpool without their husbands.'

'These are grown women you're talking about, Mr Barber,' Miss Nesfield interrupted. 'I'm sure they're capable of conducting themselves properly.'

'Capable, ay – but will they?' Mr Barber questioned. 'If I may be so bold, I'd remind you that yon place you're running is for women who've failed to do just that. We don't want to go looking for trouble, do we?'

Miss Nesfield turned on him sharply. 'And may I remind you, Mr Barber, that none of my girls would be where she is now but for the connivance of some man! Immaculate conception does not take place in Akersfield!'

'Ladies! Gentlemen!' the Reverend Francis pleaded.

John Worthing had so far taken no part in the proceedings. He seemed preoccupied, distant. But when he looked up and spoke now the others stopped to listen. It was always the same. He was a man who compelled attention.

'I agree with Matron. Our purpose is to give these women a much needed holiday, not to be public guardians of their morals. Freedom to enjoy oneself is surely part of a good holiday. So the point is, where would they do that most? Come to think of it, anyone who has a mind to do so could go astray in either Blackpool or Ilkley!'

'Ilkley is a very healthy place,' one member ventured.

'So is Blackpool,' – Miss Nesfield countered. 'I feel better the minute I get off the train there.'

Rose looked across at Miss Nesfield with interest. She had not thought of her as a devotee of Blackpool. A quiet holiday in Filey, even two weeks in Torquay, but not Blackpool. What did she do there? Did she go on the Big Wheel, or dance the night away in the Tower ballroom? But then she remembered that Miss Nesfield had nursed abroad through four years of war, serving in the thick of danger. Blackpool would hold no terrors for her.

'Well, we must put it to the vote,' the Reverend Francis said eventually.

Three were for Blackpool, three for Ilkley. 'So I must use my casting vote,' he said.

To Rose's amazement he said, 'I choose Blackpool. And now we must appoint a sub-committee who will undertake to visit some properties there.'

John Worthing, Miss Nesfield and Mr Barber, the latter presumably to hold the other two in check, were appointed. 'Perhaps Doctor Rose?' someone said. Rose looked at John Worthing, read the invitation in his eyes.

'I can't,' she said quickly. 'I'm feeding my baby. I can't be away from home for so long.'

She longed to go, to be with him for an entire day, even though in the presence of other people. But she knew it was just as well that she could not.

When the meeting was over and they were ready to leave, Rose said to John, 'Could I see you for a few minutes? There's something I want to ask you about.'

He waited behind when she showed the others to the door. When she came back into the sitting room he was standing with his back to her, looking into the fire. She doubted that he had heard her come into the room. Seeing him so, she had this deep longing to go to him, to touch and stroke the back of his neck where his dark hair, always worn a little longer than was the fashion, curled over the edge of his stiff white collar. If she could do only that, she told herself, it would be enough. She would be content. Only let her touch him.

Suddenly aware of her, he turned, and caught the longing in her face before she could hide it from him. He moved quickly towards her and took her in his arms, his lips seeking hers. There was no resistance in her and the lips she offered him were as eager as his own. How had she borne to be without him all these months? How could she ever bear it again? She stretched up her hand to touch and caress the back of his neck and his hands began to move over her body. caressing, demanding. Hunger for him rose strongly in her and she found herself responding fervently to his touch. She felt lost, as if she was moving through a dream and had no power to direct herself. And then, as he made a movement to manoeuvre her on to the sofa, she all at once came to, with a sharp, painful awakening from the dream.

She wanted immediately to return to that dream world. She resented whatever strong power had called her from it. She told herself she had heard her baby cry, but it was not true. What had brought her back was that censor in her mind which would not allow her to assuage her body's needs. With Alex she could not do so because she could think only of John Worthing. With John her sense of duty – to her husband, her child, her profession – rose up like a great barrier between them. It was impossible to give herself to either man, though the longing was there, deep and strong.

With all the resolve she could muster she tried to push John away from her, to escape from his arms.

'John, we mustn't.' It sounded childish.

He held her fast. 'Why mustn't we?'

'You know why not.'

'If you don't want me to touch you,' he said, 'you must not look at me in the way you did. How do you expect me to resist you?'

'I do want you to,' she said softly. 'To touch me. You know that, John. I don't deny it.'

He held her at arm's length now, but not letting her go; looking into her face as if he had found magic in it.

'I wouldn't believe you if you did, my love. Your body tells a different story. But do you know that it's the first time you've admitted it?'

'I do know,' Rose said. 'I'm never going to deny it again. Even so it has to stop.'

'You can't stop it,' he said. 'Any more than you can stop the sun rising each morning.'

'I can't stop the feelings,' she admitted. 'I can only refuse to act on them.'

'Such a controlled lady!' There was an edge of sarcasm in his voice which was more than Rose could bear.

'I'm not!' she blazed. 'I'm not! I don't want to be controlled, cool, contained! My blood runs as fast and as warm as yours. I want everything you want, and as desperately. Can't you see that? Can't you understand? I just have to accept that it's impossible. It's not only because I'm married – though that counts a great deal. There's more to it than that. If I weren't . . .'

'If you weren't a doctor,' he interrupted. 'I know.'

'It's difficult to explain. It's something I chose, it's part of me. Aside from those laid down for me, I set my own standards. However priggish it sounds, they don't include adultery; especially deliberately entered into, and repeated; made a way of life as ours would grow to be; a life hedged about with petty deceptions. But my feelings are real enough, John. I'm not some efficient machine. Please try to understand.'

He looked at her bleakly, let her go, almost pushing her away from him. She was trembling so that she could hardly stand. She sat down on the sofa, knowing that now he would not sit beside her.

'I try,' he said. 'Perhaps I can understand, but I can't accept. I can't live up to your standards, Rose. It's not in me.'

But you have standards, she thought. You can't leave a wife whom you think needs you. But now, even if he would, it was too late for her. She had Alex and Jenny. She wondered if, in the last few minutes, she had finally lost John Worthing.

In the silence between them he lit a cigar, making a small ceremony out of lighting it, as if to mark a change of mood. His hands, holding the flame to the tobacco, were steady, while her own hands still trembled. He puffed the aromatic smoke into the air and spoke to her as if the last few minutes had not happened.

'What did you want to see me about?'

Rose caught her breath. How could he be so cool, so calm on the instant, while her own feelings were in a ferment? She wanted to strike him, to knock the cigar from his fingers. For a moment she almost hated him for his swift change of mood, and then hated herself because she could not be so quickly dispassionate.

'The Denbys,' she said, trying to pull herself together. 'Eva Denby says that the Council is building new houses at Marton Green. She feels – and I must say I agree with her – that if only they could get out of Paradine Street, live somewhere decent, it might change their lives. You're on the Housing Committee aren't you? I wondered if you could help?'

'Has the husband applied for a house?'

'No. He thinks it's hopeless unless you know someone with influence.'

He looked stern, concentrated on the problem. The

man who had taken her in his arms only minutes ago had vanished. But it was part of the fascination this man had for her, that there were so many facets to his character. He was unpredictable, volatile; it was his intrinsic challenge which made her feel that she – she alone – could be the one to tame him.

'Tell Mrs Denby that she must get her husband to go down to the town hall and make an application,' he said. 'After that I'll do what I can. It might help if you, as a doctor, backed up Mrs Denby's case.'

'I can do that with the utmost conviction. Whether Jim Denby will like it is another matter. I'm not especially keen to tangle with him again. By the way,' she said, remembering, 'I saw a patient recommended by you a couple of weeks ago.'

'Gwen Mayfield? Yes, she told me she'd seen you.'

So did they see each other often? Rose wondered. She felt a small, sharp prick of jealousy.

'She mentioned some idea of helping you with your Mothers' Club,' John said.

'We did discuss it briefly,' Rose agreed. 'Would she be any good, do you think? Nothing against Mrs Mayfield, of course, but my mothers are important. I want the best for them.'

'Gwen would be quite good, I reckon. She's intelligent, warm-hearted, understanding under that brittle surface.'

'You sound enthusiastic,' Rose said.

John Worthing gave her a quizzical look.

'I am. All that's wrong with Gwen is that over the last year or two she's had too little to do and too much time to think. You'd be doing her – and your mothers – a favour if you took her on.'

Do I want to do her a favour? Rose asked herself. Out loud she said, 'Well I'll think about it.'

She saw him to the door, watched him as he walked swiftly down the path and got into his car. She stood there watching until he was out of sight.

*   *   *

The Babcock Street surgery was in full swing again. Rose pressed the buzzer for the next patient to enter.

'Hello, Mrs Palmer,' she said to the woman who came in. 'How are you?'

Mrs Palmer was a regular. She came with her shilling sometimes it was only sixpence – hoping that the hard-won coin would somehow buy from the doctor a solution to her troubles. She was one of several who came with the same idea. Rose knew well enough that she had no answer to the ordeal of lasting unemployment, to the burden of bringing up large families on a meagre dole, in squalid surroundings. It seemed beyond the reach even of politicians and governments to do anything about it. They had laid upon the local councils the responsibility of building houses to rent, but little had been done so far. As for jobs, there seemed no prospect of any improvement, ever.

'Is your husband still out of work?' Rose asked. She was examining Mrs Palmer carefully, sounding her heart, listening to her lungs. She needed to do none of this to know that what her patient needed was some good food, a decent place to live, a lightening of her worries; but she knew that by the act of examining Mrs Palmer she was assuring her that someone was taking notice.

'Three years since he had a job,' Mrs Palmer said. 'I reckon them politicians down in London have forgotten we exist up here! They have it easy down there. But they didn't forget when they wanted them for the war, did they?'

'You're a bit congested,' Rose said. 'I'll give you a bottle of medicine, and see you take it!' She was convinced that many of her patients came for a talk, rather than for the medicine, and who was to say which did most good? 'You can get dressed now,' she said.

'You remember that Lord Kitchener pointing his finger from the posters?' Mrs Palmer said. ' "Your Country Needs You!" Young kids like my brother rushing to join the Bradford Pals, pretending they was eighteen!'

Rose knew that Mrs Palmer's brother had been killed

183

on the Somme on the warm July day which was his seventeenth birthday.

Mrs Palmer fastened her blouse, put on her jacket.

'It was as well a lot of 'em didn't come back,' she said bitterly. 'There'd have been nowt for 'em. Thirty men after every job as it is.'

She opened her purse, scanned the contents with anxious blue eyes. 'Will sixpence do this time, Doctor? I'm a bit short this week. I'll pay you when things are better.'

'Sixpence will be fine,' Rose said.

At least, she thought, as Mrs Palmer left, she hasn't got pregnant again. At least that was something she'd been able to do for her. A sixth child would have made life impossible.

Most of that morning's patients were regulars, from the surrounding streets, their problems pitifully similar to Mrs Palmer's, but there were a couple of women from further afield who had heard that Doctor Rose Bairstow would give them birth control advice which their own doctors denied them. It was with grim satisfaction that Rose heard one of them say, 'I read about you in the *Record,* when your baby was born. I didn't agree with the letter.'

When Rose thought she had seen the last of her patients there was a knock at the door and Gwen Mayfield entered.

'Why, Mrs Mayfield, I didn't expect to see you here!' Rose said. 'How is it you didn't go to my home surgery? Not that you're not welcome here, but . . .'

'But I'm out of place,' Mrs Mayfield finished the sentence for her. 'I came out of curiosity. I wanted to see what your mothers were like.'

Rose lifted her chin, looked hard at Gwen Mayfield. She would not have her patients patronized by this young woman.

'They're women, like you and me,' she said coldly. 'Down on their luck, most of them, but like you and me inside.'

184

'Sisters under the skin?'

'Something like that,' Rose agreed. 'I'm not sure that I could cope as well as they do in the same circumstances. I don't know about you.'

'I'm sure I couldn't.' Mrs Mayfield said. 'I really didn't mean to be uppity, you know. I came because I've been thinking over what you said about your Mothers' Club. In short, I'd like to help if you'll have me, if you think I'd be any good. I was nervous about the women, about whether I'd be acceptable – to them as well as to you. But I've listened to them in the waiting room this morning, even talked to one or two. I think perhaps I could be, given a chance.'

In spite of herself, Rose liked Gwen Mayfield. And why in spite of myself? she thought. All she really had against the woman was that she came via John Worthing, that she presumably enjoyed his friendship. I'm jealous, Rose admitted to herself.

'I'm sure you could be,' she said. 'I think you could be a great help. Could you possibly come around to my home – would next Monday evening suit you? We could talk about it in detail then. We're going to my home village for our baby's christening at the weekend and I'm going to be a bit busy until then.'

As if on cue Jenny, in her basket in the corner of the room, began to cry.

'Goodness!' Mrs Mayfield exclaimed. 'I hadn't even noticed she was there! Is she always so quiet?'

Rose, picking up the baby, holding her close, laughed. 'Not always. She's pretty good, though. She doesn't always sleep; sometimes she just gurgles – don't you my precious?' She looked down with love on the downy top of Jenny's head, where the dark hair was already showing red glints.

'What do your patients think, seeing a baby in the surgery?' Gwen Mayfield asked.

'I think they rather like it. But my husband doesn't,' Rose said.

185

Alex had protested about it from the first. 'I don't want my daughter spending her time in Babcock Street,' he'd said. He didn't usually say 'my daughter', Rose thought. He must feel quite strongly about the situation.

'It's not suitable,' he objected. 'She could pick up anything.'

'Not in my surgery she couldn't!' Rose said. 'And you'd better not let Mrs Foster hear you say that! She keeps the place as clean as an operating theatre. Anyway, do you suppose I'd take Jenny there if I thought she'd come to any harm?'

'In spite of all you said beforehand, I'd hoped you'd ease off work a bit when you had the baby,' Alex said.

'But Alex, you must have known I wouldn't,' Rose said. 'I never gave you to think otherwise.'

'We could stretch to having a nursemaid,' Alex persisted. 'A girl to look after her here, at least on the days you were in Babcock Street.'

'But I don't want that,' Rose said. 'Don't you understand. I want to look after her myself. I'm just lucky that my job allows me to do that.'

'I met your husband in Akersfield,' Gwen Mayfield was saying. 'We literally bumped into each other in Market Street. I wasn't looking where I was going. He took me for a cup of tea. But I expect he told you.'

He hadn't. But no matter, Rose thought. He had no doubt forgotten all about it.

'I must get home now,' Rose said. 'Can I drop you anywhere?'

'No, thanks. I thought I might walk around here a bit. Get the lie of the land.'

'You won't like it,' Rose warned her. 'Still, it's a good idea. I'll see you next Monday evening then. Shall we say about eight o-clock?'

Within the hour, spent mostly in attending to Jenny's needs, Rose was ready for the first patient in her home surgery. In spite of her fears, most of her private patients had come back to her. In addition Dr Lewthwaite, because of her knowledge of birth control, had sent her a few new ones from his own practice. 'You know as well as I do that we were taught nothing of it in Medical School,' he'd said. 'And I think I'm too old now to enter the fray. But I approve of what you're doing, young lady, and I sympathize with your struggle. More power to your elbow!'

She had been heartened by Doctor Lewthwaite's words as she had not been by anything else in ages. It would be a long time before women could go to their physician, or to a clinic, and receive expert advice, but in the old doctor's attitude she read the signs that one day it would happen. It would be part of everyday life. She did not consider herself an expert, far from it, but she studied whatever was available and she had not hesitated to turn for advice to Doctor Marie Stopes, that much villified and maligned expert on birth control. Though Rose had never met her, Doctor Stopes had always been helpful and encouraging in correspondence.

Jenny was now six weeks old and Rose was looking forward to the weekend in Faverwell and the baby's baptism in the church there. Mrs Stanton had paid one of her rare visits to Akersfield, and Christopher had brought Emily and the girls over for the day, but it would be the first time her father had seen the baby. He could not leave the Ewe Lamb.

'I'm longing to see Dad,' she said to Alex. 'What with one thing and another, I haven't seen him since Easter. It's too long.'

When Rose saw her father, when they arrived at the Ewe Lamb on Saturday afternoon, she was shocked by his appearance. It was difficult for her not to cry out at the sight of him as he greeted her with his usual loving warmth. His wasted frame, the hollows in his cheeks which could have concealed a pigeon's egg, the overall grey of his complexion, told a story which she, as a doctor, could not help but read and understand.

Emily was there, with the children. When they had left her father in the bar, Rose took Emily's arm and led her upstairs to their former bedroom, closing the door behind them.

'Why didn't you let me know?' she demanded angrily. 'Why didn't you write, or telephone?'

'We decided not to, because of the baby. With your record so far, we didn't want to take the risk.'

'But you were over in Akersfield after the baby was born. Why didn't you tell me then?'

'You were so happy with Jenny. We didn't want to spoil it. And Mother was there. We're still not sure how much she realizes. You know what Mother's like. She won't let on.'

'All the same you should have told me,' Rose said. 'Supposing he'd . . .'

'Died? Doctor Harper said there was time. He said we could wait for the christening. Oh Rose, I did want to tell you. Even with Christopher and the children here, I felt so lonely!'

The two sisters sat side by side on the bed in the room where they had spent their childhood together. Tears streamed down Emily's face. Rose put her arms around Emily and they held each other close.

'Oh Rose, it's so awful,' Emily sobbed. 'You don't know how glad I am to see you here at last!'

It was a pity, Rose thought, that it took great unhappiness to unite people, even when they were members of the same family. She had not felt as close to her sister for a long, long time.

George Stanton was present on Sunday afternoon, with the rest of the family and many of the villagers, for the christening of his granddaughter. Rose looked across at him, standing by the font. She saw him watch closely as the Vicar performed the ceremony of baptism. The baby, quiet until now, yelled lustily as the water trickled over her forehead. It was a good sign, they said hereabouts; a sign that the devil had been driven out. Rose saw the look on her father's face as he heard the cry. It was if he, too, had been liberated. She knew as she watched him, her heart filled with sadness, for what reason she would next be in this church.

In the evening – her father agreed to let Christopher and Alex take over in the bar. It was an extraordinary concession on his part, but the afternoon had tired him.

I've a mind to listen to Evensong on the wireless,' he said. 'When I were a lad in the choir, I liked Evensong.'

He joined in the *Nunc Dimittis*, his sweet tenor voice suddenly and surprisingly strong. 'Lord, now lettest Thou thy servant depart in peace . . . for mine eyes hath seen Thy salvation . . .'

'The chap who said that had been waiting to see the baby brought to the temple,' he said to Rose. 'Didst know that, lass?'

12

'If we could rehearse in your house it would be really helpful,' Gwen Mayfield said. 'My place is too far from the centre of Akersfield for the mothers to get there. And we simply can't afford to rent a room.'

'I can only offer you the attic.' Rose said doubtfully. 'It's big enough, but it might be rather cold up there. I suppose we could put in an oil stove?'

She was ashamed that her offer was half-hearted, hoped that her reluctance didn't show. Gwen Mayfield had worked miracles in the Mothers' Club in the last six months and she was truly grateful to her. 'How do you do it?' Rose had asked.

'Well for one thing,' Gwen admitted, 'I see to it that we have a bit of fun, that we don't spend too much time improving our minds, or learning ten ways to cook a penny herring!'

She had organized a series of evening meetings and activities which had been surprisingly well attended, right through the winter. Now she had this idea of producing the women in a play.

'But Gwen, do you think they'll turn out for rehearsals two evenings a week?' Rose queried.

'Oh I know they will – if they can get their husbands to look after the children. And it will do them good to get away from home.'

'Well I agree with that,' Rose said.

'At first they weren't too sure about being in a play – none of them had done anything like it before – but now they're terribly keen. And with properties, stage managing, etcetera etcetera I've managed to involve just about everyone.'

'Well if the attic is any good to you, it's yours. Mondays and Wednesdays, isn't it?'

Pleased though she was about the success of the Mothers' Club – and Gwen Mayfield, with time to spend and with a decided flair had achieved more than Rose could ever have hoped to – she did not look forward to this invasion of her home. She faced the discomfiting fact that it was not the mothers she minded; it was Gwen. Gwen seemed, these days, to be too large a part of life in Beechcroft Road, popping in or telephoning frequently, though always with some good reason. But she was amiable, friendly, a favourite with both Jenny and Alex. Rose chided herself for her ungenerous feelings towards Gwen. But at least my prescription worked, she thought. Immersing herself in a job of work had made a new woman of Gwen Mayfield.

'That's marvellous,' Gwen said. 'I'm really grateful. And if you would let a couple of mothers come down to the kitchen to make a cup of tea, that would be a bonus. Endless cups of tea, I've discovered, is the real secret of my success with them.'

And what is the secret of your success with Alex? The thought came swift and disturbing into Rose's mind. Well not tea, that was for sure. Alex was more and more a whisky man. The demands of his job gave frequent opportunities for drinking, and he did not let them pass. She wondered how he could afford it all, even on an editor's salary. But though he drank a lot, he did not get drunk and she was thankful for that.

Whatever the secret, if there was one, Gwen Mayfield and Alex got on together famously. In Gwen's presence Alex came alive, as he had not been since the early days of Rose's pregnancy. When she was there he seemed to throw off the constraints of his job – or whatever it was which was changing him into a quiet, often morose, man.

'Expect us Mondays and Wednesdays, then,' Gwen said. 'We won't disturb you. We'll creep upstairs like little mice!' She began to pull on her gloves, fastened up her coat collar against the early April wind which was blowing outside.

'Alex should be home any minute,' Rose said. 'Stay and have a drink.'

Now why had she said that? Why, when with one part of her she resented Gwen Mayfield, with another part of her did she want the woman to stay? Perhaps because with Gwen around that first half hour of the evening was made easier. Alex would be more relaxed, not so silent. There would be less of the acrimony which since Jenny's birth had crept into Rose's own relationship with him. Almost every day of her life now, Rose decided that she and Alex must talk, must sort things out. Alex did not attempt to initiate such a discussion, and on her side Rose was too well aware of her own guilty part in the change in him, too afraid to bring the subject into the open.

'Oh he won't want me here when he gets home, tired out,' Gwen protested.

Rose looked directly at her.

'You know that's nonsense, Gwen. He's always pleased to see you.' The asperity which Rose failed to keep out of her voice, the emphasis in the sentence, was plain to both women. Now whatever made me do that? Rose asked herself. Gwen, who had been ready to leave, quietly sat down again.

'What do you mean by that?'

'Nothing. Nothing at all!'

'Why . . . why do you dislike me, Rose?'

'But I don't . . .'

'Don't deny it, Rose,' Gwen cut in. 'I'm not stupid. You tolerate me because of the Mothers' Club. If it weren't for that . . .'

Rose floundered. 'I don't! That's not true. It's nonsense!' She felt the flush which stained her cheeks.

'It's not nonsense, and you know it. But why? What have I done to you?'

'Nothing at all. I don't understand what this conversation is about!'

'Yes you do.' Gwen's voice was steady; not unfriendly. She was in command of herself. 'But I've taken nothing from you, Rose. Perhaps I could have. You seem to want to throw it away. But I haven't, I assure you.'

Had Alex offered her the chance? It was Alex they were talking about, they both knew that. And if he had, how much would I care, Rose asked herself, apart from the hurt to my pride? Was it only upset pride which was causing her stomach to churn as she faced the other woman, or was there more to it than that?

A more insistent voice asked her how much of this was her own fault. Was it true, what Gwen Mayfield said, that she was throwing away Alex's love? But Gwen did not know everything. How could she? Who was she to interfere?

'I think we should stop this conversation,' Rose said. 'I'm sorry if I sounded rude.'

Gwen managed a cool little smile.

'Oh. you're never rude. You're civilized and well-mannered, and on the whole, so am I. If we'd been two of the mothers in the club we'd have been scratching each other's eyes out by now. And maybe that's better – healthier than pushing things away, pretending they don't exist. I'd have thought as a doctor you'd have known that.'

'There are lots of things I know as a doctor,' Rose said. 'Carrying them out as a woman is another matter. I still have to contend with my own temperament.'

All at once a wave of weariness swept over her. She had an almost overwhelming desire to talk to this calm-faced woman, whom she suddenly no longer saw as an enemy. She wanted to lay before her all the problems of a marriage which in her heart she knew was deteriorating, wearing away a little every day. In her daily life, in her practice, she was always at the receiving end of other people's troubles; always the strong one, seeking solutions, offering comfort. At this moment she yearned desperately, with a depth of longing which only the strongest could experience, to be weak, helpless, to shift the burden to someone else. To lean, in fact, on Gwen Mayfield of all people.

It was naturally out of the question. Repentance she had in plenty, but confession was not for her. And there being no confession, there could be no absolution. She must sort it out for herself.

'They say the onlooker sees most of the game,' Gwen was saying. 'It's true. What I'd like you to understand is that I'm fond of you both and I wish I could help. Forgive me for speaking so frankly, Rose. But I owe a lot to you. Sometimes I think you saved my life!'

'Rubbish!' Rose said. 'You'd have done it yourself in the end.'

'I'm not so sure. Anyway, under this cool exterior there beats a heart full of gratitude.' Her tone was lighter. The mood, for both of them, was passing.

'Then you can show your gratitude by staying for a drink,' Rose said. 'I mean it when I say you cheer Alex up. In any case, I have a patient due before supper, so he'll be even more glad of your company.'

Ten minutes later Alex arrived home. Without asking, he poured a dry sherry and handed it to Gwen.

'Your tipple, I believe?'

He queried Rose with a look. She shook her head. 'Not for me, thank you. I have a patient due.'

He replaced the sherry decanter and poured himself a large whisky, almost half a tumbler, Rose noted. And he had already had some. She had smelled it on his breath when he came in. She said nothing, but could not help raising her eyebrows.

'Ah! I sense disapproval!' Alex said. 'Give me one good reason why I shouldn't drink it.' He sounded reasonably pleasant, but Rose recognized the edge in his voice. She knew that but for Gwen's presence he would quickly become argumentative. Either that, or he would lapse into complete silence. Either way, it would be another unpleasant evening. She shrugged her shoulders, watched him take a long drink.

'Because it's no good to you,' Gwen answered him. Her words dropped cool and clear into the silence. Alex looked at her in surprise.

'Oh I know it's none of my business,' Gwen said. 'I just claim the privilege of friendship to say what I think.'

'Does it matter?' Alex did not sound as annoyed as Rose expected him to be, as he would have been if she had said it.

'Of course it matters,' Gwen said. 'To anyone who cares two hoots about you, which includes your family and your friends.'

'I'm gratified,' he said mockingly.

'In any case, does it do what you want it to?' Gwen asked. 'Does it solve whatever makes you drink it in the first place? Pressure of work or whatever?'

'Temporarily it does,' Alex said. 'Pressure of work and . . . whatever.'

'I tried it,' Gwen said. 'I found everything came back next morning.'

She's treading on dangerous ground, Rose thought. Alex wouldn't stand for being lectured. So far and no further. Besides, the reasons were nothing to do with Gwen. Or could they be? Even in so controversial a discussion there was a rapport between she and Alex.

The doorbell rang.

'That will be my patient,' Rose said.

'You see what it's like being married to a doctor?' Alex said to Gwen. 'Always on the job!' His tone was bantering, falling just short of complaint.

'I'm sorry,' Rose said. 'It is rather a special appointment.'

'Don't apologize,' he said. 'We all know the job comes first, the husband last in this house.'

'You're talking nonsense,' Rose said, trying to keep her

tone light. 'You know I never see a patient as late as this unless it's for something special. Anyway, supper won't be too long. Will you stay and eat with us, Gwen?'

'Thank you, no,' Gwen said. 'I must go as soon as I've finished my sherry.'

'Then I'll say good-bye,' Rose said. 'I might be a little while in the surgery.'

She was glad to escape from the atmosphere of the sitting room. In her surgery she knew where she was, what was what. It was her domain. She was particularly happy to see this evening's patient – a young woman who was coming on Doctor Lewthwaite's recommendation, with her husband, seeking advice on planning the family they both wanted. A year ago, without breaking her patient's confidence, she would have wanted to share that small triumph with Alex. Now she would not bother to mention it.

When she returned to the sitting room, Gwen had gone.

'I'm sorry to keep you waiting for supper, Alex,' Rose said. 'It really was quite important.'

'Oh I'm sure it was,' Alex said. 'Everything to do with your job is important!' He reached for the whisky decanter and started to pour himself another drink.

'Please don't,' Rose begged. 'You've had enough for one evening.' She put out a hand to restrain him.

He shook off her hand, poured the whisky into his glass and drank deeply.

'Don't tell me what to do!' he said furiously. 'I'll drink what I like and when I like!'

'But why, Alex? Why?' Rose pleaded. 'What's gone wrong between us?'

He stared at her in disbelief. 'You ask me that? You hypocritical bitch!'

She recoiled before the anger in his eyes, the savage look on his face. This was an Alex she did not know. She had seen him lately in many dark moods, but never one like this.

196

'I don't understand,' she said.

'Oh yes you do, Madam!'

He had risen to his feet and was standing over her, his whole body trembling, the glass in his hand shaking. She put out a hand to take the glass from him but before she could do so he flung the whisky in her face. Then with a violent throw he sent the glass to smash into a hundred pieces against a table. Gasping, with the whisky stinging her eyes, Rose moved quickly to evade him, trying not to step on the slivers of broken glass which covered the carpet but hearing one crunch under the heel of her shoe. She did not move quickly enough. He caught her, and held her by the wrists, thrusting his face close to hers. She struggled to break free but his grip was too strong.

'Let me go, Alex!' She tried to speak calmly, to show that she was not afraid. How could she possibly be afraid of Alex? But now she was.

'Please let me go,' she begged. 'You're hurting me!'

As suddenly as he had attacked her, and as if he could no longer bear to touch her, he flung her away from him. She caught her foot in the rug and fell to the floor, miraculously missing the scattered glass. She lay there for a moment, her head buried in her arms. This couldn't be true! It couldn't be happening! Slowly, dizzy and shaking, she started to get to her feet. Alex moved swiftly to help her up. He sat her on the sofa and folded his arms around her.

'I didn't mean it, Rose!' he cried. 'I never meant to hurt you!' Feeling his arms around her, she burst into tears.

'What is it, Alex?' she sobbed. 'What has gone so wrong? It wasn't like this when we married.'

He moved away from her, sat at the other end of the sofa.

'When we married you were decent to me,' he said. 'Oh, I knew you didn't love me. That was the risk I took. But you acted as though you did and I fooled myself that that would do.'

'But I do love you, Alex,' she said.

'Don't lie to me, Rose. Don't insult me by pretending.' She heard the pain in his voice, and wanted to assuage it, but could not.

'I never pretended. I told you from the first that I didn't love you as you loved me. But in my own way I love you a great deal.'

'What sort of way is that? I didn't marry you because I wanted a sister or a friend.' His voice was bitter and angry. 'I wanted a wife. What sort of wife denies her husband her body for months on end, as you've done me? Do you know. just how long it is since I had you? We've made love twice since before Jenny was born!'

Guilt flushed her face crimson.

'I've tried to explain,' she said. 'A woman has odd feelings after she's given birth. It takes time. It's no reflection on you. I'm truly sorry, Alex.'

'Medical clap-trap!' He was on his feet again, pacing up and down, shouting. 'It's more than six months since Jenny was born. Is this how you teach your precious patients to limit their families?'

'You know it isn't,' she protested. 'And I'm not proud of myself for feeling like this. I'm truly sorry. But I repeat, I need time.'

'Time? What do you call time? Six months, six years? The trouble with you is, you're besotted!'

She stared at him. He could not know, he could not possibly know. What she felt was in her own heart. Only she was aware that, mixed up with her aversion to sex with Alex, which had started early in her pregnancy and showed no sign of diminishing – though she had tried, God knew she had tried – was a longing for John Worthing which never grew less. She had done everything to stifle it but it would not be stifled. The most she could do was to bury it deep inside her. It was true that she was besotted, but she had determined that it should never touch Alex.

'You're besotted by your work,' he cried. 'You think of nothing else. It takes all your strength. Even the baby comes second.'

Relief surged through her. She could cope with his accusations about her work. It was a frequent cause of minor arguments between them, but she felt no guilt about her work.

'No more than you are with yours.' she said. 'I'm in our home more than you are. But I allow for the fact that you have to work long hours, work hard.'

Alex sat down again, leaned back in the chair, his eyes closed. The fight was over, leaving them both dejected, nothing solved.

'I'll get supper,' Rose said after a while.

Supper was eaten in silence. Rose cast around for some safe topic to break it.

'Gwen is going to rehearse the mothers here in a play, Monday and Wednesday evenings,' she said. 'Shall you mind?'

'Not in the least.'

'You like Gwen, don't you?' Rose ventured.

He lifted his head and looked at her. His face was bleak, his blue eyes tired.

'Gwen Mayfield has more warmth in her little finger than you have in your whole body!'

She flinched at the bitterness in his voice. And what he said was not true. Somewhere inside her, waiting to be released, was all the warmth and passion in the world. She knew it, she felt it. But she recalled John Worthing's taunt after the Committee meeting. 'It's women like you who drive men into other women's arms.' They had been talking then of Gwen Mayfield.

'I'm sorry, Alex,' she said. I will try. I really will!'

That night she turned to him in bed, pulling him towards her. In the darkness, silently, they made love. But it was no good and they both knew it. They had gone too far away. They could never get back. When it was over they lay back to back. bodies not touching. Rose lay awake until morning and she knew, from his breathing and from his unnatural stillness, that Alex was awake too.

'Prepare yourself for a surprise,' Mrs Foster said when Rose arrived at Babcock Street with Jenny the next morning. She took the child from Rose and placed her in the playpen to which, since she had long been sitting up and could now wriggle herself around, she had been promoted.

'There you go, chicken!' Mrs Foster said fondly. There was great rapport between Jenny and Mrs Foster though they saw each other for a few minutes only before the morning surgeries.

'A pity your Dad didn't live to see her grow up a bit,' Mrs Foster said. 'He'd have been that proud!'

George Stanton had lived just a week after the christening. A wild, November storm, sweeping down the dale and bringing with it the first flurry of winter snow, had inappropriately attended the funeral of this quietest of men. He had been buried in the churchyard with his ancestors and Rose had returned to Akersfield heavy hearted. She had known her father's love ever since she could remember anything and nothing had ever spoilt the bond between them.

'I know,' Rose said. 'I know he would have loved her. By the way, my mother's coming for a short visit next Monday, so I shan't be bringing Jenny. She'll stay with Ma. Now what did you mean by a surprise?'

Mrs Foster nodded mysteriously. 'You'll never guess. And if I was to tell you it wouldn't be one, would it? So I'll be off then. Ta-ta!'

Rose did not have long to wait. She heard the doorbell and called out to whoever it was to come in, and was amazed, not so much to see Eva Denby as to see that she was accompanied by her husband. Rose felt a moment's apprehension. She had sent a letter of recommendation, on Eva's behalf, to the Housing Committee, but she had heard nothing more since then. It was possible that Jim Denby did not even know she had done it.

Eva and her husband advanced into the room and stood

before Rose's desk. It was almost three years since Rose had seen Jim Denby. Then he had been shouting drunk; now he stood quietly, cap in hand. They both looked thinner and shabbier than ever, though nothing could quite dim Jim Denby's attraction.

'We have something to say to you. Doctor.' Eva announced. She nudged her husband. 'Go on then! You promised!'

Jim Denby took a deep breath, and reluctantly spoke.

'We've come to tell you we've got a Council house.'

'I had to go in front of the Committee and a bloke there told me I should thank you. So that's what I've come to do.'

'Why, that's wonderful news!' Rose cried. 'I'm delighted. Is it at Marton Green?'

'Yes,' Eva said. 'Number eight, Firth Avenue. Three bedrooms, hot water out of the taps, a bathroom, and a lavatory to every house. Just in the doorway. You don't have to go down the yard. There's a garden back and front with railings round, and your own front gate!' The words bubbled out of her. Rose had never seen Eva so lively. 'And a school quite near for the children,' she continued.

But Jim Denby had not finished his own speech. He silenced Eva with a look and continued in a low voice, filled with embarrassment.

'I've come as well to apologize for what I done to you in the past. You didn't deserve it and I'm sorry. I was in the drink, you see. I hope I didn't muck anything up proper.'

'It's all in the past,' Rose could think of nothing else to say.

Had he 'mucked up anything proper'? she asked herself. Well, but for him she might still be at the Clinic. But for him she would not have thrown up her job, almost left Akersfield, married Alex. But that last was not true. She had married Alex because she had realized she could never have John Worthing. Perhaps, one thing leading to another, if Jim Denby had not behaved as he had she would not be here in Babcock Street. Perhaps she would be still looking after other women's babies, never have had Jenny. If things were not going too well with Alex – well, everything had a price and perhaps that was the price she had to pay. But she wished with all her heart that Alex did not have to pay it too.

'It's all in the past,' she repeated.

'Well it looks as if things might work out for me', Jim Denby said. 'This is the first bit of luck I've had in a long time.'

'Any sign of a job?' Rose asked.

'No Doctor. So if you hear . . .'

'If I hear of anything at all, you can be sure I'll let you know,' Rose promised.

'There's just one thing,' Eva said shyly. 'We wondered if . . . that is, I thought . . .'

'Yes?'

'I wondered if, when we get in, you'd come and see us? It won't be smart, of course. We've nothing new to put in the house – except Mam has promised me some lace curtains. But you'll be very welcome. It'll be after Easter.'

'I'd be glad to,' Rose said. 'Let me know just as soon as it's convenient.'

Mrs Foster was right, Rose thought when they had left. She never would have believed it, not of Jim Denby. Even now it did not quite ring true. But if things had always gone right for him, if it had not been for the war, and for all the years without a job, would he have been a completely different man? Who could tell? But she could not quite believe it.

On Monday afternoon Rose met her mother at Akersfield station. When George Stanton had died it was at first thought that his widow might take over the licence of the Ewe Lamb and continue to run it. But in her husband's lifetime she had never identified herself with the running of the inn, and she doubted that she was cut out to do it on her own, even if help could have been afforded for the heavy work. When it seemed that the Ewe Lamb must finally pass out of the hands of the Stanton family, Emily and Christopher had suddenly decided to sell the farm and take over the inn.

'How's everything going?' Rose asked her mother when they were settled in at Beechcroft Road, drinking tea, eating the curd tarts her mother had carefully carried from Faverwell.

'All right,' Mrs Stanton said. 'The alterations are finished, and with the extra built on there's a nice dining room and even bedrooms. Christopher reckons that with more people travelling about since the war – cars, and people walking and cycling everywhere – bed and breakfast will be the thing. Considering he's invested all the money he got from the sale of the farm, let's hope he's right!'

On Tuesday evening Miss Nesfield telephoned. 'I'm due to go to Blackpool again tomorrow,' she said. 'Now something's cropped up here and I can't possibly get away. Can you take my place? I think it's important for a woman to go.'

The negotiations for the house which had first been chosen in Blackpool had fallen through at the last minute and now another had to be found.

'You don't have surgery on a Wednesday and you've finished weaning Jenny, haven't you?' Miss Nesfield said.

'All except the early morning and late night feeds.'

'Well you could bring her here. Plenty of people to look after her.'

'That's all right. My mother's here for a day or two,' Rose said. 'It's just that . . .'

It was impossible to say that she did not want to spend the day with John Worthing. It would also be untrue. She longed to do so. But perhaps he was not included in this trip, in which case she could go with a clear conscience. She turned to Alex.

'Do you mind if I go to Blackpool tomorrow? Miss Nesfield suddenly can't go.'

He did not lift his head from the book he was reading. 'Makes no difference to me,' he said.

'I'll willingly look after little Jenny,' Mrs Stanton volunteered.

Rose turned back to the telephone. 'Yes, I'll go,' she said. 'Who's going and where do we meet?'

'Councillor Worthing and Mr Mortimer. Mr Barber's dropped out – he really can't stand the place. Anyway it makes more sense to have an estate agent in the party. They'll pick you up at your home at ten o-clock if that's all right.'

'I'll be ready,' Rose said. 'I'm sorry you can't go.' But she was not. She was wildly glad. And she need feel no guilt since she had engineered none of it, though she wondered if John Worthing had suggested her to Miss Nesfield.

She dressed with care next morning, pleased that in the last sales she had treated herself to a new coat. It was of dark green facecloth, with deep cuffs and a high collar of moleskin. She would be glad of that in 'breezy Blackpool'. Even in mid-April the weather could be chilly there. Her round velour hat in the same shade as the coat sat well down on her forehead and covered her ears.

'Those hats might be fashionable,' Mrs Stanton said, observing her daughter standing in the hall, nervously waiting to be called for, 'But to my way of thinking they're like overturned plant pots – or worse! Now in my days hats *were* hats. Plenty of width and lots of trimming. Still, I must say, you do look quite nice, Our Rose.'

Promptly at ten o-clock the doorbell rang and John Worthing stood on the step. He looked at Rose with appreciation but said nothing until Mrs Stanton had closed the door on them.

'You look delicious,' he said. 'I've explained to Willy Mortimer that you have to ride in the front of the car because you get travel sick.'

'But I don't . . .' Rose began.

'Yes you do. Don't argue!'

There was some traffic between Akersfield and Skipton but after that the roads were almost empty until they reached Preston. John Worthing drove fast and they were in Blackpool by lunchtime.

'We'll eat at the Imperial,' he said. 'They give you a good meal there. Does that suit you, Willy?'

'Capital, Mr Mortimer said. 'I hope you're feeling all right after the drive, Doctor Rose?'

'Fine,' Rose said.

John Worthing ordered cocktails, and a bottle of Muscadet to drink with the fish which they all chose as the main course.

'We shall see all the houses through a pleasant haze,' Rose said happily. 'Let's hope it doesn't cloud our judgement.'

She was determined to enjoy this day. Even the presence of Mr Mortimer could not be allowed to spoil it. In any case, he was a nice man.

'They're three desirable properties we're going to see,' Mr Mortimer said. 'All three different. The difficulty will be making a decision.'

After a final cup of coffee they set off to inspect. The first property was to the south of Blackpool, where it joined with St Anne's. It was a fair-sized house in a quiet avenue, ten minutes' walk from the soft sandhills which comprised St Anne's beach.

'It is pleasant,' Rose said. 'But I think it's too far out of Blackpool. It would mean a tram ride, and our mothers don't have much money for that.'

'It's a lovely house and a select neighbourhood,' Mr Mortimer pointed out. 'But let's reserve judgement until we've seen the others.'

'I don't know that we're looking for a select area,' John Worthing said. 'It won't be what these ladies come to Blackpool for.'

The second house was in the centre of the town, two

streets back from the promenade and near to the station. a tall, narrow house which had been run for some years as a private hotel.

'It's handy all right,' Rose said. 'Even a bit noisy. But perhaps that doesn't matter.'

John Worthing tapped wood, examined pipes, stared up at ceilings. 'It'll need a lot of repair,' he said. 'It's been neglected.'

But when they saw the third house there was no doubt in any of their minds that this was the one. It was brick built and solid, in an area not too quiet and not too noisy, and a short distance from the bracing North Shore. It had six spacious bedrooms which could be split up to give more privacy, and a large garden with lawns and flowerbeds, sheltered behind high walls.

'Moreover, at fifteen hundred pounds the price is right,' Rose said.

It took them no more than ten minutes to decide upon it.

'Right!' Mr Mortimer said. 'I know the agent quite well. I'll pop along and ask him to hold it, pending a decision from the Committee. But it'll have to be a quick decision. This house is a snip!'

'I'll see that it's quick,' John Worthing promised.

'And now if you'll excuse me, I'm going to leave you good people,' Mr Mortimer said. He looked a little embarrassed. 'I have this friend in Blackpool. She'd never forgive me if I didn't look her up. And I'll not travel back with you, I'll make my own way back by train. So if you'll drop me anywhere near the Winter Gardens that'll be fine.'

'Did you know he was going to do that?' Rose asked when Mr Mortimer had left them, scurrying away into the labyrinth of streets behind the Winter Gardens.

'I didn't,' John said. 'I shall be forever grateful to him and his lady friend. What would you like to do now?'

'Go home, surely?' Rose said. 'It's four o'clock.'

'Must we, Rose?'

I can't stay, she thought. I can't. I could tell him I have to see a patient, or that my mother, or Alex, expects me back. It would be untrue. Alex would be out and her mother's last words had been, 'I'll expect you when I see you.' Also, it being Wednesday, Gwen Mayfield would be holding a rehearsal, which would be company for her mother if she needed it. Above all, and with all her heart, she wanted to stay.

'Two or three hours,' John said. 'When shall we ever have two or three hours alone together? And that's all it will be, Rose. Just being together, no-one else to consider. You want it as much as I do. Be honest, Rose.'

She wanted to stay here forever: wanted time to stand still.

'I'll stay,' she said quietly. It could harm no-one, three short hours out of life.

'How shall we spend the time? What would you like to do?'

Rose was silent for a moment. She knew what she wanted, knew that John wanted it too.

'We could go to an hotel, Rose,' he said softly.

'At four o-clock in the afternoon?' With no luggage?'

'I could fix it.' His voice was husky with longing.

Her own longing was no less than his, but she could not do as he asked. If this time together was not to cast its guilt over everything that came after, they must avoid all that was too serious. They must do nothing which subsequent regret would spoil. She knew that in the future she would want to take out these few hours, like a precious jewel from a case, and look at them. She had to be able to do that without remorse.

'No John,' she said. 'I'm sorry! But maybe I'd like to do all the little things, the silly things, I've never had a chance to do. I'd like to do them just with you. Go on the Big Wheel; drive to the Pleasure Beach and try the Water Chute; play the slot machines on the pier, have my fortune told!'

She saw the disappointment on his face. Was she being

a fool, throwing away what might never come again?

'It's fatuous, isn't it?' she said. 'Perhaps we should, after all, go home. We've had a happy day so far. Perhaps we should leave it at that?'

She watched him hide his disappointment under a smile.

'No,' he said. 'We'll do everything you say. And since we're right beside it, we'll start with the Big Wheel!'

It was not as frightening as she had expected. They were totally encased in the glass carriage, which moved up and around in a slow, stately manner, the whole of Blackpool spread out below them.

'Quite staid, really,' Rose said when they were back on the ground.

The Water Chute on the Pleasure Beach was another matter. Rose screamed with the rest as the small boat shot down the steep ramp and launched itself with a tremendous splash into the pool below. She clung for dear life to John and he held her in his arms. By the time they staggered off the boat their former mood had changed – for both of them. They were happy in the simple fact of being together; free, uninhibited. Arm in arm, they sampled everything the Pleasure Beach had to offer – swings, roundabouts, coconut shies, various games at which Rose showed no skill at all, and at which John won a box of chocolates, a large stuffed rabbit, and a cheap brooch set with green stones which he insisted on pinning on her coat.

'I want to give you diamonds and pearls,' he said.

'This means more to me,' Rose told him, fingering the green glass. 'I'll keep it always.'

When they had exhausted the Pleasure Beach they found the car again and drove to the North Pier. The incoming tide brought a strong, damp wind from the Irish Sea, so strong that, getting out of the car, Rose found difficulty in standing against it. She buried her chin in the warmth of her fur collar and was glad of John's arm around her for support.

They passed through the turnstile and walked forward to the very end of the pier. It was deserted. Easter had come and gone. It was low season from now until Whitsuntide. Most of the resort's visitors would, in any case, be in the warmth of the Tower, or in one of the cinemas or music halls; or if they wanted a free show, in one of the booths along the Golden Mile where a pianist, foot on the loud pedal, thumped out the latest popular song while his partner, with the words on a huge song sheet, encouraged the audience to sing and afterwards sold them the sheet music.

John and Rose stood alone, facing the sea, their backs to the lights of the town. They watched the great waves hurl themselves against the massive iron structure beneath the deck of the pier, pitting their strength against the strength that was man made.

'The sea will win in the end,' John said. 'One day the pier will no longer exist. It will rust, and fall into the sea.'

Rose shivered at the thought. It threatened the moment they were standing in, and she wanted to be assured that this moment would last forever.

'You're cold,' John said, feeling her shiver against him.

'Not really. For a moment the sea frightened me. But only for a moment. I like the sea, really.'

'I'd like to sail away with you,' John said. 'Just the two of us. No-one else in the world.'

'Where would we get to?' Rose asked. 'If we sailed away from here, from the end of this pier?'

'Ireland. But we wouldn't land there. We'd turn south, and then west. We'd cross the Atlantic in our ship. Then we'd turn south again and we'd find an island . . .'

'A desert island?'

'What would we want with other people?'

He turned and drew her close to him, kissing her fiercely. His lips, hard against hers, were salty with sea spray. Held in his embrace she felt that life, new life, his life and vitality, flooded through her, filled her to the brim. She loved this man as she had never thought it possible to love anyone. If she could not have him, what else was there to live for, what else mattered?

'I love you, Rose,' he said. 'It's real and it's forever. There is no other woman in the world for me. Tell me you love me, Rose. I know you do. Tell me! I want to hear it.'

'I love you,' she said. 'Oh John, how I love you!'

He kissed her again. Her lips felt bruised from the strength of his kiss. She never wanted anyone else to kiss her again, ever. Like an adolescent girl who has been kissed for the first time, she felt she would carry the feeling on her lips forever.

'What are we going to do, Rose? We can't leave it like this. You know we can't!'

The tide was racing in now. The noise of the sea and of the wind enveloped them, but they were oblivious to them as they stood there in each other's arms. Looking only at each other, they did not see the giant wave which broke against the end of the pier, knew nothing of it until they were drenched in heavy spray and broken apart by its force. Afterwards, remembering, it seemed to Rose that the elements themselves, jealous observers of their love, had conspired to separate them.

John found her hand and they ran for shelter in the lee of one of the pier buildings.

'Are you very wet?'

'Not as much as I thought,' Rose said. But she was shivering with cold now; and with more than cold – with the knowledge that the moment had passed and that it would not come again. For a short space of time she had been prepared to throw everything aside. Now her mind and her spirit, as well as her body, had received a cold douche.

John took her into the shelter of his arms again.

'Rose, my darling . . .'

But the madness was over. The madness was over, but not her love or her desire. Her body ached for him.

'John, we must go,' she said.

'Where shall we go, Rose?'

There is nowhere for us to go, she thought. No warm, desert island. In all the world there is no place for the two of us. Tears, which she could no longer check, ran down her face, and while John held her close, deep sobs shook her body.

Eventually she said, 'Take me home, John. Please take me home!'

He kissed her gently.

'I shall always love you. Never forget it, Rose.'

'And I you,' she said, the words almost inaudible against the sound of the wind and the sea.

They turned their backs on the sea and began to walk towards the bright lights of the town.

When Rose arrived home her mother was waiting up for her. There was no sign of Alex.

'He took Mrs Mayfield home after the rehearsal,' Mrs Stanton said. 'It was raining and she'd missed the tram. Did you have a nice day, then?'

'Yes thank you, Mother.' Already it belonged to another world, though it was never to be forgotten. She was glad Alex was out.

'I'm rather tired,' she said. 'If you don't mind, I think I'll see to Jenny and then go to bed.'

She fell asleep thinking of John Worthing. Later, she wakened from a dream in which she was drowning in the sea just off the North Pier. She called for help but, though everyone she knew was there on the pier, no-one heard her, no-one answered.

She looked at her watch. It was two-thirty. Alex was not in bed and when she went downstairs to warm herself some milk, he was not in the house.

13

Rose had lain awake most of the night. It was not only Alex's absence, and the likely reason for it, which had kept her from sleeping, but the turmoil of her thoughts after the day in Blackpool. Round and round in her head the people spun: Diana Worthing, Alex, Gwen Mayfield, herself and, above all others and every minute of the dragging hours, John Worthing. They twisted and wove in an impossible dance of which no-one knew the steps, trying to weave a coherent pattern. It was no use. Everything was chaos; everything was impossible.

Her ears attuned to the slightest sound, just before dawn she heard Alex's car, and then the sound of his key in the front door. She waited apprehensively for him to come up to the bedroom, ready to feign sleep. There was no way they could talk to each other at this moment. But he did not come.

She heard him go into the kitchen, turn on a tap; but he moved around quietly, from which she deduced that he was sober. When he had drunk too much he tended to crash around. In fact, he had not taken a drink at home since the evening he had thrown the whisky in her face and she doubted that he had, since then, had much during the day. 'Whatever happens between us,' he had said next morning at breakfast, 'you will never have to endure such a scene again.'

It had been fully daylight when she had fallen asleep and now, next morning, she was exhausted, reluctant to obey the summons of the alarm clock. Thought came flooding back as she stretched out a hand to turn it off. She longed to sink back into a deep sleep. But it was not possible; she had early surgery at Babcock Street and she must get herself and Jenny ready to leave.

She found Alex asleep on the sitting room sofa. Standing over him, she thought how young and carefree he looked in his sleep, as if something in his dreams released him. With all her heart she wished she had not failed him.

'Alex, it's half-past eight!'

When she was sure he was awake, she left him. There was no time for explanations, for the confrontations which she knew the day must bring; nor could she bear them now.

In the kitchen Annie was preparing breakfast.

'I'll take my mother a tray,' Rose said. She did not want her to come down before Alex had removed himself.

Mrs Stanton was sitting up in bed, looking perky.

'You're spoiling me,' she said. 'I'm not used to this. I'm used to being up and doing!'

'It won't do you any harm,' Rose said. From her mother's demeanour it seemed likely that she had heard nothing.

'You don't look all that bright,' Mrs Stanton observed. 'I'd have thought a day at the seaside would have put new life into you.'

'I'm fine,' Rose said. 'Will you be able to look after Jenny this afternoon? I've promised to visit Eva Denby.'

'Of course I will, and glad to,' Mrs Stanton said.

When Rose went downstairs again Alex was in the dining room, drinking tea, eating toast.

'I'm sorry if I worried you last night, coming in late,' he said. Rose was surprised at the steady calm of his voice.

'I would have called it early rather than late!'

She realized with surprise that worry about what might have happened to him, about the possibility of accident or illness, had not been one of her emotions. She had been too occupied with other thoughts.

'We have to talk,' Alex said.

213

'Not now, Alex. I'm already late for surgery.' She didn't want to talk. Everything was too muddled.

'This evening then. No matter what you say, Rose, we *have* to talk.'

Firth Avenue was not an avenue, but a collection of houses built around a large circle of grass which had been split into four quarters by narrow concrete paths. Two or three children played on the grass but the rest were on the road, most of them with a skipping rope stretched across its width, a few playing hopscotch. Would they never get used to playing on grass? Rose wondered.

When she stopped the car outside number eight, half-a-dozen children left their games to stand and stare. No-one in Firth Avenue, and practically no-one who visited there, owned a car. 'Don't touch it!' Rose warned, getting out.

Number eight was the end house of a block of four. The whole of the estate had been built in harsh red brick, though every other building in Akersfield had, for centuries, been built in the local stone. But since all the stone buildings in Akersfield were coal black from the smoke, perhaps red brick was more cheerful. The doors were painted a dark, serviceable green and there were lace curtains at most of the windows. As Rose walked down the path, Eva opened the front door.

'Doctor Rose! Please come in!'

She smiled a welcome. How happy she looked, how different from the girl in Paradine Street. though she had been here only a few weeks. Rose followed her into the living-room – and gasped in astonishment. Everything was clean, everything was bright, everything was new. The oven range, let into one wall, shone black in its iron parts from the application of blacklead, silver in its steel trim from hard work with emery paper. The newly-plastered walls were distempered a fashionable shade of pale mauve and the floor was covered with glossy new linoleum patterned with red and yellow roses on a brown background.

'It's all quite splendid!' Rose said.

'Isn't it just?' Eva agreed. 'Look at the suite!' The three-piece suite was equally new, equally brightly flowered.

'A chesterfield with a drop end,' Eva explained. 'The tallest man can lie stretched out on it. Ten pounds the sofa and two chairs at Butterfields. It's very good value, the man said.'

There was a small, square dining table with bulbous legs, and two smaller chairs.

'It's wonderful!' Rose said. 'Jim must be doing very well at his job.'

She knew that Jim Denby was working now. Mrs Foster had told her that he'd been given a job as a chauffeur-handyman – he had learned to drive in the army – to a business man who had a large house in Marton Green. 'It'll be a miracle if he keeps it.' Mrs Foster said. 'He never has yet!' Rose. surveying the new possessions, hoped that Mrs Foster would be proved wrong.

'He's doing ever so well,' Eva said. 'Three pounds a week regular, and he likes the work. We got all this lot on easy payments – hire purchase – the first week. Thirty pounds worth of goods you can get for twelve shillings a month! When we've paid for these – we might go in for a bedroom suite.'

'Marvellous!

'But you haven't seen everything,' Eva continued. 'Come and look at this!'

On a rickety stand – one of the few pieces Rose remembered from Paradine Street – stood a square, dark oak box.

'Columbia Hornless Gramophone!' Eva said proudly. 'Five guineas, on easy payments too. And we've got two records. I could play you one if you liked. Though perhaps that's a bit silly. I expect you've got a gramophone of your own.' She was suddenly unsure of herself.

'As a matter of fact we haven't,' Rose said. 'But we have the wireless.'

Astonished delight lit Eva's face.

'Fancy me having something you haven't got!' She picked up the two records in turn, handling them with reverence.

'You can have the Black Dyke Mills Band playing *"Il Travatore"*,' she said 'Or Layton and Johnstone singing "Tea For Two".'

'Let's have Layton and Johnstone,' Rose said. Alex had taken her to see them once. It had been a happy occasion.

Eva wound up the gramophone, fixed a new needle and gingerly lowered the head. The music filled the small room and the two women sat side by side, listening; Rose deep in her own sad thoughts, Eva, a pleased smile on her face, beating time and then joining in with the chorus until, three-quarters of the way through, she jumped quickly to her feet and began to wind the gramophone handle.

'It's beginning to run down,' she explained. 'You mustn't let it run down. It sounds awful! Shall I turn it over to the other side? It's "I Want to be Happy".'

'Please!' Rose said.

The words were so slick, she thought as she listened. As if happiness was easy to come by. And yet, watching Eva with her head swaying to the music, it seemed to be so for some people. Such little things – a three-piece suite, a square of bright linoleum, two gramophone records – made Eva supremely happy. Rose's own parents had never had to seek far for happiness. So why did it run away from her, and why did she seem unable to give it?

'I'll make a cup of tea,' Eva said. 'We'll play *"Il Travatore"*, afterwards. It's a bit sad but I love it.'

'Where are the children?' Rose asked.

'Out playing. They've already made friends. There are some nice people around here, you know. A cut above Paradine Street.'

Or is it that better surroundings make better people? Rose wondered.

'Is Dorothy doing well at school?' she asked.

'Ever so well,' Eva said proudly. 'She's in the top class of the infants and she can read. She goes up into Standard One next year when she's seven. They learn to knit in Standard One.'

'And Meg?'

'She goes to school later this year.' Eva suddenly looked serious. 'If it hadn't been for you, Doctor Rose, I doubt I'd ever have reared our Meg. I owe a lot to you, one way and another. Who would have thought, five years ago, that I'd have been sitting where I am right now?'

She looked around at her home, at her beautiful new possessions. When her gaze came back to Rose her eyes were filled with happy tears; tears of gratitude for the turn that her life had taken.

Rose leaned forward and took Eva's hand. 'I'm truly glad that things are going better for you,' she said. 'It was about time you had a bit of luck. Now, are you going to show me the rest of the house before I go?'

It was quickly obvious that every resource had been put into the living room. The three bedrooms, one of them the size of a cupboard, had no floor covering and the rickety double bed from Paradine Street, plus a narrow single one in which the children slept together, comprised almost the whole of the furniture. There were no curtains at the windows except for the lace ones which looked so respectable from the outside.

'We have to get undressed in the dark,' Eva giggled. 'Lest anyone might see us! Of course we *shall* get curtains, *and* all the rest. Now that Jim's bringing money home regular there's nothing to stop us. But you can't get curtains and suchlike on hire purchase.'

'Why not?' Rose asked.

A shadow crossed Eva's face.

'Well you see, if you weren't able to keep up the payments they couldn't take curtains back, could they? Not like . . . other things.'

'I'm sure that won't happen to you,' Rose said.

217

Eva's face brightened again. "Course it won't! Not a chance!'

I wish I could believe that, Rose thought. But where Jim Denby was concerned it all seemed too good to be true. There must be a catch in it somewhere.

Every Thursday Rose held an evening surgery, specifically for the very few mothers who worked during the day, and for married couples who might wish to attend together. There were very few of the latter. Mrs Foster had popped in this evening, ostensibly to do a few odd jobs but really, Rose knew, to hear about that afternoon's visit to Eva.

'I could hardly believe it!' Rose said. 'Such a change.'

'I told you you wouldn't,' Mrs Foster said. 'What's more, I don't! It's too good to be true – knowing that Jim Dcnby as I do. There's a catch in it somewhere. I just wish I knew what it was.'

'I'm inclined to agree with you,' Rose said. 'Let's hope we're both wrong.'

Mrs Foster's answering snort expressed disbelief, derision and incredulity.

'It doesn't look as though anyone else is coming this evening,' Rose said, changing the subject. 'I'm not sure that this Thursday evening clinic is worthwhile. I doubt I'm ever going to get the husbands.'

'More's the pity.' Mrs Foster said. "Course, it's not always that they don't agree with you, but they're not going to show it in public, not going to walk into the surgery. Most of them reckon it's the woman's job, anyway.'

She took a step closer to Rose and lowered her voice. 'Would you believe, Doctor,' she said, speaking confidentially, 'that during the war, in France, they issued Our Boys with . . . well, you know what! French letters! So they could have it off with them mademoiselles and not leave a cart load of little half-breed bastards behind, I suppose! They say the Government gave 'em out like rations! Pity they don't do that now, when the men can't afford 'em.

It'd be cheaper than paying the dole for all the kids!'

Mrs Foster went off home. Rose knew that it was time she did likewise. There would be no more patients this evening. But she was loath to go, knowing that she must face Alex. From time to time, during a day in which John Worthing had scarcely been out of her thoughts, she had reminded herself that Alex knew nothing of the day in Blackpool beyond the fact that she had been, and had returned. The events of *her* yesterday were not for display. They were buried in her own heart and must remain there. Alex had other problems which Rose, though knowing herself to be deeply involved, did not want to face with him.

But face them she must. She began to gather her things together, getting ready to leave, when the surgery bell rang. When she called out to the patient to come through, Gwen Mayfield walked in. She was pale, with blue shadows under her eyes, as if she too had not slept.

Gwen seated herself in the chair in front of Rose's desk.

'You know why I'm here,' she said without preamble. 'I told Alex last night that I was coming to see you. He didn't like the idea, but I wanted us to talk. Two rational women!'

Am I rational? Rose wondered. I don't feel it. I don't know what I feel. Her heart and mind were still full of those moments on the pier. She resented anything which might usurp those thoughts.

'I haven't spoken to Alex,' she said. 'I had to leave in a hurry this morning.'

But you can guess why I'm here?'

'I think so.'

'You know Alex spent the night with me?'

Rose flinched at Gwen's hard directness.

'I took it he had,' she said.

'You might not believe it, but we talked most of the night.'

'But not all of it?'

219

'Not all. No.'

All those hours, Rose thought. What did they find to talk about? How far was all this serious and how far was Alex simply turning to Gwen for comfort? For the comfort his wife failed to give him.

'We didn't talk all the time about you,' Gwen said. Alex is nothing if not loyal. I'm not sure what we did talk about. Alex's work, our differing childhoods, my marriage, the war. Alex hadn't taken me home with the intention of staying the night, you know. It just happened.'

'Even the fact that the whole night wasn't spent in talking?'

For the first time, Gwen looked uncomfortable.

'Even that,' she said. 'And it was the first time. I'd like you to believe that.'

'I do,' Rose said.

Would I have acted any differently, she asked herself, if John and I had been in similar circumstances? If we'd been together in a warm room instead of standing on the end of the pier with the wind and the rain in our faces? Should they have gone to an hotel, as John had wanted? But that was futile thinking. It could never happen to them now.

'I have to tell you that I love Alex,' Gwen said. 'I really and truly love him. I didn't want to, I didn't seek it; but it's there. It won't go away.'

'And Alex?'

'I must leave Alex to speak for himself,' Gwen said.

'You sound confident. You must know how he feels.'

Gwen hesitated only for a second.

'I do know. He loves me. Not as much as I love him, but he loves me.'

Do two people ever love each other equally? Rose wondered. She wanted to believe that between herself and John Worthing it was so, but would it be true if they could put it to the test?

'Why are you telling me this?' she asked. 'Is it because the affair between you and Alex is to continue?'

'It hasn't been an affair so far,' Gwen said. 'There's been nothing clandestine; no secret meetings, no stolen kisses when your back was turned – though it would have been easy. You were often busy with your work. But you're my friend. I wouldn't do that to you. I won't now. What I want to say is, that if you and Alex are going to make a go of your marriage, I'm prepared to fade out of the picture. I'd leave Akersfield if I thought that would happen.'

'You must love him quite a lot.'

'I do.'

'But you don't think it will happen?' Rose said.

'Frankly, no! I don't believe your marriage with Alex has the seeds of happiness in it. You're two nice people who simply bring each other unhappiness.'

'He's stopped drinking.'

'I know,' Gwen said. 'We talked about that. It's genuine.'

Why couldn't he talk to me? Rose asked herself. Why can't we communicate? Her life was one of constant communication with people, so why not with her own husband?

'Listen, Rose,' Gwen was saying. 'Don't hang on to Alex from pride, or duty. If you can't love him as I love him – if you can't make him happy as I know I could – then let him go! Rose, I beg of you to let him go.'

'There's more to it than that,' Rose said. She felt confused, unutterably tired, deeply lonely. 'I must talk to Alex.'

Gwen nodded. 'Yes, you must. I'll leave you now. Rose.'

Rose watched her go, then gathered her things together and went home to Alex.

'Before we go any further,' Alex said, 'I have to tell you that I spent the night with Gwen. We made love. More important than that, I love her.'

'I've seen Gwen,' Rose interrupted. 'She came to see me this evening in Babcock Street.'

A shadow of annoyance crossed Alex's face. 'I didn't want her to do that. I wanted to tell you myself. I'm sorry.'

'It doesn't matter,' Rose said.

They had picked at their evening meal in near silence because Annie was in and out of the dining room, serving and clearing away. After supper Alex had rushed them both into the sitting room. The fire was lit, for the late Spring evenings were cold.

I've always known that you were attracted to her.' She didn't really know what to say to him. It was all so unreal.'

'I've made no secret of it,' Alex said. 'She's warm, she's lively. I've learnt that she's loving.'

'I'm sure she is,' Rose said wearily. 'Please spare me a recital of her virtues. I realize that I possess none of them – at least in your eyes.'

'What do you mean by that?'

'Nothing. Nothing at all.'

You used to be warm and lively,' Alex said. 'I hoped that you might grow loving.'

I tried,' Rose said quietly.

'The effort was only too clear,' Alex said.

Annie came in.

'Can I clear the coffee? she askcd.

'Please do,' Rose said. 'And we shan't need anything more this evening. I'll get my mother's bedtime drink when she comes in.' Mrs Stanton was spending this evening at the Mothers' Club, talking to the members about life in the Dales.

'So where do we go from here?' Rose asked when Annie had left the room. 'I don't see that the decisions are mine. Either you give up Gwen and we try to make a fresh start – really try, I mean – or we agree to drift along as we've been doing.'

'I can't give her up, Alex said stubbornly. 'I won't. I've told you, I love her.'

'You loved me,' Rose said. 'It doesn't seem so long ago.'

'You threw it back at me.' Alex's voice was bitter. 'You didn't want it. You wanted marriage, a child, a career. I was able to provide them. You didn't want me!'

He glanced around, she thought for the drink he would normally have had to hand. But he did not get up and pour one. He was stone cold sober. She felt sick at his words. Was it true, what he said? Possibly she had always known it, though even to herself she had never put it into words. In the beginning she was sure she had genuinely tried her best, and she was willing to do so again.

'Shall we make a fresh start, Alex?' she said.

'No,' he said. 'I don't think we can.' He was quietly implacable, no give in him. 'Not to beat about the bush,' he said. 'I want a divorce. I'm sorry, Rose, but it's the only way.'

'Divorce!' All the horror she felt was in her voice. 'We can't divorce. It would ruin both of us!'

'It wouldn't ruin you,' Alex said. 'You would be the innocent party, the wronged woman. It might even gain you a few patients!'

'Don't joke, Alex. I can't bear it. And what about *your* career?'

'I'll take the risk,' he said. 'Divorce isn't exactly common, but I won't be the first. It's easier for a man than for a woman.'

'Naturally,' Rose said. But she knew that he did not approve of divorce. He must love Gwen Mayfield very much to contemplate it. 'I suppose you've considered that every nasty little bit will be printed in the newspaper?' she said. 'Especially in the *Record*. Is Gwen prepared to face that? Or in this case will you use your God-like position as editor to suppress it?'

'I shall suppress nothing,' Alex said. 'It's not my way, as you know. But Gwen won't come into it. There are other ways, as you know.'

'A night in an hotel with a hired woman? A chamber-maid surprising you both in bed?'

'If I have to. I didn't make the divorce laws.'

Rose jumped to her feet, moved to the window, drew back the heavy plush curtains and looked out. She wanted to escape. It was a soft, dark night with no moon. Lighted windows shone in the darkness over Akersfield to the distant edge of the town where the dark moors merged into the black sky. What was taking place behind all those windows? Love, hate, birth, death – and a thousand more trivial things? It seemed to her in this moment that she was to be lonely for the rest of her life. She turned back to Alex.

'What about Jenny? Where does she fit into all this? Have you given a thought to Jenny?'

She flinched at the swift anger in his face.

'Of course I have! A thousand. But Jenny will never be mine as she's yours. You've seen to that. You always will.'

'It's not true . . . !'

'You know it is. From the day she was born you've tried to keep her to yourself. But I shall see Jenny often. It never occurred to me that you wouldn't agree to that.'

'Thank you for those kind words,' Rose said. 'And what if I won't divorce you?'

'Then I shall leave you just the same. You won't keep me by refusing to divorce me. But I don't expect you to take that line, Rose. It would be unlike you.'

The sick feeling had passed but she felt weak, all her strength spent, as if at any second she might collapse.

'I'm very tired. I must go to bed,' she said. 'I'll give you your answer in a day or two. In the meantime. where are you going to sleep? You can't expect . . .'

'I shall sleep on the sofa in here tonight. You take your mother back to Faverwell tomorrow. From then on I'll have the spare room until things are settled.'

Not only did he not expect to sleep in her bed, he had

no desire to do so. Though she did not want him, the thought was bitter.

'I'm very sorry about all this, Rose,' he said. 'Truly sorry.'

'I should not have married you,' Rose said. 'It was wrong of me to do so.'

She wanted to go to bed and sleep and sleep and sleep. She went into the kitchen and left a note for her mother on the top of the Ovaltine tin, then went upstairs. On her way up to the bedroom she looked in on Jenny. The child was lying face down, her chubby legs bent up, her clenched hands above her head, in a frog-like position as if ready to leap away. She was deeply asleep and did not stir as Rose pulled the blanket over her shoulders.

It was a silent journey back to Faverwell. Rose wondered how much her mother knew, or suspected; but Mrs Stanton was not a woman to pry. They arrived at the Ewe Lamb in time for the midday meal and Emily insisted on Rose drinking a glass of sherry before they sat down to eat. 'You look as though you could do with a bottle of whatever you give your patients when they're under the weather,' she said. 'In the meantime, a glass of this won't do you any harm.'

It was better sherry than her father had kept, Rose judged. There were other signs, too, that the Ewe Lamb was changing: flowered curtains at the windows, new display shelves behind the bar, holding a selection of drinks with which her father would have had no truck. In the built-on wing the dining room boasted an Axminster carpet on the floor and eight tables with immaculate damask cloths and small vases of flowers.

'How are things going?' Rose asked.

'Very well. We were busy at Easter – one or two room bookings as well as plenty of passing trade. We reckon we'll have a good summer.'

There was no doubt that Emily had found her *niche*. Gone was the look of discontent which had been in her eyes for so long, though to those who knew her there would always be a sadness for her son. Christopher, too, though he had little time to stop and talk, looked happy and healthy.

'It was a wrench, selling the farm,' he admitted. 'I've lived there all my life. But it turned out for the best.'

'I visited Eva Denby the other day,' Rose told Emily. 'She's in seventh heaven.' She felt that everyone's life, except her own, was prospering.

After the meal she left Jenny with her mother and went for a walk, climbing down the narrow path by the bridge to walk along the river bank. The river was in full spate from the Spring rains, and for the same reason the grass on its banks was a brilliant emerald green. A kingfisher, a blinding flash of iridescent blue, flew low over the water and was lost again under the darkness of the bridge. She had watched the kingfishers every year of her childhood. They were part, as she was, of Faverwell. This was where she belonged and, right now, she wanted to stay here forever; to make no more decisions, face no problems. It was impossible, of course. This evening she must return to Akersfield, must make decisions.

She understood, or thought she did, that Alex might love someone else. How could she not when she thought of John Worthing? But she had always determined not to let John intrude into their marriage. So was Alex being self-indulgent or was he simply more honest than she? It was beside the point. He was going. Whether she would consent to free him legally or not, he was going. She must build a new life which did not include him, a life from which it seemed marriage and love, and the prospect of more children, must be excluded.

She turned and began to walk back. By the time she reached the Ewe Lamb she had decided that she would divorce Alex. She owed him that much. But she would not tell her family just yet. They would be horrified and deeply hurt. Divorce was unknown in the family, almost unknown among all the people they knew. They would see it as disgrace. But the disgrace was not in the divorce, Rose thought; the real disgrace was in her failure to make a proper marriage.

She drove back to Akersfield on an evening so clear, so golden, that it mocked the misery of her thoughts. When she walked into the house, carrying Jenny, the first thing she saw was Alex's suitcase in the hall. She began to tremble. Dear God, not so soon? Surely not so soon? It was less than twenty-four hours. She put Jenny down on the floor and sat herself on the hall chair, her whole body shaking.

Alex came down the stairs, another suitcase in hand. At the sight of him her misery turned to anger.

'Did it have to be like this?' she cried. 'You might well have gone without me seeing you! Is that what you intended? Am I so unbearable that you can't stand me another day? Or is it that you can't wait for her?'

'I'm not going to Gwen,' Alex said quietly. 'I'm going to stay with Mrs Crabtree for a while. If you consent to a divorce I shall stay there until it's over. If not . . .'

'I'll divorce you.' Rose said. All the anger, it seemed all the life, had suddenly gone out of her.

They faced each other awkwardly. 'There's no rehearsal for this situation,' Rose said. 'I don't know the lines. Except to say that I'm sorry for whatever part of it was my fault.'

'I'm sorry, too, Rose. I'll give you the evidence quickly. And from then you understand that I mustn't see you until it's all over. The courts are hot on collusion.'

'Collusion?'

'Once you've started proceedings against me you must have no more to do with me until after the decree absolute. If it was thought that we'd agreed to this divorce, it wouldn't be allowed to go through. I'll see you don't want for money, for yourself or Jenny.'

He lifted Jenny from the floor and kissed her.

'Now please go,' Rose said.

He put Jenny down, gathered up his suitcase, and left.

Looking back, Rose realized that she measured the months after Alex's departure by the ailments among her patients at both her surgeries. There was an epidemic of diarrhoea – which among her poorer patients, with the lack of sanitation in their homes, went on all summer – followed by measles in the autumn. with its legacy of chest complaints made worse by Akersfield's cold, damp winter. Before they cleared, an early spring flu epidemic set in. Rose supposed she was thankful to be busy, though from fatigue, and from the other things which were happening to her, she felt stripped of even that emotion.

On her first birthday Jenny took her first, faltering footsteps across the sitting room and soon after that Rose engaged a young nursemaid to look after her. It was not easy to find the ten shillings a week to pay for Moira, but somehow she managed.

She was presented with evidence that Alex had committed adultery with a woman in an hotel in Blackpool – the choice of place gave her a nasty stab. Later she was granted a *decree* nisi and, six months later still, a decree absolute. She was no longer married. She was a free woman, with no idea what to do with her freedom.

On the day after the announcement of the decree absolute appeared in the *Record*. John Worthing telephoned her.

'I can't pretend I'm sorry,' he said. 'It's a step nearer. At least nothing now stands in your way.'

She was shocked by the directness of his approach. 'You're quite wrong,' she said. 'Your wife stands as much in my way as in yours. You can't persuade me otherwise.'

She wished that he could. Over the months she had seen him whenever the Committee met, but there had been nothing more. She longed for him: on some sleepless nights she had, in her loneliness, physically cried out for him. But though she longed for him, she was not ready to take him for her lover. It would, in any case, be only part of the answer. To have him as her lover, with meetings snatched in secret, when and where they could, would only accentuate his absence from the rest of her life. She wanted him not only sexually, but in every other way. She wanted the daily companionship, the shared domesticity, the evenings spent together, the births of children who would belong to them both.

As she put down the telephone on John Worthing, Annie came into the room.

'There's a Mrs Denby to see you. Says it's urgent. I told her you was busy.'

'Show her in at once, please,' Rose said. It must be important. Eva had hardly ever been to Beechcroft Road, and never without an invitation.

Eva burst into the room. She was hatless, her hair not combed; she still wore a pinafore under her unbuttoned coat. Her eyes were red from weeping.

'I had to come,' she cried. 'I didn't know where to turn! Mam's gone to see Auntie Dora in Halifax!'

'Whatever is it, Eva?' Rose had never seen her in such a state.

'Jim's been arrested! They say it's been going on for months! Something to do with his employer and some money. The police came and took him away! They took him in full view of the neighbours – handcuffed! Oh, Doctor Rose, what am I going to do? What am I going to do?'

The words poured out in a torrent, then gave way to noisy sobs as Eva collapsed on to a chair. She lowered her head to her knees, her shaking back and shoulders a long curve of hopelessness.

14

When Rose arrived at the Babcock Street surgery next morning a child, standing on the doorstep, thrust a note into her hand.

'Mrs Foster said I was to gi'e it to yer.'

'Wait until I read it, in case there's an answer needed,' Rose said.

He knew there was no answer. Mrs Foster had said so. But if he waited the Doctor was always good for a penny which, together with the one Mrs Foster had given him, would be a bit of all right.

Rose unfolded the note.

'Dear Doctor (she read)
    I can't come this a.m. on account of the bastard is up in court and I got the children here while Eva goes.
                    Yours truly and oblige
                    J. Foster (Mrs)'

Rose took a penny from her purse and handed it to the messenger. 'No answer,' she said.

In the act of unlocking the surgery door she paused. If she hurried, there was time to pop in on Mrs Foster before surgery. She felt anxious about Eva. The girl's white face, stained with tears and sick with worry, had occupied her mind since yesterday's visit. She felt she had done little to help her,

In Mrs Foster's living room Dorothy and Meg sat at the table which was spread with a clean newspaper as a tablecloth. In her darker moments Rose had sometimes thought that to have tea and treacle and soup spilled over it was just about what the *Record* deserved. Mrs Foster handed thick slices of bread and margarine to the children, then spooned skimmed, condensed milk into the cups of strong tea which she placed before them. In the area around Babcock Street most people had forgotten what fresh milk tasted like, and now they had come to prefer the sticky, sweet substance which they called 'Swiss milk'.

'This is a bad business,' Mrs Foster said. 'I can't say much, though.' She gave a warning jerk of her head in the direction of the children. 'Little pigs have big ears!'

'Where is Eva?' Rose asked.

'Already down there. He has to appear this morning though the Lord-knows what time. She could be there for hours, all on her own. I wish I could have gone with her, only I can't be in two places at once.'

She was untypically harassed and, divested of her usual hat, her sparse white hair drifting away from its hairpins and straggling around her face, she looked an old woman.

'I'll finish surgery as quickly as I can,' Rose said. 'Then I'll pop down there myself. How was she?'

Mrs Foster shook her head. 'Upset! Can you wonder? If I could speak my mind . . .' She checked herself, seeing the wary curiosity on the faces of her grandchildren. 'But it's very kind of you to offer to go down there. God bless you, Doctor!'

Fortunately the surgery was a light one. Rose reached the courtroom, and was allowed in by the constable on duty who recognized her, just as Jim Denby's case was called. There was no time to speak to Eva as she slid into the seat beside her but she took the girl's ice-cold hand and held it for a moment in her own.

In the dock Jim Denby looked diminished, all the bravado gone from him. He gazed fixedly ahead, his face expressionless. If he knew Eva was in court he gave no sign of it.

The case started, and was over, with surprising speed.

'You are charged with stealing, by a trick, the sum of five pounds, the property of the Akersfield Building Society, which trick you perpetrated by means of a bogus telephone call.'

The magistrate's tone of voice said that no tricks surprised him. He had heard them all.

'However,' he continued, 'I am informed by the police that other and far graver charges will be alleged against you. I do not therefore propose to try you in this court, but to remand you in custody for one week.'

Eva clutched at Rose's arm, gripping her until it hurt, as Jim Denby was led away.

'Let's go,' Rose whispered.

Outside in the street Rose said, 'I'm going to take you for a cup of tea. I'd like to give you something stronger but the pubs aren't open.'

The cafe to which they went was the one to which Alex had taken Rose on her first day in Akersfield. So much had changed since that day that it seemed – if indeed it had ever existed – half a lifetime away.

'Would you like something to eat?' she asked Eva.

Eva shook her head. 'It wouldn't stay on my stomach. It was good of you to come, Doctor.'

'If you like I'll come with you next week,' Rose said. 'I'll make arrangements about the surgery.' Next week's ordeal, she was sure, would be far worse than today's.

'What will they do to him?' Eva said.

'I don't know. I don't know what he's done, do you?'

'No. I swear to God I don't know anything. I thought he was doing so well with his job. When he gave me a bit extra he said it was overtime, or he'd come up on a horse. I suppose I should have known it couldn't last.

Nothing good ever does, least of all with me and Jim.'

'It might not be as bad as we think.' Rose tried to sound more reassuring than she felt. 'Grave charges' the magistrate had said. And Jim Denby had a record. 'I believe he's been in trouble before?' she said.

'Before we were married,' Eva said. 'Right from being a kid. He was in Borstal. Then he was in the glasshouse in the army. His own mother warned me. But you don't take any notice, do you? Will it be in the *Record?*' she asked anxiously.

'Only a line or two, I daresay.' Rose had seen one of Alex's reporters in the court, scribbling away.

'But next week?'

The two women looked at each other. They could not pretend that if the case was substantial the *Record* would not make a meal of it.

'That's what I dread most,' Eva said desperately. 'I can't stand for the neighbours to read it. I can't stand for the children's friends to point them out. They will, you know.'

'Surely not?'

'You don't know, Doctor. Oh, I mean no disrespect. But the people on the Marton Green estate are a cut above some. They won't like anything of this nature.'

'But they won't take it out on you and the children,' Rose said. It was strange that Eva made no mention of what it would be like for Jim, or how she would face the separation, how she would manage for money. Her entire concern seemed to be with the effect of the likely newspaper report.

'Oh yes they will,' Eva said. 'People can be very cruel. I can stand it for myself, though I was just beginning to get to know people. starting to make friends. and I suppose that'll all finish. But it's the children, you see. Other mothers won't let their children play with mine when all this comes out.'

'I think you're wrong,' Rose said. She refilled Eva's cup and for a minute they sat in silence.

'Doctor Rose,' Eva said.

'Yes?'

'I wouldn't ask you if it wasn't for the children . . .'

'You know I'll help if I can, whatever it is.'

'You're so good to me, Doctor. I hardly know how to ask. But do you think you could ask your husband . . .' She blushed with embarrassment. 'Oh dear! I mean Mr Bairstow. I know he's not your husband now and perhaps you're not on speaking terms with him any longer . . .'

'We are on speaking terms,' Eva said gently. 'And I think I know what you want me to ask him. You want him to keep the case out of the *Record.*'

Eva nodded vigorously, her face showing its first sign of hope.

'I'm sorry.' Rose said. He wouldn't do that, Eva. He wouldn't do it for me, nor for anyone. He would call it suppressing the news, and it's against his principles.'

Eva looked at her in disbelief.

'But he's the editor! He can print what he likes, can't he? He could keep it out if he wanted to.'

'I daresay he could,' Rose said. 'I'm never quite sure. But I know he wouldn't. He says the readers have a right to know.' She thought of their own divorce, which had been reported in full, every sordid detail of it, no matter how it told against him.

'But the readers wouldn't be any better off for knowing Jim had been sent to prison!' Eva protested. 'No-one would be better off. only me and the children would be a lot worse off.'

Rose saw the tears well up in Eva's eyes, and made up her mind.

'All the same I'll ask him,' she said. 'But don't build up your hopes, Eva.'

'Oh I won't, Doctor!' Eva said, immediately brightening. 'I won't, I promise!' But Rose knew she would.

'We'd better get back,' she said. 'My car's close by. I'll give you a lift to your mother's. In fact, we could pick up the children there and I could take you all back to Marton Green to save you bothering with the tram.'

They collected Dorothy and Meg and Rose drove back to Firth Avenue.

'Will you come in? Eva said.

'Well, just for a minute.'

Wanting to get home, she would have refused but for the nervous look on Eva's face as, when they saw the car approaching, a group of children gathered outside the gate of number eight. They stood there silently, curious and unsmiling; but not hostile, Rose thought. There was really no need for Eva's nervousness. The children were simply nosey-parkers. She often encountered the same behaviour when she was visiting patients.

She helped Eva and the children out of the car and crossed the pavement with them. As they walked through the group of children a girl, younger than the rest, called out to Dorothy.

'Your Dad's a Bad Man, Dorothy Denby!'

Eva took her daughters' hands and ran with them into the house. Rose turned to the little girl.

'Who told you that?' There was no way anything could have appeared in the paper yet.

The little girl looked scared at the sharpness in Rose's voice and an older girl spoke up for her.

'We saw him being taken away by the police. He was handcuffed. We saw!'

'There you are, you see!' Eva cried when Rose went into the house. 'It's started already! What will it be like next week when it all comes out?'

'My husband used to tell me that people soon forget. He said all these things were a nine days' wonder.'

'The people it happens to don't forget,' Eva said bitterly. 'It lasts a lot longer than nine days for them. Dorothy and Meg might remember for the rest of their lives!'

She sat on the bright new sofa in the bright new home, her daughters on either side of her, all three of them looking at Rose, who felt powerless to help them.

Rose had seen little of Alex since the day he had left her, almost a year ago now. They had made arrangements whereby he would collect Jenny and have her with him for a few hours at a time, but it had proved unsatisfactory. She was not yet two years old and she did not take kindly to being whisked away by this man who had already become a stranger to her. Most of the time she was with him she fretted for her mother and for the familiar surroundings of her own home. It seemed kinder, in the end, to discontinue the arrangement.

'But then she'll forget me,' Alex protested.

Rose nodded.

'Perhaps she will. I'll try to see that she doesn't. I've no wish to deprive you of your daughter, or Jenny of her father, but I suppose it's one of the consequences of divorce when a child is so young. Perhaps you can come back into her life again when she's a little older.'

She doubted that he would. By that time he would probably have a new family who would replace Jenny. He had not yet married Gwen Mayfield, but Rose was sure it was in the offing.

On the day after Jim Denby had been remanded in custody Rose went to see Alex. Yesterday's court case had been reported in the *Record*. She had known she would not be in time to stop that, but it had been a brief report, not in a prominent position in the paper. She had little hope of the same treatment in a week's time.

'You're looking well,' Alex said when she was shown into his office.

'You too,' Rose replied. He was an attractive man, no doubt of it. Since he had left her he had put on some weight, and it suited him; but his face was not so puffy, nor his colour so high. She thought that he was probably not drinking. She was interested to find that she could view him so dispassionately. Sitting opposite to him, she harboured no hard feelings, had no animosity towards him.

'How is Jenny?' Alex enquired.

Rose thought he sounded uneasy. Was he worried about her visit? Was he perhaps expecting her to ask for money?

'She's well. She's talking a lot now. New words every day. But I'm not here on my own behalf or Jenny's. We're doing fine. I'm here about Jim Denby. You know he's been remanded in custody? But of course you know! It was reported in the *Record*.'

She watched his eyes grow wary as she was speaking.

'So I'm sure you can guess why I'm here,' she continued. 'I'm asking you to keep it out of the paper . . .'

'Impossible!' He did not wait for her to finish. 'You know I can't do that!'

'Won't, not can't! Then will you promise to give it the least possible publicity, Alex? For the sake of Eva and her children?'

'I can't possibly promise that,' he said. 'It will get the amount of publicity it merits; no more, no less. But I have to warn you, it looks like being an interesting case.'

It was suddenly not true that she had no strong feelings about this man. A tide of dislike rose in her. She wanted to wipe the cool, implacable expression from his face. But even so, she realized that it was the editor in him she disliked. The man she had first known, or thought she had known, had disappeared behind the job. He was the God Almighty Editor.

'You don't care at all about people, do you?' she flared. 'As long as you can titillate your readers, feed their vulgar curiosity, that's all that counts, isn't it?'

She was shouting her accusations. She knew she could be heard all over the outer office but she did not care. She would like to shout it all from the Town Hall steps.

'Do you ever give a thought to what you do to people?' she demanded. 'Does it never worry you that you might ruin their lives? Don't you *care*?'

Alex, on his side of the desk, remained calm and imperturbable.

'I'm not the one who ruins their lives,' he said. 'I haven't ruined Eva Denby's life. Her husband did that. I shall do no more than report what the court says *he* has done.'

'My God, you make it sound like you're doing the world a favour!' Rose cried. 'Did you never go wrong? Did you never go astray?'

'When I did,' he said quickly ' – if we're to call it wrong – when you divorced me it was all reported in the *Record*. I didn't lift a finger to stop it. You must know that. You must have read it.'

I did,' Rose said sharply. 'Every sordid detail! Thank God Jenny was too young to understand. But Eva's children aren't too young. They can read – and even if they couldn't, people would soon tell them. I wouldn't have your job, Alex. I wouldn't have it for a king's ransom!'

'It's a job,' Alex said. 'I'm a professional – every bit as much as you are, though I know you like to think you're way above a mere newspaper man. But I don't tell you how to run your professional life. I leave it to you because I expect you to know best, to know where your duty lies. Why should you expect to run mine? Come to that, how many people strongly disagree with what you are doing – but you never let it stop you. Nor shall I let you interfere in mine.'

'So that's your final word?' Rose said. It was no use. She was defeated.

'I shan't give the Denby case any special publicity, any particularly prominent position,' he said. 'Nor shall I play it down. It will get exactly the space and position it deserves; no more, no less. Until the case is heard we don't know what that will be. And now can I give you a cup of tea, Rose?'

'No thank you.' She stood up, ready to leave.

'Before you go,' Alex said, 'I want to tell you that Gwen and I are getting married in two weeks' time.'

Rose began to tremble, and clenched her hands so as not to show it. She felt weak, and near to tears. How could she have thought, not many minutes ago, that she was devoid of feeling for Alex? The love, of a kind, the affection and friendship, the shared lives over five years, could not be wiped clean away by a form of words in a divorce court. It was not as easy as that.

'I hope you will both be very happy,' she said quietly.

'Thank you. And while you're here, Rose, let me say how much I appreciate your attitude to Gwen over the Mothers' Club. She'd have hated to give it up.'

'That was never on the cards,' Rose said. 'She's far better at the job than I am. I'm not really needed now. In any case, it's the club members who are important, not Gwen or myself. I have my professional standards too, you see!'

'You don't have to tell me,' Alex said.

Rose noted with some misgiving that the courtroom was almost full. She supposed the magistrate's words, duly reported, had brought people in. 'Graver charges to follow', he had said, but what did it mean? Eva had been allowed to see her husband during the past week but he had revealed nothing.

'He said he'd been advised not to,' she told Rose.

So the general public, to whom a morning in court was a way of passing the time agreeably, would hear at the same time as Eva what would so deeply affect her life. And if the case didn't take too long it would make this evening's edition of the *Record*, and the world of Akersfield, Eva's world, would know all.

Eva, pale and silent, sat beside Rose, her hands clenching and unclenching as she waited. When Jim Denby was led into the dock she closed her eyes as if she could not bear to see him. He looked even more defeated than he had a week ago, not even raising his head as the charges were read out.

'You appear on three charges,' the Stipendiary Magistrate said. 'You are charged firstly with obtaining, by false pretences from your employer, sums amounting to ninety pounds. Secondly you are charged with obtaining a cheque book from the Akersfield and District Bank; thirdly you are charged with obtaining by false pretences parts for a car amounting to twenty-three pounds fifteen shillings.'

In a voice no more than a whisper, Jim Denby pleaded guilty to all three charges.

'I don't believe it!' Eva gasped. 'All that money.'

There was plenty to interest the crowd in the courtroom, Rose thought as the tale unfolded. Doing odd jobs in the home of Mr Freeman, his employer, Jim Denby had come across the man's passbook for the building socicty. Noting the account number he had written a letter, purporting to come from his employer, saying that the passbook was lost and asking the Society to pay the bearer of the letter the sum of twenty pounds. It had worked like a dream. Denby signed for the money in a fictitious name, pocketed it, and repeated the process on four more occasions, never asking for too much. It was only when he took the short cut of impersonating his employer on the telephone, instead of writing a letter, asking the Society to pay a small sum of money to a messenger he would send to collect it, and the clerk called Mr Freeman back on some small point, that the fraud came to light.

The details of the other charges revealed equally devious plots, each of which he had got away with in the beginning, all of which were bound to trap him in the end. How could he be at once so clever and so utterly stupid? Rose wondered. Her heart ached for Eva, listening to these revelations which her husband did not deny. At one point she lifted her hands and covered her ears as if she could bear to hear no more.

The Stipendiary appeared to enjoy the summing up as much as he had enjoyed the recital.

'This case is very serious,' he said. 'The prisoner has pleaded guilty to acts which might have led him to be charged with forgery, for which I would have had no alternative but to send him to penal servitude.'

A quiet moan escaped Eva. 'It's all right,' Rose whispered. 'He's not going to.'

'You have been committing these wicked acts not-withstanding the fact that you were in regular employment. You have given no thought to the consequences for your wife and children . . .' On and on he went. Jim Denby sat as though not hearing a word. Only when the Stipendiary pronounced sentence – 'You will go to prison for twelve months in all' – did he raise his head and look across the court to where Eva sat. But Eva did not see him. Her face was buried in her hands as she wept, and she did not even see him led away. Her voice came muffled through her sobs. 'You don't understand! You don't know the worst! I'm going to have a baby! My baby will be born when its father is in prison!'

Rose gasped. 'Eva, why didn't you tell me? Does Jim know?'

'Nobody knows. I didn't tell anybody. I couldn't believe it – it's been so long. But it's true all right. What am I going to do, Doctor Rose? What am I going to do?'

It was all there in the next edition of the *Record.*

AKERSFIELD MAN'S FRAUDS
Forged Letters
Twelve Month Sentence

As well as everything about the crimes, every word of the Stipendiary's summing up, homily, dire warnings to Youth, they printed Jim Denby's home address and the names and ages of his wife and children. Nothing was left out. As she read those last details, Rose felt a tremendous anger against all newspapers and against Alex Bairstow in particular.

A week after Jim Denby had been sent to prison the quarterly meeting of the Mothers' Holiday Fund took place in Rose's house, which had become the recognized venue for them.

'The house at Blackpool has turned out very well,' Miss Nesfield said. She turned to Rose. 'You made a very wise decision that day in Blackpool, Rose!'

Rose's eyes sought and met John Worthing's. She read in his the question which had so often been in her own heart since that day. 'Did we make the right decision?' She was lonely: she admitted it. At the end of each day, when work was over and Jenny was in bed, there was nothing left for her. Often, physically tired though she was, she welcomed the urgent night calls which took her out again, pitched her into life. Work was all that was left to her, and it was not enough; even though it was going so well, it was not enough. She needed to share the success she was having, as well as the setbacks. But there could never be anyone. She would never again make the mistake of thinking that someone else could take John Worthing's place. The question burned in his eyes now as he looked at her. She turned away quickly, brought her mind back to the business in hand. There was no future in such questions.

When the meeting was over and the members were leaving, Rose standing in the hall seeing them out, John Worthing said, 'I wanted a word with you about the Denbys. Can you spare me a few minutes?'

'Of course,' Rose said.

She closed the door on the others and went back into the sitting room, John Worthing followed her.

'It's a bad situation about the Denbys,' Rose said. 'Eva is pregnant, but what obsesses her is that the baby will be born while Jim is in prison. She doesn't seem to care for his sake – though why should she. I'd say she'd lost all feeling for him. But she's bitterly upset that this is going to be the baby's start in life – as if it was a curse on the child. And she's already sure that one day it will find out . . .'

She broke off. He wasn't listening. He was standing there, looking at her. A *frisson* of fear, pleasure, wonder, went through her at the intensity of his look.

'Where's Jenny?' he asked quietly.

'Out with Moira.'

'And Annie?'

'Gone to see her mother. Why?'

'Then we're alone?'

'John, why do you . . .' Rose began.

But she was in his arms and he had stopped her words with his kiss. His mouth was hard on hers and she knew that he would bruise her lips. But she wanted him to do so. She wanted him to hold her so hard that he would crush her bones, crush the life out of her. She raised her arms and locked them around his neck, running her fingers through his hair, caressing his head, stroking his neck. And then they were on the sofa, and then on the floor. She pulled his head down to her breast and his fingers trembled as he unfastened the buttons of her blouse. A shudder went through her body as his fingers sought, and found, her nipples.

It was over violently and quickly. As the climax

came they cried out together, and then she shuddered, and began to weep. He was infinitely tender with her then.

'I'm sorry,' he said. 'I didn't mean to hurt you, Rose. I never meant that.'

'You didn't,' she said. 'I wanted you to. It had to be like that. We waited so long.'

'And now the waiting is over,' he said.

'What do you mean?'

'I mean we can't go back, my darling Rose. Not ever again.'

But she knew, it was instantly clear to her, that they could not go on.

'I love you,' he said. 'You know that. I love you as I've never loved any other woman.'

'And I love you,' she replied. 'I do truly love you, my dear one. But it's impossible.'

'What's impossible, Rose? Nothing is impossible between you and me, except marriage. I want that as much as you do. You know that's true. But what we have is better than you'll find in a thousand other marriages.'

'I know that, too,' Rose said. 'Don't think I'm not tempted, John. I am. And never more so than at this minute. I want you every bit as much as you want me. But I can't do it. I've explained to you before that for me it has to be marriage or nothing.'

He let go her hand, moved away from her. She watched the tight, hostile look come into his face.

'Don't play about, Rose. I'll not stand for that. If you're trying to blackmail me into marriage, it won't work. Diana is sick. She needs me. It's you I love, but as long as she's ill – and she is ill – I won't leave her. I've always made that clear.'

'But I need you too!' Rose cried. 'I need you every day of my life! What about my needs? As for blackmail – how can you say that?'

'I'm sorry!' John said.

'But I have my boundaries, too. You can't leave your wife while she's sick. I can't have an affair with you while you're married to Diana.'

'We always get back to the same place,' he said.

'We always will,' Rose answered.

She stood up. She felt drained, hopeless. I think you should go now, John. Moira will be back with Jenny soon.' He would never know the effort it took her to send him away. It was as if she was amputating a limb, cutting out her heart.

He gave her a long look, searching into her. 'Then he took her hand and, with that foreign way he had, lightly kissed the backs of her fingers.

'Good-bye Rose,' he said.

15

On the twenty-third of December Rose decided to go to Marton Green to visit Eva. She was ashamed that, though from time to time she had sent things by way of Mrs Foster, she had visited only once in the months since Jim had gone to prison, and that in the early days. Her excuse – she knew it was a poor one – was that with the steady increase in both her practices she had been too busy.

Before leaving home she went upstairs to the attic, which had now been furnished as a nursery for Jenny, with the adjoining smaller attic as a bedroom for Moira. The warmth and comfort of the nursery, a bright fire burning in the grate behind the heavy metal fireguard, the floor carpeted, met her as she opened the door. Jenny sat on the floor, surrounded by toys: building bricks, dolls, a teddy bear, a wooden cart. She held out her arms to Rose as she entered.

'Mummy play with bricks?' she invited.

'Well only for a minute, darling. I have to go out,' Rose said. She picked her way through the scattered playthings and knelt down beside her daughter. Jenny had far too many toys. Some must be given away. But many of them were presents from patients and it would be wrong to part with them just yet.

'You're going out yourself,' she said to Jenny. 'Moira will take you just as soon as she's finished ironing your clothes.'

She turned to Moira. 'See that she's well wrapped up. She must wear her thick leggings and her fur cap. It's bitter out. In fact I'm wondering if you should go at all. It's so snug in here.'

'She enjoys her outing, Doctor,' Moira said. She appealed to Jenny. 'Don't you, my pet?' What was more, she herself wanted to go out. She planned to change her library book again. There was a new young man in the library she rather liked the look of; moreover, he had promised to save her the new Ethel M. Dell. The doctor was a good employer, but she was so set on Jenny that she sometimes forgot that other people had their own lives to live. Much as she loved Jenny, Moira did not intend to look after other people's children forever.

'Very well then,' Rose said. 'But don't keep her out too long.' She turned back to Jenny. 'I have to go now, love. We'll have a game later, I promise.'

She kissed the top of her daughter's head. Such pretty red hair she had. 'She's the spitten image of you when you were little,' Rose's own mother had said on her last visit. 'I only wish your Dad could be here to see her.'

When Rose drove into Firth Avenue it seemed that all the children in the neighbourhood were engaged in making slides: thankfully not on the road, but on the asphalt paths which bisected the green, where the surface was like glass from black ice. They queued behind each other to take turns on the slide. The less brave went upright, one foot in front of the other, down the slope; the bolder ones shot down crouching, and the bravest of all crouched on one foot, the other held out stiffly in front of them. All over Akersfield, Rose reckoned, children were sliding on the ice. It was amazing that she did not have to deal with more broken limbs.

Eva was so long in answering her knock that Rose wondered if she was out, though she had spotted Dorothy and Meg in the crowd of children. In the end she came, opening the door no more than an inch or two until she was sure who stood there.

'Why, Doctor Rose, I didn't expect to see you!' The absence of any reproach in Eva's greeting made Rose feel more guilty than ever.

'Come in, Doctor!'

Rose, following Eva into the living room, was appalled by what she saw. She should not have been so shocked. Mrs Foster had told her more than once that things were not going well for Eva, but Rose had never pictured it like this.

Gone was the three-piece suite, with the much-prized chesterfield; gone was the bulbous-legged table and the two upright chairs. In their place were a small, deal table with a scrubbed white top, plus three old stools. The range no longer shone black and silver but, worst of all on this bitter winter's day, there was no fire in the grate.

'Why, Eva!' Rose exclaimed.

'They took the furniture back,' Eva said. 'I couldn't keep up the payments, you see.' She was ashamed to admit it, as if it was a fault in herself.

'Even the oilcloth from the floor?' Rose asked.

'Yes. Though I don't know what good it was to them. It was cheap stuff. The pattern was already wearing off.' The floor was bare now, except for a shabby, tabbed rug in front of the fireplace.

'The only things they didn't take were the two gramophone records,' Eva said. 'I reckon they forgot those. But they're not much good without a gramophone, are they?'

She picked up the records in their cardboard cases, fingering them, stroking them, as if by some magic she could bring out the music, hear the mellifluous harmonies of Layton and Johnstone once again.

'I Want to be Happy,' Rose thought. What an ill-chosen one that had turned out to be!

'Why have you no fire?' she asked – and could have bitten out her tongue at the stupidity of the question. There was only one reason for not having a fire on a day like this.

'Actually we have a little bit of coal in the coalhouse,' Eva said. 'I'm saving it for Christmas Day. The curate from Saint Thomas's said the church would be sending me a bag of coal but I'm afraid of it not coming in time. The children are out playing, so they can keep warm.'

'So they do still play with the other children?' Rose asked gently.

Eva's face shadowed. 'If it's a crowd, like playing on the ice today. But it's not liked if they're playing with just one or two others. Nothing much is said, but I watch the other bairns being called home by their mothers. And of course they're never invited into anyone's house.'

'But that's monstrous!' Rose cried.

Eva shrugged. 'It's the way things are. It's as if they were infectious. I try to make it up to them in other ways, but its not the same.'

It was freezing cold in the house. Rose resisted the temptation to draw the fur collar of her coat closer around her neck. She wanted to weep at the sight of Eva in the bare little room, where only the lace curtains remained of its former glory, hiding its poverty from the world outside.

'The worst bit was when the van came to take the furniture away,' Eva said. 'All the neighbours seeing it. They put the chesterfield down in the road while they were loading up and some of the children came and sat on it. It was worse, in a way, than when they came and took Jim.' She sat there, remembering.

'And how have you been?' Rose asked, breaking the silence. 'In yourself, I mean?'

It was hardly necessary to ask. Eva was as thin as a stick, her face chalky and hollow-cheeked, her hair lank. In contrast to the thinness of the rest of her body her belly, rilled with the coming child, swelled out in front of her like a balloon. As always, Nature had taken priority over the mother's food to nourish the baby, leaving almost nothing for Eva's own needs.

'I'm all right,' Eva said. 'The baby's due in January, a month before Jim comes out – if he gets full remission for good conduct, that is.'

'And will he?'

'Oh yes! He's a very good prisoner, it seems. Did Mam tell you I'd been to see him? The church paid my fare, though I never go there. When the baby is born I'm going to have it christened there. They've been very good to me.'

While I did almost nothing, Rose thought.

'Thank you for the things you sent with Mam,' Eva said. 'It was kind of you.'

'How do you manage for money?' Rose asked.

'I get relief. They give me a bit of cash, and a voucher for food that I can spend at the Coop.'

She did not add that she walked two miles each way to the Relieving Officer's premises, and then queued for an hour for the handout; nor that she was allowed to use the food voucher only for certain basic items. Not for her the gratification of a pregnant woman's fancy for a tin of salmon or a bit of real butter on her bread.

'I'm very lucky, though,' Eva said. 'The lady next door sends me in a bit of their dinner two or three times a week, when they have a cooked meal themselves. Just while I'm pregnant, she says. I have to promise not to share it with Dorothy and Meg, though, and that's hard. It's all right when they're at school because they get tickets to go somewhere for dinners, but it's school holidays now and they get real hungry.'

'I've brought a few things,' Rose said. 'Nothing much really.' She unpacked the bag on the table; sugar, tea, some tins of food, a packet of biscuits, cheese, a jar of her mother's home-made jam.

'Oh, Doctor, how good of you!' Eva cried. 'Strawberry jam of all things!'

'It's nothing,' Rose said quickly. Seeing Eva's poverty she felt it keenly that she had been able to pick these things from her well-filled larder almost in passing.

'It's a great deal,' Eva said. Her face shone with gratitude.

'And there are three small Christmas presents here, one for each of you. Not to be unwrapped until Christmas Day.'

At the sight of the three parcels, neatly wrapped in coloured tissue paper and tied with ribbon, Eva broke down. Tears ran down her cheeks. She collapsed on to a stool, laid her head on her arms on the table, and wept. She wept as though the misery of months was pouring out of her. She wept, not in anger or despair, but in relief that something good had happened, Rose went to her and stood with her arms around Eva's shoulders. There were tears in her own eyes that something which had cost her so little could mean so much to Eva. Hers were tears of shame at herself, and of anger against life which did this to people like Eva.

Presently Eva lifted her head, dried her eyes. 'I'm sorry, Doctor,' she said. 'But you don't know what these presents mean to me. You see I'd racked my brains as to what I could give the children. There wasn't anything. It would have had to be a Jaffa orange in each of their stockings, and some nuts. The trouble is, they believe in Father Christmas. It's one thing to be poor the rest of the time – children can cope with that somehow – but if you think that Father Christmas has left you out – well, it's too much to bear isn't it? You can't understand why. You wonder what you've done wrong.'

Rose felt anguished. She must do something more. The little she had done was not enough. There must be some fund – surely the *Record* had such a fund? She would go to Alex.

'Don't tell the children the presents are from me,' she said to Eva. 'Let them be from Father Christmas.'

There was a knock at the door. 'That'll be Norman,' Eva said.

'Norman?

'The lady's son from next door. He brings my dinner in if he's working nights. Can he tell I've been crying?' she asked anxiously.

Not waiting for an answer to his knock, Norman came into the house carrying two plates put together.

'Your favourite today, Eva! Liver and onions with fried

potatoes! Oh, I didn't know you had a visitor! I'm sorry!'

'That's all right,' Rose said. 'I'm just about to leave. Eat it while it's hot, Eva. It smells delicious.'

The door opened again and Dorothy and Meg came in. They were small and pinched-looking, red noses in faces white from the cold. Not speaking, they looked longingly at Eva's plate. Eva glanced unhappily at Norman.

'It's no use,' she said. 'How can I eat it?'

He shook his head, non-plussed.

'Ma says you've got to, for the sake of the baby. She's only sorry she can't do the same for Dorothy and Meg. She would if she could.'

'I know,' She said. 'She's a kind woman.'

'I'll tell you what,' Norman said. 'I'll take the kiddies around with me and see if I can't rake up something. Come on you two!'

'Wait a minute,' Rose interrupted. 'Isn't there a fish-and-chip shop near?'

'Five minutes away,' Norman said.

Rose opened her purse. 'Here's a shilling,' she said to Dorothy. 'Can you get fish and chips for you and Meg and me? A fish-and-a-pennyworth each? You could take Meg with you while your mother finishes her dinner.'

'A fish?' Dorothy was incredulous. 'Not just chips?'

'That's right,' Rose said. 'I'll stay and eat with you. We three will have dinner together.'

Eva beamed, was transformed. 'Oh Doctor Rose, are you sure?'

'Quite sure!'

Eva turned to the children. 'There'll be three-ha'pence change, Our Dorothy,' she said. 'Mind you don't lose it. Get off with you then.'

'I'll leave you to it as well,' Norman said.

'Now I must set some plates,' Eva fussed when they had gone. 'I'm right sorry I don't have a tablecloth.'

'Get on with your dinner before it goes cold,' Rose ordered. 'We don't need a tablecloth, nor plates either

252

for that matter. It won't be the first time I've eaten fish and chips from a newspaper.'

Eva tucked into her liver and onions with a clear conscience and a sharp appetite. 'Some say they taste better that way,' she said through a mouthful. 'Especially if they're wrapped in the *News of The World*!'

They came – hot and delicious, the white fish covered in crisp, golden batter – wrapped in the Akersfield *Record*. 'I put salt and vinegar on them in the shop,' Dorothy said.

When they had eaten the last delectable mouthful, and drunk a cup of tea which Eva insisted on making, Rose left. Her home surgery was not until six o'clock but she was determined to see Alex this afternoon.

'Close the door after me,' she said to Eva. 'Don't come outside. It's a bitter day.'

When she was getting into her car Norman came out of his house to speak to her.

'I just wanted to ask you, is Eva going to be all right? Having the baby, I mean?'

'I'm not her doctor now,' Rose said. 'But I think she should be. Thanks in no small part to your mother.'

'We do what we can for her,' he said. 'We think a lot of Eva. She doesn't get out enough. I wanted to take her out this coming New Year's Eve, but she won't come. Says it wouldn't be the right thing. My Ma agrees with her.'

'I daresay your mother's right,' Rose said. 'More's the pity. Eva doesn't get much fun.'

'I'll let you into a secret,' Norman said eagerly, 'She's going to get a wireless set for a Christmas present! I'm building it myself from a blueprint. Two valves, with a loudspeaker!'

What a pity Eva didn't meet you first, Rose thought as she drove away.

She had seen nothing of Alex since their stormy meeting in the week before Jim Denby went to prison. She had not communicated her disgust at the spread given to the case in the *Record*. It would have done no good and he already knew how she felt. She had read the account in the paper of his marriage to Gwen and a rumour had filtered through, by way of a member of the Mothers' Club who knew Mrs Foster, who told Rose, that Gwen was already pregnant.

So could I have been, Rose thought, driving into the town. I could have been carrying John Worthing's child. One sexual act, as she often told her disbelieving patients, was all it took. Nature had been at it too long to require several months of practice. On the one and only occasion John had made love to her they had taken no precautions. There had been none of the forethought she preached to others, no considerations except of the body's demands at that moment. Nothing else had mattered. She was fortunate that the episode's only legacy was a deeper understanding of her patients' actions in similar circumstances.

Was she fortunate? Above everything else she could think of she would like to have John Worthing's child in her. But no matter. It had not happened, and now it never would.

Alex was surprised to see her. He greeted her politely, though there was a shade of anxiety in his voice.

'Is something wrong with Jenny?' he asked.

'Nothing at all. She's as fit as a fiddle. You could come to the house to visit her, you know, if you wished to do so.'

His face closed up. It wouldn't do just now. Gwen is pregnant. It would upset her.'

'Surely not?' Rose said. 'I've always considered Gwen a sensible, down-to-earth woman.'

'That's true,' Alex said. 'But women are different when they're pregnant. You must know that. You see them often enough. By the way, I'm glad to hear your work's going so well. I suppose you saw the letter of appreciation in the *Record* a few weeks ago?'

'I saw it,' Rose said. 'I was encouraged. I'm sure public opinion is changing – but so very slowly. It will be a long time before more than a handful of people describe doctors in my line of work as "public benefactors". To most of the population we're quite the reverse.'

'Well, what can I do for you?' Alex asked.

'The Denbys again. Or rather, Eva. I went to see her this morning. I was appalled at the conditions she's living under. Two days before Christmas and she has no coal, hardly any food, no money in her purse. She's being fed a few dinners by the kindness of a neighbour, but until school starts again the children are going hungry. In addition to all that she's eight months pregnant. Isn't there a fund which can help her?'

'There's the Christmas Relief Fund,' Alex said. 'Run by the *Record*. Why hasn't she applied?'

'Presumably because she doesn't know about it and nobody thought to tell her,' Rose said. 'There isn't time for her to go through all the red tape of applying before Christmas. Can you cut any corners for her? To be really useful she needs the money in time to buy things for Christmas – and tomorrow is Christmas Eve.'

'I'll have a word with the Powers-that-Be. I expect they'll award her five pounds as she's in such straits.' Alex took out his wallet, extracted a note. 'I'll jump the gun and give it to you myself – and redeem it from them.'

'Thank you very much,' Rose said. 'I can't tell you what a difference it will make. I'll get Moira to go to Marton Green on the tram later this afternoon, to take it to Eva.'

There seemed nothing more for them to say to each other. She wanted to ask him if he was happy. He looked contented enough. She wanted to assure him that she felt nothing but friendship for him now. But the words would not come. Perhaps he understood all that, anyway.

'I'll be off then,' she said. 'I hope you have a good Christmas. Congratulations about the baby. I'm truly glad for both of you, Alex.'

'Thank you. We're pleased about it. What are you doing at Christmas?'

'I'm taking Jenny to Faverwell on Christmas Day. Just for a few days. Doctor Lewthwaite is covering for me.'

The two of them stayed in Faverwell until the twenty-seventh of December. Rose had closed up the house in – Beechcroft Road so that Annie and Moira could go home to their families for the holiday. When she returned there as a note on the mat from Mrs Foster.

'Dear Doctor,
     This is to let you know that Eva had her baby on Boxing Day (yesterday). A fine little boy and both well though he was before his time. The coal came Christmas Eve so they was kept warm and a big hamper from someone amon . . . anyom . . . from persons unknown.
                    Yours truly and oblige,
                    Mrs Foster

Who had sent the hamper? Rose wondered. She had not done so.

On New Year's Eve Rose attended a party given by Doctor Lewthwaite. It came as no surprise to her when, towards the end of the evening, John Worthing came in. He was alone. She had long ago realized that in Akersfield everyone ran across everyone else all the time. It was one of the reasons why she could not keep John Worthing out of her life. Even so, she had not met him or spoken with him since the day he had made love to her. Now she felt his hand under her elbow and knew without turning around that it was he. No-one else in the world could send this wave of feeling through her. A moment ago she had been with a group of people; now, as if by magic, she was just with him.

'It's almost midnight,' John said. 'A few more minutes and it will be nineteen-twenty-seven. What does this remind you of?'

'I know,' Rose said. 'I remember the first time. It's strange how we think the year just about to begin is going to be the best ever.'

At that other party, looking towards nineteen-twenty-one from the last days of nineteen-twenty, it had seemed that everything good was before her. She had been ready to start her job at the Infant Welfare Centre; Alex was her good friend; John Worthing . . . with John it had seemed no more than perhaps the lightest of flirtations ahead.

'Everything seems set to go in one direction,' she said. 'Then before you know where you are it all changes.'

'I haven't,' John said. 'I knew what I felt about you then. I haven't changed.'

'Please John, let's not talk like this!' Rose begged.

'Why not? If we can't be emotional at the end of the old year, looking into the new, when can we?'

'I can't cope with it,' Rose said. 'I don't want to make a fool of myself in front of all these people. Unless we can change the subject I shall walk away from you.'

'Then we'll talk about anything you like,' he promised. 'Only stay with me until it's midnight. I want you to be the first person I see and touch in nineteen-twenty-seven.'

'I shall be,' she said.

'So what do you want to talk about?'

She cast around for a topic of conversation. All she wanted was to be with him, not to have to talk at all. But people would notice if they stood in silence.

'Is there anything to be done about Jim Denby?' she asked. 'He's due out in February, with not much prospect of a job. If he stays out of work long, then I think that whole family will just go under. But who will give him a job now?'

'I will,' John Worthing said.

Rose stared at him in disbelief. She had asked the question with no hope of a reply.

257

'You will? But how? What?'

'I'm getting a second car. I shall need a chauffeur, mostly to take Diana around. Her health doesn't improve. Sometimes me also, if I have to go to dinners or functions in the evening. He's a good driver, I believe?'

'There's nothing wrong with his driving that I know of,' Rose said. 'But what about the risk of . . .'

'I'll take the other risks,' he interrupted. 'There won't be lot of opportunity for him to go wrong. I don't propose to employ him in the house. He'll be strictly for the car.'

'I understand he's vowed to go straight,' Rose said. 'I went to see Eva and the new baby yesterday. She'd had a Christmas letter.'

'I daresay he has,' John said. 'For what it's worth. Let's hope he sticks to it.'

A sudden thought struck Rose. Why had she not thought of it before?'

'Did you by any chance send a hamper to Eva Denby at Christmas?' she asked.

'Quiet!' he said. 'It's striking midnight.'

When the last stroke from Doctor Lewthwaite's silver-toned clock had died away John Worthing turned to Rose, gently pulling her around so that she faced him.

'A Happy New Year to you, my dearest Rose,' he said quietly. 'A happy nineteen-twenty-seven.'

She raised her glass.

'And to you, John. Happy New Year!'

Jim Denby, driving the new, maroon-coloured Daimler, felt good. It was a superb car, a pleasure to handle. Sometimes, sitting up here in front, he could almost imagine it was his own. And he himself matched the car in smartness, in his well-fitting maroon uniform with silver buttons and the peaked cap which Mrs Worthing had chosen for him. She was a woman of taste, and not mean like so many of them who had money. She had sent him to a good tailor to have the uniform made, no expense spared. It flattered his figure. Though he had lost some weight in prison, he still had a good pair of shoulders on him.

He turned into the forecourt of the Queen's Hotel in Harrogate and drew to a smooth halt in front of the main entrance. Jumping quickly from his seat, he went around the back of the car to open the rear door. No good chauffeur ever went around the front of a car: he had learnt that as he was learning many things now. It was a good job he'd landed, and he was determined to make the most of it. There would be picking, opportunities of course – of that he was sure. Now if Madam would let him handle the buying of the petrol for instance . . . Everyone knew it was a thirsty car. And in time she'd trust him to do little errands for her. He'd be happy to serve. He held open the door deferentially while Mr and Mrs Worthing stepped out.

'It's seven-thirty,' John Worthing said. 'Be back here at ten-thirty sharp, Denby.'

'I will, Sir,' Jim said. 'Do you want me to stay with the car, Sir?'

'Not necessarily. You can garage it. Do what you like as long as you're back here on time.'

Jim watched his employers walk into the hotel where they were attending a dinner. They were a smart couple; good-looking, well-dressed. She always remained the lady and she treated him all right. Come to that, so did the boss, though he didn't have much to say. Rumour was that he was sweet on Doctor Rose, but in Akersfield, that one-horse town, rumour said anything. She was an attractive bit of stuff though. He'd always thought so, even when he'd hated her – which he didn't any longer as long as she kept her nose out of his business.

He parked the car safely in the hotel garage, locked it up, and deposited the keys with the man in charge.

Nearly three hours to kill – say two-and-a-half to be on the safe side. He knew Harrogate well enough now. He sometimes brought Mrs Worthing here. While she was shopping in Parliament Street or browsing around the antique shops down by the Spa, where they said you could often see Queen Mary, he was free to explore the rest of the town. He had discovered a nice little pub near to the station and that was where he meant to go now.

'A pint of Tetley's,' he said to the barmaid, who was a new one. 'And something for yourself?'

'Ta very much. I'll have a glass of port if it's all the same to you!' She favoured him with an intimate smile, which he put down to the smartness of his uniform. It usually had that effect on the ladies. She was the type he liked: good figure, well-rounded. Eva was too skinny these days. All the same, she'd stood by him when he was inside. And then there was the boy.

At the thought of his baby son a smile played around his lips. The barmaid turned away to serve another customer and Jim went to sit with some of the regulars. He'd be back with her later if he had time. He was quite friendly with one or two of the regulars now.

'How's the bairn?' one of them asked.

'Spit of his Dad!' Jim said. 'And he'd better be!'

He called for a round of drinks, and when they came he said 'I'll ask you to drink to my lad. Wilfred – after Wilfred Rhodes. The greatest cricketer of them all – and a Yorkshireman!'

After that they drank to various people; other men's sons, mothers, wives, sweethearts. They drank to King George, Queen Mary and the Prince of Wales. The people of Harrogate were very loyal. When Jim looked at his watch he was horrified to see the time. The evening had gone by in a flash. It was twenty past ten when he reached the garage and only by the co-operation of the man in charge was he able to get the car out quickly, and be round at the front door of the hotel on the dot of half past.

He waited no more than a couple of minutes before his employer came out. Mrs Worthing was leaning heavily on her husband's arm. She didn't look at all well and the Guv'nor seemed concerned about her – which in a way was lucky because it meant that he wouldn't notice that his chauffeur had had one or two. Not more than he could carry, of course.

'Straight home. Denby,' John Worthing said. 'If the roads are clear you can step on it.'

Jim did just that, and the car responded with alacrity. He was driving well this evening. He quite looked forward to getting home, wondered if Eva would be waiting up for him and if young Wilfred might wake up.

The long, steep hill was clear of traffic. It was a still night; dark sky, touch of frost in the air and on the ground. He gathered speed down the hill, letting the car have her head, like a horse at the gallops. That fellow in the pub had given him a cast-iron tip for the two-thirty at York tomorrow. What was it called?

At the bottom of the hill, where the river ran, the road turned sharply over the bridge. The road turned, but the big car, careering down the hill, did not. It went at an angle into the wall at the beginning of the bridge. It went through the wall, which was weak at this point. As it plunged nose first towards the river it turned completely over, so that the top of the car was under water first. But it would not have mattered either way. The water was deep at this point, and swollen even more from the heavy Spring rains. In no time at all the whole car was submerged. The bubbles which rose to the surface were lost in the torrent of water. A peaked cap, maroon. with a shiny black neb, floated to the surface and was quickly carried downstream by the current.

16

Rose knocked hard on Eva's door, a second time, but to no avail. No wonder, though, that she couldn't be heard. Loud music filled the house, escaping through the open window, floating in the air around number eight, Firth Avenue. Rose turned the knob and went in. Neither Eva nor Norman, who sat on either side of the table, heard her. They were visibly enraptured by a spirited brass band rendering of the 'William Tell' overture from the gramophone. In the split second before the baby, playing on the rug by Eva's feet, looked up and gave the alarm, Rose thought how totally happy they looked. She was glad that, for Eva at any rate, things seemed to have worked out.

'Oh, Doctor Rose! I'm sorry! I didn't hear a thing!' Eva sprang to her feet, shouting over the music. Norman lifted the gramophone head from the record and stopped the sound.

'I didn't know you had a gramophone,' Rose said. Just in time she stopped herself saying 'again'. Now was not the time to remind Eva of that earlier instrument which had been so cruelly snatched from her.

'Norman bought it me for a wedding present,' Eva said. 'And three more records!'

How different the house was since that sad visit she had paid last Christmas, Rose thought. It had not been restored to the shining glory of that first easy payment splurge, but there were some comfortable chairs. and a decent table with a crocheted runner and a glass vase filled with marigolds. Eva, following Rose's glance, said:

'Norman grew them. He's done wonders in the garden

in such a short time. We've got lettuces and radishes and other things too!'

Norman Ackroyd had come to Eva's aid from the first awful moments of her widowhood and had looked after her ever since; and always would. Perhaps they would have children of their own? At twenty-seven Eva was young enough, and the way this kind man looked after her, she would soon regain her strength.

'I had to make a visit out this way,' Rose said. 'I thought I'd call and see how you were getting on.'

Eva's smile as she looked at Norman was full of pride. 'We're getting on very well, aren't we, love?' she said. 'We've been married six weeks now, you know!'

'I know,' Rose said. She had been a guest at the quiet wedding in the church which had been so good to Eva when she was in need.

'Wilfred looks well,' she said.

Eva looked fondly at the baby. 'He's into everything now that he's crawling around,' she said with pride. 'He was in the coal scuttle yesterday. You should have seen him. Black as the fireback he was! Ma's looking after him tomorrow. Me and Norman and the girls are going to Morecambe on a *charabanc* excursion, it being Akersfield Tide Saturday.'

'So Mrs Foster told me,' Rose said.

'I've promised Eva that one of these days we shall go for a whole week's holiday,' Norman said. 'I've made up my mind on it. Perhaps in two or three years. I'm one of the lucky ones, you see – a steady job in the dyeworks. I manage to put by a shilling or two each week.'

He was such a good man, Rose thought, looking at his round, pink face, his earnest brown eyes. He had taken Eva's three children as if it was a privilege for him to do so, showing them as much love as if he had fathered them. He must love Eva a great deal.

'How is that nice Mr Worthing?' Eva asked. 'Is he keeping well? I shall never forget how good he was to us when Jim came out of prison. And then to me when Jim . . .'

263

She faltered. Norman stretched out and took her small hand into his huge one.

'It's all over, love!'

'I know,' Eva said. 'All the same, I don't forget a kindness. I often think what a miracle it was that he wasn't drowned when his wife and poor Jim were. The *Record* said if he'd been trapped like them he couldn't have saved himself. He came to see me, you know. After he came out of hospital.'

At first, when Rose had visited John in hospital, he had not wanted to talk about the accident, but gradually over the weeks, from the little he had said and from the report which had appeared in the *Record.* she had pieced together the story.

In the seconds after the car had plunged into the river John Worthing, finding himself free, had tried at once to save his wife and his chauffeur, but it had been impossible. In any case he had recognized that they were already dead – most likely from shock. He had swum to the river bank, heaved himself out of the icy water, and gone to look for help. The rest of the story had been told to the *Record* by the couple whose cottage John had reached.

'It were a bitter night, with a keen frost,' the man said. 'Me and the wife had gone to bed when the knocking came on the door. I shall never forget the sight of him standing there, like something from the grave; shaking and shivering, the water running out of him and making a pool at his feet; his face bleeding. The wife looked after him – got his wet clothes off, wrapped him in blankets – while I ran to the vicarage to get them to phone for the ambulance.'

As a result of that night, John had taken pneumonia. On the day of his wife's funeral he had a raging temperature and could not leave his bed in the private ward of Akersfield General Hospital. For several days, when it seemed that he might die, life to Rose had seemed cold, black, hopeless. She could not envisage a world without him. Now, though she had seen little of him since he had left hospital, she was grateful every day of her life for his recovery.

'I think he's quite fit again,' she said, answering Eva's question.

When she had drunk the cup of tea which Eva insisted on giving her, she said, 'I must go. I have several calls to make. I'm glad to see everything is going so well.'

Eva went out to the car with her.

'Doctor Rose . . .' she said hesitantly.

'Yes?'

'I hope you don't think it's disrespectful of me, marrying Norman so soon after Jim died. I did try with Jim, you know. And there was nothing went on between Norman and me, no funny business, even when Jim was in prison. I wouldn't have had that, nor would Norman.'

'You did the right thing,' Rose assured her. 'It's clear to me that Norman worships the ground you walk on.'

'And I love him the same,' Eva said. 'I shall try to be a good wife to him. I hope one day you'll be as happy as me, Doctor Rose.'

Rose drove to Babcock Street. She had an afternoon surgery there today. It was, in many ways, a replica of most of her surgeries. And yet they were all different and she never tired of them. People were not carbon copies of each other even when, as in Babcock Street, their problems were so similar.

There were problems among her patients she was powerless to solve. Unemployment was fractionally better than when she had started in Akersfield, but there were still hundreds of men who had not worked for years and perhaps never would, their families existing on the small dole for which the men queued. Rose saw those long queues day after day, in all weathers, as her route to Babcock Street took her past the Labour Exchange. And until the problems of bad housing and overcrowding were dealt with, no doctor would ever eradicate the diseases and infections which arose from them. Eva had shaken it off, but Paradine Street still stood, its bug-ridden houses still inhabited, the rats still playing on the middens. Such places should be razed to the ground.

The last patient at that afternoon's surgery turned back as she was on the point of leaving.

'There's one thing you've done for us, Doctor, those of us who take advantage. You've shown us how not to have children we can't afford to feed, having to watch them starve, sharing out too little food amongst too many mouths. It isn't that women don't want children, Doctor. Most of us do, and life wouldn't be the same without them. It's that we want to be able to look after them properly. I reckon children are best born to folks who love 'em and want 'em *afore* they're born.'

Rose smiled. 'I know that, Mrs Laycock. It's what I've been trying to get across for years.'

'But things *have* changed a bit,' Mrs Laycock said. 'It's not all that long ago that working-class wives like me had to insert a bit of sponge, soaked in olive oil – or cooking oil if you couldn't afford better – if we didn't want to have a bairn. Sometimes it worked, sometimes it didn't, but it was a right messy business, I can tell you. And then all that douching afterwards!'

It was the attitudes which needed to change, Rose thought as Mrs Laycock left. She was convinced that as attitudes changed, research would produce what was needed. It seemed to her – it always had – that attitudes lagged a long way behind science.

She packed her bag and left for home. When she arrived, Jenny was in the hall to greet her.

'You promised to take me to the Tide,' she said.

'I know, and I will,' Rose assured her. 'Straight after evening surgery. Did you do as I suggested and have a good sleep this afternoon? You're going to be staying up rather late for a little girl.'

'She slept well,' Moira said, coming into the hall.

'Good! Then we'll have tea, and then it'll be time for surgery.'

It would be a short surgery this evening. Apart from the fact that there were fewer illnesses in the summer months, the first week in August was Akersfield Tide. 'Tide' was the West Riding word for 'fair'. It was the week when all the mills closed down and those who could afford to go on holiday flocked to the seaside. But there were far more for whom a holiday was impossible and in the tide they had a substitute. It could, at a pinch, be enjoyed for nothing. It cost nothing to walk around and look. But it was far better if one had even a little money.

Rose saw a few patients – stomach upsets, insect bites, sunburn; a stye on the eye of a pretty girl who was mortified by her appearance on the eve of her holiday.

'Bathe it with boracic lotion. Also I'll give you some ointment,' Rose said. 'Cheer up! It doesn't look half as bad as you think. It'll clear up in a day or two.' Rose had long ago concluded that there were a great many ailments which would clear up as quickly of their own accord as from any remedy she might hand out, but it was another matter getting patients to believe this.

The girl was the last of her patients, but as she started to clear her desk there was a knock at the door.

'Come in,' she called.

When she looked up, John Worthing stood before her. Her heart gave its customary lurch at the sight of him. However calm her outward demeanour she could never, in his presence, control what went on inside her.

He looked well. Leaner. perhaps, since his illness – but more handsome than ever. He was better looking, even, than he had been seven years ago. the few grey hairs amongst the dark ones merely adding to his distinction.

'I thought you were a patient,' Rose said.

'I decided I would be. It seems the easiest way, these days, of seeing you. Do you ever do anything but work, Rose?'

'I've been really quite busy,' Rose said defensively.

'Nonsense! I know perfectly well that this is the slackest

time of the year for you. You paid me more attention when I was in hospital than I ever get from you now.'

'Well that's a doctor for you! The sicker the patient, the more attention they get.'

'I wasn't your patient.'

'Well, no. But I always have one or two people to visit in hospital.'

'So you fitted me in? Thank you!'

'You know that's not true,' Rose protested. They both knew that she had visited him night and day, had hardly been able to keep away, But as a doctor she had been able to do that inconspicuously. Now that he was home again . . .

'Have you come for something special?' she asked.

'Very special. I've come to ask you to marry me.'

'Oh John, what am I to say?' They were the words she had waited so long to hear, but now that he had said them she was suddenly unsure of herself, afraid. She wanted, at one and the same time. to shout with happiness and to burst into tears. Why was she being such a fool?

'You are to say "Yes", my darling Rose!'

'But I don't know . . .' She fended him off. 'It's too soon . . . Your wife . . .'

'Nonsense!' he said. 'Look at Eva Denby. She's been married nearly a couple of months already.'

But to Eva life seemed so much less complicated. In spite of her disastrous experience of marriage, she had had no hesitation in accepting Norman. She had that simple faith in the future which Rose longed to possess.

'I want an answer, Rose.' He was stern, demanding.

'You'll have to wait, John.'

He looked at her for a long time before speaking again. When he did so his voice was quiet, yet firm.

'It's nearly seven years since I fell in love with you, Rose. You sat buried in that big chair in the Committee room. Your hair was escaping from under your severe little hat and I thought that your spirit was as fiery and irrepressible as your hair. I fell in love with you then and

I wanted you for my wife. Whatever stood between us then, Rose, is past.'

She was trembling from head to foot. What was she to say to him? Her mind was in a turmoil.

'Do you remember the bit in the Bible?' he said.

'What bit?'

'"And Jacob served seven years for Rachel and they seemed unto him but a few days for the love he had to her." That's what it says. Well, I've served it, Rose, but it hasn't seemed a few days to me. It's seemed a long, long time. An eternity.'

It had been a long time. So much had happened. She had gone through all the things they had told her would make her a better doctor; marriage, motherhood, the death of her father – even the break-up of her marriage. Had it made her a better doctor? She didn't know. What she did know was that she wanted to be a doctor for the rest of her life, that nothing would ever take its place. But could she at the same time be the kind of wife John Worthing wanted – and deserved? She didn't know.

'Yes,' she said. 'It's been a long time. Don't think I don't feel that, John. But it's myself I don't trust. I've failed so badly at marriage once, caused a lot of unhappiness. And the reason is – as far as I can tell – that I want more out of life than marriage. Even marriage to someone I love as much as I love you. I'm greedy, John. I want the best of all worlds.'

'Are you trying to tell me that you can't give up your career?' John said. 'Well I don't expect you to, any more than I expect to give up mine.'

'I don't even think of it as a career any longer. I'm not looking for personal advancement. But I couldn't give it up, and I know that sometimes I would put it before you.'

'I'd not stand in your way,' he said. 'I'd not prevent you doing anything you wanted to.'

'There's more to it than that,' Rose said. 'Alex felt sometimes that I belonged to my patients, not to him. He was right.'

'But this is different, Rose. You and me . . .'

'I know. I love you so much. But it could happen.' Seeing him standing there on the other side of the desk, she wanted to rush into his arms, to be held by him forever.

'I do understand, Rose,' John said. 'I don't think you have anything to fear. I can cope with it if you can – and I know you can. We can face anything if we're together.'

Rose looked at him – and her eyes pricked with tears at the love in his face. What had she done to deserve it? She could never do anything which would let this man down.

'John, I can't give you an answer yet. I want to, but I can't. But I promise not to keep you waiting long.'

'How long, Rose?'

'I don't know. Not long. And whatever I say, that will be final. John, I have to go now. I promised to take Jenny and Moira to Akersfield Tide. They're waiting for me.'

He looked at her without speaking, and then in the end he smiled. She felt an enormous relief that he was not angry with her.

'Then I'll come with you if I may,' he said. 'You can't refuse that. I haven't been to Akersfield Tide for a long time. I don't suppose you've ever been?'

'No. Moira put the idea into Jenny's head but I didn't want Moira to take her alone. If you're coming with us you'll have to go on the tram. That's part of the bargain with Jenny.'

They took the tram, also at Jenny's request riding outside on top. For the past two days Rose, out and about in the town, had seen the tide engines arrive; giant steam engines whose big iron wheels clanged over Akersfield's cobbled streets, whose size held up the trams and all other traffic. 'Mighty in Strength and Endurance', one of them had in letters of brass on its side. It was a good motto since they pulled behind them caravans and trucks, or platforms holding the big roundabouts, and once on the fairground they would generate power.

'We must keep close together,' Rose warned Jenny as

270

they alighted from the tram and walked up the lane to the tide field. 'It's going to be very crowded.' It was wage night in Akersfield. Anyone lucky enough to have a little money would be here.

With Jenny between Rose and Moira, holding hands, and John Worthing at Rose's elbow, they walked around.

'You may have some brandy snaps,' Rose said. 'It's a very clean stall.' There was fresh sawdust on the ground around the stall and the woman who weighed out the crisp, golden curls of brandy snap wore a clean white coat.

Rose took Jenny on the big cockerels, both of them clinging for dear life to the twisted brass rails. Then John took them all on the luxuriously appointed motor cars. From the centre of each big roundabout the music – each with a different tune – blared out, mingling with all the other noises of the fairground. Moira alone tried the 'Waltzer', each seat of which whizzed around independently as the roundabout also circled. When she came from that, looking as pale as winter, they watched while John tried the 'Test Your Strength' machine.

'I was a dab hand at this when I was twenty,' he said. 'I don't know about now!' He raised the big hammer above his head, swung it violently, hit the pin, and was cheered by the crowd as the indicator shot up the steel slide and rang the bell at the top. He acknowledged the cheers with a satisfied grin.

They patronized the coconut shies and moved on to the 'pot' stall, where John bought 'fairings' for the three of them; china kittens for Moira and Jenny and a pair of china lovers, entwined in each other's arms, for Rose. Next to the pot stall they admired the rippling muscles of 'Samson' in his leopardskin leotard.

'And now we really must go home,' Rose said. 'It's way past your bedtime, Jenny.'

'I want to go on the children's roundabout,' Jenny pleaded. 'I want to go on by myself.'

'It's safe enough,' John said to Rose. 'It can only go

as fast as the lady in the middle can turn the handle. Let Moira watch Jenny while she goes on this. I want to take you on the "Shamrock".'

Rose gasped. 'I wouldn't dare to go on that thing! I'd be terrified!'

'Not with me you wouldn't,' John said. 'Remember how I looked after you on the Big Wheel, and the Water Chute in Blackpool?'

'I remember.'

She had been recalling that all evening as they had walked around the fairground. Did he hold in his mind every moment of that day, as she did? Did he think back to the moments on the pier when they had seemed to be alone, only the sea and themselves in the whole world? Such a brief time, but she would never forget it.

'Shamrock' was the name of the huge steam yacht. It was fitted with brass rails to which the passengers clung as the Shamrock gathered speed and swung ever more violently. The underside of the Shamrock was painted with the Union Jack, and when it reached the greatest height of its swing the whole of the flag was visible to the people on the ground. There was always a crowd around to watch the Shamrock and their screams were drowned only by the louder ones of the Shamrock's passengers. John took Rose's arm and led her towards it.

'I can't!' Rose cried, though with part of her she knew she wanted to. She enjoyed the physical thrill of such things.

'Yes you can,' John said.

When the Shamrock came to a standstill and disgorged its passengers, John led Rose up the steep steps and they climbed aboard.

The huge boat swung gently at first, lulling its passengers into a false security. Then it started to go faster – and faster, higher and higher. It was horrific! Terrifying, breathtaking, wonderful, and deliciously frightening. As the violent movement flung them first in one direction and then in the other, Rose clung desperately to John. He folded his arms around her and held her close. Only then did she feel safe. He spoke to her, but the screaming and shouting of the other passengers drowned his words.

'WHAT DID YOU SAY?' Rose shouted back.

'I SAID WILL YOU MARRY ME? I'VE WAITED TWO HOURS SINCE I ASKED YOU. WILL YOU MARRY ME?'

Hurtling through the air, swinging to and fro, though now the Shamrock was slowing down again and she was being rocked gently in John's arms, Rose knew, suddenly, in this most incongruous of places, as she had never known before, what her answer must be. There could be no other.

'I shan't let you go,' John said. 'I shall keep you in this contraption until you say "Yes".'

'Yes,' Rose said. 'Yes, I will marry you. Oh John, my love, I will, I will!'

The Shamrock slowed down, and finally stopped. Arm in arm they descended to where Jenny and Moira were waiting.